NOTHING
BUT
TROUBLE

BY

ERIN KERN

Nothing But Trouble
by Erin Kern
Published by Erin Kern

NOTHING BUT TROUBLE
Copyright © 2014 ERIN KERN
ISBN 13: 978-1500831837
ISBN: 1500831832
Cover Art Designed by P.S. Cover Design

ONE

"DID YOU KNOW the probability that a woman will marry by the age of forty is eighty-six percent? You have eleven years to beat that statistic Rebecca Lynn," Rebecca's mother stated matter-of-factly in a serious tone that was supposed to strike fear into Rebecca's heart.

"Good morning to you too, Mother," Rebecca said with a smile plastered on her face that she hoped was cheerful. Good grief, her mother never said "hello" anymore. Every time Rebecca stepped through the front door of her childhood home, she was greeted with another ridiculous marriage statistic. Like the information was going to make her run out and wed the first man she came in contact with. The woman acted as though Rebecca had a hoard of admirers and she'd turned every single one down. Like it was her choice to remain alone, so she could single handedly defy the all-mighty marriage gods.

"And you know what else I read?" Patsy Underwood said as she closed the stained-glass front door on the early morning cool air.

"I can't imagine," Rebecca replied automatically.

Her mother hurried after Rebecca down the hallway. "The risk of miscarriage rises twenty-five percent over the age of thirty-five. Are you listening to me, Rebecca?"

"It's way too early in the morning to start reciting baby stats, Mom." Rebecca bit back a groan of frustration as she entered the living room. The thick draperies were still pulled closed so the sun couldn't bleach out the brown and orange plaid couches. Because that would make them look so much worse than they already were. The things looked like they'd been transported from nineteen-seventy-four, and they sagged in the middle. Their appearance was almost as ungodly as the comfort. Her father insisted they were just as comfortable as the day they bought them. Rebecca had decided to take his word on that one.

Patsy adjusted her floral robe, or "housecoat" as she referred to it. "I know you don't want to hear any of this, but I was twenty years old when I had your sister."

This time Rebecca did groan. She dropped her purse on the kitchen counter and rifled around in her mother's "junk mug" for her father's car keys. "Mom, it's barely seven a.m. Do you think we could at least wait until lunch time to break down the nitty-gritty details of my life?"

"Rebecca—"

She kept her attention on finding the car keys, digging past discarded pennies, paperclips and a green button. "I know you mean well, Mom. But I need to get Dad's car dropped off so I can get to work. I have back to back patients and a ton of paperwork to catch up on." When Rebecca faced her mother it was to a scowl and pinched lips, a look often associated with annoyance. She wrapped her arms around her mother's shoulders. The housecoat was thin from years of use, yet soft at the same time. "I love you very much, Mom. But I can't have this discussion right now." She turned back to her task of locating the keys. "Where are Dad's keys?" she asked in exasperation.

One of her mother's strawberry blonde brows lifted in disapproval. "Hanging up right there on the hook, where we always keep the car keys."

Rebecca yanked the keys down and looked at her mother. "Since when do you keep keys hanging up on the bulletin board? Nevermind," she interrupted before her mother could answer.

"Be sure to tell them not to paint the car black. You know your dad hates black cars."

Despite her mom's "mother hen" tendencies, Rebecca couldn't help but smile as she picked up her purse. "Paint's usually the last thing they do, but I'll be sure to tell them."

Patsy's house shoes were silent on the laminate flooring as she hurried after Rebecca. "Don't forget that first gear sticks. And try not to come to a complete stop, otherwise the car will stall."

"I got it, Mom," Rebecca reassured her mother. Even if she could be a bit exhausting, Rebecca's mother had the biggest heart of anyone she knew. Patsy Underwood would give a person her last dollar if they needed it. Then she'd lecture them on being more responsible with their money. *Then* she'd sign them up for a finance class at the local junior college and drive them there herself. At the end of the day, the person in question would probably have rather moved into a cardboard box than deal with Mrs. Underwood.

"Wait," Patsy said as Rebecca opened the front door. "How are you getting to work?"

"I can walk," she replied. "It's not that far," she insisted when her mom pinned her with a look.

"You don't need to be losing the weight, but whatever, Rebecca. And give R.J. a hug for us," she added as she placed a hand on the door and started to close it.

I'd rather sit on a cactus.

Instead of voicing her disdain for he-who-must-not-be-named, Rebecca smiled and hoped her true feelings didn't show. "Sure, Mom."

The sun was barely able to penetrate the low-lying clouds, but Rebecca slid her sunglasses on anyway. Mostly because they would give her a defense against R.J., however false it was. Those green eyes of his had always been her weakness.

It had been her mother's idea to restore the old 1967 Chevrolet Camaro as a surprise for her husband's retirement. Her father had put in more than thirty years at the wheat plant and had reached his limit, mostly because his body wouldn't allow him to do manual labor anymore.

Don't ever get old, Rebecca, her father had once told her.

He'd developed a serious case of arthritis in his hands and could no longer pull fourteen hour days. After June, Donald Underwood would be free do to as he pleased, which would include driving his wife crazy.

The car, which Rebecca had learned to drive on, was a hideous shade of gray primer with standard tires and the original seats. The five-speed transmission was fickle at best and stalled at the most inopportune times. Her father had called this car his baby ever since he'd bought it for next to nothing back in '83. Rebecca hated the thing and had dropped hints for him to sell it. After realizing Donald Underwood cherished the Camaro almost as much as his kids, she gave up her quest.

She and her mother figured, if they had to look at the car, the least they could do was fix it up for him. Replace the engine, get some more comfortable seats and slap some shiny paint on it.

The front window was slightly open and the door was unlocked. Her father was too trusting.

Rebecca slid in the car and winced when her spine came in contact with a spring beneath the upholstery of the seat. The car roared to life when she turned the keys over in the ignition. After saying a silent prayer that her father's pride and joy would get her to R.J.'s shop, Rebecca pulled out of the driveway.

As luck would have it, she only stalled twice. Once at a stop sign. And once right in front of the shop, where one of R.J.'s employees looked at her like she was some imbecile who didn't know how to drive a car.

Her dignity was barely intact when she parked the car, turned it off and got out. Luckily, he-who-must-not-be-named hadn't seen her display of amateur driving. Or, maybe he had and was waiting for the right moment to rub it in. Such was the way with R.J. Devlin.

Even though he was nowhere to be seen, she found herself trying to smooth her curls back anyway. Like he was hiding behind one of the bushes and would jump out and scare the panties off her. Just like he did when she was fourteen.

"What can I do for you, ma'am?" The kid with the shaggy brown hair who approached her didn't look like he was much over twenty-years-old. A grease-stained towel was slung over one of his shoulders.

"Well, this my father's car—"

"I'll take it from here, Sam."

Oh, good. He decided to show up and torture her after all. And here she thought she could escape unscathed. She should have stopped expecting that a long time ago.

"Why don't you go see what you can do with the carburetor in that Pontiac?" R.J. suggested.

The kid shrugged his shoulders and whipped the towel off his shoulder. "You're the boss."

R.J. watched Sam walk away, then pinned her with that penetrating stare of his. The sunglasses on her face were useless at blocking him out, just as she suspected. Hell, she would need an entire suit of armor in order to protect herself from his devastating effects.

It was only seven a.m. and his white t-shirt, which was

just tight enough for her to see the outline of those fantastic pecs, was already stained with grease. Dark splotches riddled his faded jeans, which molded and hugged his world-class rear-end. It was so damn unfair how he could throw on the most basic of clothes, yet look good enough to pour chocolate syrup all over so she could lick it off.

Rebecca cleared her throat and took a step back from him. She couldn't stand to be near him because he'd always made her feel itchy and uncomfortable. Like all he had to do was look at her and he knew every sordid thought that swirled through her head. The bastard had always known exactly how he affected her, and never failed to point it out. That had become a nasty game between them many years ago, that had started out innocent enough. Then... well, then it wasn't so innocent. In fact, her innocence was the one thing she hadn't been able to hold on to.

"So, what can I do for you, Dr. Underwood?" he asked in that deep baritone which never failed to make her toes curl.

Okay, you're an adult. He's an adult. There's no reason why you can't conduct this business like a mature person.

"It's my father's car," she gestured lamely behind her, like he hadn't already figured it out. He knew good and well whose car that was.

"And?" he prompted

"Well, he's retiring and my mom and I want to get it restored as a surprise to him."

He shifted his attention from her to the vehicle behind her. "No shit?" he muttered. Those long, powerful legs of his took him to the old Camaro. "I've been waiting a long time for your father to let me get my hands on this baby." He ran his palm over the surface of the hood; much like a man would touch a woman in a lover's caress. The thought sent a chill running down her spine, because she knew exactly what those hands felt like on her skin. Cradling her face as he kissed the bejeezus out of her. Trailing the tip of his thumb over her lip as he told her how beautiful she was.

That was a long time ago, and you need to stop thinking about it.

R.J. circled the car and his eyes darted over every square inch, taking in all the details and perhaps already coming up with ideas. When he came to the taillights, he squatted and studied the back end. He touched his fingers to the gas cap in between the taillights with the "SS" emblem. "It's in damn good condition," he muttered.

Rebecca wouldn't know anything about that. Her knowledge of cars didn't go far past how to start them and where to put the gas nozzle. But R.J. was the best at what he did, so she trusted his judgment.

He stood from his position and crossed his arms over his thick chest. "Do you know what you want done to it?"

The man was so damn distracting that she had to think about her answer. Hadn't she and her mom talked about this? What was it they wanted again?

She adjusted her sunglasses higher up her nose. "It needs a complete overhaul. You'd probably have to rebuild the entire thing. But we want to put in an automatic transmission."

"This has a three-hundred and twenty-five horse power manual transmission and you want to take that out?" he asked as though she were insane for even thinking it. "That's sacrilegious."

Rebecca didn't know enough about engines to comment either way. That had been her mother's decision, probably because of her father's arthritis. R.J. walked to the front of the car and popped the hood. He leaned over the engine and rested his hands on the edge of the hood. The movement lifted the hem of his stained shirt, and gave Rebecca a peak of the white elastic of his boxer-briefs. R.J. was a Fruit of the Loom kind of guy, standard white like the men who advertised the underwear on the packaging of the product. All lean muscle and powerful lines. Not an ounce of fat on him. And she knew for a fact the man could put away food like nobody she'd ever seen. How in the hell he managed to burn off that many calories was a mystery to her.

His brows pinched together as he reached an arm down and tinkered with the stuff under the hood. Rebecca had no clue what was under there. She assumed whatever it was made the car go — or stall as sometimes was the case. He turned some knobs and touched a few other things before slamming the hood shut. The loud thump matched the thumping of her heart.

"I'm probably going to have to strip it down to the metal frame and replace everything. The engine is in okay condition but it won't last much longer. And the timing belt is about to go." He turned to face her. "You're positive you want to put in an automatic transmission?"

"Yes." The heat from his green gaze had her breasts tingling inside her hot pink bra. When his attention wandered down to her mouth, which was still unpainted, her already unsteady heartbeat turned erratic.

"Let's head into my office and talk," he said in a gruff voice.

That sounded so much more sensual than it should have been. Like, he'd meant to say, "Let's go into my office so I can make you scream." Which, at this point, Rebecca wasn't sure she would refuse, but knew she should if she wanted to keep her sanity intact.

She followed him into the shop, past other employees who were working on cars, some of which were nothing more than bare metal frames. A stereo in the background blasted AC/DC over the sound of metal clanking against metal. One of the technicians lifted his chin in greeting to R.J., and a woman with long mahogany hair was in the reception area with a telephone pressed to her ear. She was an Amazon of a woman who probably towered over Rebecca's average five-six frame by at least four inches. Her fair skin and pale blue eyes were a striking combination with her dark hair. Rebecca lifted the corners of her mouth in a friendly smile, then the smile faded when she got a load of the way the woman looked at R.J. That she looked at R.J. wasn't what made Rebecca uncomfortable; lots of women looked at R.J., and R.J. usually looked back. It was the pure hunger and territorial gaze coming from her that had Rebecca looking away from her. R.J. didn't seem to notice. He kept right on walking until they came to a hallway and a bank of offices.

He stopped at the first one and opened the door for her, gesturing for her to enter before him. She brushed past him and tried not to breathe, so his clean, bar-soap scent wouldn't make her eyes roll back into her head. And if that didn't do it, then the pure heat coming off of him would.

The office was small and seemed even smaller when he closed the door and stepped around her. His shoulder brushed hers, and probably not by accident either. He'd always used every opportunity to knock her world off its axis, so why would now be any different?

The man had made a career out of torturing her.

He stopped directly in front of her, with about enough room to slip a hand between them. Maybe she ought to try it so she could feel those steely muscles beneath his dirty shirt. No, because then she'd want to rip the thing off like some crazed animal. This was a very bad idea, coming inside. They should have stayed outside, because outside had an unlimited amount of air that R.J. couldn't consume.

He lifted his hands, and she braced herself for him to touch her, to feel those long, blunt fingertips smoothing over her skin. And she would welcome it, because R.J. Devlin had the ability to send her to another planet. But he didn't touch her. Exactly. His fingers slipped her sunglasses down her nose until they were all the way off. Then he nestled them on top of her head.

"There we go," he said. "Did you really think I was going to let you keep hiding behind those?"

Was she supposed to answer him? Like, with an intelligent answer? Because she couldn't think about anything other how easily she'd almost succumbed to him. Again.

"The sun was bright," she said lamely but with as much conviction as her wired brain could manage.

"The sun inside the office?" he countered as he settled in his desk chair.

"Shut up." The only reason she sank into the other chair, was because her legs were about to give beneath her anyway.

One corner of his mouth quirked in a half-smile. "There she is. I thought maybe you were having an off day."

She pulled in a deep breath and tried to realign her focus on why she came. What was it again? It certainly wasn't to be near R.J. The man was bad for her mental health.

Oh, yeah. Her father's car.

"So, about how long do you think this will take?"

He paused before answering. "I could go all day."

Just take a deep breath so you don't reach across his desk and strangle him. Or kiss him. Because the last time that happened, things ended so well.

"The car, R.J. Can we focus on that please?"

He swiveled back and forth in his chair, and the whole time his eyes remained fixed on hers as though he were trying to figure her out. She didn't want him figuring her out, thank you very much.

"When do you need it by?" he finally asked.

"My dad's not retiring until June."

"I think I can manage that." He faced forward in his chair and grabbed some papers, which he jotted notes on. "And other than the transmission, is there anything specific you want done with it?" he asked without looking up.

"Other than the paint color, no," she answered while roaming her eyes over his blonde locks. They were soft, she knew that. And only because she remembered how they felt on her fingers. R.J. wasn't the type of man to get his hair professionally styled at a high-priced salon. The man he saw did nothing more than snip off a few inches with a pair of scissors. Such a low maintenance thing, and it suited him perfectly. She couldn't say for sure, but he was probably one of those guys who didn't waste time combing his hair. He most likely shook the excess water out with a towel and went on his way. Rough and carefree. That was R.J. all the way.

He finished making notes and leaned back in his chair. The pen rolled back and forth between his big, callused palms. "What kind of color did you have in mind?"

"Orange. My dad loves orange." She adjusted her positing in the chair and tugged the hem of her skirt down. Had the thing been that short when she'd put it on? "And those double white stripes. You know the ones that go over the center of the car?"

One of his blonde brows lifted. "Z stripes?"

"If that's what they're called, then yes."

He nodded and folded his hands behind his head. "What else?"

She shrugged. "That's it."

"So I can have free reign over this thing?"

"Pretty much."

"And you trust me to do that?"

Were they still talking about her father's car? "You're the best at what you do." When he lifted both his eyebrows, she clarified. "With cars."

Oh my Lord, stop talking!

A sneaky grin crept along his mouth, broadsiding her with a wave of sexual awareness. "I know what you meant, Ms. Underwood."

They stared each other down like two people planning their battle strategies, only R.J. had never played fair. He was a sneaky bastard who always struck when she seemed to be the most defenseless. She rarely had time to prepare herself for him and always walked away exhausted, yet... strangely pleased.

Just as she was about the gather her purse and get the hell out of Dodge, his office door opened. A nauseating and over-powering perfume swirled around Rebecca as the woman from the reception area let herself into R.J's office. In her arms she carried a stack of papers and a sack from a fast food restaurant. When she set the papers down on the desk, her balloon-like breasts damn near fell out of her Argyle-printed v-neck sweater. Incredibly long legs were encased in a pair of jeans so tight, they look like they'd been sprayed on. Rebecca's natural competitive side rose full force, but she held back the urge to stand up and fluff her hair.

Who was she trying to impress, anyway?

"I need you to sign these," the woman said in a sing-song voice, like she was a breath away from a really good orgasm. "And I have this for you." She plopped the sack in R.J.'s lap. "But without the cheese, because I know you don't like that."

"Thank you," was all R.J. said as he picked the bag up and moved it to the desk. He nodded his head toward the papers. "What are those?"

She glanced at the papers. "Accounts that need to be closed. And don't even think about putting them off until later," the woman replied as she placed a hand on R.J.'s shoulder. "Because you'll stick your head under a hood of one of those cars and you'll forget all about these." She pinned Rebecca with those clear blue eyes of hers. "He thinks a world doesn't exist outside of a transmission. And if you think this is dirty," she went on, pointing to R.J.'s shirt. "You should see him at ten o'clock at night." She ended the statement with her deep red lips turned up in a grin, as though the sight of a dirty R.J. brought an exceptional amount of pleasure.

Now, Rebecca wasn't about to argue with that. But what she really wanted to do was scratch the woman's eyes out.

Which was ridiculous because The Amazon could have been a perfectly nice woman. Underneath all that makeup and exorbitant amount of cleavage could beat a heart of gold.

The familiarity between the two of them had something twisting deep inside her. Something that Rebecca wasn't about to name because it felt very similar to jealousy. The only reason she knew that was from all years of practice; all those years of R.J. going from one woman to the next and leaving Rebecca to wonder why...

Why what?

She'd been nothing more than a flash in the pan to him, which he'd acted perfectly okay with. The dark-haired woman seemed a lot more than that to him, if the way she caressed his shoulder was anything to go by. That hand of hers, with red shimmery painted nails, floated back and forth over his shoulder like he was some pet.

Unable to stomach anymore, Rebecca gathered her purse and stood from the chair. "Call me with the bill, and I'll come by to drop off a deposit." She just stepped through the doorway when R.J stopped her.

"Wait."

She turned, but his attention wasn't on her. His hand flew over the papers as he scrawled his signature at the bottom of each one.

"Actually, we require a deposit now." The woman's blue eyes zeroed in on Rebecca, daring her to challenge the statement. "Ten percent."

R.J. tossed the pen down, stacked the papers together and held them out to The Amazon. "I'm sure we can trust Ms. Underwood. In the meantime, I need you to start a file for her."

In other words, I'm-dismissing-you-so-you-can-go-do-your-job. Ms. Amazon didn't take well to the dismissal. Her fingers tightened on R.J.'s shoulder before releasing him. Rebecca stood aside as the woman took the papers and hurried out of the office.

Lover's quarrel? That's what it seemed like to Rebecca, but it was really none of her business. There were surely a lot of scorned women running around this town who had a bone to pick with R.J. Devlin. For a long time, Rebecca had been one of them, until she'd accepted her fate as such. She and R.J. weren't destined to be anything more than... well, she wasn't sure what they were.

The term "frenemies" came to mind, but even that didn't suit.

Even sitting in his chair, R.J. consumed so much space that the office felt like it was about to close in on her. She supposed that was his commanding side coming out. But when he stood, she felt the need to back up, even though she was already standing in the doorway.

He removed a set of keys from his pants pockets. "How are you getting to work?" he asked.

She lifted her chin. "I'm walking."

He lifted a brow in doubt and Rebecca felt her independent streak come out in spades.

"Why does no one think I'm capable of walking two miles?"

"I can't imagine," he said with a pointed look at her heels.

Okay, yes. They weren't the ideal footwear for walking to her practice. And yes, they pinched her toes after several hours. But what other choice did she have? She'd left her car in her parents' driveway, and she had to get to work somehow.

R.J. rolled his eyes at her obvious lack of common sense. "I'll drive you."

I'd rather walk barefoot. Over hot coals. "I'm fine," she said instead.

He came toward her with slow movements, and she tried not to focus on those long, powerful legs. "I have to go out anyway, and your practice is on my way."

She studied him for a moment. The brown flecks in his green eyes were especially pronounced today. They looked like specks of gold in contrast to the emerald irises. The combination of his blond hair and green eyes had always made him look like a good ol' boy. Or maybe the good ol' boy's evil twin.

"You do not have to go out," she countered.

"Always so technical," he said. "Humor me anyway."

And with that, he placed a hand on her lower back and ushered her out of the shop. Even through her blouse, the heat of his hand warmed her skin. The heat travelled down her legs, paying special attention to her loins, which had been painfully neglected over the years. As though her body remembered his touch, her nerves ignited with a fire they hadn't felt in nine years. Nine long years of mundane love-making that could barely light a match. One touch from R.J. and she remembered why no other man had measured up.

They reached some kind of muscle car that was in pristine condition. The flawless, shiny vehicle was white with a thin black stripe going around the base of the car. The thing was mean-looking and only had two doors, each probably weighing more than she did. With no emblem visible, Rebecca had no clue what kind of car this was. Nor was it the same one she'd seen R.J. driving a few months ago.

"What happened to the Firebird?" she asked as he unlocked her door and went around to his side.

"I sold it a few months ago and picked this up for pennies," he answered as they both climbed in the car.

The leather seats were cool and in perfect condition. They were shiny and the same color as coal.

"I fixed this up in my spare time."

"What kind of car is this?" she asked while running her hands over the soft interior of the door.

"It's a '68 Chevelle." The engine was loud and rumbly, just as a muscle car should sound. The vehicle vibrated with power around them. R.J. slid a pair of dark sunglasses over his eyes and glanced at her. "Want to drive it?" he asked with a smile.

Her heart beat up to her throat when he grinned at her like that. That smile always meant trouble, and it was usually something Rebecca wasn't prepared for. One of his many talents was catching her off-guard. But that wasn't entirely his fault. The fault lay with her for being too unaware for whatever devious plan he had for her.

"I think I'll stick with modern cars."

His big hands shifted the gear as they pulled onto the road. "You should step outside your comfort zone every once in a while."

Thanks, but I did that once already.

She'd been left without her virginity, and loving a man she knew she'd never have.

TWO

R.J. WAS CONVINCED that Rebecca Underwood was placed on this planet to drive him out of his mind. Long legs, high heels, and a sassy attitude were all the key ingredients for an irresistible woman. And he would know all about irresistible.

He'd spent the better part of fifteen years trying to resist her and the weird spell she had over him. Ninety-nine percent of the time he'd succeeded. Unfortunately that one percent was what had kept him up a lot of nights and drove him into the arms of other women. Women like his office manager, Danielle.

Danielle wasn't an easy woman to deal with, and Rebecca had handled her like a champ. Even though R.J. had seen right through that calm exterior. The woman was quite a plotter, which he'd been victim to many times in his youth.

They cruised down the almost deserted road in silence. His passenger had her legs and arms crossed like she expected him to jump over there and all but molest her. What kind of guy did she think he was?

Okay, maybe Rebecca wasn't the best person to answer that question. He'd left a bad taste in her mouth, and he didn't blame her for how little she thought of him.

Her loose, red curls looked especially soft and picked up the sunshine like little red magnets. He knew she hated those curls, and one time, about ten years ago, she'd tried to have her hair relaxed. Seeing as though she'd never gone straight again, she hadn't been pleased with the result. Personally, he always thought curls were sexy as hell. But Rebecca's curls went beyond sexy.

"I'm sorry for Danielle's behavior," he found himself saying, mostly because he couldn't stand her icy silence. "She can be a bit territorial."

Rebecca glanced at him, but her expressive eyes were hidden behind those damn sunglasses. "Over you?"

The woman really didn't miss anything. They came to a red light, even though there was no one in the intersection. The pause gave him an opportunity to place his attention on her. "I was going to say the shop. But yeah, me too."

She tilted her head, as though trying to figure out why without making him say it. "And why would she do that?"

He grinned in spite of himself, because Rebecca was smarter than that. "Because we used to sleep together."

The only reaction she showed was her teeth gnawing on her full lower lip. Then she did something he didn't expect. She laughed, and it carried on until she had to wipe moisture away from her eyes. Somewhere in the midst of her laugher she muttered something. He couldn't make the words out, but he swore he heard "stupid."

The light turned green and he shifted gears to press on down the road. "You disapprove?"

She held her hand up as though to silence him. "What you do with your employees is your prerogative, R.J."

"Don't look now, but you're actually turning green," he teased and skimmed the back of his index finger down her cheek. So damn soft. "It's a good look for you."

She smacked his hand away and actually scooted closer

to the door. She was good and pissed now. Excellent. *This* Rebecca he knew how to handle.

"Why the hell would I be jealous?" she asked in a sharp voice.

He pulled into the parking lot of her practice and stopped in front of the building. Just as she opened the car door, he said to her, "Because you know what you're missing out on."

If it were humanly possible, there would be actual steam coming out of her ears. As it was, the rosy hue coloring her cheeks gave him enough satisfaction.

"You know, on the outside you look quite normal. But on the inside you're the Angel of Death." The smile on her face was dripping with ire, a look he put there so many times he was unused to seeing anything else.

She slammed the door shut, but he wasn't about to let her have the last word. He rolled down the window and pulled up alongside her as she strode with angry steps.

"You're welcome for saving your feet from those deadly weapons you're wearing." Without giving her a chance to respond, because he just knew she would have something to say, he sped out of the parking lot. He flipped a U-turn, shifted gears and headed back to his shop. A glance in the rearview mirror showed she'd already entered the building. But he was damn sure she'd glared at him from behind those black sunglasses. How could he expect anything less from her? Over the years, he'd learned to read her body language and facial expressions. Lip biting meant nerves. Lip biting coupled with laughter? That was a whole other extreme beyond nerves. R.J. would label that as hysteria. Rebecca would label it something different just to spite him.

She was annoyed as hell with him, but he loved it. Anything else threw him off-guard because that was the routine they'd fallen into about nine years ago. Actually, if one wanted to be exact, it was eight years, four months, seven days and however many hours. Not that he was counting. Or *still* thinking about it.

If he were a smart man, or didn't have a death wish, he'd stay the hell away from her. While he couldn't help her coming to his shop, because he was the best, as she'd said, he could have let her walk to work. After all, she'd insisted, and he wouldn't be driving the short distance back to work cursing himself. Or suddenly needing a bucket of ice cold water dumped over his head.

He *should* have let her walk. Because, while he enjoyed getting her panties in a twist, he almost always paid for it later. Usually by having to go home and take a freezing shower. But all the cold water in the world couldn't get Rebecca Underwood out of his head. And he slipped into the same old patterns every single time. And Rebecca was smart. She was one of the smartest people he knew. Not only did she have his number, but she always saw through his bullshit. She was one of the few people he knew who had that talent.

That's why he hadn't sugar-coated his relationship with Danielle. Okay, getting involved with an employee hadn't been the smartest thing. But R.J. hadn't always been very smart when it came to his choice of women. In the past, he'd always gotten involved with whatever female had shown interest. And Danielle had more than shown her interest in him. Shortly after hiring her, she'd cornered him in his office and rubbed her hand over his crotch. His body had instantly responded, and he'd taken her right there on his desk.

He'd thought those days of indiscriminate, anytime, anywhere sex had been behind him. His hormones had had other ideas. For the next year, they'd jump into bed together every once in a while, until R.J. had called it quits. The signs of complications, a.k.a. Danielle developing feelings for him, had started to surface. Suffice it to say, Danielle hadn't been pleased and had all but begged him to give them another chance.

The truth was, he valued his work environment too much

to let things get too sour with his office manager. And, to be honest, Danielle was the backbone of Devlin Motors. She did everything from the bookkeeping to face-to-face time with the clients. Her outgoing personality and personable ways with them made her good at wooing even the pickiest clients. She knew the business inside and out, almost as well as he did.

Damn, but she'd been dynamite in bed and had always been up for a good round of sex whenever he needed it. But he feared letting her go would have been detrimental to the shop. So he'd kept her, but made sure she knew to keep things professional.

He pulled into the back parking lot of the shop and turned the car off. Danielle's behavior toward Rebecca had toed the line of inappropriate. R.J. couldn't figure it out because Rebecca hadn't done or said anything to elicit that reaction from Danielle. And it's not like women hadn't come into the shop for business before. He'd never had an issue with Danielle behaving in such a way.

His guys were hard at work restoring a Pontiac Lemans, a GTO, a Buick Skylark, and two Mustangs. Two had only needed new engines and paint, but the others had to be stripped down to the chassis. And all this wasn't including the Camaro Rebecca had just dropped off. Luckily for him, his team was damn good and efficient.

Rebecca said he could have free rein over her father's car, which made him downright giddy. Sometimes a client would ask for something a little unorthodox, and R.J. always felt like he was committing an act of treason against the car. Ideas were already swirling around in his head, but before he could get started, his best client and biggest money maker rolled into the parking lot. Charlie McGready parked his sweet little 1949 Oldsmobile coupe and stepped out. R.J. had restored that one for Charlie about a year and a half ago, and it hadn't been easy. He specialized in muscle cars, but every once in a while he'd get an older classic that posed more of a challenge. The

Oldsmobile had taken him several months to bring back to glory, but it had been worth it.

R.J. put his issue with Danielle on hold and walked to greet his best client. Charlie was in his late forties, medium height and had a limp in his left leg from an injury sustained during the first Gulf war. He also had an unlimited amount of cash flow for his cars. R.J. had decided the man must have inherited from a wealthy relative. Not many people in this town could afford a forty-seven-thousand dollar classic car, not to mention the countless other cars he paid R.J. to fix up for the annual car show in Reno.

"Charlie, how are you?" R.J. greeted with a shake of the other man's hand. Charlie's grip was firm and solid.

"Business as usual. She still drives like a dream," Charlie said with a gesture to the Oldsmobile behind him.

"I'm glad." R.J. was especially pleased, considering what a challenge the car had been.

"I'm sure you know the Reno show is coming up in a few months." When R.J. nodded, Charlie continued. "I found two gems at an auction recently that I want to show. They aren't much to look at now, and one of them is pretty beat up. But I think you can work your magic on them."

R.J. crossed his arms over his chest. "What kind of cars are we talking about?"

"A '35 Mercedes 500K and a '32 Packard Deluxe. I know you don't normally deal with cars that old, but after fixing up that old thing," he said with a wave of his hand toward his car. "I figure you can do just about anything."

It was true, R.J. preferred cars from the sixties and seventies because the older the car, the harder it was to find parts for them. But he'd never backed down from a challenge before, and he'd done enough pre-war era cars to take the project on.

"All right, why don't you bring them in when you can and I'll take a look at them. When's the show this year?"

"I'm doing the Silver Dollar Car Show in August. They welcome any make and model."

R.J. rubbed a hand across his chin. That gave him four months to find the parts, strip down and rebuild two cars. "Okay. That's doable. The sooner you can bring them in, the sooner I can get started on them."

"My boys and I will be by this afternoon. I already have a list of things I want done to the cars. But I know you'll do them justice."

Charlie was one of the clients who wanted to control every detail of the rebuild, down to the seatbelts. R.J. didn't usually mind that, but Charlie had a habit of changing his mind a dozen times before the project was finished. At the end of the day, as long as the checks cleared, Charlie could control whatever he wanted.

"Sounds like deal," R.J. said, and he shook the man's hand again.

Charlie sauntered off, and R.J. went inside the shop to find Danielle. Donald Underwood's car had already been wheeled inside, waiting its turn. R.J. wanted to see to the details of that one personally. Not that he didn't trust his guys; they were as good as he was. But something of Rebecca's would be left up to him.

Danielle was in the front office, typing on the computer. He headed that way, but was intercepted by Alex who was wearing a white jumpsuit to protect his clothes from the paint sprayer.

"We've run into a little snag with Walter Hamilton's Mustang," Alex said.

"What's up?"

"The paint color we ordered for him had been discontinued. And they don't know if they can send us a replacement by our deadline."

R.J. rubbed the back of his neck. A headache this early in the morning was not a good sign of the day ahead. "And why are they just now telling us this?"

"Apparently there was a mix up in their computer. He tried to make me feel better by telling us we weren't the only ones this happened to."

"I doubt that," R.J. muttered. "Okay, find a suitable replacement so we can get Walter's approval. Then we'll have to put a rush on it. If not, then we'll have to explain to Walter what happened and hope he'll understand." He turned to the office, then stopped himself. "Be sure to get on that ASAP," he reminded Alex even though R.J. knew the employee wouldn't have to be told twice.

Things like this popped up all the time. A part would go on backorder or an engine would be in worse shape than they anticipated. What separated R.J from other shops was his ability to ease the client's fears and turn out a spectacular car despite bumps in the road.

"You're the boss," Alex answered with a salute.

R.J. refocused his attention to the matter at hand. Danielle wasn't going to like this, but he didn't really give a damn. The woman was opinionated to a fault and just as hard-headed, a combination that could be combustible. When he entered the office, she was typing at a rapid rate on the keyboard and muttering to herself. The scene was odd. For one, he'd never known her to talk to herself. And two, she was twitchy. Both her knees were bouncing up and down, and she kept pausing to nibble on her fingernail.

The latch on the door clicked, and she turned in her chair to face him. Her brow was pinched in tension, but immediately smoothed when she saw him. Her lips turned up in a welcoming smile, and she crossed her legs. Probably trying to be provocative, which would have worked at one time. Not anymore.

"Was that Charlie I saw?" she asked.

"Yeah, he came to talk to me about the Reno show."

Her eyebrows tugged together in disbelief. "Already?

Isn't that several months away?"

"August." He stepped farther into the office but made sure to keep his distance from Danielle. If he came too close she might get the wrong impression. "But the cars he wants done will take a lot longer. They're both pre-war and could take some time to locate the parts."

Danielle turned toward the computer and hit a few keys. "What are they?"

"A 1935 Mercedes 500K and a 1932 Packard Deluxe."

"No kidding?" Danielle said with wide eyes. "That Packard might be a challenge, but I think we can do it."

His office manager had always been resourceful and efficient when locating rare parts. Her ability to pull this off didn't worry him.

"So, you want me to start finding parts even though we haven't seen the car yet?" Danielle asked while still typing.

"Yeah, just start making a list so we can be prepared. Charlie and his sons will be by later today to drop the cars off. In the meantime…" His words trailed off when his eyes landed on a pink invoice sitting on top of some client folders.

He picked the paper up and scanned the information. "Didn't we close this account out several months ago?"

Danielle snatched the invoice out of his hands and placed it in an empty space on the other side of the computer. "Don't worry about that. It must have accidentally been placed with the to-be-closed accounts."

"And how did that happen, Danielle?"

She spun around in her chair to face him and pinned him with an irate look. "I don't know, R.J. Maybe because I do everything around here, and sometimes things get overlooked?"

Whoa, what the hell? Since when did Danielle get all snappy with him? And when did she take to biting her nails? Nails that she spent a lot of time and money to keep up?

The narrowed look on his face must have conveyed his

displeasure with her outburst. Her shoulders slumped over. "I'm sorry. I didn't sleep much last night so I feel out of sorts today. I promise this will get taken care of."

"Well, according to that, the guy still owes us two hundred dollars, so see that you make it your first priority." Normally R.J. didn't bust his employee's asses like some drill sergeant, unless the situation called for it, and this one definitely did. Two hundred dollars was a drop in the bucket compared to how much the shop brought in every month. What he was more concerned with was potentially losing a client because they'd failed to collect the entire bill. But Danielle should be able to charm the guy into forgiving them. If she could get her act together.

"I was going to tell you to open a file for the Underwood car, but that needs to be put on hold until you take care of this other account."

Danielle shook her head. "I still can't believe you let her walk out of here without getting a deposit from her. Don't you remember the last time that happened?"

Hell, yeah he remembered. The man who'd brought his car in said he hadn't had the money to pay ten percent up front. So R.J. had started on the car anyway and ended up finishing the whole thing without being paid a dime from the owner. In order to be collect, they'd had to take the guy to small claims court. A year later, R.J. had finally received the money owed him, but the process had hardly been worth it. Since then he'd made the shop's policy to collect money up front before he started the restoration process.

Knowing Danielle, her consternation had more to do with Rebecca herself than the shop's rules.

R.J. leveled her serious look. "Trust me, Rebecca won't stiff us for the bill. She's good for it."

Those icy blue eyes of hers stared back at him as though trying to figure out whether or not there was more to the story. There was, but he wasn't about to share that with Danielle.

"You know her that well?" she finally asked.

Should he clue her in on how well he knew Rebecca? Knowing Danielle, she wouldn't take it well, especially given her weird behavior today. "Well enough," was all he said.

Danielle leaned back in her chair and crossed her legs. He knew that look. Gone was the bundle of nerves and in its place was the bold vixen who'd practically ripped his clothes off a week after hiring her.

"Let me take you out to dinner." Danielle always slipped into that tone of voice when she was trying to make him melt at her feet. The kind of tone one would dub a "bedroom voice." It had always amazed him how she could transform herself that fast.

"Not a good idea, Danielle. Besides I'm going to be working late tonight." He would only work late if he needed to, but he really didn't. Going out to dinner with Danielle was out of the question. Setting aside that line he didn't want to cross again, he had no interest in her anymore. No, these days his thoughts were more on red-haired women with green eyes and a spunky attitude. A woman who still elicited reactions from him even though those reactions were bad for his sanity. Because he was supposed to have exorcised her from his brain nine years ago, but that had only had the opposite effect. Rebecca still lingered in his mind and crowded his thoughts with how she'd felt — underneath him.

Danielle waved a hand in the air and turned back to her computer. "Yeah, you and your *no dating* rule. It would only be a problem if you allow it to."

Which was exactly why he couldn't allow that anymore. It had almost gotten out of hand one time, and he could never go there again. He'd built this business from the ground up, and he wouldn't destroy it for anyone.

"We've talked about this and things haven't changed." He turned to walk out of the office and said over his shoulder, "Get that account straightened up, then start finding parts for

Charlie's cars."

With that, he left her alone in the office and walked back into the main shop. There were a few things that needed his attention, and he'd already gotten a late start. From his back pocket his cell phone vibrated. R.J. withdrew it and glanced at the screen.

Just so you know, walking in heels can tone your calves more than walking in flats.

Rebecca had probably been waiting all morning to say that to him, because she couldn't stand letting him have the last word. With an ear to ear grin, he responded to her text message with one of his own,

What textbook did you get that out of?

In that moment Alex approached him about some issue with after-market gauges. R.J. was only half listening to his tech, which he waited for Rebecca to respond, because he knew she would. No way would she let that question slide. A few seconds later she shot him a return text message.

Bite me.

R.J. laughed the whole way to the GTO that had been giving Alex fits.

THREE

TURNS OUT HE'D had to work a lot longer than anticipated. The longer hours were due to little problems that kept popping up throughout the day. Some of them had been nothing more than a nuisance that he'd been able to fix with little effort. Others had been more troubling because they'd been caused by Danielle's mistakes. Mistakes she hardly ever made. One had set them back quite a bit on the Pontiac and would cause R.J. to miss his deadline for completion. The incorrect ignition coil she'd ordered hadn't even come close to fitting. Luckily the client was a family friend and would likely not mind the extension on finishing the car.

Frankly, R.J. hadn't really been worried about that. Yes, the car would have to be put on hold for the time being. What concerned him was Danielle and the little slip ups she'd been making. Normally, he'd been able to trust her with anything. But over the past few weeks, his confidence in her and been shaken a bit. At first, he hadn't really noticed that a bill had been filed in the wrong place or double-booking an appointment. After all, no one was perfect. A few mistakes he could overlook, but Danielle's recent behavior was out of character for her. She blamed lack of sleep, which was entirely conceivable.

Unfortunately he'd been too busy to question her about it. Just as he'd had a moment of down time, Charlie and his two sons had come in with their cars. The consultation alone had taken two hours, then R.J. had spent the rest of the day on the computer software with Rodney, one of his techs, starting the design process. The cars were going to be difficult, to say the least. But R.J. had never backed down from a challenge, and he wasn't about to start now. His only worry was Danielle. She'd assured him she was already on locating the rare parts, but after her recent unsteady performance, his confidence was slim.

Now all he wanted to do was hit his weight machine then settle on his leather couch with an ice cold beer. Maybe if he drank enough he wouldn't go to bed thinking about Rebecca. Then again, that wouldn't be any different from any other night.

As he pulled into his driveway, he let out a groan at the sight of his sister's compact car. Normally he loved spending time with his little sister. But tonight he wanted to be alone. Courtney could be exhausting on her best day. Shortly after recovering from her car accident, she'd lost her way a little. She'd put her design degree in the back of her mind and took up cleaning houses, a decision that left his whole family scratching their heads. And he really wasn't up to hearing a story about how some homeowner's weird cat had left a trail of fur balls for her to clean up. God love her, but the girl could talk. Luckily she'd pulled herself out of her weird depression and landed a job with Wright on Design, where she now worked as an interior designer.

He turned off the Chevelle and exited the car. Lord only knew what Courtney wanted. She had a habit of appearing at the oddest times. Just last week, she'd showed up and was eating a bowl of cereal by the time he'd gotten out of bed. And he was an early riser, so there was no telling how long she'd been awake. Possibly, she'd never gone to bed.

Three years ago, Courtney had been in a devastating car accident and she'd never been the same. For months she'd suffered from temporary memory loss, not to mention the physical damage done to her body. Even with time to heal and physical therapy, she still suffered from memory problems. The simplest things, like a conversation she'd had a day before were fragmented in her mind. It was as though the wires in her brain were crossed and she had to concentrate extra hard to remember her own cell phone number.

As he opened the front door, the scent of burnt toast blasted him in a wave of nauseating toxic fumes. Great. Not only had Courtney broadsided him, but she'd made his whole house smell like a fire pit.

"I'm rethinking my decision to give you my spare key," he announced as he shut the door and walked farther into the house.

"Then who will you call when you lock yourself out?" she countered as she just came out of the kitchen with two pieces of toast on a plate.

"That only happened once." R.J. stood back as Courtney settled at the table and took a small bite of her meal. Ever since her accident she'd left her hair its natural blonde, which was unusual compared to the outrageous shades she used to color it. She rarely ever did anything with it. The long strands were often pulled back into a high ponytail. Long ago, she'd removed her nose ring and her face was almost always make-up free. The woman in front of him resembled his sister in looks, but underneath was someone he didn't recognize. The most troubling thing was that she repeatedly insisted she was fine.

"Why does everyone keep worrying about me?" she used to demand when R.J. had questioned her about her *maid services*.

"How many pieces of toast did you burn?" he asked after taking a chair at the table with her.

"Just two. I'd sat down to go over my appointments for tomorrow and lost track of time."

Now, *that* was typical of his sister.

"You look like you had a busy day," Courtney observed with a nod to his greasy shirt.

R.J. leaned back in his chair to stretch his tired legs out. "And how busy was your day?" he countered.

"Yes, I was busy. My boss, Cynthia, put me in charge of my first project today. It's a redesign of a guest cottage."

"These poor people aren't going to end up with zebra stripes on their walls, are they?"

She shoved a piece of toast in her mouth and swiped away stray crumbs. "I know I have eccentric taste, but I'm not that outrageous. And there's nothing wrong with infusing a little personality into your home. Mr. I-Love-Beige," she added.

He narrowed his eyes at her. "What's wrong with beige?"

"Nothing," she answered with a lift of one shoulder. "If you have no flare."

"I have plenty of flare."

Courtney picked up her toast, and gazed at him. "Your choice of women doesn't count."

R.J. scrubbed a hand down his face. Damn, he was tired. "Court—"

"When have I ever given you shit about how you've screwed practically every single woman in this town, that your love life has become a revolving door? I haven't always agreed with it, and I think you know why, but that's beside the point."

Whoa, what the hell?

She picked up her cell phone and glanced at the screen. "Everybody's busy tonight. Rebecca never returned my text message, and Lacy says Abigail has croup and she's stuck at home with all four kids because Chase is at work. I thought about going over there, but those boys give me a headache."

She kept rubbing her head, right around the faint scar that ran from the side of her forehead to her cheek bone. The scar wasn't that noticeable, just the remnants of a nasty gash. But R.J. knew Court was sensitive about it. She'd always claimed that was the reason her ex-fiancé Grant had skipped town; because he hadn't been able to handle the physical scars of her accident. R.J. suspected there was more to the story. The details behind her mysterious engagement, then abrupt break-up, had been fuzzy. That was something she hadn't been willing to share with the rest of the family. Although he respected his sister's privacy, R.J. was more than curious about it.

"What's the matter?" he asked when Courtney kept rubbing her head.

"I just have a headache." She tossed the last bite of toast in her mouth. "And I keep feeling like there was something I was supposed to do today, but I can't remember what."

"I hope it was nothing important."

"Me too." She stood from the table, gathered her trash and disposed of it in the kitchen. When she came back she asked him, "By the way, what did you do to piss Rebecca off?"

He waited before answering, but he wasn't sure what to say. What she should have asked was "When do you *not* piss Rebecca off?" The answer would be "not very often." Of course, her feathers were so easily ruffled. And they were such pretty feathers. Sexy and irresistible feathers.

He leaned back in his chair and grinned. "I dragged her into a closet and ravished her."

Courtney shot him a droll look. "And that would be just like you, wouldn't it?"

No need to mention that he actually had done that, though not with Rebecca. It had been one of many impulsive, and stupid, moments as a teenager. But it had been damn fun.

"Don't answer that," his sister said with a roll of her eyes.

"I wasn't planning to. And what makes you think I did anything to her in the first place?"

Courtney lifted her shoulders in a half-shrug. "I don't know. She sounded... odd. Like she was distracted. She kept asking me to repeat myself when we talked earlier."

"Again, why would you assume I did that to her?" Was it a coincidence that Rebecca sounded distracted on the same morning she had an encounter with him? Not likely. R.J. gladly took full credit for that.

Courtney studied him for a moment, her blue eyes zeroing on him like insights into his darkest thoughts. "No reason," was all she said.

Okay, then. Whatever the hell that meant. Courtney could be annoyingly cryptic when she wanted to be.

"Something's going on in that strange head of yours," he said.

"Nothing stranger than usual," she said with a half-smile. "I know you think you're sly, dear brother, but I have your number."

R.J. didn't doubt that for a moment. No one knew him better than his sister.

"One of these days, you're going to see what's right in front of you." With those pearls of wisdom, she gathered her bag and keys and walked out the front door.

Shit, R.J. saw Rebecca just fine. In fact, he saw her too much. Too deeply. Wanting things he couldn't have and had no business going after in the first place because Rebecca was too good for him. Had it been smart to climb the trellis to her bedroom room window? Smart to steal her virginity like the thief he was?

No and hell no.

That night had started with a scorching kiss in his parents' driveway when Rebecca had stopped by looking for Courtney. She'd gotten him instead, and after he'd spent the day seeing her everywhere he went in town, he'd reached his limit.

Rebecca had deserved better than someone like him taking what he hadn't had a right to take. Sure she'd willingly given it up because she'd been half in love with him. He'd gone to her knowing how she felt about him, which made him the lowest of assholes. But after spending summer after summer watching her run around in cut off shorts and blooming into a gorgeous young woman, he'd snapped.

Okay, yeah, underneath his care-free exterior were feelings for her he'd been unwilling to explore. Because they'd scared the shit out of him. They started with the letter L and ended with a white picket fence.

****

It was only 8:05 and already her day had the makings of a Twilight Zone episode. Actually, it had started last night when she'd received a phone call from Dr. Gross, the man who owned the practice where Rebecca worked. Apparently he'd received a jury summons for which he was unable to get out of. He'd suggested having all his appointments rescheduled, but Rebecca couldn't bring herself to do so. Besides, he had a light patient lineup for the day, and there was no reason why Rebecca couldn't work double time and see his patients too.

At least, that had seemed like a good plan until their only nurse came down with a nasty case of food poisoning. Now Rebecca was supposed to see a day full of patients with only herself, Erica, the physician's assistant, and Janet, who manned the front desk. Of course she thought she could do it. There was no reason why she couldn't juggle her patients and Dr. Gross's as well.

Because Trouble was such a small town, and they were only one of two practices, Rebecca knew all her patients personally. She knew their names, their birthdays, and their personalities. She knew her first patient, five year old Benjamin, was ticklish on the bottom of his feet and always asked for a grape sucker. Dr. Gross's patients, on the other hand, she knew next to nothing about. Rebecca didn't like going into an appointment, not knowing what she was dealing with. Studying charts helped. But those were just numbers and information.

She hit a few keys on her laptop and pulled up the next patient file. A ten year old girl named Lindsey, who was scheduled for an 8:30 checkup. The girl was on a double-dose of Adderall for ADHD and was due for her routine three month checkup. Because Adderall was a highly addictive drug, all patients were required to have an exam every three months, to make sure they weren't abusing the drug. Rebecca thought it was odd that a girl as young as ten was on a double dose of the drug. But, then again, this was Dr. Gross's patient and Rebecca didn't know anything about the situation. But according to her chart, she was diagnosed with Type 1 classic ADHD, meaning she had a combination of hyperactive-impulsivity and inattentiveness. It was the most common form, and people tended to respond well to stimulant medications. However, Rebecca noted in her chart, that Lindsey had been switched from Adderall to Adderall XR, which was a once-a-day tablet. Then Dr. Gross had increased the dosage to 30mg. The usual dosage was 20mg, because that was simply a double dose of regular Adderall. 30mg for a ten year old girl seemed rather high, but maybe her ADHD had proven difficult to manage.

Rebecca pushed away from her desk and took a sip of coffee. A second cup by eight a.m. was usually an omen of how her day was going to go. Meaning, not good. Could be because she'd gotten hardly any sleep the night before. Why? Well, she wouldn't go there. The big, blond man with wide shoulders and green eyes had already wreaked enough havoc with her nights. She did not need him messing with her day.

Soon enough, she'd see him. After all, she still owed the deposit for her father's car, which she was paying for and her mother would cover the rest. But she really did not want to go back down there and be near him. And smell him. And hear his deep voice. And see those callused, grease-stained hands and remember how they'd felt on her.

She glanced at her watch and saw that it was almost time for her first appointment. After that her day would be a blur of one child after another. Most days, Rebecca wasn't able to think straight until her day ended. Just as she stood from her chair, her cell phone rang.

"Hello?"

"Is this a bad time?" R.J.'s deep voice sounded very close and intimate in her ear.

It's always a bad time for you.

She sank back down into her chair, and smiled in spite of herself. "I have about ten minutes to spare."

"You're not still mad at me are you?"

"That depends on whether or not you want me to be mad at you."

He paused before answering. "You're going to do the opposite of whatever I say anyway, so does it really matter?"

"No," she admitted.

His chuckle had the hair on the back of her neck standing up. "Well, now that we have that cleared up, I have the estimate on your father's car."

Rebecca had no earthly clue how much it would cost, but her mother warned her it would be expensive. She was expecting some ungodly amount, but the one R.J. hit her with just about knocked the breath out of her.

"Are you there?" he asked after she hadn't said anything.

She shook her head. "Yeah, sorry. It's just a lot of money for one car."

"It's a long, detailed process. But trust me, honey, I'm worth every penny."

Oh, why did he have to use "honey" in that tone of voice? Like he was in the mood to drip actual honey on her sensitive skin and lick it off.

When she found her voice, which wasn't easy, she asked. "And the deposit is ten percent of that?"

"Yeah, you can come drop off a check anytime."

Why don't I mail it instead? Or carrier pigeon perhaps? "It'll be after six," she said.

"I'll be here."

She swore he was going to add the word *alone*, like he was inviting her to some forbidden tryst.

You already had one of those with him. You do not need to have another one.

"One more thing," he said as she was going to hang up before she started panting.

"What?" she asked in a near whisper.

"Your calves don't need toning."

The call ended without giving Rebecca a chance to respond. But what would she have said? "I'm thrilled you were checking me out?" Even if the thrill came from the deep place inside her where all her R.J. feelings were stored. Every once in a while that vault would open and a little zing would sneak out. It always caught her by surprise, even if she really wasn't that surprised.

She set her cell phone down and refused to think about R.J. Devlin anymore. Or, at least the next few hours. Seeing him later would ensure another sleepless night. Because every time she crawled into her bed, she remembered what it had felt like to have him crawl in there with her. The memory of his weight and how his long legs had hung off the end of her bed.

She rubbed her head in order to ward off the start of a headache. "Stop thinking about that night," she whispered to herself.

Pulling in a deep breath, she stood from her chair and

took one last bite of her bran muffin. The thing was roughly the equivalent of eating cardboard. Topped with sand. She barely managed to swallow the bite, and walked out of her office. The second she stepped into the quiet hallway, Erica greeted her with a smile. The girl wasn't that much younger than Rebecca, had curly brown hair, thick black lashes and dimples in her cheeks. Erica always wore a smile and had a kind word to say to everyone she was around. Rebecca had always liked her. She was wonderful with the kids and was just about the best P.A. Rebecca had ever seen.

"Your first appointment is in Exam Three," Erica announced.

"Thanks." Rebecca walked to the sink and washed her hands. After scrubbing up, she went through the door to the third exam room and was greeted by the blue eyes of Danielle. Rebecca managed to keep the surprise off her face when locking gazes with the woman. Seated on the exam table, with a cell phone in one hand, was a thin girl with long blond hair. Danielle smiled, though Rebecca would call it more of a grimace, as though the sight of Rebecca made her skin crawl.

Whatever. Rebecca hardly had enough room in her head to worry about what R.J.'s former lover thought of her.

Rebecca sat at the round stool in front of the counter and plastered a smile on her face. Erica had left the laptop open to Lindsey's chart. "Good morning, Lindsey." She turned to face the girl. "How are you feeling?"

"Good," she responded with a small smile.

"She just needs a refill of her Adderall," Danielle jumped in, as though Rebecca had just crawled out from under a rock and had no clue what she was doing.

She gestured toward the laptop. "Yes, I see she's due for her three month checkup. Let's start with your blood pressure."

The girl didn't so much as glance up from her phone as Rebecca performed the necessary tests. If any signs of loss of sleep, appetite or change in vitals were present, then either the dosage had to be changed or the drug was to be removed from the patient all together.

All of Lindsey's vitals were normal. Still, Rebecca had a hard time understanding why Dr. Gross would put the girl on such a high dose of the medication, especially since Rebecca didn't see an ADD evaluation form in the girl's file. Normally, the parent was given a sheet to be filled out by themselves and teachers at school to evaluate the child's level of inattentiveness. There wasn't one. And Lindsey seemed like a normal ten year old. She wasn't twitchy or talkative. Not so much as a finger moved, aside from the thumbs that were flying over the keypad of her phone. From what Rebecca could tell, the girl was very low key.

"Yes, she's been doing well," Danielle butted in. "No signs of change." She glanced at her watch. "I hate to rush you, but I have to get to work."

Rebecca retained her focus on Lindsey and tried to ignore the girl's mother. "We're almost finished. I just have a few questions to ask. Your weight looks good, but how's your diet been? Any change in appetite?"

"She eats like a horse," Danielle chimed in again. Her words were accompanied by an awkward laugh that Rebecca didn't find comforting.

Despite her dislike for the woman, Rebecca smiled at her then turned her attention to Lindsey. "Okay, Lindsey," Rebecca said, so that Danielle would get the hint to let her daughter answer for herself. "How have you been sleeping?"

"Good," she muttered with a lift of one shoulder, that Rebecca thought was supposed to be a shrug.

Rebecca referenced the girl's chart. "I see no change in weight, so that's good. And everything else seems to be normal. I'll go ahead and write you another prescription." Even though Rebecca wasn't comfortable giving a ten year old 30mg of Adderall XR, Dr. Gross had been doing so for several months, and all Lindsey's major vitals were in good shape. She made note of the information in the computer program.

"Are still using the same pharmacy?" she asked, while typing on the keyboard.

"Yes," Danielle answered briskly.

Rebecca shut the laptop and stood from her stool. "Okay, then. Tina at the front desk will fax the new prescription to the pharmacy. Just check out with her and go ahead and schedule your next three month checkup."

"We'll do that. Come on, Lindsey."

Rebecca left the exam room and washed her hands again. Even though they weren't dirty, just being in the presence of that woman made her feel unclean. That was an unfair statement, she knew, because she didn't know the woman from Adam. But something about her rubbed Rebecca the wrong way.

Could it be because she was R.J.'s lover? And obviously still had some kind of feelings for the man?

Ridiculous.

Preposterous.

Okay, maybe there was some thread of truth to that. But Rebecca wasn't naïve. R.J. had always drawn women to him like bees to honey. It was something she'd accepted a long time ago.

With Danielle, there was more than that. It was something more than just rubbing Rebecca the wrong way. She knew it had something to do with Lindsey's appointment. Rebecca had treated kids with ADHD and had prescribed Adderall many times. From what she could tell, Lindsey didn't fit the typical profile of Type 1 ADHD.

On the other hand, the girl wasn't even her patient. It wasn't her place to question Dr. Gross. He'd been practicing pediatrics for twenty-five years and was well-known in the town. It was her hope to someday take over his practice and run it herself. Over the past two years, Dr. Gross had earned her respect. He treated every child like they were his own. She'd learned a lot from him, and hoped she could continue to learn even more.

She pushed thoughts of Lindsey aside and prepared for the next patient, who was due to arrive in fifteen minutes.

So, why couldn't she help but think that something wasn't right?

FOUR

IT WAS 7:15 before Rebecca had been able to call it a day. And thank goodness she'd opted to wear flats, because what a day it had been. There had been too many patients for her to be able to stop and eat lunch. The mediocre bran muffin had hardly satisfied her appetite. By two o'clock dizziness had set in, and she'd had to force herself to stop and eat a sandwich. That hadn't lasted long either, and now she was so hungry she felt nauseous.

All she wanted to do was soak her aching bones in a hot bath, sip some red wine, and say *buh-bye* to the world for the next ten hours. Unfortunately, reality always had other plans. Her pantry was down to the bare bones, and her dry cleaning had been ready to be picked up for over a week.

Oh, and there was the little matter of paying R.J. his deposit. If her luck were to hold out, he wouldn't be there. Or maybe she could toss the check in the general direction of his shop and hope he received it.

She shook her head as she locked up the practice and walked to her car. Hadn't she just said the other day that she was adult enough to handle him? That R.J. still shouldn't be affecting her like this? For some reason, these days it seemed worse. Like every time she was around him, her resolve grew weaker. Her body had a harder time not reacting to him, as though it were tired of resisting him and was ready to give up. But she had to be strong. There had never been any future for them. Hell, there had never been a present for them. Just that one night when R.J. had snuck in through her bedroom window, slowly lifted the nightgown over her head and took her virginity like the bad boy thief he was.

She'd turned nineteen the week before and had been in no hurry to give her body over to just any guy. But, then again, R.J. had never been just any guy. She'd known from the moment she'd met him, that he'd be different.

As he'd laid himself on top of her, she'd screamed to herself, *Don't do this! He'll shatter you!* At that point, she'd been beyond listening to her own warnings. Just seeing him standing in her room had obliterated what willpower she'd had left.

In the years before, Rebecca had considered R.J. a friend, even though she'd always had the hots for him. But after that night, things had changed between them, just as she'd known they would. R.J. had made a point of staying away from her, and even his demeanor around her had taken a subtle shift.

It had become clear that R.J. had no longer considered her a friend. Not only that, but she'd watched him move on from her to one woman after another until she'd lost count. The reality had been hard to swallow, and she'd been forced to accept R.J. for what he was: a carefree playboy. And definitely not for her.

Even still, she'd fallen for him hard and fast. At first it had seemed impossible to live with the feelings, knowing he didn't reciprocate them. Like walking around with heart outside her chest. Being held by a man who'd taken it with little effort. After time, she'd learned to bury the feelings and live with them. Of course, that hadn't been easy, and the years she'd gone off to medical school had been a huge relief.

Then she'd moved back home and all it had taken was one look from those deep green eyes for all the feelings to come bubbling to the surface.

Despite all that, and the years since then, she still wanted him. Her insides still turned to Jell-O when she was around him. She still heard him whispering in her ear, telling her how incredible she felt. Even now, as she started up her car and headed to his shop, her body reacted.

She'd given her virginity to R.J. Devlin, and in return he'd ruined every other man for her. Part of her resented the hell out of him for that. And the other part smiled, because she knew she'd take the secret of them together to her grave.

A few minutes later she pulled into the shop's parking lot, and parked her car close to the office entrance. A few days ago, the place had been hopping with music and men tinkering with engines, or whatever men do in a car garage. Now the place was so quiet, Rebecca wondered if anyone was around. She assumed his Chevelle was parked around back. Or not. Maybe she could get away without seeing him after all.

The door to the front reception area was open. She walked, in but didn't spot anyone. From there, she walked through the back door that led to the shop. All she saw were cars; some of which were high up on lifts and others were nothing more than the metal frames. She spotted her father's car on the other side of the room. Still no R.J. And he didn't answer when she called out his name. He knew she'd be coming, so where was he? Would it be inappropriate for her to walk back to his office? She went anyway, just because she was dead tired and wanted to get this over with.

As she got farther down the hallway, she heard voices, one male and one female. The male's was definitely R.J.'s and she was pretty sure the other one belonged to Danielle. She came to a stop in his office doorway and spotted the two of them working. R.J. was seated at his desk, doing something on the computer. Danielle was next to his chair, leaning over so far that Rebecca swore those breasts of hers would come toppling out of her shirt and smack R.J. upside the head.

And yeah, that was probably the woman's plan.

Stop hating. You don't even know her.

The other woman spotted Rebecca first. She straightened and pinned her with those freaky blue eyes. They held an accusatory glare, as though to say, "What the hell are you doing here, you inadequate little thing?"

Yeah, I'm not too pleased to see you either.

Funny, how they'd just met and had already developed a dislike for each other. Rebecca wasn't the sort of person to go around disliking people for no real reason. In her book, everyone got a fair chance. Until they screwed it up. Danielle was the first person that Rebecca had disliked on sight. And every time the woman opened her mouth, Rebecca's displeasure grew even more. The feeling was so out of character for her, and Rebecca couldn't figure out why Danielle rubbed her the wrong way.

"Hey," R.J. said when he finally laid eyes on her.

Her heart rate immediately picked up, and she tried to squash down the light-headedness that always accompanied being near him.

"I have your check," she announced as she took the folded slip of paper out of her purse.

He leaned back in his chair and looked her over. "Okay," he responded. "Why don't you go finish this up?" he said to Danielle. He held out a stack of papers to her, which she took without saying a word. The woman must have sensed R.J.'s dismissal and not liked it. She stalked out of the office with sharp clacking sounds made by her platform heels. Rebecca would have taken a moment to admire the woman's exceptional taste in shoes if she hadn't found herself alone with the man who could turn her brain into mush with a simple tilt of his mouth. And then Rebecca was left alone with R.J.

Just the two of them.

All. Alone.

He stood from his chair and came around the desk toward her. His long legs took slow and deliberate steps, bringing him closer and closer to her. She refused the back away, because she needed to prove, both to him and to herself, the she could handle being that close to him. Because if R.J. knew, which he probably did, he would no doubt use it against her. She refused to allow him that tactical advantage.

"Thank you." He plucked the check from her hands and shoved it in his pants pockets. The sleeves had been ripped off his black t-shirt, which was noticeably cleaner than the white shirt he'd had on before. Powerful shoulders gave way to defined, muscled biceps. The tan cargo pants he had on sat on lean hips and accentuated his long legs. All in all, R.J. Devlin was a spectacular specimen of a man. Not an ounce of fat riddled that fantastic body of his.

He perched on the edge of the desk and crossed his arms over his chest. Goosebumps rose on the surface of her skin as his green gaze swept down her body. His attention lingered on her feet, the slowly rose back up.

She couldn't control the shiver that washed over her. "What?" she asked after he'd done nothing but stare at her.

"There are just a few things I want to run by you about your dad's car," he finally said.

She blinked at him. Had that announcement required scorching her clothes off with his eyes? "All right."

"Is your dad going to care how much horsepower I put in?"

How the heck should she know? She lifted her shoulders in a shrug. "He's always liked his cars mean and powerful. I'm guessing however much you put in would be okay."

"How about the seats? Do you know if he has a

preference for fabric?"

"I would go with leather."

He rubbed a hand along his jaw and stared over her shoulder, as though thinking. "Okay. Do you know how he wants the overall integrity of the car? What I mean is, does he prefer to keep it classic, or would he care if I put in some modern touches?"

Rebecca thought about that for a moment. None of these things she'd thought to find out. Over the years, she'd heard her father mention features that he wished he had in the car. Things like better tires and a newer sound system. The small details completely eluded her.

"I honestly don't know," she admitted. "But I think mostly he would rather the car remain true to its original form. But he does like conveniences. I know he would love to have a modern sound system and a high tech engine. Other than that, I would keep the car in its classic shape."

"And you're sure you don't want to keep the manual transmission?" he asked.

Rebecca held her hands up. "I agree it shouldn't be changed. But those are my mother's orders."

He stared at her for a moment, then nodded. "Okay."

"Have you started on it yet?"

"I've got a few sketches over there. They're all pretty rough."

Her heart rate kicked up in excitement. "Can I see them?"

Without saying a word, R.J. straightened from the desk, and circled around to the computer. A few drawings lay haphazardly on top of other various papers. He gathered them up and held them out to her.

She paid careful attention to not touch his fingers. There were so long and thick; strong and masculine as a man's should be. Unwanted memories of them floating over skin, along her abdomen and down her hips flooded her. She remembered with perfect clarity how his fingertips had bit into the soft flesh of her hips as he'd held her in place.

Yes, it was best for her sanity if she didn't touch him.

She tried to ignore how his gaze bore into her, so she could focus on his drawings. They were quite good. No, they were better than good. R.J. had a real talent for sketching. In each drawing, the car looked just how she imagined her father's car would look completely restored. Each one had a different variation of orange, with a different color or width of Z stripes.

"We usually use a computer program to come up with a design. But sometimes drawing them out by hand helps me come up with more ideas."

She glanced from one paper to the next. "These are really good. The single black stripe is nice. But I think I like the double white ones the best."

"Good, because that's the design I've decided to go with. I just needed to know a few things from you before I have Danielle order the parts."

The mention of Danielle made Rebecca remember her odd behavior earlier that morning. Since Rebecca legally wasn't allowed to talk about patients, she kept her thoughts to herself. "Good." She handed the papers back to R.J. He took them and set them down on the desk.

"Is that everything then?" she asked, because she really needed to get away from him. His scent, which Rebecca knew was Old Spice, was about to make her eyes roll back into her head. The office space, while decent-sized, felt suffocating and small. His big self filled every nook and cranny with his wide shoulders and tall frame. Rebecca wasn't considered short. At 5'7", she was typically considered above average height for a woman. But next to R.J. she felt like a dwarf. She was pretty sure he hovered around six-two or maybe six-three. Every time he stood near her, she was reminded of how small and curvy and feminine she really was.

"I think so," he answered. "Unless there's something else

you want."

Now that was a loaded question and one she had no intention of answering. And he knew it, which was why he'd asked.

She cleared her throat. "No, that's everything."

He came around the desk and stopped directly in front of her. For a moment, he didn't say anything, nor did he move. He just stared down at her in the unnerving way of his. She attempted to pull in a steadying breath because she feared that he was actually going to kiss her. Which she wasn't prepared for, yet at the same time she kind of was. Or perhaps she was confusing prepared with wanting? Because the want was definitely there, which was totally confusing the heck out of her.

A feeling she was well acquainted with.

Then his hand came up and tilted her chin until his mouth was a breath away from hers. Close enough to feel the heat on her own lips, but too far away to extinguish the sudden aching in her chest. And he didn't kiss her. His thumb swiped across her jaw line, sending shock wave of electricity all the way down to her toes.

"You had an ink smudge," he said in a husky voice.

She couldn't tear her eyes away from his. But she had to in order to keep her head on straight and mind in the game. That meant she needed to hightail it away from Devlin Motors to the comfort of her own home. Otherwise she'd find herself in the exact same position she had nine years ago.

"I have to go," she blurted out. Without saying another word, she spun on her heel and practically fled the scene of the almost-crime.

The cool outside air felt like a refreshing blast on her heated face. Her heart had yet to slow down to normal, but she'd worry about that later. For the time being, she needed to focus on putting one foot in front of the other. And as many miles in between her and R.J. as she possibly could.

What happened to the days of innocent teasing? When had he gone from making wisecracks to tying to scorch her clothes off? The teasing she could handle. The wisecracks could always put a smile on her face and send her into a combative mood. This sensual side that held all kinds of secrets she'd yet to unlock? That made her want to run for the hills. Which she was currently doing as she beat ground toward her car.

R.J. hadn't shown this side of him in a long time. Too long, that she'd almost forgotten how hard it was to resist him. She needed to stay away from him. If she valued her mental health, which she certainly did, she'd conduct all further business with him over the phone.

****

He knew damn well that touching her would be a mistake. But he'd been unable to help himself and now he wanted to kick his own ass for ignoring his common sense. Lately his iron-clad resolve had slipped, which he couldn't afford. Rebecca was hard enough to resist. If he went around ignoring his own rules, he'd be up shit creek.

The desk between them hadn't been big enough, yet it had been too much. Her skin was flawless and so damn creamy. It always had been, and he'd needed just one sample to remind himself. And he'd been right. Her skin was just as smooth and satiny as it had been nine years ago.

Good thing she'd booked. If she'd stayed, he would have kissed her. Those full, sexy lips had looked too good for him to ignore. The flush that had colored her cheeks had been amusing and a turn on all at once. Good to know he could still get a reaction out of her. Gave him a healthy amount of male satisfaction.

He remained in his office for several minutes after she'd hightailed it. Mostly to allow time for his hard-on to deflate. If he went to the shop with his pants tented, Danielle would likely get the wrong idea and act on it. In fact, he knew she would, and that was the last thing R.J. wanted. All he had to do was enter the room, and Danielle practically got herself in a tizzy. Not that he was trying to toot his own horn. He couldn't help how the woman felt about him. He had to constantly remind her of their professional relationship, and it was becoming wearisome. If she wasn't so good at her job, he would have let her go and found himself a man to run the place. Not that he didn't trust a woman to do a good job. He just wouldn't trust another female not to hit on him. A man wouldn't present the problem of sexual undertones.

When the throbbing in his pants finally subsided, he left his office and went into the front reception area. There were still a few things he needed to go over with Danielle. Before Rebecca came, he and Danielle had been making a list of all the rare parts she'd need to order. They'd been in the middle of Charlie's list and needed to finish. If he was going to restore the man's cars in time, Danielle had to hit the phones tomorrow.

She wasn't in her office, nor was she in the reception area. But a parts list was. One that she was supposed to have taken care of last week. Whenever Danielle completed an order, a note was made on the list, and the paper filed in the proper client's file. No such note was on this list, and R.J.'s deadline for the car was one month away. He picked up the paper and went into the shop looking for his manager. There, on the other side of the large space, was Danielle shaking some pills out of a prescription bottle. She downed a couple, or maybe just one, since he couldn't really tell, without using water. Since when did she take prescription medication? Was she ill and he wasn't aware of it?

"Are you sick?" he asked her when she spotted him.

Two slashes of red colored her cheek bones. With a pinch of her lips, she tucked the bottle in the back pocket of her jeans. "No," she answered with a quick shake of her head. "I uh..." she rubbed the back of her hand across her nose. "I've been having problems with migraines, so I had to go to the doctor."

He watched her carefully for a moment, not sure if she was telling the truth. Danielle had never been a liar, and he had no reason to doubt her explanation but... something nagged at him. She didn't seem like herself, but he couldn't put his finger on what it was.

Shoving the thoughts aside, he walked close to her. "What's the story with this?" he asked, holding up the paper in his hand.

She came toward him, her high heels making annoying clacking sounds on the concrete floor. Why did she insist on wearing those God-awful shoes? "What do you mean?"

"These parts were supposed to be ordered last week. I found it sitting on the desk in reception with no note that they'd been ordered. Please tell me that you ordered them, but forgot to file the work order."

Her blue eyes zeroed in on the parts list, but no sign of recognition flashed across her features. She took the paper from him and scanned the information. "I don't remember seeing this. Are you sure you gave it to me?"

Was she for real? How could she not remember? "Positive. We stood right in that room and talked about it. You said you'd get right on it. Don't you remember?"

Her dark brows pinched together, as though trying to remember the conversation. She shook her head. "Well, maybe I did order them, but I just didn't make a note of it. I honestly can't remember."

When he lifted a brow, Danielle rushed on. "Look, it's too late tonight to call them. I'll come in early in the morning and call them first thing. If, for some reason I overlooked this order, I'll put a rush on it, and you can take the charge out of my paycheck. I'll get it straightened out. Okay?"

Was that desperation he heard in her voice? Danielle was never desperate. She'd always been the epitome of professional and efficient. One or two mistakes, he could overlook. But if she continued on this path, her days here would be numbered.

"All right," he found himself saying. "But if you cost me this deadline, so help me, Danielle, you'll see a side of me you'd wish you'd never seen."

He left the discussion at that and walked away from her. The mistakes she'd been making were befuddling to say the least. R.J. couldn't wrap his mind around the Danielle he knew being forgetful and absentminded. On the other hand, maybe she was overworked. The hours she pulled could rival his. In fact, tonight was rather late for her to still be here. And lately she'd been coming extra early. He had no clue where she found stamina, plus being on her feet all day.

Maybe the problem wasn't really her. Maybe putting everything on her shoulders was asking too much. Perhaps it was time to hire some more help. Someone who could answer phones and take care of billing. That way, Danielle could see to the more important jobs without as much distraction. Just as he was about to try to figure out her situation, his cell phone vibrated. He pulled the device out of his back pocket and glanced at the screen.

He recognized Rebecca's number immediately.

The market has beef jerky for buy one get one free.

Her comment had him laughing because Rebecca had always teased that he survived on a diet of pure beef jerky. One year for his birthday, she'd placed a wholesale-size package of jerky on his doorstep.

How was he supposed to stop thinking about her, if she was constantly everywhere he turned?

FIVE

"DID YOU CHECK out the dad in exam one? Gorgeous," Erica announced with a sly smile.

Rebecca glanced up from her paperwork and grinned at the P.A. "After yesterday I am perfectly content to stay in my office." Even though she loathed paperwork, Rebecca welcomed the break to her feet.

Erica adjusted the stethoscope around her neck. "Can you believe Dr. Gross sat at that courthouse all day and they didn't even call his name? What a waste of time."

"I know, that's why I always try to get out of jury duty," Rebecca responded. "But it's good to have him back. With my workload today, I don't know if I could have filled in for him."

"I know, right? I don't know how he does it."

Erica turned to leave, but Rebecca stopped her. "Hey, wait a minute. Do you know if Dr. Gross has any ADHD patients coming in for their checkups today?"

The younger woman thought for a minute. She glanced up at the ceiling, then shook her head. "I don't think so. Why do you ask?"

Rebecca leaned back in her chair and rolled her pen

between her palms. "No reason." At least none that Erica needed to know about.

The P.A. walked away, leaving Rebecca to her work. But she was too distracted to get anything done. It hadn't been until she'd gone home last night that she'd realized how many ADHD patients Dr. Gross had. Since he'd been out, she'd had to have access to his patient files, which required a password. Just yesterday alone, she saw six kids who'd been diagnosed with ADHD. And every single one of them was on 30 mg of Adderall XR. The kids ranged in age from thirteen to seven. That high of a dose of Adderall XR was downright dangerous for a seven year old. Not only that, but every single one of them checked out as normal. And none of them had the ADD evaluation paperwork in their files.

The incident wasn't anything alarming, but it did leave Rebecca with some unanswered questions. And a strange feeling in the pit of her stomach. One possibility was that Dr. Gross was misdiagnosing the kids and wasn't doing a thorough enough job with the exams. These days a lot of kids were just distracted in school, and that distraction was mistaken for ADD or ADHD.

Rebecca had always been extra careful when diagnosing someone with that particular disorder. Mostly because Adderall was so addictive and easily abused. In a lot of cases the kids just needed a diet change or maybe a natural supplement like an Omega3 and the medication wasn't necessary.

Could it be possible that Dr. Gross had been swayed by some of these parents? One common thread they all had with the doctor was personal acquaintance. They all had some kind of personal relationship with Dr. Gross, whether it was a friend of the family or a relative.

If that was the case, it would have been easier for the doctor to give in to the parents' desires.

Either way, something didn't sit right with Rebecca. She

would never prescribe an unnecessary drug to a child no matter who their parents were.

The man in question strolled by her office, holding his laptop. "So, you survived yesterday, did you?" he said with a kind smile.

She'd always like Dr. Gross. He had an easy disposition and calm demeanor, which worked perfectly as a pediatrician. At the age of forty-nine, he still looked good with a full head of light brown hair and a relatively trim waist. He and his wife, Heather, had been married for twenty-four years and had three children, who were all grown and out of the house. His plan, he'd told her was to turn the practice over to her after he retired. Having her own practice had always been her life's dream, and Patrick Gross had built a solid, reputable business over the past ten years.

"It certainly was a challenge, but that's what I thrive on. Do you have a heavy work load today?" she asked him.

"Not too bad. My last appointment is at 4:15, so I might cut out of here early. Maybe get in a little golf."

Dr. Gross could always been found in one of two places: his practice or the golf course.

Rebecca stood from her desk, and walked toward him. "There's just one thing I'm wondering."

"Shoot," he said.

"I saw quite a few of your patients yesterday who are all on high doses of Adderall XR. Is that pretty normal for you? I mean, I don't have that many kids who are on the medication, but it seems like you have a lot." When he didn't respond. She rushed on, "I'm not trying to question you, or anything. I just thought it was a bit odd."

He rubbed a hand along the back of his neck. "Can this wait until later? I have a patient waiting."

Great. Now she'd gone and offended him. "Yeah, sure. It's not like it's a pressing issue..."

But Dr. Gross was already walking away, effectively

ending her inquiry.

She leaned against the doorframe of her office, and sighed. Dammit, she should have kept her mouth shut. Why in the world would she think her mentor would break a doctor's code of ethics, not to mention the law, by passing out illegal prescriptions? Her first thought was that Dr. Gross was writing these prescriptions for the adults, and using the kids as an excuse to hand out the medicine. But wasn't that preposterous? Why would he risk everything he'd built to dope up some of his friends? Unless...

No. That thought was too far-fetched. No way, would Dr. Gross be accepting money under the table for illegal prescriptions.

Good grief, she'd watched way too many true crimes shows.

He wasn't that sort of man.

And yet...

There was a way for her to put her suspicions to rest. She did have his password to access his patient files. She could easily pull them up and see just how many ADHD patients he had, compared to her. And she could see how many of the patients had some sort of personal relationship with him.

What kind of person would that make her? To go snooping through his patient files, trying to prove he was committing prescription fraud? What kind of person did that?

On the other hand...

If there was something fishy going on, it was her duty to find out the truth. The future of the entire practice could be on the line.

Rebecca sat back down at her desk and pushed away the papers she'd been working on. After pulling in a resolving breath, she opened the program that held all the records and started trolling through them.

She shouldn't be doing this. She shouldn't be writing down names of the patients who'd been prescribed Adderall by Dr. Gross. Shouldn't she trust his judgment? So what if almost all the names on the list were acquainted with Dr. Gross in some way. Did that mean the man was committing prescription fraud with his close personal acquaintances? It was so unfathomable to her.

And yet, something wasn't right. It all went back to Danielle's behavior and the surprise, borderline panic, in the woman's eyes when she saw Rebecca. As though she'd been expecting Dr. Gross, which she had, and hadn't wanted Rebecca to question Lindsey. But why? It was a routine checkup, and Danielle had been fidgety and nervous. Lindsey had been fine. More than fine, actually. She'd seemed like a normal ten year old girl. Her mother, on the other hand, hadn't seemed normal.

Almost like...

Rebecca shook her head at the thought as she perused more records. Danielle did not seem like the type of woman to be addicted to Adderall. She was a professional woman who ran an office. And office full of men, no less As much as Rebecca didn't like her, she had to give the woman credit for what she did for a living. That kind of work environment, surrounded by that much testosterone, could not have been easy. She must work long hours and be on her feet all day long. Actually, she was the perfect candidate for a drug like Adderall. The medicine, when used correctly, provided energy, discipline and a focused mind. Perhaps Danielle needed that extra pick-me-up, but didn't have ADHD so she couldn't get a prescription. Was she using her daughter to get the medicine illegally from a friend?

But what Rebecca didn't know was the connection between Danielle and Dr. Gross. Almost all Dr. Gross' patients, who were on Adderall XR, knew the doctor on some kind of personal level. That much Rebecca knew because Trouble was such a small town, and almost everyone there either went to high school together or were distant relatives.

How was Danielle connected?

The even more disturbing thought was Danielle's work at the shop. If in fact, Danielle was addicted to the drug, then how was that affecting her job? Adderall was one of the most dangerous drugs to abuse. It could cause loss of sleep, headaches, anorexia and even heart attacks.

During medical school, Rebecca had excelled in the drug and medicine curriculum. Because of that, she was especially good at recognizing signs of withdraw and abuse. In just the short amount of time she'd seen Danielle the other day, she'd thought she'd picked up subtle signs of withdrawal. The only thing was, Rebecca didn't put two and two together until hours later.

When she finally had her list made, Rebecca sat back and stared at the names. Most of the patients were middle-aged, and all had kids who saw Dr. Gross and had been diagnosed with ADHD and were on 30 mg of Adderall XR. To sum things up, Dr. Gross had three times as many patients on Adderall XR than she had. In fact, Rebecca only had five patients on Adderall XR. All her other patients were on the lowest dosage of Adderall.

The whole thing was so strange, and Rebecca was kicking herself for not noticing this before.

The other question was, should she say something to R.J? But how could she do that without violating the patient confidentiality she was bound to? On the other hand, shouldn't he know if his manager was having problems with drug abuse? Maybe she could drop hints about Danielle's behavior without actually talking to him about it and telling him things she wasn't supposed to.

Rebecca leaned back in her chair and stared at the ceiling. She shouldn't be doing this. Her worry over R.J.'s manager was conflicting with her guilt for snooping through Dr. Gross' records. She'd invaded his patients' privacy and that was inexcusable. She wasn't that sort of doctor. Hell, she wasn't that sort of person.

The low rumble in her stomach reminded her she'd worked through lunch. The practice closed down for an hour so they could grab something to eat. Without even realizing it, Rebecca had sat in her office while everyone else had left for their lunch break. But, instead of leaving, she decided to dig into her tuna salad. If she finished up early enough, she could take off for an early weekend. So she worked through lunch on the monotonous things she hated doing. She'd much rather be tending to a newborn or treating an eight year old for the flu. Paperwork always put her to sleep, but it was a necessary evil.

Hours later, she was finally finished and had seen Dr. Gross stroll by her office. Going on gut instinct, Rebecca shot out of her chair and followed him down the hallway. She tried to tell herself this was just to alleviate her own suspicions. Dr. Gross would deny everything, tell her she was crazy for even thinking that, and everything would be peachy keen.

In a perfect world...

When she came to Dr. Gross's office, the older man had just sank down into his chair. He leaned back and dug the heels of his hands into his eye sockets. Her mentor worked just as many, if not more, hours than she did. Sometimes he even saw patients on a Saturday morning. The man had to be exhausted.

"I bet you're ready to hit the sack," she said from the doorway.

He arched a brow. "Are you kidding? I have a 5:30 tee time. My pounding head won't keep me from that."

Rebecca laughed at the man's dedication to the old sport. Dr. Gross was nothing if not predictable. She stepped farther into the office, then glanced back at the hallway. She didn't want to start broadcasting her suspicions and have Erica stroll by.

"Do you mind if I ask you a question?"

He lifted a hand toward her. "Not at all."

She crossed her arms under her breasts and tried to figure the best way to word her question. No way would she mention she'd spent the morning perusing his patients' files. She cleared her throat and prayed for the strength not to put her foot in her mouth.

"I just wanted to apologize for this morning. I didn't mean to overstep my boundary." When Dr. Gross didn't say anything, nor did he move, Rebecca forged on. "But I was thinking maybe some of those kids are a little young for 30mg. When I was examining them, they didn't seem to exhibit the normal behavior for ADHD."

"That's because the medication's working," Dr. Gross joked.

Was it just her, or had his laugh been strained?

Rebecca tried to laugh along with him, only to make light of the situation. "Yes, that is true," she admitted lamely. "But don't you think there are too many kids on the drug? I mean, is it possible some of them were misdiagnosed?"

One of Dr. Gross' brows rose as though surprised she would question him. *She* was surprised. But her nagging suspicion wouldn't go away. Something wasn't right with these diagnoses and she wanted to get to the bottom of it. Otherwise, she'd start to lose sleep over it.

She shook her head. "I'm sorry, I'm not trying to step on your toes or anything—"

The doc held up a hand. "It's all right. You've always had a good eye for medication. But I've known most of those kids since they were born. I know their parents really well. I'm positive I'm not misdiagnosing them. It's probably because you don't deal with as many ADD kids as I do, and not everyone has the same symptoms."

The number of kids on the drug wasn't what bothered her. The dosage was the issue.

But she didn't press further. Questioning him twice was

toeing the line of inappropriate. So, she plastered a smile on her face and apologized again. "You're right. It's also been a long week, and I'm really exhausted. I'm going to call it a day and head out."

"Have a great weekend," he said with a wave of his hand and a smile. Rebecca noticed, as she turned to leave, that his smile didn't quite reach his eyes.

She tried to get the look on his face out of her mind, even ten minutes later as she sat in her car. She knew the problem wasn't a misdiagnosis. ADHD was very easy to spot, especially to a trained eye. The more concerning issue was whether or not Dr. Gross was using the kids as an excuse to give the medication to the adults. Prescription fraud could strip a doctor of their medical license and land them in jail. Rebecca would most likely be guilty by association, and she'd lose everything she'd worked for. Nine years of her life, she'd spent studying medicine with the ultimate goal of running her own practice. If Dr. Gross was committing prescription fraud, he'd ruin everything for her.

But how could she dig deeper, without out-right accusing him? Danielle's face flashed across her mind again. Going on gut instinct, Rebecca pulled out of the parking lot and headed toward R.J.'s shop. She wasn't sure what she hoped to find there. If nothing else, she could at least gauge Danielle's behavior.

Lord, she felt like such a parasite doing this. But she couldn't shake the feeling that Dr. Gross was up to something very, very wrong. There were too many coincidences. All the kids on the same high dosage, none of them displaying signs of ADHD and none of them having evaluation charts in their folders. The odd behavior of the parents when they realized that Rebecca would be examining them instead of Dr. Gross. And, finally, the fact that almost all of them knew Dr. Gross on some sort of personal level.

Within minutes, Rebecca reached the shop. She pulled

her car into the almost full lot and walked toward the building. Her sweaty palms were probably a sign that she should skedaddle. She didn't want to see R.J. anyway. Lately he'd been bringing the worst out in her. Instead of thinking how being near him was so bad for her, she kept fantasizing about him. But that was nothing new.

Just last night, she'd had another dream about when he'd snuck into her bedroom window, locked her door and lifted her nightgown over her head. She'd woken up from the dream, in the middle of the night, as though she'd lost her virginity all over again. Her body had been achy, and the extra-long shower hadn't helped. The hot water had only irritated her already sensitive skin. She'd arrived at work with R.J. competing with her thoughts about her patients.

As she walked across the parking lot, she spotted R.J. inside the shop, standing at the open hood of a car. One of his employees stood by, and the two of them were conversing while they worked. And her heartbeat kicked up just at the sight of him. For a weak moment, she allowed her gaze to travel down to his drool-worthy rear-end. The faded, worn jeans molded over his hard cheeks like they'd been specifically designed just for him. In an instant, the memory of how they'd felt underneath her fingers, how firm and toned they were, slammed into her. Because she couldn't face him with the heat flaming her face, Rebecca bypassed the shop and walked to the reception area. Danielle was in there with the phone pressed to her ear. Rebecca took a chance and stepped into the area, to get a good look at the woman.

Judging by the stiff set of her shoulders, Danielle wasn't happy to see Rebecca. She continued her conversation while raking her gaze over Rebecca in close scrutiny. Once again, Rebecca was struck by how stunning the woman was. Her fair skin and bright blue eyes were an odd combination with her black hair. She had Rebecca by at least three inches and had full pouty lips that most men probably fantasized about.

Rebecca could see why R.J. would have been attracted to her. Tall, busty women had always been his Achilles' heel.

However, her sharp collar bones and bony fingers sent Rebecca's radar on high alert. Adderall could often curb an appetite, so a lot of people on the medication could go all day without eating. People who were on the drug needed to be careful about not dropping too much weight.

Rebecca stopped in front of the desk and tried to think of a good reason for stopping by. Danielle hadn't acknowledged her past a casual glance. She continued her conversation while typing on the computer. Her soft laughter led Rebecca to believe it was not a business-related phone call. Rebecca was a paying client, so being ignored did not set well with her. She cleared her throat in a subtle attempt to get the woman's attention. Danielle slanted Rebecca a look and said, "I'll call you later," into the receiver.

She turned in her chair and pasted just about the fakest smile Rebecca had ever seen. "What can I do for you?"

"I just came to check on my car," Rebecca fibbed.

Danielle just stared at Rebecca as though she wanted to call Rebecca out for the liar that she was. Just as Danielle stood from her chair, the phone rang, which she answered. After reciting a crisp greeting, the woman placed the call on hold and walked out of the office.

O-kay. Was she supposed to stand there and wait for Danielle to come back? Was she supposed to go into the shop? She already figured that R.J.'s manager had lukewarm feelings for her, to say the least. But to treat a paying client like this? Very strange.

Danielle came back in the room a moment later. She picked up the phone, told the caller that R.J. would call them back, then hung up.

"They're making good progress on your car," she finally answered. "Looks like they'll finish on time."

"Good," Rebecca nodded, unsure of what else to say.

"How's your daughter?" she blurted out.

"Fine," Danielle answered immediately.

"And the Adderall is still working for her?"

Danielle picked up a pen and twirled it around. "Yes."

Okay, then. It was clear the two of them would never brush each other's hair and gab about their first kiss. Fine. Rebecca could take a hint. But she wasn't finished.

"Have you ever thought about dropping her dosage down a bit? 30 mg is an awful lot for a girl her age. And she seemed good enough to me that maybe she could get away with taking a smaller dose."

A tight-lipped smile didn't make Danielle look any friendlier. "Dr. Gross has been Lindsey's pediatrician for a long time. I trust he knows what he's doing." She crossed her arms over her chest as though ready to battle. "How do you think he'd feel if he knew you were down here questioning him?"

"I'm not questioning anything," Rebecca said hastily. "I'm just offering my professional opinion. I think Lindsey would do just as well on regular Adderall. It's a less severe drug than its counterpart."

"Well, until Dr. Gross tells us otherwise, I'll keep her on what he's been giving her."

That's because you're taking the medication instead of your daughter.

Rebecca immediately pushed the thought from her mind and decided to change the subject.

"You sure have your hands full with this place. Is there another manager here to help you out?"

"No, it's just me," Danielle answered.

"So, you basically run everything on your own? You must have endless amounts of energy." Which was something Adderall XR helped with. Danielle no doubt worked long hours in order to cover all the business that needed taking care of. Maybe she had started to feel stretched thin and needed a little pick-me-up. Adderall could definitely gear a person's thoughts toward focus and give them steam they didn't even know they had. The idea of Danielle going that route in order to keep up with things wasn't inconceivable. Thousands of people across the country resorted to such measures all the time. They felt they were immune to the dangerous side-effects. Or the boost in progress outweighed the risks.

"I do just fine," Danielle responded with another tight-lipped smile. The phone rang again, and she used the opportunity to dismiss Rebecca. "Excuse me please."

Rebecca took the distraction to her advantage and slipped out of the office. When she entered the shop, she spotted R.J. rooting around in the guts of the same car he'd been working on before. He straightened from the car and his hands were covered with grease. Strangely enough, the sight of his big, callused hands blackened from a hard day's work sent tingles down to her stomach.

"We're going to have to order another one," he was saying as Rebecca approached him. The dark scowl on his face would scare anyone away, but not her. R.J's bark had always been worse than his bite. He'd clearly had a rough day, and now Rebecca was thinking twice before voicing her concerns to him.

"Is this a bad time?" she asked him.

"Depends on what you want," he said to the car instead of placing his attention on her.

"Just a quick word." *Although I have no clue what I'm going to say without risking lawsuit.*

He straightened from the engine he'd been tinkering with and glanced at her. His penetrating stare bore down into hers and she had to force herself not to fidget where she stood.

"All right," he said.

She followed him to his office, the whole time trying to keep her eyes on the back of his head and not his ass. Because it was such an impressive ass.

"Make it quick," he stated after they arrived in his office. He folded his arms across his thick chest and waited for her.

Focus on what you want to say and not how fantastic he looks.

Rebecca's heart thumped harder against her ribcage. "I was just..." She cleared her throat and steeled her nerves because she'd never thought she'd find herself in the situation of talking about a patient like this. Not only wrong on so many levels, but she could be sued for breaching patient confidentiality. "I was just wondering if you've noticed anything odd about Danielle's behavior lately."

R.J.'s brows pinched together, and he took a moment before answering. "Why?"

Yes, Rebecca why?

"No reason." *Liar!*

He stared at her for a moment. "You came all the way down here to ask about Danielle's behavior just for shits and giggles?"

Well, when he put it that way it sounded stupid. It *was* stupid.

A puff of breath left her lungs on along exhale. "I can't tell you."

He gave her another long, hard stare. "Would this have anything to do with migraines?"

Huh?

When she didn't respond to that, he added, "Or a prescription medication?"

His question piqued her interest, but she didn't say anything. Did he already know what was going on? But why would he ask about migraines?

"I just need to know if you've noticed a change in her recently," Rebecca said instead of answering his question. "I can't say anything beyond that because of patient confidentiality."

"What kind of changes?"

"Is she having mood swings? Acting tired? Have you

noticed a change in her weight? Is she working extra-long hours?" Maybe he could fill in the holes without her actually having to tell him.

R.J. shook his and leaned against his desk. "All those things could be because she works long hours. She has a lot to get done on her own."

Rebecca took a step toward him. "You just mentioned migraines. Does she get those?"

He didn't answer her right away. Could it be because he didn't want to? Did he not want to admit that Danielle had a problem?

He shook his head again. "The other night I caught her taking a prescription and she said it was for migraines."

Bingo.

But Rebecca had to keep her mouth shut from telling him it was likely the Adderall she'd prescribed her daughter. But having to stay quiet about the whole thing was killing her! R.J. needed to know if his manager was abusing a dangerous drug, because it would affect the entire work environment, not to mention put Danielle's health at risk. But her hands were tied, unless she wanted to get slapped with a lawsuit.

"What aren't you saying?" R.J. asked when she'd been quiet.

"Did you get a look at what she was taking?" she countered.

"No."

She wanted to keep on, to ask if he'd noticed Danielle taking those pills before. But the whole conversation was toeing the line as it was. If she were smart, she'd leave and not say anything else.

Another sigh left her wracked and wired body. She turned from him. "I have to go."

Before she could depart, and go home to drown herself in a bottle of wine, R.J. grabbed her arm. Not one of those gentle touches where his fingers pressed into her soft flesh. His grip was tough, firm, and impatient.

"I've had a long, shitty day, Rebecca. Did you come here to accuse Danielle of something?" The look in his normally playful eyes was hard, and one she was used to seeing.

Something about his words created a shiver of unease through her. She had to remind herself that R.J. and Danielle had once been lovers, even though she didn't *want* to remind herself. Because of that he might feel defensive of her. But he was right; Rebecca really didn't know Danielle. Apparently not the way R.J. did, which seemed to be really well.

She took a step back from him, suddenly uncomfortable with the way R.J. was so quick to defend the other woman. Rebecca knew her medications and the signs of addiction when she saw it.

"Something's not right with her," Rebecca stated. "And I think you know it."

He straightened from the desk, which made him tower over her. "What I know is for some reason you don't like Danielle. I don't really give a damn if you're jealous, but you can't come in here and toss around and ask questions like that."

His words threw her for a loop. Jealous? Okay, yes a very small part of her resented the hell out of the woman. But enough for Rebecca to do something vindictive?

"What?" she stammered. "Why would I do something like this if I didn't have a good reason?"

His warm palm cupped her chin and tilted her head up. "Jealousy sounds like a good enough reason to me." His voice dropped down to that delicious husky that always had her toes curling and her eyelids dropping.

Not this time though. Her blood was too boiling to allow her body to react in a sexual way. She slapped his hand away. "Go to hell, R.J. I came here because I care about your business. I'm sorry that I can't tell you more, but I think you already know there's an issue."

White hot anger had her storming out of his office. Just to drive her point home, she slammed his door shut, then spun around on her heel. Her high heels made an annoying clacking sound on the concrete floor which she ignored. Let him listen to her walk away. And let this be the last time she tried to help him.

How dare he? What kind of person did he think she was?

Tears of frustration burned her eyes. Why did it always have to be this way between them? Why couldn't they have an amiable relationship like two normal human beings? Whenever they got to good terms something would happen and she'd go back to hating his guts. Whoever coined the phrase "thin line between love and hate" must have had a personal relationship with R.J. Devlin. The man was so maddening, she didn't know whether to strip his clothes off or punch his lights out.

But why was she surprised? And why did she continue to do this to herself? She couldn't logically blame anyone else. She was a glutton for punishment who always came back for more. Every time she walked away from R.J., confusion created a sick feeling in her stomach because she had the hardest time figuring him out. Bouncing back and forth between love and hate gave her enough whiplash to last her a lifetime.

She finally got in her car and whipped out of the parking lot.

Not once had R.J. defended her the way he defended Danielle. No, he always went out of his way to make her as uncomfortable as possible. It was like it gave him some kind of sick satisfaction. She told herself she didn't care. But if she truly didn't, why couldn't she stop the tears from rolling down her cheeks?

****

By the time Rebecca pulled onto her street, she'd been drained of all her anger, and in its place was plain old exhaustion. Enough that she didn't even have the energy to groan when she spotted her mother's car on the other side of the driveway.

Rebecca had a good relationship with her parents. They often had dinner together a few times a month, and sometimes she and her mother would go shopping together. But she was not in the mood to deal with either of them tonight. In fact, she wasn't in the mood to deal with anyone. All she wanted to do was soak in the tub and sleep off her stress. Even Yoga didn't sound appealing. And Rebecca was *always* in the mood for Yoga.

Lord only knew what her mother wanted. Probably to scare her with some ridiculous statistic about having babies. Like maybe Rebecca had a better probability of being abducted by aliens than having kids after the age of thirty-five. With the mood she was in, Rebecca would welcome little green men whisking her away to the far reaches of the galaxy.

Despite that, she pulled into the garage and let herself inside the home. Her parents were painfully predictable people. Whether at home, or at someone else's house, they could always be found doing the same things. Her father had made a home for himself stretched across her couch. And her mother was at the kitchen sink, running the water over some dishes. Something smelled absolutely heavenly, which did little to lift her spirits.

"Hey baby doll," her father greeted. "Hope you don't mind us crashing here."

"Honey, we got struck by termites," her mother called from the kitchen.

"Of course I don't mind," Rebecca replied even though she didn't want her parents all but living here for who knows how long.

She set her things down in the hallway that led to her

bedroom and walked toward the kitchen. Her mother greeted her with a hug, which chased away some of Rebecca's worries.

"What are you cooking?" she asked.

"Your favorite. Chicken fried steak with rice and gravy," her mother said with a cheerful smile. The apron tied around her waist read "I bake with love" and had various stains on it from years of use. The yellow color of the apron was faded and the memories of her mother wearing that went back a long time.

"That sounds good," Rebecca said even though she wasn't hungry, which she didn't have the heart to say. "So how bad are the termites?"

Her mother waved a hand in the air and stirred the gravy. "Oh, they're all over the place. The house is all covered up, and I don't have a clue how long it will take to fix the damage. Will you hand me the milk?"

Rebecca withdrew the two percent from the fridge and handed the carton to her mother. The older woman poured some into the brown gravy, then swirled it around with her wooden spoon. Her mother had always been a magician with gravy. Somehow she knew the right amount of drippings and milk to make it perfect. A second ago she wasn't hungry. But the sight of the homemade gravy had her stomach rumbling.

"Honey, are you okay?" her mom asked. "You look tired."

Rebecca leaned against the counter. "I am tired. But I'm okay. I'm just going to eat and turn in early."

Patsy Underwood stirred the gravy and shook some pepper into it. "Your daddy and I can go somewhere else. I'm sure there's a hotel we can stay at. I don't want to put you out if you're worn."

She smiled to reassure her mother. "Don't be ridiculous, Mom. You and Dad can stay here as long as you need to. The second bedroom is more than big enough."

"We sure appreciate it, honey. I think I finally have this

perfect," she said about the gravy, which was a mouth-watering shade of brown and just thick enough to Rebecca's liking.

The meal, though low-key with mundane conversation, was as delicious as anything her mother had ever cooked. Rebecca took care not to overload her plate because she was already feeling uneasy.

Her mother questioned it of course, saying things like, "You're not eating very much," and "Do you not like the meal?" The meal was delicious, but her appetite was non-existent. Rebecca was smart enough not to tell her parents that because they wouldn't stop until Rebecca spilled every last detail. Patsy Underwood was a human lie detector. When coupled that with Rebecca's poor lying skills, came a situation Rebecca wouldn't be able to escape from. So she ate, even when her stomach told her to stop.

Thankfully she was able to plead a headache and escape to her bedroom. Her mother assured Rebecca not to worry about the dinner dishes, even though Rebecca felt bad for leaving her parents to clean the mess. Even so, she was grateful for a chance to escape. Thousands of thoughts still churned through her mind. All those kids and whether or not they were taking Adderall. R.J. and his weird defense of Danielle. Or, maybe not so weird, given they used to be involved. And now having her parents share space with her.

In order to wash the day away, Rebecca took a long bath and soaked for longer than she needed to. Her skin was nice and pruny when she wrapped herself up in a robe. By the time she crawled into bed, she was just drowsy enough for her eyes to drift shut. Just as she was about to drift off, her cell phone vibrated on the nightstand.

With a groan, Rebecca snatched it up and glanced at the screen.

Sorry for being an ass. It's the damn mango.

The reference to the fruit had her laughing. When she

was fifteen, she and Courtney had been sitting on a high branch in a tree of her parents' yard. They'd been talking and eating mangos when R.J. had come strolling by, right under where they'd been sitting. Rebecca had been feeling extra frisky and looking to get back at him for something he'd done, for what now Rebecca couldn't even remember. On a whim, she'd dropped a whole mango and it had hit him right smack on top of his head. He'd cursed and threatened to end their lives, but his anger hadn't been able to stop hers and Courtney's laughter. For weeks after that R.J. had been surly and snappy with her. When she finally questioned him, his response had been, "Why don't I drop a mango on your head and see how you like it?"

From that point on, she'd never been able to look at mangos with a straight face. And R.J. always referenced them when Rebecca called him out when he was in a bad mood. "It's the mangos," he'd always say.

The year after that incident, she'd taken her life in her own hands by putting a mango in a gift bag for his birthday. The next day, she'd found a note in her mailbox that said. "Run and hide, Ms. Underwood."

She stabbed her teeth into her lower lip and returned his text message.

Mango season is coming up, so watch out.

Taunting R.J. was the equivalent to playing with fire. He always found a way to get even. Her cell phone vibrated again, and she glanced at the screen.

Your bedroom's on the first floor. If you're smart, you'll lock your window this time.

This text didn't have her smiling. In her smile's place was a tingling heat that spread all throughout her body. Why did her girly parts have to get themselves all worked up like that?

This was his way of getting back at her; sending her to bed sexually frustrated.

She dropped her cell phone back on the nightstand with a

heavy sigh. Why couldn't she have said something really simple like, "Hey, no sweat."

"You'll never learn, will you?" she whispered to herself just as her eyes drifted shut.

SIX

HE OUGHT TO HAVE his head examined for coming in to the shop on a Sunday. A normal person would be at home reading the paper and catching a ball game on T.V.

But the tingling sensation going down his spine wouldn't allow him to relax with the sports section. Since waking up that morning, he'd been unable to shake the feeling that something wasn't right. He could thank Rebecca and her questions for that one. But however much he could ignore Rebecca's words, he couldn't ignore Danielle's odd behavior.

Had he noticed a weight change in her? Come to think of it, she did seem thinner over the past few weeks. Was she working longer hours? Actually, she'd been staying later, and arriving even before him in the mornings. The weight thing could be because of a diet, even though she didn't need to diet. And maybe she'd been working longer hours because she had too much of a workload. If that was the case, then the fault fell on him for overloading her.

All reasonable explanations, and yet... something still wasn't adding up. Was it just a coincidence that Rebecca's warning came on the heels of Danielle's recent mishaps? Then there were the sudden outbursts of her snapping at him over the littlest things. Forgetting to place orders, mixing accounts up. Very un-Danielle-like.

Besides that R.J. was restless and felt the need to get dirty. After a sleepless night of fantasizing about Rebecca, he needed to get his hands into some grease. He had a few new arrivals that needed to be stripped down to the bare chassis. So that's what he did. After whipping his shirt off, R.J. went to work on the first car

For the next hour, he dove into what he loved best: Getting into the inner workings of a classic vehicle to reveal the inner beauty. The sound of metal on metal was like music to his ears in the quiet shop. As he worked, he tried to align his focus to the '71 Corvette Stingray. Vehicles like this didn't come in very often, so when thoughts of Rebecca kept intruding on his concentration, his frustration grew. He tossed aside an old timing belt with more force than he needed to. The thing clattered to the ground and skittered under the wheel of the next car.

He had no business touching her. Past experience was enough for him to know that even the simplest touch always led to more. Once he got a taste of that downy skin, his body wouldn't rest until it had more. And more had never been enough. Dammit, he knew better. Even climbing through her bedroom window and making love to her hadn't been enough. For weeks he'd been tortured with the memory of sinking into her welcoming body, of hearing her moan and sob and feeling her quiver around him.

The experience had shaken him and created feelings inside that scared the shit out of him. The next night after taking Rebecca's virginity, he'd called an old girlfriend. But the hours of vigorous sex had only pronounced his feelings for Rebecca. She wasn't just someone he'd slept with. She'd never been just another notch in his bedpost, no matter how much he wanted her to be. She'd been something else, but admitting to it was something he'd been unable to do.

From an early age, R.J. knew he had no desire to be in a committed relationship. After seeing what his mother had gone through with his father, R.J. figured it would be best for women in general if he kept commitment out of it. Sex was okay. In fact sex was out of this world, as long as the relationship stayed on that level. Rebecca was better than that. She deserved a guy who would take her out to dinner on Valentine's Day or cooked her breakfast in bed. R.J. wasn't built that way, and he cared about Rebecca too much to lead her to believe otherwise. So he cut her loose with the idea planted that he didn't care. She needed to think he didn't give a rip either way, so she would go find that guy who could give her what she wanted.

But the truth was he did care. He cared way too much and those feelings had been bordering on something more for a long time. Whenever he saw her, a strange feeling twisted in the pit of his stomach. And when he touched her, something shifted inside of him. No other woman had been able to elicit those reactions from him. It scared the shit out of him, and that's why he needed to stay away from her. She'd fall in love with him, and he'd break her heart. The same way his father had broken his mother's heart, over and over again.

He wouldn't be able to live with himself if he turned out to be the man to put that same hurt look on her face. She was too special for that.

Too good.

Too pure.

Everything he wasn't and never would be.

But why did she have to make it so damn hard for him? Didn't she know she needed to stay away from him? How could he do the right thing if she kept batting those green eyes at him and shaking her sinfully sexy hips? Shit, he had will power but it wasn't iron-clad. If she kept pushing him like this, he was going to push back. He feared both of them would like the result too much to stop.

Where would that leave them?

After gutting the engine of the Corvette, R.J. stepped back to survey his work. Not bad for one guy. He snagged a nearby towel and swiped it across his greasy hands. His throat was so damn parched he felt like he'd swallowed a handful of sand.

He walked toward the office and to the mini fridge that stored several bottles of water. Danielle had brought the appliance in about a year ago, so she could have a place to store her lunches. Plus the bottled water came in handy, especially for mechanics buried under a car on a hot day. He tossed aside the towel and opened the office door.

There, in the desk chair, hunched over the keyboard of the computer was his office manager, fast asleep. What the hell? How did he not see her car when he'd pulled into the parking lot? And what was she doing here on a Sunday morning?

He stepped toward her and was about to nudge her shoulder when his gaze fell on an orange prescription bottle. On the desk, right next to Danielle's elbow with Lindsey's name on the label.

What the hell?

Why would Danielle have Lindsey's medicine here, with her, on a Sunday morning?

Instantly, thoughts of all Rebecca's questions and catching Danielle taking medicine and claiming migraines, came back to him. Rebecca hadn't given him shit to go on with all her I-can't-talk-about-its and odd questions. But he knew something with his office manager wasn't right. Just as Rebecca had said.

R.J. picked the bottle up and scanned the label. 30mg of Adderall XR for a ten year old girl? Lindsey had ADD?

"What the hell are you doing?"

Danielle's sudden exclamation yanked him out of his questioning thoughts. He barely had time to glance at her when she snatched the bottle out of his hand and shoved it in the desk drawer. If her daughter had ADD, wouldn't she need the medication at home and not at her mother's office? And especially not in a drawer, where Danielle could forget to bring it home?

"I could ask you the same question, Danielle," he retorted instead of answering her demand.

Her bloodshot, blue eyes narrowed at him. "What were you doing with that bottle?"

He stared back at her for a moment, noticing the lack of makeup, the hollow cheeks and lines of stress bracketing her full mouth. "What were *you* doing with it?" When she stood from the chair, he wrapped a hand around her elbow, preventing her from dismissing him. "Do you have a problem you need to tell me about?"

"That," she emphasized with jerk of her arm. "Is none of your business."

"What goes on in my office is my business, Danielle. So I'll ask you again: Do you have a problem?"

Her lips tightened and for a moment he wasn't sure she was going to answer the question. "Taking an Adderall every once in a while to get me through the day isn't a problem. Lots of people do it, so get off my back. Okay?"

Except he wasn't sure it was just once in a while. And why would the prescription be made out to Lindsey if Danielle was the one who needed the Adderall?

She must have taken his silence as not accepting her explanation, because she added, "It's all under control."

"Is it?" he countered. "Because you don't seem like yourself."

"If I tell you it is, then it is. I don't have a problem and I'm not an addict." She gathered her stuff off the desk, dropping her car keys twice before swiping them off the floor with trembling hands. Hands, he just noticed where thinner than he remembered, with bony fingers clasping the keys and shoving them in her purse. The office door slammed behind her, echoing in the quiet interior and making the metal mini blinds clang against the window frame.

R.J. stood in the wake of her departure and tried to make sense of what had just happened. The woman in the office this morning was not the woman he'd hired two years ago. Danielle had always been vibrant, with bouncing shiny hair and a light in her eyes that was unique to her. In fact, that was one of the things that had always drawn him to her. Not only was she gorgeous and held her own in an environment of men, but there'd always been a fire in her. She was a go-getter who'd earned the respect of his other employees.

Her behavior the last few days threw him for a loop. She didn't look like herself. With the weight she'd dropped and the dull, uncombed hair, it was like a different woman had taken over her body.

But beyond that, he was concerned for her. And not just the business. He cared about Danielle, and if she was doing something that could potentially harm her, she needed help. He didn't know much about ADD and even less about Adderall, but taking any drug that wasn't prescribed couldn't be good.

He turned to walk out of the office, but his eyes landed on the list of parts for Charlie's cars. Immediately, he knew the list was incomplete. No way could the couple dozen parts listed be everything they needed to restore the two classic cars.

A small shiver of panic coursed through him as he sat down at the desk and rifled through the papers. Danielle had a very efficient storage system. Every file had a code and was stored in its own place. R.J. hardly ever delved into the files or micromanaged Danielle's system. She knew it inside and out. Unfortunately, he didn't know more beyond typing in the client's name to pull their information. He only hoped Charlie's file would have a note about an order placed for his cars.

No such note was in the client's file. So R.J. pulled up the history of recent orders placed and hadn't found one for Charlie for at least a year. The panic pulsing through him a second ago, turned into full-blown hysteria. Had Danielle ordered these parts on time, they'd arrive next week. That would give him and his guys plenty of time to restore the cars by August. If, in fact, they hadn't been ordered, it could be another month before he received enough of the parts to start. Getting them finished by August, if that was the case, would really be pushing it. R.J. would have to pull extra hours and overnighters to get the job done.

Even though it was Sunday, he placed a call to his supplier and left them a message to call him back first thing tomorrow morning. Before jumping to conclusions, R.J. needed to verify that the order hadn't been placed. If it hadn't, then Danielle would have a shit storm come down on her like she'd never seen. Charlie was his biggest client and R.J. could not afford to screw up this job.

He stood from the chair and worked the kinks out of his back. After walking back into the shop, he swiped his shirt off the floor and tugged it over his head. He owed Rebecca an apology, and not another quick text message like the one he'd sent two nights ago.

Chances were she was right about Danielle, and he shouldn't have snapped at her like that. Rebecca wouldn't have come to him with concerns if she didn't have good reason. Not only that, she'd never been a vindictive person. She had an enormous heart and had always lived to help others. She'd come to him out of concern for him, and instead of being thankful he'd accused her of being jealous. What kind of insensitive asshole reacted that way?

She'd been completely within her rights to tell him to go to hell.

For the rest of the day, R.J. worked on his cars, getting as much done as one person could. Only when his stomach rumbled for dinner did he stop. On the way home, he grabbed a burger and Coke, then made a detour to Rebecca's neighborhood.

His balls hardened at the thought of seeing her again. Would her hair be free, with its wild curls calling out for his fingers to tame them? Would she have reading glasses perched on that petite nose? One thing he could say for sure, was that no matter how she'd look, he'd want her. He'd stopped trying to control his body's reaction to her a long time ago. All she had to do was breathe and he was a goner.

Her mother's late model sedan was parked in the street along the curb. He'd hoped to have some privacy with her, but perhaps this was better. With her parents there, he wouldn't have the opportunity to drag her to bed and peel her clothes off one article at a time. Which was a good thing. At least that's what he told himself.

You don't need to take her to bed again. Just say your apology and get the hell out of there.

His car purred into the driveway where he turned it off and stepped outside. Before he reached the front door, it opened and Rebecca stepped out.

Short-ass, frayed denim shorts, if one could even call them shorts, barely covered all the essential parts. A t-shirt which read, *If You Can Read This You're In Roundhouse Kick Range* clung to her curves and the words were stretched across her breasts.

The shirt brought a smile to his lips. Rebecca might be the collected, professional pediatrician but she had a kickass sense of humor that always made him laugh.

She came to a stop in front of him. "I heard your car," she greeted.

He glanced at the house and wondered why she could come outside and not wait for him to come to the door.

She gestured behind her. "My parents are in there, and my mother will make you eat and talk your ear off. Plus it's just better if we're out here anyway."

"Because you don't want me inside your house?" Where he could survey the lay of the land and one day drag her off to her bed? Or was it just the thought of him being inside her home that made her uncomfortable?

"I wouldn't go that far. But it is better if we're not near a bedroom."

He raised a brow at her comment. "What do you think I'll do to you with your parents here?"

She crossed her arms over her chest. "Nothing you haven't done before."

A slow smile curled along his lips. "Touché. But don't pretend like you didn't love it."

The pulse at the base of her throat fluttered, bringing satisfaction where stress had once occupied. She stared back at him and didn't reply to his comment. Because she knew she didn't have a leg to stand on. He may have climbed through her window, but her enthusiasm had matched his.

She cleared her throat. "Did you come here torture me?"

His smile grew. "No." He flicked the end of her nose. "That's just an added bonus."

She blinked at him for a second, then rolled her eyes and turned back toward the house. That spectacular ass of hers, which was barely covered in those shorts, just about brought him to his knees. When he realized she meant to leave him standing outside, he bolted after her.

"Rebecca, wait," he said with a laugh. "I'm sorry. I didn't mean that."

She stopped directly in front of the door, where the porch light could pick up the brilliant red in her hair. The curls were piled on top of her head, with a few wispy tendrils teasing her neck. It took all his restraint to keep his hands to himself and not brush the hair away so he could replace them with his mouth.

"Yes, you did," she accused. "You never say anything

you don't mean."

She's got your number, asshole.

He exhaled a defeated breath. Why did he bother pretending around her? "Okay, you're right. I did mean it. But I shouldn't have said it. You're just so damn cute when you get mad, that I couldn't help myself."

"Is that supposed to flatter me?"

He opened his mouth to answer the question, when he noticed the flush in her cheeks and the firm set of her mouth. Only one thing could get Rebecca tense like that. Actually two things, if he were to count himself.

"What's wrong?" he asked.

She narrowed her eyes at him. "What do you mean?"

"Something's bothering you." He lifted a hand and rubbed the spot in between her eyes with his thumb. "You get tense right here." He allowed his hand to linger longer than necessary, which was a mistake. Her skin was velvety and her warm breath tickled his hand.

She moved back from him and rubbed the spot where he'd touched her. "My parents are driving me crazy. They got hit by termites, and now they have to bunk here for who knows how long. Plus I've had a stressful few days at work."

"Speaking of work, I came to apologize." When she raised both her eyebrows in confusion he added, "For barking at you on Friday."

"You mean that text message wasn't a heartfelt apology?" she asked around a smile.

He found himself grinning back. "No, it was. But I still felt guilty."

"It's all right. And I'm sorry for telling you to go to hell."

"No you're not. You enjoyed that."

She shrugged. "I never said I didn't enjoy it. I just said I was sorry."

"Apology accepted."

She nodded and he couldn't help but notice how her gaze

kept wandering to his mouth. "Is that all you wanted, then?"

Honestly? He wanted a hell of a lot more than a few *I'm sorrys*. "Actually no." He rubbed a hand over the back of his neck. Why was this so hard for him to say? "I've been doing some thinking, and I think there might be something to your suspicions about Danielle."

Both her brows creased her forehead. "You mean, like I'm right?"

Oh, she was going to twist the knife good and deep. Didn't he deserve it though, for all the goading he'd done to her?

"Yeah, I think you might be right. Even though I don't want to think she'd do anything like that, your explanation seems to be the only one that makes sense."

She exhaled a long breath. "I know it's hard to admit someone you care about has a problem, but I know my medications. I excelled in that particular course in school. And I know the signs of an addiction when I see one. She shows all the symptoms. But you spend more time with her than I do. Have you noticed a significant change in her?"

He folded his arms over his chest. "Yeah. She does look thinner and she's been complaining about not sleeping and working longer hours. There are times when it seems like she has this sudden burst of energy, and other times she can barely stand on her feet. She's been really up and down recently."

"Look, I don't want to sound morbid or anything, but people who are addicted to Adderall generally go downhill really fast. It's a very easy drug to OD on. You might think about talking to her, and try to get her in some kind of program. Because before you know it, she'll be beyond help."

He thought about that for a moment. People who had a problem usually didn't want to admit they had a problem. Rock bottom needed to come before the admission. As far as he knew, Danielle hadn't hit rock bottom. On the other hand, how could he continue to allow her to run his business if she wasn't up to par?

Then, a startling thought occurred to him. "What about you?"

"What about me?" she wanted to know.

He lifted one shoulder. "Where did you get your suspicions about her? Is Lindsey one of your patients?"

Rebecca shook her head. "I told you I can't talk about patients I treat. I could get sued.

"So you can't tell me anything?"

She tucked a wayward curl behind her ear. "Only what I've already said. I can only warn you about the dangers of an addiction to Adderall. You would have to find out for sure if she's taking it."

"I think I already know that she is," he answered.

One of her brows lifted in response.

R.J. blew out a heavy breath. "This morning I went into the shop to get some work done and she was there. I found her asleep at the desk with a bottle of Adderall prescribed to Lindsey."

Rebecca took a step forward. "Did you question her about it?"

"Hell yeah, I questioned her about it. At first she denied it, then she said she only takes them every once in a while and she doesn't have a problem."

"That's the first thing addicts always say."

He rubbed the back of his neck. "Yeah, so what am I supposed to do now?"

"Get her to admit it, then get her help."

He gazed back at her for a moment, trying not to react at the way she kept licking her lower lip. "And what about you?"

She shook her head and opened her mouth to speak.

"Yeah, I know you can't talk to me about it," he stated before she could say the words herself.

Damn, he wished there was something he could do. Just

seeing the helplessness on her face tore his guts up. He supposed he could do his part by talking to Danielle. She'd always opened up to him, usually in hopes they'd end up back in bed. It was the least he could do, considering the position Rebecca was in, even if he wasn't sure what position that was.

"I'll see what I can do about her," he added.

The lamplight just beyond Rebecca's head glanced off her cheek, casting it in a soft yellow glow. His will power was crumbling at a rapid rate, and when she nibbled on her lower lip, he wanted to drop to his knees and howl like a wild animal. Her mouth was unpainted and so damn kissable that he couldn't help but reach out and tease her lower lip with his thumb. It was still moist from when she'd been gnawing on it.

He stepped closer to her and tunneled his hand into her hair. The strands were thick and soft and blanketed his fingers with her heat. Her round, pliant breast pressed against his chest, and the memory of how they'd looked and felt from all those years ago was just as vivid as though it had been yesterday.

He shouldn't be doing this. Touching her and being this close to her was a mistake. Yet, he couldn't stop himself from lowering his mouth and brushing it over hers. She inhaled a sharp breath, and tightened her hands on his forearms, digging her sharp nails into his muscles. Oh, she wanted this even if she told herself she didn't. He confused her and infuriated her. That much he knew. A small, and sick, part of him thrived off the havoc he wreaked on her senses. Then her mouth moved along his, until her tongue darted out and tentatively touched his lips.

The contact was like lightning exploding inside his head. If they weren't on a suburban street, he'd press her against the wall, remove those shorts and glide into her. Damn the world if they heard her scream.

The kiss deepened, both of them opening up for the other. Their tongues slid along each other, swirling around exploring heat. His hand on the back of her head tightened, holding her closer to him, refusing to allow her to push him away. To his satisfaction she didn't. Instead she inched her arms higher up his until they rested on his shoulders. She sucked in a breath when he plunged his tongue deeper into her mouth. Then she moaned and the soft sound traveled through him, causing a rash of goosebumps to coat the surface of his flesh. A squeak here, a groan there.

He pressed himself closer to her, and backed her to the front door. Both of his hands went to her hips, then wound around to her rear end, where he was able to cup the soft mounds in his hands. They were just the right size for him to grip. He gave a testing squeeze, and the action prompted a gasp from her. She kissed him harder and tangled her hands in his hair.

And oh, yeah. This was what he'd wanted. No, *needed*. Until the very moment when her lips came into contact with his, R.J. hadn't realized just how much he'd missed touching her. Feeling her heart smack against his rib cage. Hearing her breath whoosh in and out of her lungs. Knowing he was doing that to her?

Heck, yeah, he needed this.

But before he could get to the really good stuff, the stuff with the fireworks, Rebecca gave him a hard shove. He'd been so preoccupied with... well, *her*, that the action caught him off-guard. Enough that she was able to put some distance between the two of them. They'd gone from kissing to parting so damn fast that R.J. almost got a case of whiplash.

In the midst of his what-the-hell moment, Rebecca made an attempt to smooth back her hair, which he'd messed up with his hands. It was a good look for her, to have little curls flying away. Knowing he could still muss her up that way gave him a small amount of satisfaction, even though it felt like he had an iron post in his pants.

She licked her lips and gripped the handle of the front

door. "You can't keep doing this to me," she whispered. Then, without another word, she disappeared inside the house.

What about what she did to him?

SEVEN

THE WEATHERMAN WAS predicting a storm to pass through their part of Wyoming, with a slight chance of grape-sized hail. Storms like that were pretty normal and could often pop up and dissipate in various locations. The dark clouds overhead matched R.J.'s mood as he left the house early, the morning after The Kiss Heard Around The World. He was pissed off, sleep-deprived and horny as hell. Agitation coursed through his restless bones as he shifted gears in his car and cruised toward his shop, lowering his foot harder on the gas pedal with each mile he ate up.

His guys better steer clear of him today because he was sporting for a fight. Unfortunately no one was there yet, including Danielle, whom he wanted to growl at right then.

In order to work off his tension, he walked down to the coffee shop and grabbed the blackest cup of coffee they had and a breakfast burrito. He'd barely dodged the storm, and by the time he returned, Alex and Sam had arrived and were hard at work on Charlie's cars. The red message light glowed on his phone. R.J. took a monstrous bite of the burrito and picked up the receiver to check the message. His mood grew dangerously blacker when the message turned out to be Danielle, informing him she'd overslept, then woke up with a headache. She'd be in later, was all she'd said.

Later his ass. He was so damn tempted to call her back and tell her to not bother coming in at all. But the whole thing with the order for Charlie's cars was something only she could answer. So he held off.

As he finished the last of this breakfast, R.J. picked up the phone and placed a call to his supplier. Even though he'd yet to hear back from them, he took a chance someone would be around this time of morning. The receptionist had to put the manager on the phone in order to find out the information R.J. needed. He paced back and forth like a caged animal while he waited for the man to come back on the line. He snagged the cup of coffee from the desk top, blew on the hot liquid then took a shallow sip. The coffee was hotter than sin, but he didn't really give a damn. The temperature closely matched the blood boiling in his veins.

"I don't have any orders from you dating back for at least a year," the guy told R.J. after coming back on the line.

He damn near crushed the paper cup in his hand, so the hot drink could give him a third degree burn, not that he would care. Thankfully his anger hadn't disabled his common sense. He set the cup down and tightened his grip on the phone.

"Son of a bitch," he cursed into the mouth piece.

"When did you say your deadline was?" The guy was clearly trying to calm R.J. down, but it wasn't working.

He closed his eyes and tried pulling in a calming breath. That didn't work either. "No later than the end of July."

"And you've got two cars?"

R.J. stopped his pacing and leaned heavily against his desk. "Yeah."

The other man didn't say anything for a moment. "Well, you could put a rush on them, but it'll cost you extra. And even with the rush you'll be pushing it real close."

"Yeah, no shit," he muttered. "How soon could they get here if you rush them?"

"I won't be able to say for sure until I see a parts list. But it sounds like you're going to have a lot. Depending on how rare they are, two weeks at the earliest. Maybe three."

Three effing weeks. He was so screwed.

He pinched the bridge of his nose. "Okay, I'll get the list off to you ASAP. Just see what you can do about getting them here in two weeks. I don't care how much extra it costs. The shop will cover it."

"All right, then."

They hung up and it was all R.J. could do not through the damn phone against the wall. If Danielle had done her job accordingly, they would have gotten the parts within the next few days. Now it would be at least two weeks before he could start rebuilding. He had designs and colors all picked out, and he couldn't do a damn thing on them yet. Made him feel antsy as hell, and he didn't like it.

What in the world had she been doing? R.J. picked up the phone again and placed a call to Danielle. Not surprisingly, she didn't answer. He didn't bother with a message because he knew she'd be in sometime. Besides, the time would give him a chance to calm his murderous temper down. He'd be damned if he'd let Danielle and her addiction destroy what he'd built from the ground up. He told himself if she messed up again she'd be gone. No matter how valuable of an employee she was. He hated to throw away a working relationship, but his business came first.

Until Danielle showed herself, there wasn't a whole lot R.J. could do about the situation. So he buried himself in good old-fashioned back-breaking labor. For the next three hours, he tore apart Donald Underwood's car. Charlie may have been the bigger client, but the deadline for Donald's car would hit sooner. He needed to get the thing gutted so he could start the rebuilding process.

The skies had opened up overhead, and a decent thrashing of hail beat down on the shop's roof. It wasn't anything R.J. hadn't experienced before, but the sharp sound of ice hitting metal got on his nerves. After twenty minutes of mild thunder, the hail turned to rain and the atmosphere outside was as dark as evening. It was right around that time Danielle came in, looking like a drowned rat with wet hair and a panicked expression on her face. As though she sensed R.J. was just chomping at the bit to ream her six ways from Sunday. He couldn't imagine why.

She disappeared into the office, came out a second later and said something to Alex. After Alex's reply, Danielle went back into the office. R.J. leaned against the front bumper of Mr. Underwood's car and watched Danielle through the only office window. She stood at the desk, shuffling through papers, then went to the filing cabinet. She thumbed through some files for a moment, then turned to the computer.

R.J. decided it was time to confront her about her detrimental mistake. He pushed away from the car and walked toward the office.

"Sam," he called out to the mechanic. "Grab the phone if you hear it ring."

"You got it," the kid answered.

There was also a phone in the shop, so one of them could answer it in case Danielle wasn't in the office. This was one of those conversations that needed to happen without any interruptions. He didn't want to give Danielle a chance to escape him if the telephone rang.

When he opened the office door, Danielle jerked around in her chair, as though she'd been caught with her hand in the cookie jar. Her eyes widened for a moment, then she smiled. Her relief would be short-lived when she heard what he had to say.

"Hi," she greeted. "I'm really sorry about the tardiness. I

woke up in the middle of the night with a horrible headache and I couldn't go back to sleep. My pain relievers finally kicked in, but they make me really drowsy and I overslept."

When she said "pain relievers" the Adderall instantly came to R.J's mind. Would Danielle take it in the middle of the night? Would it make her go to sleep like that? He didn't know much about the drug, but he knew it was meant to treat ADD, and he guessed something like that wouldn't make a person sleepy. Unless she was mixing it with other medications...

R.J. filed that information away for later and decided the business was the most pressing matter.

"We have something we need to discuss," he started.

The muscles in her throat worked as she swallowed. Nerves?

"Okay," she replied.

He crossed his arms over his chest and braced his feet apart. "I found the incomplete list of parts for Charlie's cars on the desk in here—"

"Oh don't worry, I got that done," she interrupted.

R.J. paused, more out of astonishment than anything else. Had she really just outright lied to him? His conversation with his supplier directly contradicted her. And his supplier had no reason to lie. And there was no work order or any record that the purchase had been made.

"Actually, Danielle it hasn't been taken care of," he said with more patience than he felt at the moment. "Because I looked in Charlie's file and there's no record of any parts order—"

"I have that here, I just never filed it," she interrupted again.

R.J. stared at her for a moment and noticed how her pupils were dilated. She also didn't have any jewelry on, and Danielle never came into work without her heart locket and mother of pearl ring.

"Really?" he asked. "Because when I called our supplier, he had no orders for Charlie dating back a year." He left the statement at that and waited for Danielle to say something. They both knew she had no argument, at least none that he would accept. Dropping the ball on something this big was inexcusable. No matter how loyal she'd been, no matter how much he relied on her to run the business side of things, he could not ignore a blunder of this magnitude.

Danielle stared at him, speechless. Her brow wrinkled in display of her obvious confusion. How could she be confused after the evidence he'd just given her?

"No, that's—" she paused and shook her head. "That's not possible. Look, I have Charlie's file right here. I can show you." She spun around in her chair and yanked the filing cabinet open. Her slender fingers trembled as she rifled through the files, and came away unsuccessful. "I know I have it here somewhere," she muttered as she turned to the desk and searched through a stack of files next to the computer.

"Danielle," he interjected, but she either didn't hear him or she ignored him. Her soft mutters were incomprehensible to him, but he gave her a minute to pull herself together.

"Here's his file." Her voice held a twinge of relief, but R.J. knew that would be short-lived. She wouldn't find what he was looking for because he'd already gone through Charlie's file. Was it possible she was getting his best client confused with someone else? But how could she since Charlie's order was so large?

And R.J. had already placed the order and had the information folded up in his back pocket.

"It's in here somewhere, because I know I did it." She got to the end of the file and started at the beginning again, clearly convinced she'd missed the work order.

R.J. was out of time and out of patience. He had cars to work on and couldn't do this song and dance with her. "You're not going to find it, Danielle, because it's not in there."

"It is," she snapped at him. She stared back at him with a wide, panicked gaze that was so uncharacteristic of the woman he'd known for two years. Danielle never panicked over anything, nor was she stupid. She knew R.J. fired people for a lot less than what she'd done. How could she justify keeping her on staff?

"I'm telling you, I made that order. In fact, they should have come in by now," she said.

R.J. unfolded his arms and took a step toward her. "You didn't, Danielle. I don't know what's been going on with you, but you dropped the ball on this one." He pulled the invoice out of his pocket to show her he'd had to make the order instead of her. Clearly something was wrong with her memory and needed a good jogging.

She grabbed the paper from him, her blue eyes scanning the information, unblinking. Slowly, her face crumbled and R.J. knew that she knew she'd been caught red-handed. Or maybe she didn't think it was red-handed. It was very possible that Danielle really thought she'd taken care of the matter. She could have gotten this account confused with another, and ultimately, it got neglected. Whatever the case, R.J. needed to take action.

She handed the paper back to him with a shake of her head. "This can't be right. I know I made that order."

"You didn't. And now I may not have the parts in time to get the cars finished. I don't know what happened, Danielle, but I can't have you making these kinds of screw ups. This..." He picked up the invoice. "Is inexcusable, and quite frankly you've been making a lot of mistakes like this lately."

She stood from her chair and was almost eye-level with him. The pleading look on her face didn't achieve any sympathy from him. "I understand you're mad, and you have every reason to be—"

"You're damn right I'm mad. This place is everything to me, and I cannot allow you to put that in jeopardy because you have a problem."

"I already told you I don't have a problem—"

"You have a problem. I don't know what you've gotten yourself into, but it's affecting your performance here. And that's where I have to draw the line."

She jabbed her fists onto her hips as an angry blush colored her cheekbones. "What problem do you think I have? I mean, yes I've been having sleep issues and headaches, but other than that, I don't have a problem."

He leaned in close and whispered, "We both know you're popping those pills more than you should be. It's dangerous and you need help. I'm sorry, Danielle but I have to let you go."

She opened her mouth as though she had a response all ready but wasn't expecting him to say that. What else would she expect from him? A slap on the wrist? A time out? She knew him better than that.

"Okay look, I'll just take a few days and come back when you've cooled off." She turned to walk away from him, but he stopped her with a hand on her arm.

"This is permanent, Danielle. Once you walk out that door, you won't be coming back."

He allowed time for his words to sink in, because he knew she thought he wouldn't really let her go. She thought herself too indispensable to the shop, which she was. But he had to draw the line somewhere.

"You can't let me go, R.J.," she said with a hysterical laugh.

"I can and I just did."

Her lips flattened to a thin line, a sign that her blood was right at the boiling point. Of course, he understood her anger and fully expected it, but he didn't care. His shop had to come first.

"And who's going to run this place?" she demanded. "Who's going to answer the phones, and deal with clients, and do the bookkeeping or the payroll or order supplies, and basically everything that I do around here?"

While she did have a point, R.J. wasn't going to relent. "You're not the only woman in this town who can run an office."

"That may be so, but I know this place inside and out. Do you have any idea how much time it will take you to train someone else? Not to mention getting them to learn the filing systems and all the coding for our clients?"

R.J. shook his head. "That's not your concern, Danielle. I'll find someone else."

She snatched her purse off the floor and yanked it onto her shoulder. "Fine. But be warned," she said with a finger pointed at him. "You're not going to find anyone as good as I was."

He stood back while she marched toward the door. "Do yourself a favor and dump those pills down the drain."

"Go to hell," she snapped just before slamming the door behind her.

****

That stupid asshole!

How dare he fire her after everything she'd done for his business? She'd dedicated two years of her life, doing the bullshit grunt work no one else in that shop wanted to do, and he fired her? Just like that?

Danielle marched toward her car as tears built up in her eyes. There was still a light rain coming down, which soaked into her hair and left wet droplets on her clothes. Like she gave a damn. Let it pour on her for all she cared. Sopping wet clothes wouldn't faze her right now.

She let herself into her car and tossed her purse onto the other seat. It landed with such force, that it fell onto the floorboard, spilling the contents inside. She dug for her keys with trembling hands from the spilled mess and jabbed the key at the ignition three times before she get the thing inserted. Damn key.

What she needed was her pills. They kept her thoughts organized and gave her the motivation to keep busy. R.J. told her to get help, but she didn't have a problem. She didn't need anyone's help, thank you very much. She'd been raising Lindsey on her own for seven years, successfully ran this shop, until today that is. Sometimes she felt a little overwhelmed and needed the stimulant to keep her going. What was the harm in that? Lots of people took Adderall in order to channel their energy. Danielle didn't have excess energy she needed to tame. The Adderall kept her going when she would otherwise want to quit.

What bothered her was how R.J. found out. She'd been on the drug for about a year and had always been able to mask the effects, which had never been out of control. A few sleepless nights here and there. And yes, her appetite had been curbed, so she'd dropped about fifteen pounds. She hadn't thought the weight loss had been noticeable.

Danielle backed out of the parking space, her tires peeling on the concrete beneath the car, and left the shop.

It had to have been the red-head, the doctor bitch that R.J. always undressed with his eyes. The second that woman had come into the exam room, Danielle had known she'd be in trouble. She should have listened to her instinct and rescheduled her appointment for when Dr. Gross had been there. But what Danielle hadn't expected was for Rebecca to be so damn observant. She must have said something to R.J. But wasn't she bound by confidentiality, or some shit? How much was she legally allowed to say? If Rebecca had kept her nose in her own affairs, Danielle would still have a job and no one would have been the wiser.

Now she was jobless and had R.J. sniffing around where he shouldn't have been.

Rain pelted her windshield as Danielle headed down Main Street toward home. What had the hairs on the back of her neck standing up, was too many people finding out. If word got out what Dr. Gross was doing, the shit would really hit the fan. Dr. Gross wasn't a bad man, just helping out a few friends who needed something extra. Other doctors hadn't been able to give Danielle what she needed. She hadn't displayed the symptoms of ADD, so they'd turned her down when she'd asked them to put her on Adderall.

Then, one day the answer came to her like a Heavenly choir of angels from above. Danielle had been talking to one of her neighbors, whose son saw Dr. Gross. The woman had mentioned she'd recently been taking her son's Adderall in order to get her through her day easier. She'd made the whole thing sound completely harmless, as though people across the country took their kids' medication every day. Danielle's interest had immediately been piqued. But Danielle had been concerned because Lindsey didn't have ADD.

Her neighbor's response had been, "Don't worry, Dr. Gross will take care of you. He's very accommodating."

Danielle had no clue what that had meant, until meeting the man himself and realizing he had no qualms about writing a bogus prescription for her daughter. At first it had kind of made Danielle sick to her stomach, like she was using her baby girl for her own personal benefit. But, after a short time, Danielle realized the whole thing didn't really have an effect on Lindsey. All she had to do was see Dr. Gross once every three months, have her blood pressure taken and tell the doc she was fine. Dr. Gross then handed Danielle the slip of paper, and all was good with the world. What was wrong with that?

Plus, Danielle loved the way the Adderall made her feel. She could go for hours and not even think about being fatigued. She got shit done. She'd been better at work and actually had energy to spend time with her daughter in the evenings. It was a win-win situation for everyone.

Now the thought of being jobless was stressing her out. What she needed was another pill. She'd taken one this morning, and wasn't supposed to take more than one in a twenty-four hour period. But what harm could one more little pill cause? It would send her on a work-spree around her house and she wouldn't have time to think about her current unemployment. Or how R.J. had obviously banged the doctor bitch, and clearly wanted to get in her pants again. Danielle was very familiar with the looks he gave the other woman. Because he used to look at *her* that way. Until he decided to go all ethical on her with his "I can't do this anymore" bullshit.

She was getting irritable, and that wasn't a good sign. Another pill would take the edge off. Just one more and she could float through the rest of her day stress-free.

EIGHT

REBECCA TOOK ADVANTAGE of the practice's lunch hour and drove to the pharmacy. This was pure instinct and something she probably shouldn't be doing. If information got beyond her, the potential of Dr. Gross getting in serious trouble grew exponentially. Not to mention she could get slapped with a lawsuit, so she had to be careful with what she said. But she'd graduated high school with one of the pharmacists, and she trusted him to be discreet. At least she hoped. One could never tell with people these days.

She still hadn't worked out what she was going to say to him. But she needed more solid evidence of Dr. Gross's activities and she wasn't sure how else to go about it. If her suspicions were true, which she was sure they were, she'd be forced to leave the practice. In that case, she might have to find a practice in another town. However, that was a small sacrifice to make in order to keep her medical license.

The sun was a bright yellow disc directly overhead. After yesterday's storm, Rebecca was grateful for the warm weather, even if it was a bit toasty for her taste. Her feet were sweating in her brown high heels.

In just a few short minutes after leaving work, Rebecca pulled into the pharmacy. It wasn't one of those that was tucked in the back of a drug store. It was one of those mom and pop places located at the end of a small strip center. Luckily there were no other cars. Rebecca didn't relish anyone else overhearing.

With a pounding heart, she parked her car and went inside the pharmacy. The place wasn't very big. Wall-to-wall shelving held over-the counter medicines and vitamins, along with a few chairs for those who wanted to wait for their prescriptions. Rebecca spotted Josh behind the counter with his white coat and light brown hair. The phone was cradled between his ear and shoulder as he worked on the computer.

She'd always liked Josh. He had a warm smile and never had a bad word to say about anyone. He was also a newlywed, and he and his wife were renovating an older home in the neighborhood where Lacy, R.J's sister-in-law, used to live. She came to a stop in front of him and waited for him to finish his phone call. After a few minutes, he hung up and greeted her with a grin.

"Hey, Rebecca. Are you dropping off, or picking up?"

She inhaled a deep breath. "Neither. I actually have a favor to ask you."

"What do you need?" he asked.

"I need you to let me know if any prescriptions for Adderall come in here that are written by Dr. Gross. Would you be able to do that?" she asked, knowing good and well he wouldn't.

Josh shook his head and frowned. "I can't really give you that information."

That's what she was afraid of. Did she really expect him to give her a glance of all their confidential files and keep a personal record of Adderall prescriptions just for her? She wouldn't do that for anyone either. But still... without that information, she was that much further away from getting to the bottom of this.

"Why do you need to know?" Josh asked.

The look on her face must have shown her disappointment. Now, face to face with Josh, Rebecca wasn't sure she could divulge this information. "Uh…" she started, not feeling the confidence of a few moments ago.

Josh leaned forward across the counter. "You know you shouldn't even be in here talking to me about this. And you also know I can't give you that information."

"I know," she admitted, unable to look at her own reflection in Josh's eyes. What had she been thinking, coming in here? That Josh would allow her access to confidential information and answer all her questions? She knew better than that and could get in trouble for even asking. "Forget I said anything," she added.

Josh didn't respond, probably because he couldn't forget she'd asked. Now she'd probably raised a red flag for him that would likely come back to bite her in the ass.

She turned and left the pharmacy with a heavy and oppressing weight pressing down on her shoulders. It was sort of the same dread she used to feel the night before an exam, the ones that she hadn't been as confident about. And not only had she not gotten anything accomplished, but Josh probably thought she was nuts.

As she drove back to work, she tried to keep her thoughts aligned to her patients that she still had to see today. Thoughts of impending doom, such as losing her medical license, kept interfering with normalcy. While examining her first patient after lunch, Rebecca pulled up the wrong file and it took her several minutes to fix the problem. Dr. Gross had been scarce, going from one exam room to another, then back to his office. It was just as well. She didn't have the wherewithal to broach the subject again.

Not only that, but she couldn't look at him with a million questions in the back of her mind.

Thankfully the rest of her day went by pretty smoothly. Her last patient left at quarter to six, giving her time to stop by the grocery store to pick up things for dinner. However, after arriving home, the chicken and asparagus all of the sudden didn't sound very appetizing. Her mother already had a pot spaghetti on the stove, while simultaneously arguing with Rebecca's father. As mouthwatering as the garlic bread smelled, Rebecca really didn't want to listen to her mother and father argue about whether or not to take advantage of the termite invasion and remodel the house.

"The shag carpeting is thirty-five years old and needs to get ripped up anyway, Donald. Why leave old carpeting?" Her mom was saying as Rebecca walked into the house.

"Because there's nothing wrong with it," her father shot back.

Twenty minutes into the wood paneling debate, Rebecca excused herself to her room and packed an overnight bag. No home-cooked dinner was worth this headache. She'd had a long day and the last thing she wanted was to listen to her parents volley back and forth for Lord knows how long. She'd grab a quick dinner and go see Courtney. The two of them were overdue for a girls' night anyway.

"Honey, where are you going?" her mother asked as Rebecca walked through the kitchen to the garage door.

"Over to Court's. Don't feel like you have to wait up."

Patsy eyed the overnight bag with a suspicious gleam in her eye, but shrugged her shoulders. "All right."

Her car was so blessedly silent, that all Rebecca could do was sit there. Maybe she ought to just sleep in her car. The seats were leather and pretty darn comfortable. No, because then her mother would really think she was crazy.

So she pulled out of the garage and headed to her friend's house. On her way there, she grabbed some dinner and a sweet ice tea. The tea was entirely too watery and not sweet enough, but she didn't care. It was cold and wet and that was all the mattered.

Courtney's house was pitch black when Rebecca pulled up to it. She knew, even as she rang the bell, that her friend wasn't home. Even still, she rang the bell two more times, but no one answered. No one answered the phone either when Rebecca called on her cell phone. Disappointment had her taking slow steps back to her car. She tossed her overnight bag in the back seat and climbed behind the wheel. Over the next few minutes, Rebecca munched on her brisket tacos and stared out over the darkened street. After finishing dinner, she grabbed her cell phone again and called Lacy. She'd been dying to see the little girl Lacy had given birth to three months ago. But Lacy informed her the newborn had croup.

Rebecca hung up her phone again and stared at the thing. She thought about calling Erica but then remembered the girl saying something about going out for her birthday. With a defeated sigh, she tossed her phone back in her purse and laid her head on the steering wheel. Her only sensible option was to go back home, but she really, *really* didn't want to go there. She loved her parents dearly but they'd been suffocating her since they'd come to stay with her. Rebecca had never realized how much she valued the quiet of her home, until her home was no longer quiet. Questions about why she wasn't dating and her biological clock ticking away, was not what she wanted to deal with right now.

A completely crazy idea came to her mind, and she knew better. She turned the car back on and pulled away from Courtney's dark house. If she had any sense at all she'd turn around and go back the other direction. It would be much safer for her to go home and listen to her parents.

But she was tired of being safe. Safe was boring. Safe was predictable. All that had earned her was one lonely night after another and a mother who constantly nagged her to procreate. At this point, Rebecca would rather deal with the torture to her deprived hormones.

By the time she pulled up to the well-lit two-story home, Rebecca's heartbeat was in overdrive. An old muscle car, covered in gray primer that she didn't recognize, sat in the driveway. Without giving herself a chance to change her mind, Rebecca got out of the car and walked to the front door. She leaned on the doorbell and waited.

A few seconds later, the door swung open. No amount of pep talking or preparation could ever brace her for R.J. Devlin. He stood, silent in the doorway, with one arm braced against the door frame. His eyes, which were especially green at the moment, swept over her in slow appraisal. Every inch of her body, down to her toes, felt the touch of his gaze. It made her feel alive, wanted, and incredibly sexy. No one looked at her the way R.J. did. The man made an art out of the act. Usually she had to fight the urge to run for cover, or throw a turtleneck and a pair of sweats on. Now, she reveled in his attention. It was a pleasing thing to know she could still elicit a reaction out of him after all these years.

His gaze landed on hers, and he lifted a brow in question as though waiting for an explanation.

"My parents are driving me insane," she blurted out. "And no one else was home."

"Good to know I'm a last resort," he said in a low voice.

She tilted her head on one side. "Does it really matter?"

For a moment he just stood there and stared at her, his attention dropping down to her breasts, which were still covered by her work blouse. Then he pushed away from the door and stood back for her to enter.

As she brushed by him, she tried not to breathe too much because his scent always made her feel light-headed. She felt his scorching gaze on her as he closed the door, then led her into the great room. She forced her attention away from how spectacular his ass looked in those jeans, and placed it on the interior of the home. She'd been to his house before, but had never stepped foot inside, mostly because of the whole comfort factor she always struggled with around him. Being inside his home just felt too... well, personal. Rebecca didn't do personal with R.J. Devlin.

The inside was nothing like she expected. The soaring ceiling with exposed dark-wood beams was awe-inspiring to say the least. Two sets of French doors, framed by more dark wood, led to a backyard that was heavily-treed. Where she expected sparse furnishings, which was usually typical of men, she found rich décor and over-sized couches that were high class, yet masculine. A large archway to the left led to what she assumed was a kitchen. Rebecca got a glimpse of an enormous stainless steel fridge adjacent from a black granite island. From the outside the house didn't look any bigger from the other places on the street. But from the inside the home felt huge and airy.

Despite the space, it suddenly felt small and suffocating as R.J. brushed past her. He stopped by the couch and gathered a pile of newspapers, which he stacked in a much neater manner, then set them on the coffee table.

"This is really nice," Rebecca said lamely. If she didn't say something she'd stand there and gawk at him.

"Thanks." He straightened from his task and shoved his hands in his pockets. "Noah oversaw the construction and Courtney decorated it."

Noah was R.J.'s oldest step-brother and was in construction project management. And that would explain why everything was so coordinated and well put together. Not that R.J. couldn't put together a house. But Courtney had always had an eye and a flare for this kind of thing. She'd decorated Mason's — Lacy's and Chase's oldest son — nursery and had done a fabulous job. She hadn't used the typical blue for a boy. She'd mixed in yellows and greens and had pulled together a very tasteful and appropriate baby room. Her friend's unique eye for design was what had landed her the job as a decorator that she was currently soaring at.

"How's my dad's car coming?" she asked, because R.J. was staring again, and if she didn't put some words between them, she'd do something really stupid. Like say, "The hell with this, take me already."

"It's moving along smoothly. I was going to start rebuilding next week, but I might have to put that on hold."

"Why? Are you having problems with the car?" The last thing she needed to hear was an unfixable problem with her father's car.

R.J. shook his head. "No. We've just had some staffing changes so I have to re-shift my focus temporarily."

"What do you mean?"

He picked up a beer bottle from one of the end tables, and took a long swallow. "I fired Danielle," he stated after lowering the drink.

Rebecca stepped toward the couch. "You fired her?" When R.J. didn't respond she asked, "Because of me?" All she wanted was for the woman to get help. She never imaged her accusation would cost Danielle her job.

What did you think would happen?

"Partly," he said after a moment. "But that's not the only reason. She screwed up an order for one of my biggest clients. Now I may not finish the job in time. She was always a good employee." R.J. shook his head, as though he still couldn't believe it himself. "But I can't overlook something like that."

Rebecca lowered her gaze to the brown leather sofa, trying not to feel guilty for Danielle losing her job. What if Rebecca had kept her mouth shut? What if she'd ignored the signs and chose to mind her own business? But what would that have done to R.J.'s shop?

And had she said too much about her practice, even though she hadn't given any details?

A dull pain bloomed inside her chest, and all Rebecca could think about was Lindsey, Danielle's daughter. How would the woman support a child with no income? In a moment of uncertainty, and borderline panic, Rebecca had taken matters into her own hands, and hadn't thought about anything else. What kind of selfish person did that make her? That her lack of thought had cost a single mother her job, even if that single mother needed substance abuse help?

A sudden wash of shame shadowed over her, feeling the momentary guilt for interfering where it hadn't been her place.

But perhaps there was something she could do.

But what? Beg R.J. to give Danielle her job back? After she'd all but suggested her let her go?

"Hey," R.J. said as he came around the couch, toward her. He placed his index finger under her chin and forced her to look at him. "You didn't do anything wrong. I fired her because she screwed up, not because of what you did."

"I know, but it was still none of my business," she whispered and lowered her eyes from his. "I should have stayed out of it." His thumb went back and forth along her jaw line, making it hard for her to think about anything else but how good it felt to be touched by him.

"You did the right thing. And you came to me because you have a big heart, not because you were jealous. I shouldn't have said that."

Now probably wasn't a good time to tell him the jealous thing was partly true, even if that had never been her motivation. And how could she ever feel any other way when he always looked at her the way he was looking at her now? Like he wanted to devour every inch of her. Slowly, until she slipped into unconsciousness.

"I'm sorry you had to go through that," she admitted. "What are you going to do about replacing her?"

His wide shoulders moved beneath his gray t-shirt. "Find someone else." He pinched her chin and grinned. "You want the job?"

She plastered her sweetest smile on her face. "Not if you paid me all the money in the world."

"You're a tough woman to please, Ms. Underwood."

She took a step back from him because he was way too close and his body heat had her breasts tingling. "Not if you know how." *Why did you say that? Do you have a death wish?*

He tucked his hands in his pants pockets and raked his sensual gaze down her frame. "Oh, I know how. And don't pretend like you forgot."

That would be your cue to run out the front door.

If she were smart she'd go home and listen to her parents argue over wood paneling. But something about being here, sparring like old times, had her rooted in her spot. She couldn't leave even if she wanted to. R.J. made her feel too alive, which was something she hadn't experienced in a long time. Her job required long hours, then she went home to an empty home. No boyfriend, no husband, not even a cat to greet her at the door. Wasn't she entitled to a little fun? Wasn't she allowed to be naughty every once in a while? There was no one better in this town to be naughty with than R.J. Devlin. She'd experienced his version of naughty once before and had been craving another taste ever since.

And, judging by the look in his eyes, his thoughts were running along the same lines as hers. That was extra dangerous.

She eyed the beer in his hand. "Do you have another one of those?" *Yeah, add alcohol to the mix. Great idea.*

He raised the bottle to his lips. "Are you sure you want to drink around me? I might feel a little wicked and try to take advantage of you." The muscles in his throat worked up and down as he took a deep gulp.

To be honest, Rebecca wasn't sure she'd stop him if he made a move on her. At this point, if he so much as blinked at her, her will power would disintegrate.

"I think I can handle it," she retorted.

His grin grew downright wicked. "I'm going to hold you to that."

Yeah, you do that. She turned away from him when he walked to the kitchen, mostly because she didn't trust herself to keep her eyes off his ass. She could probably bounce a quarter off those cheeks.

The fireplace, which was the focal point of the room, was a massive thing surrounded by stone and a giant wood mantle. It was easily double the size of hers, but looked like it had never been used.

On the dark wood mantle were several family photos. Rebecca scanned her eyes over them, smiling at R.J.'s sentimental side. The largest one in the middle was a group photo of R.J., his parents, all the siblings and their kids. There were a few of just him and Courtney, one of him and his step-brothers, and one of him with all his nephews. There was one of just him and his mother, in which he had his college graduation cap and gown on. Rebecca made her way to the end of the mantle where she spotted a little four by six photo. The picture was pretty old because R.J. couldn't have been more than five or six at the time. In the scene were he and Courtney, along with another little boy Rebecca didn't recognize. They were all obviously related given the strong resemblance, but Rebecca didn't have a clue who the kid could be. A cousin maybe?

"I don't have light beer, or any of that shit, so you're stuck with this," R.J. said as he came back into the room.

Rebecca turned from the mantle and took the bottle from him. He'd already popped the top for her, so she took a sip. It was cold and spicy and burned all the way to her stomach. She normally didn't drink beer, mostly because she couldn't stand the taste of it. White wine was much more her thing, but this stuff wasn't that bad.

"Thank you," she said, and wiped a bead of moisture off her bottom lip. R.J.'s gaze strayed to where her thumb swiped across her mouth, as though he wanted to do the deed himself.

She was just about to ask him about the boy in the photo

when he jumped in with a question of his own.

"How are things at the practice? Are you still having a hard time?"

"Things have been pretty normal. Though, I did go to see Josh at the pharmacy to see if he can help me out. Even though I shouldn't have," she added.

"What would he be able to do for you?"

Rebecca turned around and lowered herself onto the oversized couch. "I just asked him to notify me if any suspicious prescriptions come through."

"Could he even do that?" he asked as he leaned against back against the fireplace mantle.

"Well, no." She paused to take a sip of her beer. "He said he couldn't help me and reminded me not to talk to him about stuff like that."

R.J. pushed away from the fireplace, came around the coffee table and sat down on the couch next to her. "You can't even tell me what's been going on at your practice? Does it have something to do with Dr. Gross?" he asked as he leaned back into the cushions and stretched his long legs out in front of him.

And how could bare feet be so sexy on a man?

Rebecca pulled her gaze away from R.J.'s feet. "I think Dr. Gross might be writing illegal prescriptions." Lord, just saying it out loud was like someone jabbing an ice pick through her heart.

R.J. choked on his drink. "Say what?"

"I know, it sounds crazy," she answered.

"I have a hard time imagining Patrick Gross doing anything like that."

That made two of them. And Rebecca still didn't believe it, despite her own gut instinct.

"You can't tell me anything else, can you?" he asked when she'd remained silent.

Rebecca shook her head, wishing she could confide in

him. Or anyone. Normally being bound by doctor/patient confidentiality wasn't an issue, but this time it was killing her. Keeping her worries, fears and suspicions to herself felt like a cancer, eating away at her insides.

"I can't without breaching my confidentiality agreement." She lifted her bottle in mock solute. She took a long deep sip, keenly aware of R.J.'s eyes on her as she tilted her head back. That unnerving look was back, the one he always got when he was plotting something devious. Not to mention the alcohol was working its magic, loosening her limbs and chasing away the day's tension. Even with that, she still couldn't fully relax around him. Being in close proximity like this always brought back memories of the night she'd lost her virginity to him.

They'd never discussed it, probably because there'd been some weird unspoken rule to never talk about that night ever again. Besides, if he could pretend like it had never happened, then why couldn't she? Only she couldn't pretend, at least not much longer. It *had* happened, and no amount of pretending could change that. The lasting effect on her had been profound and life-changing. She'd never been able to look at him without remembering what he'd looked like naked. Watching him walk from her bed to the bathroom, his firm round butt cheeks, framed by lean hips, then flaring up to wide shoulders. Until that night, Rebecca hadn't realized how good of shape R.J. was really in. Oh, she knew he took good care of himself, but the definition in his muscles had been fascinating. And incredibly sexy. Now when she looked at him it was with a different kind of appreciation. She knew his shoulders were as wide as they looked, and his thighs really were that powerful.

Cursed heat flamed in her cheeks and went all the way up to her hairline. She took another sip of cold beer to chase away the feeling, but it didn't work. And the more she sat there the more acutely aware she was of him, of how he seemed to sprawl himself on the couch with a comfortable ease, even though he really wasn't that sprawled out. He was just that big. And there was a hole in his jeans, right near the pocket and dangerously close to the most impressive part of him. If she shifted the tiniest bit, she'd be able to see a sliver of flesh through the worn threads.

She downed the last of her beer on one gulp, and set the bottle down on the coffee table. "One more of those and you'll be carrying me right out of here."

"Maybe that was my plan all along," he said in a low voice.

She slanted him a look out of the corner of her eye. That one was debatable, so Rebecca decided not to answer. She dropped her head back against the couch cushion. "This couch is really comfortable." Her body felt heavy and blissfully relaxed. If she closed her eyes for more than ten seconds, she'd be out like newborn baby.

"Thanks. Courtney picked it out."

She rolled her head to the side and looked at him. "Is there anything in this house you picked out?"

"The bed," he replied with infectious curl of his lips. "I wanted to make sure I got the biggest one."

"Somehow I don't doubt that." The longer she sat there, the more her feet throbbed in her tight shoes. Her toes had been jammed at the very end a narrow point, because they were borderline too small, so she slipped them off and stretched. "My feet are killing me," she groaned. She really needed to start wearing more comfortable shoes. Even the flats smashed her toes together until they felt broken. But she had a weakness for shoes, and style usually overrode common sense.

"I was really looking forward to soaking in my tub tonight," she added, as she tucked her feet on the couch so she could rub them.

R.J. stretched his arm along the back of the sofa. "And how much longer are your parents going to be staying you?"

"Who knows? My mom is trying to convince my dad to

do some renovating, but my dad doesn't want to spend the money. Especially since he's going to retire." She glanced at R.J. to find him watching her. "That's why I had to get out of there. I couldn't listen to another night of their mindless arguing. Plus my mother uses every opportunity to remind me that twenty-eight is too ancient not to be married." She slipped into an imitation of her mother's voice. "Rebecca, by the time I was your age, I had two kids." She shook her head. "She keeps trying to convince me that my biological clock is a ticking time bomb that's going to explode when I'm thirty."

R.J. chuckled. "Mothers are supposed to nag. It's their job. How much damage was done to their house?"

"I think it's pretty bad. They have to all but rebuild the house." She ran her thumb over her pinky toe, which was especially red.

"Give me those."

She swallowed a gasp when he grabbed the foot she'd been working on and placed it in his lap. Her heel rested on his right thigh, which was just as hard and big as she remembered. When he shifted, her foot came dangerously close to brushing up against that magnificent muscle of his. She leaned against the arm rest and forced herself to relax. Her other leg was tucked awkwardly beneath her, but she couldn't bring herself to sprawl both her legs across his lap. One leg was enough contact, thank you very much.

For a moment, neither of them spoke, and Rebecca studied R.J.'s profile while he dug his thumb into her arches. An all day's worth of beard growth coated his strong, square jaw. His mouth was set in a firm line as he focused his attention on her foot. Looking at his mouth made her think of the other night, when he'd kissed her and they'd come dangerously close to taking things too far. On her front porch. When had she become so inhibited?

But what had surprised her was how much she'd wanted it. She'd welcome the contact with him with open arms. Then she'd done the cowardly thing by getting mad at him. She hated herself for always reacting to him, and she'd needed someone to take it out on. In the heat of the moment, she'd felt better. But afterward she'd felt like a parasite for putting all the blame on him. She'd been just as enthusiastic, but had been unable to admit how much she'd really wanted it. Or enjoyed it.

"I owe you an apology for the other night," she found herself saying. Begging R.J.'s forgiveness had never been an easy thing. It was a pride swallowing siege that always gave him way too much satisfaction. However, guilt had eaten away at her for the way she'd left things between them. No matter how tumultuous their relationship could get, Rebecca still strived for an amiable friendship with him.

He slanted her a look out of the corner of his eye, and rubbed the tips of his fingers over her toes. "What ever for?"

Was that a grin she saw? She resisted narrowing her eyes at him. Barely. "For talking to you the way I did." She sucked in a breath. "It was wrong of me to make you feel like it was all your fault."

"You mean it wasn't?" His words were accented by a smirk, followed by digging his thumb extra hard into her calf.

She squirmed as much from the contact as she did from his feigned ignorance. The smile she plastered on her face was tight-lipped and forced. "You know it wasn't."

"Wow. And you were so convincing."

"Keep going and I'll dig my heel in so hard, you'll be talking like girl for the rest of your life."

The comment earned her a laugh, a hearty and deep one that sent a shiver running down her spine. Ironically, she smiled back and her earlier annoyance melted away. R.J.'s laughter had always been infectious and sensual at the same time. Sort of like an intimate whisper in her ear.

"No matter how well I think I know you, Rebecca, you always manage to surprise me," he said with a grin.

She leaned against the arm of the couch and rested her head on the back cushion. His hands felt sinful, yet magical on her feet. Every once in a while, he'd creep his touch up to her leg, and dig his fingers into the soft skin on the underside of her knee. It took almost all her will power to keep her from snatching her leg away and curling into a ball. His touch had always had a strange effect on her. At the same time, it was one she'd always welcomed because she knew only he could make her feel this way.

The languid movements of his hands made her limbs feel heavy and relaxed. The muscles in her legs and feet hadn't felt this loose in a long time, especially given how many hours she spent standing up. After a few moments, R.J. finished his work on her first foot. He set that one aside and grabbed her other leg.

"Thank you," she muttered in a sleepy voice.

"For what?" he asked without looking at her.

"For rubbing my feet. For listening." She took a deep breath and swallowed past the lump in her throat. No one confused her like R.J. One minute she despised him, and the next he was unbearably sweet. "For a million other things," she added.

He glanced at her with a somber expression. "You're the only woman I would do this for."

She couldn't stop the soft groan from flowing out of her when he worked his magic on the arch of her left foot. She hadn't realized how tense she was until she'd been forced to relax. After a moment, her eyes drifted shut and the last thing she remembered was R.J. telling her to have sweet dreams.

NINE

STEAM CURLED OUT of the cup of R.J.'s black brew as he stood next to his bed and watched Rebecca sleep. She was one of those people who hugged the edge of the mattress and left the rest of the bed un-rumpled. It amused him, because he was the opposite. In the mornings, he left his bed looking like it had been hit by a hand grenade. He usually slept spread eagle and almost always kicked the sheets to the floor.

The condition of the bed this morning only reminded R.J. of how different he and Rebecca were. She was gentle where he was hard.

Rebecca was selfless and spent her days taking care of other people. For years, R.J. had only thought about his own happiness.

But that didn't mean he didn't like to watch her sleep. Gazing at her in slumber was like watching a child; an innocent little girl who dreamt of things like unicorns.

Last night, he hadn't thought of anything other than taking care of her. When had he ever gotten that urge?

Never.

He hadn't been shocked when she'd fallen asleep on the

couch. The fatigue in her eyes had told R.J. she'd be a goner within seconds. As her eyes had drifted shut, he'd kept rubbing her feet until sure she was completely out. Then, he'd lifted her from the couch and, like a foolish dumbass, had bypassed the guest room and placed her in his bed. For years he'd imagined her there, seeing her bright red hair fanned out over his pillow. He'd selfishly played out his own fantasy by tucking her under the sheets and removing her clothes as carefully as possible. Any dirt bag would have taken advantage of the situation by ogling an unsuspecting woman. That wasn't to say he hadn't savored the sight of her creamy skin. However, he'd known that last night wasn't the night to engage in a little mattress dancing. Even still, it had taken all his will power not to slip her underwear over her hips, place a kiss on her inner thigh and wake her up with a nice little orgasm.

Instead he'd tucked her under the sheets and turned from the bed with a raging hard on. The ice cold shower he'd taken hadn't done a damn thing to ease the pounding in between his legs. As a result, he hadn't slept for shit and was paying for it now with a pounding headache. The coffee helped slightly, but he'd need a lot more if he had any hope of getting through his Saturday like a normally functioning human being.

So far he hadn't made a whole lot of progress. Right now all he felt like doing was grumbling like a bear.

He took another sip of the extra strong brew just as Rebecca stirred beneath the sheets. She turned over, exposing a slim back and teeny-tiny pale blue underwear which were molded her over delectable little ass.

The bastard between his thighs reacted instantly, pushing painfully against the zipper of his jeans. He adjusted himself accordingly and left the bedroom. It was clear she wasn't going to wake up anytime soon, and she needed her sleep. She worked too hard, and now had the stress of possibly losing her medical license.

R.J. didn't know Patrick Gross very well, but the man had a sterling reputation. He'd been Trouble's pediatrician for as long as R.J. could remember. He was well trusted and highly respected. But that didn't mean he was a stand-up guy, just a good doctor. He had no clue if Dr. Gross really was engaging in illegal activities, but Rebecca seemed certain he was. For that alone, R.J. wanted to bust his perfect pearly white teeth through his skull.

Even though it was none of his business, and R.J. didn't know shit about anything involving a medical practice, he felt the need to help her some way. But how? He couldn't very well pound on Dr. Gross's front door and ask him if he was handing out illegal prescriptions. Maybe he could pay Danielle a visit. That is, if she wasn't still too pissed at him.

How could she not be? You fired her.

Knowing Danielle, she'd cut his brake lines and smile while he wrapped himself around a telephone pole.

On the other hand, she could have answers for him. If he approached it carefully enough she might be able to tell him something.

He tossed back the last of his coffee and immediately poured another cup. The house was quiet save for the hum of the dishwasher, which was still pretty quiet. Rebecca would likely sleep for a while longer, so he used the opportunity to get in a good workout. He finished his second cup of coffee and headed upstairs. Once there, he stripped off his shirt, pulled on a pair of sneakers and fired up the treadmill.

The soles of his shoes pounded on the rubber of the exercise equipment for the better part of forty-five minutes. After that, he moved to free weights, and pumped iron for another thirty. A good workout always helped clear his head and gave him a sense of accomplishment. It also chased away any lingering feelings of fatigue. When he left his workout room, it was with a rapid beating heart and a thick coat of sweat from head to foot.

He jogged down the stairs, ready to hit the shower. But first, he made a detour to the kitchen for a bottle of water. When he came to the archway leading into the room, he spotted Rebecca, opening cabinets, clearly looking for something. She hadn't heard him and he used the opportunity of her ignorance to watch her. Man, she was something else.

She'd changed her clothes. Where she'd gotten them, he had no clue. Unless she happen to have a change of clothes in her car, which she must have retrieved while he'd been upstairs. The outfit was nothing more than a tank top with dental floss-sized straps, and cotton shorts. When she stretched to a cabinet overhead, the tank lifted above the waistband of her shorts, exposing a creamy sliver of skin. The shorts were so damn short, that he had the urge to back her into the counter so he could wrap her long legs around his hips. She'd love it, just because he knew her a lot better than she thought he did.

His heart kicked up as memories from the other night on her front porch slammed into him. Her passionate kisses. Her hands all over him, trying to eat him up. The noises she made, encouraging him to do more, to take it all the way. Damn, she had him tied up in knots. But that had always been the way with Rebecca. Every time he allowed himself around her, she got inside his head and scrambled up his thoughts. He didn't feel like himself. He felt unsure about everything, which he hated.

From across the room she sighed and opened another cabinet. He leaned against the doorway and grinned. She may mess with his head, but she was so damn cute when she got fired up. As if sensing his presence, she whipped around and caught him staring.

"I was just looking for a mug. Someone's going to get hurt if I don't get some coffee."

He chuckled and pushed away from the door. "The cabinet to the left of the sink."

She snagged a mug and poured the coffee in practically one move. Desperate, much?

"Do you have any cream?" she asked as she placed the carafe back in the machine.

He narrowed his eyes at her. "What do I look like, a woman?"

"Do you at least have any sugar?"

Without saying a word, he reached into a drawer and tossed out a couple of sugar packets onto the counter.

She eyed them like they were maggots. She licked her lips and picked one of the packets up. "This looks like you hijacked these out of a restaurant."

"Maybe I did." He slanted her a look as he took a bottle of water from the fridge, then took a long gulp.

"Don't you have, like, regular sugar?"

He lowered the bottle and leaned against the counter. "Why would I need regular sugar?"

"Everyone needs regular sugar." She tore open one of the pink packets and dumped it into her coffee. She opened three more, then stirred the drink.

"Only people who bake. I don't bake."

She took a sip of her coffee. "That's a shock." Her eyes darted down to his chest, which sported left over sweat from his workout.

He hadn't bothered wiping it off because he'd planned on showering anyway. Didn't women love sweaty men, or some shit like that? She'd tortured him enough last night and this morning. Hell, he'd stood under ice cold spray for damn near twenty minutes, trying to wash her away.

Payback was a bitch, baby.

Her chest expanded when she took in a breath. Eventually, she lifted her gaze back to his. "So, what happened last night? I mean, obviously you carried me, but why didn't you just wake me up? I would have gone home."

Because I wanted to see you in my bed.

Yeah, say that to her and see what happens.

"You were out, and in no condition to drive home. I could tell you needed a good night's sleep."

She rubbed the back of her neck, then cradled the mug in her hands. "Yeah, I think everything kind of caught up with me. I didn't mean to fall asleep like that, and I certainly didn't mean to kick you out of your bed."

For one brief and wicked moment, R.J. had considered crawling into the bed next to her. It was a king-sized bed and he could have easily stayed on the other side without ever touching her. But that had always been the problem with Rebecca. He didn't trust himself around her. She weakened his resolve, and even in sleep, she would have tempted him. What would have stopped him from getting them both naked? Or, even curling himself around her just to feel that satiny skin?

Nothing, that's what. That's why he'd gone to the other bed. Eliminate the temptation altogether.

He lifted one shoulder, as if to shrug the matter off. "It was no big deal. And my bed is the most comfortable."

"I'll say," she said on a breathy sigh.

Good God, if she didn't stop that he'd kiss her. Then she'd walk away asking for a cigarette.

"What kind of mattress is that?" she wanted to know.

"The expensive kind."

She leaned back against the counter and hugged the cup of coffee to her chest. "That thing is so heavenly; I don't know how you get out of bed in the mornings." She took a sip of her drink, then lowered the mug. "I bet women love it."

He lifted his brows at her comment, but didn't say anything. Not because he was offended. Things like that didn't bother him. But because of her honesty.

Her eyelids dropped closed, and she expelled a defeated sigh. "That was uncalled for. I'm sorry."

Women did love it, but R.J. didn't tell her that. No need to twist the knife.

"Do you want a shower or anything?" he asked her. Just because the thought of her naked, in his shower with the water cascading down that beautiful body of hers, was too much of a temptation.

"No," she replied quickly.

A little too quickly.

"Are you sure?" he asked, just because he enjoyed pushing her. "It's really big. I have two shower heads and they both massage."

To pink slashes stained her cheeks. One of his favorite things in the world was to make her blush, because it was so easy to do. She'd get all flustered, then get mad at herself for reacting so easily. Then she'd take her frustration out on him, and that's when the fun really started.

One time he'd gotten her so riled up, that she'd dumped a bottle of ice cold water on his pants. In public. So he'd had to walk around looking like he'd pissed himself.

"I'm positive," she finally said. He watched in amazement as she gulped the rest of her coffee in one final swallow. She set the cup on the counter with a loud clack. "I know what you're trying to do, and it won't work."

When she moved away from him, he stopped her with a hand on her arm. "Actually, I think it did." His thumbed caressed the base of her throat where her pulse beat at a rapid pace. He knew he was the only one who would get such a reaction out of her, even though she'd say otherwise. Mostly because she wouldn't want to give him the satisfaction.

She jerked away from his hold and stepped back from him. "I don't know why I thought you could actually be nice for a change."

"I'm a very nice guy," he countered. But what was the fun in that? Nice was boring. *Nice* didn't make her blush.

"You must save that side of yourself for really special people."

With those words hanging between them, she left the

kitchen and the opening and closing of the door followed a few seconds later. He glanced out of the window above the sink in time to see her backing out of the driveway and speeding away.

Good. If she knew what was good for her, she'd stay away from him. He felt like the biggest bastard in the world putting that look of hurt and confusion on her face. But it was necessary to keep her in check.

This was why they couldn't be alone together. Rebecca was dangerous. He'd stepped outside of his comfort zone last night and they'd toed that same sexual line they'd crossed nine years ago.

R.J. had never regretted having sex with her. The climb up her mother's rickety rose trellis had been worth it. He'd take his own life in his hands and had risked getting his bare ass shot off by her father's twelve gauge. Since then, he'd yet to experience a night like that. So, no. He didn't regret it. Her tight body and desperate moans had been a sweet memory he'd carried with him since then.

After Rebecca had flown out of his house like the place had been stuck by lightning, R.J. had finally grabbed a shower. Only, he'd made sure it had been nice and cold. Which had helped momentarily, until his traitorous brain and turned its thoughts back to the woman who had his guts turned in knots. His thoughts trailed from the look of fury on her otherwise delicate features, to her in the shower with him. Wet skin. Slicked back hair. Soapy hands gliding over the taut muscles of his flat belly.

Yeah, maybe a shower had been a bad idea. Stinking to high heaven would have been preferable to the images he'd suffered through while rinsing shampoo from his hair. Because he was predictable sap who couldn't keep his priorities in line.

Whatever. She was pissed at him, and just as well. That meant she'd stay away for a few days, and R.J. could use the break in order to rein in his sanity.

Later he left the house to grab some lunch from The Golden Glove on the way to his shop. While in the car, he single handedly dialed Danielle's number, while keeping one hand draped over the steering wheel. Why he thought she'd answer for him, he had no clue. And why he should care how she was doing, after she'd royally screwed him over, was another question he couldn't answer.

But despite what some people thought of him, R.J. did have a soft side, especially when it came to women. Danielle might have a problem, and she might have put him in a major bind, but he still cared about her. Something inside him kept nagging to make sure she was okay.

Just as he expected, she didn't answer. He left a brief message asking her to call him back if she felt up to it. After hanging up, he swung his car into the parking lot of his brother's restaurant. He was later getting to work, something he never did, but his morning with Rebecca had been oddly worth it. Even if their encounter resulted in her sticking another needle in her proverbial voodoo doll of him.

She probably had that thing so riddled with holes, it was likely falling apart.

He entered the restaurant, prepared to have a bacon cheeseburger and fries ordered to go. Behind the bar was Joel Garrison, the quiet, ex-military, rough-around-the-edges man Brody had hired to replace Anthony, the other ex-military guy who'd moved from bartender to chef.

At first, R.J. had been wary of Joel, mostly because Joel was one of those people who kept his feelings, or everything really, close to the vest. That had immediately made R.J. suspicious. But after getting to know him a bit better, R.J. realized Joel was just one of those guys who got his point across in as few words as possible. He was a private guy and R.J. could only respect that.

"A bit early for slinging drinks, isn't it?" R.J. commented

as he approached the bar.

One side of Joel's mouth kicked up. "My work is my life." He jerked his chin in R.J.'s direction. "What brings you by?"

"I need a bacon cheeseburger and fries to go."

Joel tossed the towel down he'd been holding. "You got it." The guy disappeared behind the kitchen doors for a moment, then reappeared. His too-long hair just barely brushed the neckline of his black shirt, which was just a shade darker than his hair. And his eyes. The edges of an equally black tattoo peeked just beyond the hem of the shirt sleeves, giving Joel that rough-around-the-edges feel many people had come to associate with him.

"About fifteen minutes," Joel commented, cutting right to the point.

In the meantime, R.J. perched on a stool, prepared to wait for his food, knowing it would be worth the fifteen minutes. "You still thinking about opening your own place?" R.J. asked, remembering when the other guy had mentioned running his own bar.

"Hell, yeah," Joel answered. "I've never been that guy to work for someone else, know what I mean?"

Yeah, R.J. got that. And if anyone was suited to run a bar, it was Joel Garrison. The guy had *hard-ass* written all over him.

"Have you said anything to Brody yet?" R.J. wanted to know, seeing as though Brody, R.J's step-brother and the man who ran the restaurant, had a difficult time keeping the bartender position filled for more than a year or two. People seemed to come and go like they were spinning through a revolving door.

Joel tossed him a quick glance while he refilled glasses. "Of course. I wouldn't leave your brother hanging like that."

Because underneath that hard-as-nails exterior was a good guy. R.J. had sensed that just as he'd sensed Joel's checkered past, probably filled with some kind of tragedy. People like Joel didn't become reserved and wary of their surroundings because they had a picture-perfect Norman Rockwell childhood.

The two men chattered for a bit longer before Anthony came out of the kitchen with a plastic sack filled holding a to-go container. He passed the food over, which R.J. took while reaching for his wallet.

Anthony waived a hand in the air. "It's on the house, bro," the big man announced.

R.J. shook the chef's burly hand. "Thanks, man." He turned to Joel and gave the man a hearty fist pump. "Check ya later." Then he was out the door, sliding his sunglasses on to shield from the bright overhead sun.

As he made his way to his car, he happened to glance down the street where Rebecca's practice was. And just like that, he was thinking about her again. Because all it took was a simple glance in her general direction and his mind was all over her like a kid on sugar.

He'd had a lot of sex over the years with a lot of different women. No matter how fantastic some of it had been, none of the women had quite measured up to Rebecca. They'd been nothing more than passing conquests who'd given him the release he'd needed. Rebecca was better than that. He had a tremendous amount of respect for her. Too much for him to bang and run. Even though that's basically what he'd done.

Despite that, he'd been willing to tarnish her own image of him so she could go and find happiness with someone who could give it to her.

But if she didn't stay away from him, he'd give her what she was all but begging for.

TEN

MONDAY AND TUESDAY had been frighteningly uneventful days, which really irritated Rebecca because it gave her time to think about R.J. and how they'd parted ways on Saturday. How stupid of her to think they could have a normal conversation that didn't end with some kind of altercation. With him looking at her the way he always did and making some kind of smarmy comment. Why couldn't he just be nice? Why couldn't he say something like, "Hey Rebecca, how's it going?"

But really, why was she mad at him? He was only being R.J. The person she was furious with was herself. Why did she always have to react like that? Why couldn't she be cool as a cucumber and let his comments roll off her back? The man had a way of bringing her ugly side out, and she let him do it every single time.

Even on Wednesday morning, she was still irked about their encounter. Until her cell phone vibrated and she glanced at the screen.

I just bought a five pound bag of sugar. See what you do to me?
Despite his evil ways, R.J. could always make her smile.

She'd never been able to stay mad at him for long.

She leaned back in her desk chair and answered his text message.

So bake yourself some cookies and smile.

A second later her phone vibrated.

Only if you come eat them with me. Or, better yet, off you.

She ignored that last line because she knew why he'd said that. She refused to react. Her next patient was due soon, so Rebecca pocketed her cell phone and decided not to respond to his message at all.

Five hours later, she'd felt like she'd already put in a full day's work. Back to back patients had made the time fly, and she was grateful to have her mind taken off R.J. for the first time in weeks.

They'd just locked their doors for lunch when her cell phone rang. Rebecca glanced at the screen, but didn't recognize the number.

"Hello?"

"Rebecca, it's Josh. I was wondering if you could spare some time and meet me for lunch."

She sat straighter in her office chair and tried not to sound too eager. "Of course. We just closed for lunch so I could give you about an hour." Had he changed his mind after telling her he couldn't help? But why would he do that, knowing he could get in trouble too?

"That should be more than enough time. You know the deli that just opened on Beach Street?"

"Yeah, I know it."

"Meet me there so we can talk."

The line disconnected and Rebecca set her phone down. Something wasn't right with this. It hadn't been that much time since she'd spoken to Josh, and his voice sounded funny. As though he knew she wasn't going to like what he had to say. But what choice did she have? Things at the practice had been pretty normal, almost like she'd imagined the entire thing with Dr. Gross. And yet, she knew it wasn't over, just as she knew Josh didn't have good news for her.

With a sick feeling in the pit of her stomach, Rebecca gathered her things and left the practice. Everyone had already left for lunch, so she made sure to lock the door behind her.

It took her no time at all to reach the deli. She'd eaten there only one time before and absolutely loved their chicken salad sandwich. Josh was already there, seated at a table along the wall. Next to him was a middle-aged man with dark hair and silver streaks at his temples. A dark jacket sat over narrow shoulders, and was accented with a black tie and white shirt. The bored expression on his face told Rebecca he'd rather be anywhere but a deli in Trouble, Wyoming. The sick feeling in her stomach didn't lessen. She had a feeling this guy wasn't a friend of Josh's who decided to join them for lunch. Given the nature of their business, she doubted Josh would invite an outsider to join them.

The realization didn't make her feel better.

Instead of going to the counter to order lunch, since she'd suddenly lost her appetite anyway, she approached the table and sat down.

Neither man had food in front of them, which wasn't a good sign. The other guy was nursing lemonade, which had barely anything drunk out of it. Josh was just sitting there, in his white pharmacist coat, tapping his fingers on the table.

"Are you hungry? Do you want to order something?" Josh asked her.

"No, I'm fine," she said as she set her purse next to her.

Josh cleared his throat and gestured to the man next to him. "Rebecca, this is Agent Reinhold."

Agent?

"He's with the DEA," Josh continued.

Oh, God.

Oh, my Lord.

Rebecca glanced at the agent and tried to swallow past the bile rising in her throat. What had Josh done?

Agent Reinhold handed her a white business card, which she accepted but didn't bother looking at it. What was the point? It would only tell her what Josh had already said.

"Dr. Underwood, I need to speak with you about the activities going on in your practice."

She tossed an accusatory glare at Josh, but he wouldn't look at her as though he knew he'd betrayed her confidentiality. His focus was fixed on the tabletop, so Rebecca glanced back at the other man, even though her stomach turned over at the thought of what was happening.

It was too soon for this. She wasn't ready to involve the authorities. All she'd wanted was to get to the bottom of everything and put a stop to Dr. Gross's activities. The DEA would shut the practice down. They'd take her medical license and possibly even throw her in jail. Her name would forever be tainted and she'd never be able to practice medicine again.

Now she was glad she hadn't had anything to eat, because she'd likely have thrown it up by now.

She shook her head and tried to sound light-hearted. "I'm not sure what you mean, because I don't really have anything to go on."

How could she explain herself without outright lying? She had no way of knowing what Josh had told the man, and she didn't want to start contradicting herself. That would only make her look guilty.

"They're just suspicions—"

"Actually, we've been investigating Patrick Gross for several years now, but we've never been able to pin anything down." He accentuated his statement by pulling out a thick file and laying it on the table.

"His reach goes far beyond his practice, Dr. Underwood."

Was he still speaking? Rebecca couldn't think past his initial statement. Several years? As in, as long as she'd been working with Dr. Gross?

The agent kept speaking and Rebecca forced herself to remain in her seat. And listen. Even though she wanted to puke.

"How long have you been employed by Patrick Gross, Dr. Underwood?" he asked her.

She shook her head and forced herself to think. "I don't know. A few years."

"Hmm," he replied, and flipped through his file. His head remained down when he asked his next question. "Does three years sound about right?"

Rebecca didn't like where this conversation was going. Would he chase after her if she ran out of the deli? "I suppose."

"Because three years is how long we've been investigating Patrick Gross."

Had one of the deli employees cranked up the heat? Perspiration coated the valley between her breasts. "You don't think I had anything to do with this, do you?"

Agent Reinhold ignored her question and pulled out a piece of paper. On it was a photocopy of a prescription.

He held it up in front of her face so she could see her own signature. "Did you write this prescription, Dr. Underwood?"

"Well, yes but—"

"And this one?" he interrupted with another photocopy of a prescription.

"That child actually has ADD." The words came out in a rush because she was so desperate to defend herself. It wasn't until after she'd said them that she realized what it sounded like.

"And this child doesn't?" Agent Reinhold asked, as he pointed to Lindsey's prescription.

Rebecca waited before answering because she needed to choose her words very carefully. "Lindsey Parker isn't my patient. I was filling in for Dr. Gross that day and she came in for a refill on her Adderall. I had never examined her before and all her vitals were normal."

"Even though you suspected prescription fraud of Adderall XR?"

"At that time I didn't suspect anything. I was just trying to take care of the patient." She glanced at Josh but his expression was unreadable. After a moment, he looked away and fiddled with the napkin holder.

For the next thirty minutes, Agent Reinhold peppered her with questions in that bored, monotone voice of his. As though he did this sort of thing every day. And maybe he did. But she certainly didn't. She'd never had her ethics questioned before, never had the possibility of having her medical license stripped. His calm demeanor was driving her crazy. It made her want to reach across the table and strangle him with that ugly-ass tie of his.

He didn't even know her! And yet he thought her capable of writing fraudulent prescriptions, when the very idea made her sick to her stomach. It defied everything she stood for. Unfortunately just her association with Dr. Gross and that bullshit 'scrip made her look guilty has hell.

Then he slapped her with the words she knew was coming, yet still was like a punch to the stomach. Worse even. A knife through the heart.

"We're suspending your medical license until further notice, Miss Underwood. Your practice will receive a cease and desist order and will we be confiscating all of your patient files."

"Those are confidential," she argued, as though that was a bigger deal than being told she couldn't practice medicine anymore.

Agent Asshole packed up his stuff, all nice and neat in that stupid file of his. Which she wanted to burn. "Not anymore, they aren't."

"You can't take those," she reiterated with borderline

hysteria. "What about the practice? What's going to happen to that?" She leaned forward and came *this* close to latching onto the man's scrawny neck. "When can I go back to work?"

Agent Reinhold tossed her a casual glance, as though it was all so damn easy for him. "We'll know more after we take Dr. Gross into custody and question him further."

Everything around her stopped. The waitresses stopped chatting when they should have been serving customers. The speakers in the ceiling stopped playing the dull elevator music. And her heart stopped beating.

"Custody," she repeated. "I don't even know what that means. What does that mean?"

"It means," he answered in a low voice. "That we have a warrant for the doctor's arrest. You can legally continue to operate until you receive a cease and desist order. Then you'll have to surrender your license."

Unable to stomach anymore, Rebecca stood from the table and bolted for the door. Somehow she managed to fend off tears of frustration and fear until she got to the car. She thought she heard Josh call out her name, but he was the last person she wanted to talk to right now.

Moisture pooled beneath her eyes and spilled over as she fumbled with the stupid keys. They fell from her hand three times before she got the car started.

Arrested? They were actually going to place handcuffs on Dr. Gross's wrists and book him? Wasn't that what they called it in the movies? Take them downtown and book them?

How could you compare this to a movie?

This was as real as it got. Fear, like she'd never even felt in her whole life, gripped her like a hard fist trying to choke the breath from her.

Why had Josh called the DEA? Yes, Dr. Gross needed to be stopped, but why had he broadsided her like that? She would have rather he told her to go screw herself than *help* her the way he had. She'd gone to him in confidence because she hadn't known where else to turn.

She gripped the steering wheel tighter and tried to compose herself. Walking back into work sobbing hysterically wouldn't be good for business and would hardly look professional to her patients.

Her cell phone vibrated somewhere in the depths of her purse, but she ignored it. There was no way she could hold a conversation and sound normal.

The rest of her day passed in a blur, and Rebecca kept going over the recent turn of events in her mind. How had the DEA gotten a hold of the prescription she'd written? He'd seemed particularly interested in Lindsey's 'scrip which was no coincidence she was Danielle's daughter. And no coincidence that Danielle had just been fired by R.J.

Rebecca didn't want to think it was possible, but had Danielle ratted her out? But why would she do that? Wouldn't she only be pointing the finger back to herself? It was no secret Danielle didn't like Rebecca, and Rebecca was basically the reason the woman had lost her job. Would she go so far as to call the authorities and blame the whole thing on Rebecca?

None of it made sense, but something told her Danielle had played a part in this. Rebecca didn't have a clue how, and to what extent, or even who Danielle knew to call.

The only thing Rebecca knew was that after today nothing would be the same. Her work was the reason she got out of bed in the morning. If she didn't have that, what did she have?

****

R.J. didn't know how much more of this shit he could take. Danielle had coded all the files in effing hieroglyphics, so he couldn't find a damn thing. The phone rang every five minutes, and he was pretty sure bills were supposed to be paid this week, but fuck it if he could find the checkbook. Or the bills.

He'd finally delegated Alex to phone duty so R.J. didn't rip the bastard out of the wall and smash it over somebody's head. After that was taken care of, he'd located the checkbook in a locked drawer. But that hadn't been until he'd searched for twenty minutes for the key. However, a checkbook wouldn't do him any good without the bills to refer to. Danielle had probably filed them somewhere with some weird ass code that didn't make sense.

A line of cars were in the garage, but R.J. couldn't get anything done for chasing his own ass. None of the guys knew where Danielle kept the bills, nor did they have a clue what her filing codes meant. To top that off, the computer was locked with a password, which was probably Greek symbols or some stupid shit.

"I need a vacation," R.J. muttered to himself as he dug through another filing cabinet, hoping to find the bills.

"Don't we all, man?" Alex said.

How did he not know his own office? It was obvious he'd placed way too much responsibility on Danielle's shoulders. Shouldn't he have at least known the password to the computer?

"Why the hell did she lock everything?" R.J. asked as he found yet another locked drawer that wouldn't unlock with the key he'd found.

"Maybe she had some freaky shit she wanted to hide," Alex chimed in.

R.J. didn't want to think about how right Alex might have been about that. He moved to the next drawer as the phone rang. His employee picked it up and recited the shop's greeting.

"Devlin Motors." Alex paused and glanced at R.J. "Yeah, he's right here." He held the phone out. "It's Charlie."

Great. He really didn't need this right now.

"Hey Charlie," R.J. greeted with as much enthusiasm as

he could.

"Just calling to check on my babies. How are things coming along?"

Luckily he'd gotten a call from his supplier that morning to let him know the parts for both the cars had shipped. He'd put a rush on them and they should arrive next week.

"Moving along on schedule," he lied. Charlie didn't need to know of the little hiccup. As long as R.J. could finish the cars on time, no harm done.

"Great. That's good to hear. Listen I have some drawings and ideas I wanted to run by you. Would you mind if I stopped by this afternoon? I wanted to see the cars anyway."

Wouldn't that just be the perfect end to his day? Having Charlie show up to micromanage R.J.'s design style, then see that he hadn't really done anything yet to the cars.

"Actually, today's not good. Would you mind coming in the morning?" That would give him time to at least look like he'd started working on the cars. And maybe he'd be too busy to shoot himself.

"I guess I could wait another day," Charlie said with resignation.

R.J. knew the drill with the man. He always tried to disagree with whatever R.J. did to the cars, but in the end he'd always loved the way they turned out.

He ended the call and rubbed a hand down his face. "We need to place an ad for an office manager. Call the paper and get information on running an ad in the employment section," he told Alex.

Alex turned in the desk chair and lowered his brows. "You said this needed to get done first." Alex gestured toward the computer where he'd been sorting through the payables.

"I changed my mind. None of us is going to get anything done until I get someone in here to pick up where Danielle left off."

"All right."

R.J. left Alex to the task, then he walked down the hallway to his office. Even though he had a shitload of work to do, he needed some time to himself. Someplace where there was no noise and no phone ringing. He shut his office door behind him and sank down in the desk chair.

Maybe he'd been too hasty when firing Danielle. Maybe he should have found a replacement first, then shown her the door. His impulsiveness had gotten the better of him again. In the past, he'd had a habit of acting without thinking. Quitting a job without thinking of how he was going to pay his bills. Selling a car without having other means of transportation. Screwing a woman without thinking about the next morning.

He'd thought that hasty behavior had been over with.

On the other hand, Danielle had been exhibiting worrisome behavior and she'd needed to go. He didn't regret firing her. But he should have been more prepared with a replacement.

He dug his cell phone out of his back pocket and dialed Rebecca's number. They really had no reason to speak, other than he wanted to hear her voice. He desperately needed some sweetness in his shitty day.

The phone rang several times before she picked up.

"Hello?" The word was breathy, yet strange. She sounded distracted and not like herself.

"Did I catch you at a bad time?"

"What?" she asked as though it were an afterthought. "Oh, no. I've just had a busy day. I can't seem to get out the door."

She accented her statement with a quick laugh, but it wasn't the sort of chuckle he usually associated with Rebecca. Her laughs were always carefree and airy. This one was strained and short. Put on, almost.

Come up with a reason you called so she doesn't think you're psycho.

"I was just calling to let you know we started the rebuild

on your father's car."

That was lame, asshole.

"Oh, good," Rebecca responded as though she wasn't paying any attention.

He didn't blame her.

He cleared his throat and tried to regain control of the conversation. "Are there any last minute changes you need to make?"

She was silent for a moment and some background noise came through. Shuffling papers maybe. "What was your question again?"

"Is something wrong?" he asked her.

"What do you mean?" she asked with a strained laugh. "Everything's fine."

The woman was a terrible liar. Always had been, especially to him. But R.J. accepted the statement even if he didn't believe her. Rebecca was not what one would consider an open book.

"All right. Looks like we're coming slightly ahead of schedule on the car. You can come by and see it anytime." *That way I could see you too.*

"I trust you to do a good job. I don't need to come see it."

A wise idea. So why did that leave him deflated? "Okay."

Her heavy sigh came through the line. "I gotta go."

"Don't work too hard, Rebecca," he told her. Sometimes he wondered how she had time for herself. She deserved some pampering.

"Thanks," she responded in a low voice.

She hung up and R.J. stared at the phone before setting it on the desk. Rebecca was perpetually upbeat person who rarely let anything get to her. The defeat in her voice was uncharacteristic of her and left him wondering what had happened. It had to have been something profound to have that much of an impact on her. Damn his protective side for wanting to strangle whoever had taken the laughter out of her voice.

And damn the person for making him want to commit violence.

He ought to bring her something or... do something. Hell, he didn't know what. One of his many faults was wanting to fix everything. Something was wrong with Rebecca and R.J. felt the uncontrollable urge to make it better.

Especially since she was so much more beautiful when she smiled.

ELEVEN

REBECCA WANTED TO crawl into a dark hole and die.

She wanted to pound on Dr. Gross's door and demand to know why he couldn't have stayed a straight arrow.

She wanted to bash Agent Reinhold's knee caps in for taking her license away.

Without her work, what did she have?

Helplessness like she'd never experienced before washed over her and hovered like a black cloud. It followed her as she left the practice and clung as she drove home.

Home, where her bed waited and she could crawl under the covers and not think about anything.

But going home didn't appeal to her. Her parents where there, waiting to talk to her about things like termites and her biological-flipping-clock.

It was a good thing she didn't have kids. How could she support them now that she was unemployed?

As much as she loved her mother, and often sought her council, Rebecca didn't want to talk to her about this. Patsy had called about six times today asking Rebecca the most mundane questions.

She was doing a load of clothes and wanted to know if Rebecca would like her to throw in some of her clothes for her.

Then she'd wanted to know if Rebecca was going to be there for dinner. And, just as she'd walked out of the office, Patsy had called again to let her knew there was a suspicious stain on the living room ceiling.

"It looks like a water stain," her mother had warned.

Well, wasn't that just the greatest thing ever?

Unemployed *and* a leaky roof.

She was really on a roll.

Never in her life had she felt so out of control. And Rebecca lived and breathed control. However, it had all been taken away before she'd even realized what had happened. All afternoon, she'd bounced back and forth between red hot anger and unbelievable despair.

Normally she was pretty even-keeled. Current events made her feel not like herself.

As she cruised through town, Rebecca racked her brain for a solution, even a temporary one. But what?

Perhaps she could change her identity and move across the country.

Going into work, knowing the clock was ticking, made her sick to her stomach. But she'd never been one to quit, even if she didn't hold out very much hope.

How long would she be out of work? Months? Years? Would she ever be able to go back? More importantly, would she be able to practice medicine with the same sterling reputation she'd worked so hard for? Could Dr. Gross single-handedly toss out everything she'd killed herself for? The sleepless nights of being on call. The endless hours of studying. Making rounds after listening to hours of lectures.

It would not all be in vain, dammit!

There had to be something she could do. She couldn't just sit back and watch her career be taken from her like this.

She drove past her street but didn't turn. She couldn't

face her parents in this condition. Her mother would see right through the fake smiles and put-on cheerful tone. The woman would pepper her with questions, and Rebecca wasn't in the mood to deal with them.

In fact, she wasn't in the mood to deal with anyone. No one would understand. They would ask questions, for which she didn't have the answers to. None of this made sense to her, so how could she possibly explain it to others?

Only one person on the planet knew what she was going through. Only one person was connected to this, and he was the only one she wanted to be around at the moment.

How strange.

Against her better judgment and all logical thinking, Rebecca cruised through her neighborhood until she came to the other side where it dumped onto a side street that ultimately ended on Main Street. Rebecca took a right on the main drag and drove for several minutes to the newer part of town. Two small strip centers gave way to an apartment complex. She took a right past the apartments and drove down the four lane road, cruised through a green light and eventually came to R.J.'s neighborhood.

It was a newer development surrounded by nothing. Not big, stately homes like the complex R.J.'s oldest step-brother, Noah, lived in. These were smaller and modeled after sixties, ranch-style homes. She'd always loved this neighborhood but the price tags were beyond her reach.

Everyone thought doctors made shitloads of money. Yeah, those were the guys in their fifties and head of their departments. In the meantime, Rebecca was too busy paying off her student loans.

She drove to R.J.'s house without any real thought of which way to go. Funny how she knew this route like the back of her hand, even though she'd spent so many years telling herself to stay the hell away.

His house came into view and she pulled along the curb

just as R.J. came out the front door. She stepped out of the car and her stomach dipped just at the sight of him. Faded jeans and a white t-shirt were nothing spectacular, but on R.J. it was a dangerous thing. Dangerously sexy that made her skin itch and her heart take a nosedive to her stomach.

She squashed her reaction to him because the last thing she needed was to add lust to what she was already feeling.

He came to a stop next to his car, holding some kind of drink in one hand and a baseball glove in the other.

R.J. played baseball?

Rebecca didn't say anything as she walked closer to him. But really, what was there to say? They'd never been good at conversing anyway. Sexual tension had a way of muddling the conversational waters. Perhaps it was time that she accepted her fate as such. She and R.J. would never be pals who sat around and shot the breeze. They fit into some other category she'd yet to label.

R.J. braced a muscled forearm on the roof of the car, and watched her. She stopped a few feet from him and tried not to notice how the denim of his jeans cupped that magnificent package to knee-weakening perfection.

She licked her lips. "I had a really shitty day," she blurted out.

One corner of his mouth kicked up and his gaze lowered down her body. A second later, he opened the driver's side door.

"Hop in," he stated.

She shouldn't be doing this. Getting in the car and being alone with R.J. Devlin was complete and utter madness.

On the other hand, Rebecca hardly had a choice in the matter. Her feet moved across the concrete, taking her to the passenger door. Even though the logical side of her brain screamed at her not to, she pulled the handle, opened the door and lowered herself to the seat. The loud clunk of the door closing sounded like a vault door trapping her in. As though there was no going back. As though getting in the car was finally crossing that line she had no business crossing.

The classic car roared to life when R.J. turned the ignition over. He tossed the glove in the backseat and settled the bottle in the drink holder. His big, strong hand gripped the gearshift as he maneuvered the car down the driveway and through the neighborhood.

She should demand that he stop. She should make him pull over so she could get out and run the opposite direction.

But what she should do and what she wanted to do were two different things. And, dammit, Rebecca was tired of doing what she *should* do. For once she was going to do what she wanted to do and damn the consequences.

Because there would no doubt be many.

Neither of them spoke as R.J. drove through town, working the gearshift with an expertise of someone who was born to handle powerful cars. His right hand gripped stick with just the right amount of confidence and pressure, moving it back and forth without any real thought. The muscles of his left thigh flexed when he pressed down on the clutch at just the right time.

Rebecca had tried driving a stick-shift once, but gave up at that first awful grinding sound. R.J. had probably mastered it the first time because he was that talented and always excelled at anything involving a motor.

They came to a red light just before the interstate and R.J. used the break to hand her the drink. She eyed it for a moment before accepting it from him.

"What is it?" she asked.

"Root beer," he answered.

Not her favorite, but it was cold and that was all that mattered. She took a sip and lowered the bottle. "Got any pumpkin beer in here?"

He accepted the bottle from her. "What the hell kind of girly shit is that?"

"Girly shit," she answered with a smile. "It's good stuff."

He snorted and muttered, "Says you," just before chugging half the bottle.

"You should step outside your comfort zone every once in a while." She grinned at being able to throw his own words back at him.

The look he tossed her could have scorched the clothes off her back. "Why do you think you're here?"

Okay, touché.

The light turned green and R.J. drove them onto the interstate. Where they were headed, Rebecca had no clue, nor did she care. Just getting away, leaving her problems behind, if only temporarily, felt so... freeing.

They drove east toward Cheyenne, but R.J. quickly merged onto 287 North toward Casper. Her family had traveled through this area several times when she'd been a child. The scenery up here was breathtaking and peaceful. Aspens dotted the hillsides, their little leaves dancing in the breeze. The winds had grown gustier in the past hour, bringing with it dark clouds that chased away any remaining sunlight. The sight promised a wet evening, and perhaps a few thunderstorms.

R.J. had removed his sunglasses, giving Rebecca the opportunity to study his profile. A sexy layer of stubble covered his square jaw, giving him a disreputable, carefree look. Her fingers itched to trace the edge of his chin just to feel the roughness of those whiskers.

You can't fall in love with him again.

Loving R.J. was an impossible thing. She'd learned that the hard way many years ago, but her heart didn't seem to care. It always succumbed to him no matter how wrong she knew it was. Nine years ago she'd mistaken his love-making for something deeper, but he'd quickly proved it had been nothing more than scratching an itch. She'd jumped into the situation as a naïve girl and had learned a hard lesson:

Don't fall in love with R.J. Devlin.

Such a simple thing shouldn't have been so hard for her to grasp.

If she kept gravitating toward him like this, she'd be in the same position she'd been in nine years ago.

Then she'd have no one to blame but herself.

They drove for quite a while longer, away from the clouds which seemed to be chasing them. Finally R.J. pulled off the interstate and headed east again. They drove a while longer, until the sky was almost dark. Several times Rebecca wanted to ask R.J. where they were going. But the hard set of his jaw told her he wasn't in a conversational mood. His left hand held a tight grip on the steering wheel, while his right rested on the gearshift.

She wanted to reach out to him and ease the tension that had him wired so tight. Was it her mere presence that did this to him? Was it something else? Could it have to do with where they were going?

Rebecca kept her mouth shut and studied their surroundings, which weren't much to look at. Finally they came to a stop at a place called McCarger Cemetery.

A cemetery?

With a baseball glove?

He parked in front of the entrance and killed the engine.

Rebecca didn't know of any close relatives of his that had passed away. Courtney had never mentioned anyone in their family being buried here. Come to think of it, she'd never mentioned visiting any gravesite before.

R.J. reached into the back seat and grabbed the baseball glove.

"I'll be right back," he muttered just before exiting the car and leaving her alone.

Translation: *Stay in the car.*

Screw that.

He asked her to come along and expected her to wait in

the car?

Okay, so she did kind of show up unannounced.

But she was dying to know why he brought a baseball glove to a cemetery in the middle of nowhere.

His fine backside disappeared to the other side of the graveyard, baseball glove hanging loosely from one hand. His gait was slow and relaxed but the hard set of his shoulders completely contradicted that. She'd learned a long time ago how to read R.J.'s body language. It was pretty easy once she'd gotten the hang of it. Feet braced wide meant relaxation and comfort. Add hands in the pockets and he was settling in for a long haul. Shifting from foot to foot meant agitation. Crossing his arms over his chest meant trouble. Kicked back in a chair with his hands behind his head, and he wasn't going anywhere anytime soon.

She also knew he got quiet when he had a lot on his mind. R.J. had never had trouble telling it like it was or speaking his mind. He'd barely spoken to her the whole ride up here.

Despite his order of staying in the car, Rebecca threw the door open and followed the path he'd taken.

Some people were creeped out by graveyards. They'd never bothered Rebecca. Death was a natural part of life. She just made sure not to step on the graves. Something about walking on another person's resting place made her skin crawl.

She spotted R.J. kneeling in front of a small headstone, with the glove on top. The lack of light made it hard for her to read the names or see anything for that matter. R.J.'s white shirt was like a beacon in the darkness that she followed until she reached him.

He straightened and glanced over his shoulder with an unreadable expression when she approached. She expected him to reprimand her or make some smartass comment about not listening to him.

Nothing.

The muscle in his jaw ticked, but he didn't speak.

He turned his attention back to the headstone and shoved his hands in his front pockets.

When was the last time R.J. had been this quiet? How long had it been since he'd tossed out some careless, smarmy comment designed spark her temper.

Very un-R.J. like.

With a hesitant movement, she placed a hand on his shoulder. If anyone needed someone to lean at that moment, it was R.J. Even though she didn't know why.

Not knowing was killing her.

The muscles in his shoulder were hard and big. As she rubbed her hand over the sleeve of his t-shirt, she felt every groove, every sinew. Nine years ago, he'd been big and defined, as a man should be. At thirty-two he seemed bigger, taller even. His shoulders were broader, his forearms more chorded. Even his back muscles were more mouth-watering than ever.

What is wrong with you?

Something weighed heavily on his mind and all she could do was ogle him. All she could think about was his hard muscles and how good he felt under her touch.

"How did you know him?" Rebecca asked softly.

R.J. was silent for so long she didn't think he was going to answer her. Then he said in a low voice, "He was my brother."

His brother?

Rebecca knelt down so she could see the name on the headstone. It was so dark that the wording beneath the name was unclear to her.

Trent Michael Devlin.

R.J. and Courtney had had a brother?

In all the years Rebecca had known the Devlins she'd never heard any of them mention a brother or anyone named Trent.

153

He must have died a long time ago for Rebecca to never have known him.

She glanced at R.J., but he was stony silent and motionless. Trent's death must have left him terribly wounded and maybe even permanently scarred.

"He had a rare form of cancer," R.J. said into the quiet night. "He was diagnosed with Osteosarcoma at the age of eight. They only gave him six months to live but he held on for a year. I was ten when he died."

Rebecca shook her head, trying to digest the information. A brother who'd died from cancer. What a horrible and tragic thing for a family to endure. The only loved one Rebecca had lost was her great-grandmother. But she'd been a hundred and two so her death hadn't been a shock to anyone. More of a relief.

But a child? And one who'd been battling such a nasty disease? She couldn't begin to imagine what Trent's death had to done R.J. and his family. Just the fact that they never talked about it was telling of how painful it probably was.

"I never knew," she finally said. There had to be something more she could say. But what?

"No one ever knew. Except Martin."

His voice was strained and low, as though speaking about it tore at some deep dark place inside him, scratching the wound raw and bleeding. He'd watched his brother whittle away and had lived with the pain for twenty-two years. Was that why he always kept everyone at a distance? Or was there more to the story that he wasn't ready to share with her?

"Today's his birthday," R.J. continued. "He'd be thirty-one."

Oh Lord.

Her heart broke open at the agony in his voice. Did he do this every year? Alone? Come to his brother's grave and grieve for the little boy who'd died?

No one should have to go through something like that alone. No one should have to bear the weight of such a life-changing event by themselves.

Rebecca slid her hand down R.J.'s arm, over the sinew of his forearm and slipped her hand into his. His fingers were warm and so much bigger and rougher than hers. She gave his hand a gentle squeeze if only for the reassurance that he didn't have to grieve alone. How much comfort it actually afforded him, she didn't know. Probably not very much. But she was at a loss of what else to do. She felt like she had to do something. Say something.

"I'm sorry," she murmured lamely.

"We used to play catch together. Because we were so close in age we were always on the same little league team. We always wanted to be better than all the other boys so we practiced together." He paused and shifted his weight to his left foot.

Agitation.

"I stopped playing after he died."

"Oh, R.J." She turned to face him and cupped his stubble-covered jaw with her free hand. "I'm so sorry. That must have been devastating for your family."

He lowered his forehead to hers and inhaled a shaky breath. "I've never told anyone about him. I hate coming here."

His breath was warm against her lips, reminding her how mind-numbing his kisses were. She wrapped both arms around his neck and whispered in his ear, "So let's leave."

TWELVE

THE DARKENED SKY swallowed up the surrounding foothills as R.J. flew down the interstate toward Trouble. The woman next to him was playing with fire. She kept rubbing his thigh and threading her fingers through his hair. Every slight touch, every small smile and his gut tightened until he felt like his muscles were about to shatter. It was damn painful and his balls felt like they were going to explode.

The second she'd stepped in the car she'd sealed her fate. R.J. told himself to keep his hands off her, but screw that. She should have known to stay away from him and she hadn't. He only had so much will power and his had snapped.

Talking about Trent had opened up that old wound that always oozed for days. His brother's death had altered their family forever. He hated dealing with it. Hated remembering the pain and the unanswered questions of why this had happened to them. Why Trent had to be the one whose bones had been infected with rare tumors. Why R.J. had to sit back helplessly while his younger brother had fought for his life. And lost.

Every year he dreaded this. Dreaded the day that marked

another year that Trent wasn't with them. Visiting his brother's grave wound R.J. up so tight that only two things would relieve the tension. Drinking and sex.

Only R.J. had really had no desire to bed one of the many women he had in his proverbial Rolodex. His only plans had been to come home and drink until the memory of that bleak time in his family's life was gone. Because the only person he'd been interested in taking to bed was the woman sitting next to him.

Since he'd known doing that would be bad for both of them, he'd only planned on drinking the night away.

But damn, how was he supposed to resist her when she kept looking at him like that? How could he keep her away when she'd held his hand and told him how sorry she was? Then she'd wrapped her arms around him, giving him ample opportunity to feel those spectacular breasts against him. After that he'd tossed his rule out the window.

Trying to stay away from Rebecca had always been exhausting and he no longer had it in him.

He turned off the interstate, not bothering to slow down even though the speed limit warned him to back it off. If he went any slower he'd have to pull over and take Rebecca in the car. That would be no good because he needed his big bed in order to fully enjoy her.

His muscles twitched again when she squeezed his thigh. "Hurry," she said.

"If I go any faster they'll throw my ass in jail."

"No they won't," she responded with an evil grin. "Martin knows the sheriff too well. Plus, you could always use that R.J. charm on them."

"You mean the charm that always worked so well on you?"

"It worked better than you think," she answered quietly.

Luckily he lived on the edge of town, so they reached his house that much faster. Which was a good thing because he was about to shoot off in his pants. Rebecca had no idea how her nimble little fingers really affected him.

He had the car in the driveway and was out the door in practically one move. When Rebecca came around the car, he took her hand in his, mostly because he needed to keep touching her. Her skin was the softest thing he'd ever touched. As though she'd never done a hard day's work of manual labor in her life. Unlike him, who'd spent his days beneath the hood of a car, covered in grease and abusing his hands.

Where he was rough she was soft.

And curvy.

She had curves in all the right places that made him want to drop to his knees and howl at the moon.

He fumbled with the lock on the door like some horny jackass who couldn't handle a key. Rebecca's insistent, wandering hands didn't help. She kept cupping his rear end and making his eyes cross.

"Stop if you know what's good for you," he warned.

"Or what?"

He shoved her against the door and took her mouth in his. Without hesitation, he swept his tongue inside her slick heat, prompting a startled gasp from her. The kiss was hot, a flat out demonstration of all their pent up sexual frustration for each other.

"Or I'll take you right here where all my neighbors can see," he whispered in her ear.

That shut her up.

Her teeth stabbed into her lower lip, which was still damp from his ferocious kiss. But he could have sworn he saw her smile, as though satisfied with herself.

Witch.

He'd show her satisfaction.

When he finished with her she'd have a smile on her face like no man had ever given her.

He finally got the damn door open, mostly because

Rebecca had stop distracting him with her hands.

After kicking the door closed, R.J. whisked Rebecca in his arms and carried her to the bedroom. She muttered something about having to use the bathroom. He actually had no idea because her face was buried in his neck and she kept sniffing.

Why were women always trying to smell him?

Once in his bedroom, which seemed like a ten mile walk, he dumped her on the bed. Not much finesse behind the move, but there'd be time for that later. Right now all he cared about was getting inside her.

He kicked off his shoes, then ripped his socks off. "Clothes. Off," he ordered.

She sat up on her elbows and watched him as he whipped his shirt over his head. "Wouldn't you rather take them off yourself?"

He tossed the shirt on the floor and went to work on his pants. "Next time. Just get naked."

Her eyes went wide and she fumbled with her shoes. "Yes, sir."

That's right, *yes sir*. R.J had been waiting for this moment for nine years, and he wasn't about to wait another second. All he could think about was Rebecca and getting lost in her. Feeling her hands on him and all that silky hair tickling his nose and getting tangled in his fingers. Right now was about the two of them and he planned on making every moment something she'd never forget.

****

Rebecca lay back on the pillows and stared at the dark ceiling. Her whole body felt like Jell-O and weightless, as though she was floating a foot above the bed. She knew R.J. was good in bed. Nine years ago had been phenomenal. So much so that every other man she'd been with hadn't measured up.

But this… This had been something entirely different. The lovemaking had been deep and intense and the force of her orgasm had shocked her. She felt as though she'd entered into another realm, one which she was unfamiliar. One which she felt she couldn't return from unscathed.

There'd definitely be no returning from this. If making love with R.J. nine years ago had rocked her world, then this would leave her a changed woman. A woman who'd given her heart away and most likely wouldn't be getting it back. Or receiving one in return.

Of course, she'd gone in with her eyes wide open. She'd known what she'd been doing when coming here earlier. A part of her had hoped they'd end up right where she was. And that part of her wasn't sorry at all, nor was there any regret.

R.J. had the ability to bring her unbelievable pleasure, and that's exactly what she'd needed. She couldn't remember the last time she'd had a release this satisfying, and it had momentarily erased the day's stress.

Unfortunately her heart had been a casualty. Then again, Rebecca supposed she'd never really stopped loving R.J. How could she? When that kind of unrequited love was involved, there was no recovering from it. The only thing that surprised her was that she hadn't figured it out a long time ago.

Or maybe she hadn't wanted to.

All those years of telling herself R.J. Devlin meant nothing to her, and she started to believe her own lies.

The shower in the bathroom turned off. She heard the glass doors open, then close. The image of him naked, with water running down that gloriously hard body of his, invaded her peaceful reflective time. The urge to leave the bed and press her own nude body against his was almost too strong. That would be a mistake. She'd be unable to resist those scorching looks he always gave her and they'd end up having sex again.

No. No more sex.

She needed her mind clear in order to sort through the mess of her life.

The clock on the dresser next to the bed read eight-thirty. Not nearly early enough to go to bed, and she wasn't tired anyway. She leaned over to the nightstand and clicked on the lamp, which was next to the T.V. remote. The wall-mounted television had to be at least sixty inches and probably had a killer picture. Rebecca leaned against the headboard, pulled the sheet up over her breasts and turned the T.V. on.

Lame nighttime dramas and reality shows. All garbage.

Where was a good movie when she needed one?

R.J. came out of the bathroom, followed by a thick cloud of steam. A single drop of water ran down the middle of his sculpted chest, in between the ridges of his six pack and was absorbed by the towel secured around his waist. Though it looked like one single tug and the thing would come right off.

"Eyes above the waist lady or suffer the consequences," R.J. commented with a lifted brow.

Okay, so she'd been caught ogling. What else was new?

"I hardly think I'd be suffering."

He dropped the towel and faced her, feet braced apart. The man was too big for his own good.

"Care to give that statement a test?" he asked.

"No," she answered quickly and secured the sheet tighter around her boobs. "There's nothing good on T.V. to watch."

R.J. rooted around in the top drawer of his dresser and pulled out a pair of black boxers. Disappointment washed over her when he pulled the garment up and covered the package she'd been trying not to stare at.

"Here." He picked up the remote, hit a few buttons and dropped the thing on the bed.

Rebecca tossed him an annoyed look. "That's sports."

"And?"

"And it's boring."

He crossed his arms over his thick chest. "If you're that

bored, I could think of something else to do."

She turned her attention back to the T.V. because just looking at him weakened her resolve not to get naked with him again. Even though she was still naked.

"On second thought, it's not that boring."

"That's what I thought," he muttered, then he turned around and left the room.

Damn him. One minute she was swearing to herself not to get tangled up with him, literally, again. All he had to do was walk in the room with a towel and her own declaration withered away. Why was he the one man who could strip away her defenses like they were made of tissue?

Of all the men in town, why him?

Again she was deflecting her anger with herself onto him. He hadn't done anything wrong. He was just being R.J. The man she loved. Flaws and all, cocky attitude and everything else that came with him.

She would never stop loving him no matter how hard he tried to push her away.

Some baseball game went into the sixth inning. Rebecca didn't follow sports, never had really, and the game held no interest for her. But she stared at the screen anyway without really processing the information. There was nothing else on, and R.J. would probably change it back anyway.

He strolled back into the room with a plate in his hand. Some kind of shredded meat was piled on the entire plate. The smell, something like BBQ, had her stomach rumbling and reminded her of how long it had been since she'd eaten.

She scooted over on the bed to make room for him. He set the plate down next to her and stretched out on his side, leaning on his right elbow.

"What is that?" she asked him as he plopped a piece of meat in his mouth.

"Pulled pork."

The stuff was slathered in sauce and smelled divine. She

picked a piece off the plate and studied it. "Where'd you get it?"

He glanced at her and swallowed another bite. "I made it. It's not poisonous, Rebecca," he said when she only stared at the food.

"*You* made this?"

"Don't sound so impressed. You'll ruin my confidence."

Nothing could ruin his confidence. She dropped the shredded piece of meat in her mouth and chewed. It was actually pretty delicious. Smoky, tender, and full of flavor.

"I just never pegged you for a cook," she responded and reached for more food.

He swallowed a bite and licked his fingers. "There's a lot you don't know about me, Dr. Underwood."

Apparently. "Such as?"

The look he gave her was so intense, she thought he was going to tell her to back off. Or maybe remove the bed sheet. She had no intention of doing either.

"I play the piano."

Huh?

Of all the things he could have said, that was the last thing she expected. Maybe something like "I'm can ride a bucking bronco," or "I'm an excellent shot with a rifle."

But playing the piano?

"Get out of here; you do not play the piano." Because she could not imagine big, hard R.J. Devlin, who spent his days ripping apart cars, running his fingers over ivory keys.

He crossed his legs at the ankles and picked up some more pork. "You think I'm kidding?"

"Well, yeah."

The grin that broke across his face was reminiscent of the ones he used to flash her when they were teenagers. And it had the same effect too. Her toes curled and a deep flush heated her face.

"I know I've had a habit of jerking you around in the

past, but I'm being serious."

Well, then. What was she supposed to say to that?

"Do you have a piano here?"

"No." He plopped a huge piece of meat in his mouth, then licked his fingers. "My mother has it."

What a shame. Seeing him play the piano would be the ultimate catalyst. She could die a happy woman.

"Before Trent died, my mother used to force all three of us to play. The only one who enjoyed it was Courtney. When my mother realized her efforts were useless she gave up."

Rebecca chewed thoughtfully for a moment, then swallowed. "And you still know how to play?"

He lifted one thick shoulder. "Some."

The sheet slipped a millimeter, so she tugged it tighter. R.J. had been eyeing her breasts ever since he'd lain down, and she didn't need that on his mind again.

Even though it probably already was.

"Do you ever practice?"

He tossed another piece of pork into his mouth. Just the sight of his throat muscles working turned her on. "Some," he said with a grin. "It really turns women on."

"You're just saying that to get a reaction out of me." At least she hoped. Yeah, she was pretty sure.

"Never could get anything past you."

Didn't mean it wasn't true. R.J. had a poker face like she'd never seen. But she tapped the slight feeling of jealousy down, because she did *not* need to go there again. The better part of her adult life was spent feeling jealous of whatever woman he was with at the moment.

And there'd been a lot.

Hence the reason why she stayed away from him.

They munched on pork for several minutes, falling into a comfortable silence. The baseball game played in the background and the one nightstand light cast a yellow but weak glow around the room. R.J.'s length took up almost the whole bed. Seeing him sprawled out, half naked reminded her of how much bigger and harder than her he was. His thighs were chorded with muscle and dusted with a soft layer of dark hair. The black boxers were form fitting and really left nothing to the imagination. They cupped the bulge between his thighs, showing off just how big he really was.

His shoulders were thick and broad, his chest smooth and sculpted.

Basically his body could have been carved from marble. Or better yet, marble statues could have been carved from his example. Either way he was perfection personified and Rebecca's body always reacted to him. She hugged the sheet tighter around her breasts to conceal the flush that bloomed across her chest.

"So, tell me what happened today," he said after they'd been silent for several minutes.

"What do you mean?" Her feigned innocence wouldn't work, she knew. She'd never been able to lie to R.J.

He lifted a brow and held out a piece of meat to her. Her attempt to snatch it from his fingers was unsuccessful. He held it out of her grasp and clucked his tongue at her.

"Open up," he ordered.

"I can feed myself."

"I know, but what fun is that?" The pork in his hand was inches from her mouth.

This was all just a little too intimate, a little too comfortable.

You just had sex with him! What's more intimate than that?

Strangely enough him feeding her felt so much more intimate than making love. As though their relationship was transitioning to something she wasn't comfortable with. Because, in the end, she knew, R.J. would leave her. Because R.J. always left.

"Rebecca," he growled. "If you don't open your mouth, I'll be forced to punish you."

Admitting defeat, she opened her mouth just wide enough to accept the food. R.J. placed it inside her mouth, somehow managing to slip his index finger in between her lips. The tip of his finger was blunt and tasted like all man.

Something she enjoyed way too much.

When she swallowed, he grabbed another chunk of pork and held it to her lips. She obeyed and this time he used the opportunity to swipe his thumb across her lower lip.

"Proud of yourself?" she chastised after swallowing.

"You have no idea," he replied with a wicked tilt of his lips. "Now tell me what happened today."

She scooted farther down the bed and laid her head back on the pillow. "I told you, I don't know what you mean."

"Rebecca," he said with a sigh. "I know you a lot better than you think I do. Something bad happened today. Tell me about it. I'm not letting you out of this bed until you do."

Even though talking about it was like rubbing salt on the wound, she knew she had to get this out. And hadn't she come here with the purpose of telling R.J. what had happened? Given his relationship with Danielle, there might be something he could do. What that was, she had no idea.

With a deep breath, she recounted her day, explaining to him her meeting with Josh and Agent Reinhold. She also included her suspicions about Danielle ratting her out about the 'scrip she wrote for Lindsey. When she'd finished it felt as though she'd relived the day all over again. The frustration, confusion, and fear were back, clouding her mind and preventing her of thinking about anything else.

"Why would Danielle rat you out?" he asked after she finished her story. "Sounds to me like Josh was the one doing the ratting."

"That doesn't make any sense. Josh doesn't have anything against me."

R.J. placed the empty plate on the nightstand and returned to his position. He propped himself up on his right arm so that he was practically looming over her. His right bicep looked huge next to her face.

"What would Danielle have against you?" he countered.

She shot him a droll look. Men were so clueless. Rebecca knew a jealous woman when she saw one.

Both his brows lowered over his green eyes. "Are you talking about me?"

"Yes."

"What would Danielle have to be jealous of?"

Something about his words rubbed her the wrong way. Did he not think their relationship was enough to spark the tiniest bit of jealousy in the other woman?

Rebecca sat up and leaned on her elbow. Her curls, which she'd taken down, slid over her left shoulder. "I don't know, R.J. You tell me."

He shook his head. "Danielle's not a vindictive kind of person. You don't know her."

There were those words again. They didn't go over well the first time he'd said them, and she liked them even less now. They only reminded her of his intimate relationship with the other woman, and the whole jealousy thing came back, which she was sick of. But more, his words sparked the tapped down emotion from earlier in the day.

She bolted from the bed, yanked the sheet and wrapped it around her. "I don't understand you. You've known me a hell of a lot longer than her. Why do you always defend her?"

"I wasn't defending her," he said casually from his relaxed position on the bed.

Fury had her nostrils flaring and a scream of frustration bubbling in her throat. She wanted to pound on him and make him understand the severity of the situation. One would think, that after admitting Danielle had a problem and firing her, he'd be more inclined to believe Rebecca.

"You are," she argued. The familiar heat flooded her cheeks again. "And don't say it's because I'm jealous. That has nothing to do with this." Lie, lie, lie. "My career and future are on the line here and I don't think you get that."

By the time she'd finished her rant, tears of helplessness pooled in her eyes and threatened to spill over. Dammit, she did not want to cry in front of him. Seeing her weak was one thing she never allowed in front of R.J.

And what's worse, she'd thought he would understand. After going through what he went through with Danielle, she was sure he'd be more sympathetic.

He held up a hand as though to calm her down.

It didn't work.

"Honestly, I'm not trying to defend Danielle. She's obviously a touchy subject for you. But the woman I know wouldn't do anything like that."

A traitorous tear leaked out, and Rebecca furiously swiped it away with the back of her hand. "Drugs have a way of changing a person, R.J." She paused as a horrific thought occurred to her. "Do you still have feelings for her?"

He shook his head. "It was just sex. There were never any feelings."

Rebecca lifted a shoulder and clutched the sheet tighter to her. Now, she wished she'd gotten dressed while he'd been in the shower. Even with a sheet, she felt horribly exposed and vulnerable. "Maybe not on your part."

"I can't help the way she feels about me."

He tossed the words out so casually, as though he dealt with this kind of thing all the time. Come to think of it, he probably did.

The thought caused another tear to leak out. The emotion was a combination of who R.J. really was and the nightmare that started at lunch today.

"Hey," he said softly, coming off the bed and walking toward her.

She turned from him, ashamed of her display of emotion and hating herself for it. His strong, warm hands gripped her shoulders and tried to turn her toward him.

"No," she protested.

"Rebecca, come on," he prodded gently.

"No," she tried again with more conviction. Somehow she managed to disengage herself form R.J.'s strong hold. She stalked toward the bathroom. "Just leave me alone."

He called out her name one more time, but Rebecca had already slammed the door. Nothing he had to say at the moment interested her. Nor did the lavish bathroom with its dark marble shower and jetted tub. The room looked like something out of a five-star hotel. Normally she would have ogled the dual shower head and spacious interior.

All she could think about was losing her license for something she didn't do, and the mind blowing sex she'd just had. Which had given her the misconception that R.J. actually cared.

How could he still defend that woman?

Rebecca paced from one side of the bathroom to the other, while dragging the stupid sheet behind her. Why hadn't she put her clothes on?

With an exhausted sigh, she lowered herself to the toilet and stared at the tiled floor. What was she supposed to do now? She had no one. No one to confide in, no one to help her. There was no way she could tell her parents, though she figured they'd find out soon enough. Her sister was all the way in Utah and had enough going on with her two kids and running a business. Courtney only came around when she wanted to be found.

R.J. was the only one who'd been affected by this, and he seemed so nonchalant about it.

That's because he still has a job. Agent Reinhold hadn't shut his business down.

She lowered her head to her hands as another tear leaked out.

The only person she could rely on was herself. Hadn't she

learned that a long time ago when she'd applied for her own student loans, paid for her own books and bought her own house?

Her parents were wonderful parents, but they'd raised her to be independent. They'd always taught her to never rely on anyone.

The only person you can depend on is yourself, Rebecca, her mother used to always say.

For Pete's sake she'd gone through medical school, residencies, internships, and all night studying. She'd thought for sure medical school would have killed her, but she'd lived to tell the tale. She'd always claimed to be a resourceful woman who could make her own way, and here she was, in R.J.'s bathroom whining and sniveling because she didn't have anyone to lean on.

It wasn't R.J.'s fault. And what could he possibly do anyway?

He hadn't patted her shoulder and told her everything would be okay. That had pissed her off. But R.J. had never sugar-coated anything. It was one of the qualities she'd admired most about him. So why had she expected anything different?

Agent Reinhold didn't have anything solid on her, because she hadn't done anything wrong. The authorities would eventually see that, and she could go back to practicing medicine.

She inhaled one cleansing breath and stood from the toilet. The bathroom sink was one of those clear contemporary things that sat above the counter. It wasn't really Rebecca's style, but it suited R.J. She turned the faucet to warm and splashed water over her face.

Thinking about R.J. out in his bedroom caused a twinge of guilt to twist in her stomach.

He'd only been honest with her and she'd gone all bipolar on him. As though it were his fault. He'd been an innocent bystander just like herself.

She patted her face dry and knotted the sheet in between her breasts. The damn thing kept falling down.

When she opened the door, she was mildly composed, meaning she didn't want to take R.J.'s head off, which was progress. However the blasted lump in her throat was still there, and if the man so much as looked at her the wrong way she'd lose it.

He was leaning against the wall, staring at the television when Rebecca came back into the room. When he spotted her he pushed away from the wall and came toward her. She clutched the sheet as he stopped in front of her.

His warm, comforting palm cupped her cheek and tilted her face to his. "I'm sorry," he whispered. "I didn't mean to upset you."

The lump in her throat grew until it was almost impossible to swallow. "You didn't do anything wrong. I'm just..." She leaned her forehead against his smooth, solid chest. "I'm really scared."

Rebecca practically melted when R.J. folded her into his arms. His presence was so reassuring and strong, like a sentinel who would beat away any bad guy. Realistically she knew there was nothing he could do, but just being with him, having his arms around her made her feel like she could fight any fight. And win.

He tilted her face up and swiped away the stray tears with his thumbs. "Let me take you back to bed."

Hadn't she just told herself not to be intimate with him again? That voice in the back of her mind told her to get dressed and go home. But looking into his very green eyes and seeing the promise of pleasure they held, she gave in. Only R.J. could make her feel better. Only he had the ability remove her twisted reality; if only for a few hours.

He took her hand in his and led her back to the bed. She undid the knot in the sheet and allowed the material to fall to the floor. Surprisingly, her nudity didn't make her blush. Probably because there was nothing but raw hunger in R.J.'s gaze as he took in every inch of nude flesh. Her teeth sank into her lower lip when he hooked his thumbs into the elastic band of his briefs. The glorious muscle beneath the cotton sprang free, reminding her of how he'd made her feel a short time ago.

R.J. lowered her to the bed and blanketed his body over hers. He was so much bigger than her, so much harder. Yet this time, when they made love, he showcased a gentleness she never expected him to have. As promised, he brought her to another planet then held her trembling body close to his.

And for a few blissful hours, Rebecca forgot the trouble that awaited her tomorrow.

THIRTEEN

If Danielle had been a man, R.J. would have beat the shit out of her.

And enjoyed it.

Anyone who put tears in Rebecca Underwood's eyes deserved to have their ass handed to them.

Her tears had just about been the undoing of him. And seeing the hopelessness cloud the usual vibrancy of her eyes made him realize how serious the situation was. Admittedly, at first, R.J. hadn't believed Danielle was the crux of the problem. Or rather, he didn't want to believe the woman he knew would have such a hateful streak inside her.

Drugs have a way of changing people.

Rebecca's words floated through his mind the morning after she'd said them to him.

Hell, he'd seen the evidence of that change at his own expense. But if Danielle was going to seek retribution, why go after Rebecca? Why ruin her future? R.J. was the one who fired her. If she wanted revenge against anyone it ought to be him.

Unless she really was that jealous...

What the hell would she have to be jealous of? He and

Rebecca were just friends.

Weren't they?

Before last night his answer would have been an unequivocal yes.

A big fat *hell yes* without a smidgen of doubt.

After spending the better part of the night buried inside her tight body, R.J. wasn't as confident. How many times could he sleep with her and still call her a friend?

And if she wasn't, what was she to him?

You've known the answer to that for a long time.

Dammit all to hell.

R.J. had always hated liars. His father could take the credit for that one. As a result, he'd always been honest to a fault. Some people would say he was almost too truthful for his own good. At least that's what Court always said to him.

So why was Rebecca the one thing he always lied to himself about?

Why could he never admit how he really felt about her?

Because she's too damn good for you. Because she deserves better than some horn dog who doesn't know the meaning of the word commit.

Damn it all to hell and back.

Even though he was no good for her, he loved her anyway.

That morning, Rebecca had slipped out just as the sun had edged its way above the Wyoming foothills. She had patients to see. Even if her days were numbered, the woman still took her job stone-cold seriously. She had every intention of seeing every last patient until they dragged her away kicking and screaming.

That was his Rebecca.

He admired the hell out of her.

After her departure, R.J. showered and went to the shop so he could continue another day of cleaning up Danielle's mess. The day before he'd delegated Sam to checking and double checking all the recent orders to make sure Danielle hadn't made any more boo-boos.

As R.J. had suspected, Sam had found a few blips in the radar. And he'd only gone through half the workload.

They'd gone back to the grind today, while finding time to restore all the cars on his lineup. *And* finding a replacement for Danielle.

Yeah, he really had his work cut out for him.

If it hadn't been for his crew, R.J. would have thrown himself in front of a Mack truck.

Hell, it was barely noon and he was halfway there already.

"Not one call this week?" R.J. asked Alex, who'd been answering the phones. The kid was a damn saint, doing the grunt work no one else wanted to do, when he'd much rather be buried in a car.

"Not one," he answered.

R.J. rubbed a hand through his hair. "Shit." There had to be at least one woman in this town who was desperate for a job. Maybe he could convince Courtney to fill in for a few weeks.

And she'd drive you insane in the process.

"Keep at it," R.J. said with a nod of his head toward the back log of work.

Alex muttered something under his breath. What, R.J. had no clue, but he'd bet it had something to do with his disdain for the tedious task.

Yes, technically it wasn't the tech's job, but they were a team. And until a new manager could be found, they'd all have to pitch in. Tomorrow it would be Sam's job.

In the meantime, the cars on the bays weren't going to build themselves. Two of them had gone for their paint jobs this morning and would return tomorrow. In their absence three more cars had been brought in for rebuilds.

Lately the workload of this place had felt like more than

he could handle. His five man staff was stretched thin and busted their asses every day to deliver. Two engine guys were hardly enough, and Mitch was the only electrical technician R.J. had. The forty-two year old was already working extra-long hours just to keep up. They were coming down to the wire to have Donald Underwood's car ready, not to mention Charlie's two babies.

As long as they were advertising for a new manager, he ought to throw in an ad for some more mechanics.

For the next several hours, he and Tim buried themselves in Charlie's vehicles. Knowing the guy, he'd stop by earlier than planned and would want to see some progress. R.J. would have to deliver, especially if he wanted the repeat business.

But the damn itch on the back of his neck wouldn't go away. The one that always told him something wasn't right.

And he wasn't talking about the cars. They were coming along beautifully. Tim stepped back and swiped dripping sweat off his brow.

"This is the most frustrating God damned car," Tim said with a sigh. "I hate pre-war vehicles."

So did R.J. They were unpredictable because one never knew what sort of shape the engine would be in. And finding parts for them was often a lottery.

They'd gotten extremely lucky with the antique vehicles. But they were still complicated to rebuild.

"I have to run out," he told Tim. "Do you think you can handle this for a bit?"

"Yeah, I think so," Tim answered.

"I won't be gone long." Hopefully.

And here's hoping Danielle didn't castrate him when she saw him.

She hadn't returned the message he'd left for her, not that he expected her to. And there was a good chance she wouldn't admit to anything. But, dammit, R.J. felt like he owed Rebecca something. He'd been the one to fire his manager, and if she had gone after Rebecca it was his fault.

He owed it to her to at least find out anything he could.

Someone needed to come to her rescue and dry the tears from those beautiful eyes. No one should have to go through something like this alone.

But they absolutely, positively could not have sex again. No matter how much she tempted him, no matter how seductively she wagged her hips. It was high time he kept his pants zipped.

Because going to bed with her again would catapult him so far into oblivion there would be no coming back. She would fall in love with him, if she wasn't already, and he'd break her heart.

Sweet, vulnerable Rebecca Underwood deserved so much better than him. If they kept gravitating back together she'd start to expect things from him. And he couldn't come through with those expectations. He simply wasn't built that way.

He had too much of his father's blood in him.

If he did the same thing to Rebecca that his father had done to his mother, R.J would never forgive himself. He'd spend the rest of his life wallowing in the self-hate that his father should have had.

Nick Devlin had been too much of a selfish bastard to feel anything but love for himself.

In the years since his childhood, R.J. had done everything he could *not* to be his father. If that meant not settling down with one woman, than that's the path he'd chosen. The thing was, his lifestyle had always suited him perfectly.

Until last night.

While the sex had been amazingly fantastic, it had also been dangerous. R.J. needed to keep his head clear and make sure last night remained a one-time thing. From now on he needed to go back to keeping his distance from her. Other than her father's car, there was no feasible reason for them to see each other.

They'd grown too comfortable with one another and he needed to put a stop to it.

The first thing R.J. noticed about Danielle's house, when he pulled in front, was how neglected it looked. The normally bright flowers that had intricately lined the base of all the trees were nothing more than droopy, forgotten weeds. The grass sprouted up at uneven levels and would probably be long enough to flirt with his knees. A week's worth of newspapers were piled in the driveway from where the delivery service had tossed them.

The place looked so different from the last time he'd been here, that R.J. had to look for the house number to make sure.

Number 5482.

Definitely the right place.

He parked his car along the curb and walked to the front door. The concrete path leading to the door was half-covered with wayward crab grass and overgrown dandelions.

A few seconds after rapping his knuckles on the door, Danielle's ten year old daughter Lindsey answered.

The girl was tall for her age and had her mother's blue eyes and midnight dark hair.

"Hey kid," he greeted. "Is your mom around?"

"Um…" Lindsey tossed a look over her shoulder and tucked a strand of hair behind her ear. "Yeah, but she's not feeling very good. She's just been lying on the couch."

How un-Danielle like.

"Can you do me a favor and tell her I need to talk to her for a minute?"

Lindsey shrugged her shoulders. "Okay."

R.J. was left standing on the front step for so long, he actually thought Danielle was intentionally ignoring him. Her house wasn't that big and he was sure she'd heard him talking when Lindsey had opened the door. She had every reason to avoid him, but he wasn't leaving until he got some answers.

The woman who finally came to the door didn't at all resemble the woman who used to work for him. The lack of makeup and hollowed cheeks aged her by a good ten years, and the lines of stress bracketing her mouth didn't help either. Unwashed, uncombed hair was pulled back in a sloppy ponytail that only held half the strands. Dull blue eyes glared back at him, surrounded by bags upon bags from lack of sleep.

Man, if looks could kill, he would have dropped dead the instant she laid eyes on him.

She crossed her arms over her stained shirt. "What the hell do you want?"

No need to beat around the bush. It's not like he came over to ask for a stick of butter.

"Did you rat Rebecca out to the DEA? And don't pretend like you don't know what I'm talking about."

Something flashed in her eyes, something that looked suspiciously like panic. Then the look disappeared and in its place was stone-cold ire. Her mouth tightened at the same time that her hand gripped the doorknob.

She almost got the door slammed in his face. Luckily for him, he was a quick on his feet and was able to slap his palm on the door to stop her action.

"Fuck you and your high horse, R.J.," she spat out.

His hand remained on the door, even though the irate woman in from of him was trying her hardest to get him off her porch.

"I no longer give a shit what you do to yourself, Danielle. But your actions are now affecting other people and it needs to stop. You can lie to me all you want, but I know what you did."

"You don't know shit, and you can't prove I've done anything to your little girlfriend."

Fully aware of Lindsey within earshot, R.J. kept his voice as even as possible. What he wanted to do was get in the woman's face and demand an honest answer.

He kept his hand on the door, because Danielle's arm was too twitchy for his comfort.

"Get mad at me for firing you, Danielle, but don't ruin other people's lives because you're pissed at me."

"She brought this on herself because she couldn't keep her mouth shut," she spat out while jabbing a bony finger against his chest.

Two angry splotches of red colored her cheeks. Her blue eyes glistened with unshed tears, giving him a small glimpse of their former vibrancy.

Hell. This really wasn't the woman he'd known. She'd done something horrible to herself until she no longer resembled the Danielle he'd first met.

While he was furious with her for getting Rebecca into trouble, he was also concerned for her. She'd entered into a dangerous place where she'd put her health at risk. Hadn't Rebecca said something about Adderall being a very dangerous drug to abuse? That it could cause death?

Why would Danielle risk herself like that? And what about Lindsey?

R.J. took a step closer to her and lowered his voice, hoping to appeal to whatever sensitive side was still left in her. "Danielle, I don't know how deep you've gotten yourself, or how you got into this situation to begin with. But you have a daughter to think about—"

"Don't you dare bring her into this," she whispered with vehemence. "Everything I do, I do for my daughter. Now, thanks to you I have to figure out how I'm going to feed her."

"Cutting the drugs out of your life would be a start," he shot back.

Danielle jerked as though he'd slapped her. Then she shot a look over her shoulder and stepped out onto the porch. "What I put in my body is no one's business but my own. And I'm hardly the only person who does it. Everything was fine until that bitch opened her mouth. She should have left well enough alone."

Shock at Danielle's audacity rendered R.J. speechless. How many times in the past few minutes had she blamed Rebecca? As though there was nothing wrong with becoming addicted to prescription drugs and potentially getting an innocent person arrested. The person who belonged in jail was Dr. Gross. Was it possible the man would walk free? And keep drugging up the parents in this town?

There had to be a way to get Danielle to see how wrong this all was.

He attempted to soften his voice even though fury still pumped through him. "Danielle, you need help. Let me take you to rehab."

"I don't need help," she said with a desperation R.J. almost believed.

"You do need help. I'll drive you there myself, and even pay for it."

Danielle stepped through the door. Just before slamming the thing on his face, she said. "What I need is for you to leave me the hell alone. And for your girlfriend to keep her nose out of other people's business."

Well, that went as well as he expected.

Had he really thought she'd surrender herself and apologize for anything? Danielle was headstrong to a fault, and it seemed as though the drugs only heightened those traits.

He was convinced she was responsible for the DEA agent, even though she hadn't come out and admitted it. But he could hardly go to the authorities with such flimsy evidence. Rebecca had told him they had some bullshit prescription she'd written Lindsey which did look pretty damning, even though she'd only been doing her job. R.J.'s only hope was that the DEA would do their jobs accordingly and base their case on the facts they found. If they investigated correctly, they wouldn't find anything against Rebecca and she could clear her name.

But with someone like Danielle having a vendetta against her, things could get tricky.

There was no way she would think clearly while her brain was on drugs. He had to get the woman sober and convince her to come clean. The Danielle he knew would never get an innocent person in trouble the way Rebecca was.

As R.J. left Danielle's house and headed back to work, he racked his brain for some kind of solution.

But maybe Danielle wasn't the key. Maybe what he needed was to cut the head off the snake.

Perhaps it was time to pay a visit to Dr. Gross.

FOURTEEN

THE UNIVERSE WAS conspiring against her.

That was the only way to explain why absolutely nothing was going Rebecca's way. Yesterday, she'd gone to pick up her contacts only to find out her insurance company had screwed up, and her eye doctor had been unable to fill the prescription. Sometime next week, was what they'd told her.

Great. On top of everything else, she had to deal with wearing her cheap glasses, which kept sliding down her nose. That was *after* the practice had received its cease and desist letter from the DEA. Dr. Gross had conveniently been sick that day, probably because they'd arrested him, which left Rebecca to deal with the mess of explaining things to the nurses, while seeing patients.

Some parents had been confused and even angry when Dr. Gross hadn't been there to examine their children. Rebecca didn't blame them. She was angry and confused herself.

The nurses had taken turns between crying and peppering Rebecca with questions.

Was she sure the DEA had the correct information?

How had they found out?

How could Dr. Gross do such a thing?

The most frustrating part was that Rebecca didn't have answers to any of those questions. She was just as much in the dark as the rest of them. Except for what Agent Reinhold had told her, which hadn't been a lot.

Tina had been tasked with the unpleasant chore of calling all their patients and explaining the situation without actually telling them anything. All their patients would have to be referred to another pediatrician, whom Rebecca had already spoken to.

As she'd left the practice yesterday, essentially closing its doors indefinitely, Rebecca had been consumed with so much rage, so much bitterness she hadn't known what to do with herself. She's sent R.J. a couple of text messages but he hadn't returned any of them.

Dr. Gross had done this. He'd spun their lives into a vortex of uncertainty and chaos and now he wasn't even around to clean up his mess. Several times, during her last work day yesterday, she'd called him. His house and his cell phone. Not surprisingly he hadn't answered.

That's because he's sitting in a jail cell.

Rebecca had been unwillingly thrust into resolving the aftermath of his bad choices, and it wasn't fair. She was a good person. She paid her taxes and helped old ladies load their groceries into their cars. She'd dedicated her life to helping children when they were sick and to keeping them healthy.

Now she was being punished for someone else's mistake. What's worse she was so utterly depressingly alone. The only person who had a smidgeon of an idea what she was going through was ignoring her.

When she'd woken up that morning, she'd sent R.J. another text. No answer.

The man was avoiding her. Probably because he regretted sleeping with her and was hoping she'd take a hint.

Normally, Rebecca would obsess over his lack of

attention, but she had too many other things on her mind.

Her parents had been gone when she'd emerged from her bedroom at ten after seven. When she finally wanted to be around someone, had craved one of her mother's home-cooked breakfasts, they hadn't been there. Her mother had left a note, saying they'd gone home to check on the cleanup from their termite situation. Rebecca had no idea how long it took to cleanup from termites. It had already been several weeks, plus they had taken the opportunity to remodel part of the house. Chances were they'd be staying with Rebecca for quite a bit longer.

Her mother had also said in her note she wanted to change part of her father's car. Manual transmission instead of automatic. She was leaving it up to Rebecca to tell R.J. before it was too late.

Fan-freakin'-tastic.

After inhaling a cup of coffee, Rebecca placed a call to the shop and talked to some kid named Sam. He'd sounded distracted and said he would pass the message along. She didn't trust it to get taken care of, so she followed the call up with a call to R.J.'s cell. Like before he didn't answer, so she left a message. Which he probably wouldn't return.

Because he was ignoring her.

Just like nine years ago.

You just can't learn your lesson, can you?

Sleep with R.J. and get ignored. Fall in love with him and get blown off.

Why had she expected anything else?

It was just so perfect considering everything else going south in her life.

Because she required control, Rebecca was going to attempt one last thing to put things back together. The last conversation she'd had with Dr. Gross about the matter had been unsuccessful. Maybe, now that things had gotten worse he'd be willing to answer some questions.

Hell, he owed her some kind of explanation. His actions and thrown her life upside down. And she owed it to herself to try, considering everything she'd sacrificed to make it this far.

She took a quick shower, while eyeing the seventies' wallpaper she still planned to remove. Honestly, what person in their right mind would put giant brown, gold, and orange flowers on their wall?

In less than fifteen minutes, Rebecca was dressed, without bothering to dry her hair. She wasn't going to work, so who the hell cared what she looked like? Nor did she bother with make-up.

Dr. Gross would just have to look past the frizzy curls and freckles bridging her nose. Because she no longer cared what he thought. She wanted some kind of explanation. An apology or any kind of remorse for getting their practice closed down.

Ten minutes later, she realized her wishes would remain pipe dreams. No one was answering at the Gross residence and all the curtains were pulled over the windows. A newspaper sat forgotten in the driveway and their porch light was on.

Odd.

She placed one more call to his cell phone, but no answer. Mrs. Gross didn't have a job, so Rebecca couldn't seek her out at for questions about her husband's whereabouts, nor did she know the woman's cell phone number.

Desperate for answers, Rebecca tried one last option for a resolution. She walked across the sprawling green front lawn to the neighbor's house. A Cocker Spaniel was tied to a tree while a little girl drew pictures on the driveway with sidewalk chalk.

"Hi," Rebecca said to the girl, who looked to be about nine years old. "Is your mom or dad here?"

"My mom's inside," the kid said.

A tiny glimmer of hope unfurled inside her. She rang the bell and a second later, a tall woman with short, dark hair opened the door. A baby boy with a pacifier stuck in his mouth was perched on the woman's hip.

"Hello," the lady said.

Rebecca slid her sunglasses to the top of her head so she could look the woman in the eye. "I work with Dr. Gross, and I was looking for him, but they don't seem to be home. Would you have any idea where they would be?"

The woman hefted the baby higher on her hip. "If you work with him, then I'm sure you know he was arrested."

Rebecca attempted to hide the surprise from her face, because really it wasn't a surprise.

The woman continued. She shook her head, as though confused. "But his wife said he was wrongfully booked, so they released him. Which is kind of strange how anyone could confuse Patrick Gross for a criminal." She hefted the child higher on her hip. "Anyway, they came home, then last night, at around ten-thirty or so, I saw them put some suitcases into the trunk of his car and left. I haven't seen them around today."

Dr. Gross had left town? After being arrested? Even if he'd paid bail to go free, would he be able to leave Trouble? Wouldn't that make him a fugitive?

"And they didn't say anything to you about where they were going or when they'd be back?"

The woman shook her head and pursed her lips. "No. Their daughter usually comes by and brings in their mail, but I haven't seen her around either."

Damn! Why couldn't she catch a break?

Rebecca attempted to hide her frustration with a deep breath. She hoped it worked.

"I'm sorry," the young mother said. "Is there anything I can help you with?"

Rebecca smiled. "No, unfortunately I have to speak with

Dr. Gross." She glanced back at the Gross home. "Thanks for your time," she said, then turned around and headed back to her car.

It seemed as though she'd have to wait longer to get her answers.

Or not.

Once in her car, she pulled out her cell phone and Agent Reinhold's business card. Just calling the man made her feel like she was conversing with the enemy. Which was ridiculous. The man was just doing his job. Dr. Gross was the real enemy, yet she still couldn't bring herself to think of him that way.

The DEA agent answered on the third ring. "Agent Reinhold."

"Agent Reinhold, this is Rebecca Underwood," she stated, using her most confident voice. "I understand you took Dr. Gross into custody."

He hesitated. "Yes, that's correct. But he posted bail and was released."

Ah, so that would explain why his neighbor saw them come back. She debated whether or not to ask her next question when the agent beat her to it.

"But he was instructed not to go far. We may have to bring you in for questioning, Dr. Underwood, so don't go far either."

"When you say, 'Don't go far,' what do you mean?"

"To put it bluntly, don't leave town. But we're already aware of Dr. Gross's activities and are monitoring him closely."

In other words, he was one step ahead of her elementary detective skills. Which was why they were the professionals and she wasn't.

"Okay. I just needed to talk to him—"

"I wouldn't advise that Dr. Underwood. I strongly recommended you sever all contact with him. Anything you say or do with him could be held against you. As of right now, our interest in you is purely evidential."

A mixture of relief and unease, which was a strange enough combination, settled over her. So she couldn't talk to Dr. Gross at all? How was she ever supposed to understand why he'd done any of this?

"I understand," she said in a quiet voice.

"Good," he responded shortly. "I'll be in touch."

****

Several hours later, Rebecca still hadn't returned home. Though she'd struggled to find things to fill her time. An hour-long grocery shopping trip had been thanks to her rumbling stomach. Never shop for food on an empty stomach. After that, she'd gone to her parents' house to the see damage the termites had done.

The destruction hadn't been nearly as bad as her father had made it out to be. The work was mostly confined to the living room, to her mother's disappointment, who wanted to redo the kitchen. Instead they would be replacing the wood paneling and tearing out the shag carpet. The home was still unlivable so they would be staying with Rebecca for a while longer.

Her mother, Patsy, had immediately picked up on her daughter's despair and had shot off a barrage of questions. Rebecca had shrugged it off as PMS, then felt guilty for lying. They would eventually find out about the practice closing. One of the parents of a patient would say something to their mother, and their mother would undoubtedly know Patsy. Then Rebecca would have to face the wrath of hell for not telling Patsy sooner.

But today wasn't the time. Later

After visiting her parents, Rebecca had no choice but to return home only because the milk in her trunk would spoil.

At three-fifteen she walked in the door, even though she didn't want to be there. It took forever to put all the food away, which she'd gone way overboard on. How many boxes of brownie mix did one person really need?

She stored all the food but kept the bottle of wine out. She fully planned on making good use of that baby tonight.

Because getting drunk by one's self was so cool.

Was four p.m. too early to start chugging Merlot?

Just as she checked her phone to see if R.J. had returned any of her messages, which he hadn't, the thing rang. Lacy's name flashed on the caller ID.

Rebecca smiled and answered the phone. "Hello?"

"If you have plans tonight cancel them," Lacy said instead of a greeting hello.

No need to tell her friend Rebecca was too pathetic to have plans. "Why, what have you concocted?"

"We've planned a girls' night at Courtney's. Because all I do is raise children and I need a break. So you're coming whether you want to or not."

Rebecca leaned against the kitchen counter and shook her head. "Your timing could not be more impeccable. What do I need to bring?"

"Lots of alcohol. Be there at seven."

The one bottle of wine she'd picked up from the store would not be sufficient for whoever would be there. And it beat getting drunk by herself. Lacy had just saved her some private humiliation.

But what was she supposed to do for the next three hours?

She thought about swinging by the shop just to see if R.J. was still alive. Since he was obviously ignoring her and regretted sleeping together, she decided not to. She knew when to take a hint and decided she didn't need the pain of being rejected again.

However much his silence hurt her, she needed to make

sure he got the message about her father's car. That was more important than anything else.

She placed a call to the shop and Sam answered again.

"Yeah, he got the message. He said he'd take care of it," Sam replied after she asked him about her earlier call. Setting aside the fact that he chose not to call her back, Rebecca held in a sigh and thanked the kid for being honest.

At least her father's car would be done right.

Whatever.

R.J. wanted to blow her off, that was his prerogative. She'd survived falling in love with him and being cast aside before. There was no reason she couldn't get through it again.

Yeah. She could do it.

No sweat.

For one whole night she could do it. With enough alcohol in her system, she'd forget about R.J. Devlin.

With a heavy sigh, Rebecca pushed away from the counter and went to the bedroom to change her clothes and put make-up on. She may not have cared what Dr. Gross thought, but she didn't want her friends to think she was some pathetic hobo who couldn't take the time to blow dry her hair.

So she changed into jeans, a long-sleeved t-shirt and a pair of flats. Minimal amount of make-up made her feel like less of a loser even if her hair still kind of looked like a rat's nest. Thus the hazard of having curly hair.

A second trip to the market was in order because the one bottle of wine wouldn't be enough. Lacy hadn't said who all was coming, but she knew there would at least three of them. Megan, Lacy's sister, would probably be there, as would Avery, Noah's wife. Elisa, Brody's wife, was a question mark given how sick she'd been.

She'd managed to kill a half an hour at the store, then made a trip to the hardware place. It was way past time she did something with the wallpaper in her bathroom. The flowers were atrocious and an eye sore she could no longer stand. Since she would have an endless amount of time on her hands, there was no reason she couldn't do a little updates. By the time she left with her wallpaper stripping supplies, it was five-fifteen.

Great. Another hour and forty-five minutes to kill.

Rebecca wasn't one of those people who reveled in time off. Keeping busy was of the utmost important, so having nothing to do was killing her.

R.J.'s shop was on the way home from the hardware store. Unfortunately. It took all her willpower not to glance inside to see if she could catch a shot of him. The fact that she kept her head averted was pretty damn impressive, if she did say so herself. Now wasn't the time to storm in there and demand an explanation. It had only been a few days since she'd slipped out of his bed. And judging by how full the bays were, he was swamped.

The light turned green and Rebecca headed toward her house. Since she'd be drinking Lord only knew how much, it wouldn't be smart to drive home. Bringing an overnight back and crashing at Court's would be the wise thing to do.

Once at home, she put her wallpaper supplies away, then tossed some essentials in a small duffle bag. Her parents hadn't returned yet, and she didn't want them to worry. She scribbled them a short note, then looked for things to do around the house to kill the last hour and fifteen minutes.

She checked the mail, discarded a handful of junk and set aside some bills. The flowers needed watering so she took care of that as well. It took twenty minutes to scroll through e-mail, half of which was spam. One was from her sister, checking on the progress of the car. Rebecca shot her a quick response, and tried not to let the mention of the car force her to think of R.J.

A girls' night out could not have come at a better time.

With thirty minutes to go, she decided now was a good time to head to Court's. The sooner she got there, the sooner she could start drowning her problems away. She gathered the bottles of liquor in a paper sack, and loaded everything, including her overnight bag, into the car.

Courtney's farmhouse rental, which Rebecca used to share, wasn't in town. The place was one of those turn of the century Victorian farmhouses that hadn't seen an update in two decades. Every corner of the place creaked and groaned and the single pane windows were a nightmare in the middle of a harsh Wyoming winter. The forty acres the house sat on still belonged to the family members of the original owners of the home. They raised beef cattle, but had built a newer home and decided to keep the original structure as a rental.

Rebecca took the back roads through various neighborhoods. She told herself the wayward route had nothing to do with avoiding R.J.'s shop, and more to do with killing time.

Yeah, that was it.

She arrived at her friend's house fifteen minutes early, only to see Avery was already there. R.J.'s sister-in-law never did anything late. She was always on time or early. Rebecca had no clue how she managed to do that while raising two kids and devoting so much time to the youth center.

The sun was inching its way toward the foothills as Rebecca climbed out of her car. She gathered her belongings from the back seat, walked to the six-foot wide wrap-around porch and knocked on the stained-glass door.

Rebecca had always loved it out here. The hundred-year-old home was surrounded by nothingness and lent a peaceful solitude not found in town. At first she hadn't understood why Courtney had decided to remain in the home after Rebecca had moved out. But being out here reminded her of why her friend stayed.

No one answered her knock, so she rang the bell.

A second later, her childhood friend opened the door. For as long as she'd known her, Courtney had always taken liberties with her appearance. Especially her hair. Courtney had always gone for bold colors. A strip of hot pink here and there. Short spiky and red. Several years ago, she'd pierced her nose with a tiny silver stud.

That all changed three years ago when Courtney had been in a horrible car accident. Ever since then she'd been understated and natural. Not at all like the Courtney that Rebecca had grown up with.

"Oh, good, you brought lots of drinks," Courtney said with a sigh of relief. "It completely slipped my mind so I don't have anything here. But," she continued as she stepped back to let Rebecca enter. "I do have a blender."

It wasn't uncommon for Courtney to forget something. Or a few things. Like a conversation she'd had the day before.

Courtney closed the door behind them, and they made their way through the small foyer and down the narrow hallway. The original wide-planked wooden floors creaked beneath their footsteps, just as they had done when she still lived there.

"Luckily for us, Avery was smart enough to bring lots of ice and margarita mix. I like to feel like I'm contributing by providing the blender."

"And a place for us to all crash," Rebecca added.

Courtney let out an airy laugh. "That too. Lacy called; she's going to be late as usual. She said Chase was freaking out at the idea of being with all four kids alone. So she had to make out a list of their routines and get them set up with dinner before she could make her escape."

Lacy had married Courtney's and R.J.'s step-brother five years ago, and was a tremendously talented artist. Somewhere in the middle of raising four kids under the age of five, she managed to sell her drawings that earned her a nice living.

Rebecca had one hanging in her bedroom.

Courtney pushed through the kitchen door so Rebecca could set her bag of drinks down. Avery, who looked sleek and stunning as always, was rinsing something in the sink.

The way the woman put herself together so flawlessly always made Rebecca feel like she needed to smooth down her own hair.

Because Avery was so genuinely nice, Rebecca forgave the woman her perfection.

"I don't know how Lacy does it," Avery said, who must have heard them talking in the hallway. Sounds tended to carry in the old house. "As much as I always wanted a big family, I'm kind of glad we only have the two girls."

"Who are the sweetest things ever," Courtney added.

Avery grinned and turned the tap off. "Tell me about it. I don't know how Noah and I got so lucky."

Rebecca didn't know many of the details, but Avery and Noah had suffered from infertility for many years. They had Lily, who was now five and a half, and a one year old adopted daughter named Amanda.

Courtney had told her that about two years after having Lily, Avery found out she had endometriosis. The condition was fairly common and could make conceiving a child very difficult or even impossible. Over the span of three years, Avery had suffered from three miscarriages. Rebecca couldn't imagine enduring so many losses, especially for such wonderful people like Avery and Noah.

After all that, Noah hadn't wanted his wife to go through the agony of losing another child, so they'd adopted. Rebecca had never seen Amanda, only a few pictures of her around Courtney's home. The child had dark hair, dark eyes and had captured everyone's hearts from the moment they met her.

"Well, now that half of us are here, I say we go ahead and get smashed," Courtney announced.

Rebecca removed wine bottles one by one from the sack.

Avery had the blender set up with a bag of ice next to it. She had fresh limes and watermelon, which she'd already started slicing.

"What's with the watermelon?" Courtney asked.

Avery tossed Courtney a surprised look. "For the watermelon margaritas. Remember?"

Rebecca started uncorking the wine bottles as Courtney rolled her eyes. "Duh," she said. "And you're surprised I forgot that?"

Avery chuckled and squeezed lime juice into the blender. "Actually, no."

"I feel like my Chardonnay is a little too fancy," Rebecca stated. "Did I overdo it with my five bottles?"

"Trust me, they'll get used," Courtney said as she pulled glasses out of cupboards.

Avery poured ice in the blender, then lifted a bottle off the counter. "What are we using the Grenadine for?"

"Shirley Temples for Elisa since she can't drink," Courtney answered.

"I hope she doesn't throw them up," Avery muttered.

"Brody says she's been doing better."

Avery grinned, then hit the power button on the blender. "Maybe she can be our designated driver."

"Uh-uh," Courtney jabbed a finger at both Rebecca and Avery. "A girls' night means all night. You're staying here whether you like it or not."

Avery winked at Rebecca. "Good thing I packed clean underwear."

FIFTEEN .

"SO INSTEAD OF taking Kevin to the potty where he's supposed to go, Chase takes the kid outside and tells him to pee in a bush," Lacy said as she waved a hand in the air, gently sloshing her margarita over the side of the delicate glass. Courtney's sister-in-law was toeing the line of smashed.

"That's what little boys are supposed to do," Courtney announced as she poured another glass of wine.

Rebecca was still nursing her second margarita two hours after everyone had arrived. She was considerably behind pace with everyone else, with the exception of Elisa, who'd consumed three Shirley Temples.

"Not when you're trying to potty train them," Lacy shot back. She slid from the couch to the floor, next to Megan, and crossed her legs.

"Think of it this way," Lacy's sister said. "That's less pee to clean up off the floor."

For some reason Courtney found Megan's statement hilarious. Her burst of laughter caused her to spit some wine on the area rug, but she didn't seem to care. She took another sip and set the glass on an end table.

"I think Court's had enough to drink," Avery stated.

"You've had more than I have," she argued. Then she giggled. "You just hold it better than I do."

"Actually, I think you have us all beat," Rebecca said.

Courtney pulled her hair-tie out and shook the strands free. "Hey, don't judge me. We were supposed to do this a long time ago, but someone could never commit," she said with a pointed look at Lacy.

"That's because your brother kept knocking me up," she argued without any heat in her voice.

"Maybe you should have tried birth control," Court said.

Lacy chucked a pillow at her friend. "Bitch. Only one of my children was a surprise."

Elisa giggled.

"Actually all four of your kids were surprises," Megan chimed in.

Yes," Lacy agreed while holding up her index finger. "But I was on birth control with the last three, which was the whole point of our discussion." Her brows lowered over her eyes and she shot questioning glances at everyone. "Wasn't it?"

Courtney laughed so hard that she actually squirted some of her drink out. "I don't know," she managed in between chuckles.

"I don't think any of us has a clue what's going on," Rebecca added as she drained the last of her margarita.

"Except for Elisa," Avery added. "She's the only one here smart enough to stay sober."

"Only because I'm pregnant," Brody's wife complained from her spot in front of the fireplace. "Otherwise I'd be right there with you."

"I'm sorry, but I do not envy you," Lacy said with more laughter.

By Rebecca's estimation, Lacy and Courtney had been laughing for fifteen straight minutes. She figured they'd finally entered the drunk realm where everything was funny. Avery was close behind them, because she was starting to sway in her chair.

Rebecca figured the women were just so excited to be kid-free for one night, they planned on taking advantage of the situation.

"I'm taking this away from you," Megan said, then she plucked the watermelon margarita out of Lacy's hand and placed it on the coffee table.

"Hey," Lacy complained.

"Don't let her have any more," Elisa said.

Courtney waved her glass in the air. "You're too uptight, Megan. We need to get you laid."

"I have plenty of sex, thank you very much."

Her words had Avery guffawing, and even Rebecca giggled.

"In a non-whorish kind of way," Megan added, then sniggered at her own words. "Shut up," she said to the room in general.

"We're all grown-ups here, it's okay to talk about sex," Avery countered.

Courtney gasped and set her drink down. "That's what we should do. We should take turns telling each other about our first times. And who we did it with. Or," she continued. "You could opt for the craziest place you've ever done it. You go first," Courtney said with a nod to Lacy.

"Why do I have to go first?" Lacy complained.

"I'll go first," Avery offered. "The craziest place I've ever done it is in one of Noah's construction trailers on a job site."

Silence followed her statement, and someone coughed. They all stared at Avery, as though expecting her to elaborate with something naughtier.

Finally Lacy said, "That's really lame."

Avery threw a discarded cherry at Lacy's head. "Then you come up with something better, Miss I-didn't-want-to-go-first."

"All right, fine." Lacy flipped a chunk of hair over her shoulder and set her glass down. "I'd say it's a toss-up between a fitting room and a restaurant bathroom."

"Ew," Avery said.

"Do you have any idea how many germs are in a public bathroom?" Elisa asked.

"A bathroom, Lace?" Courtney asked with raised brows. "Even I have my limits."

"You're the one who wanted to play this game," she shot back. "I can't help it if my husband finds me irresistible. And I think the twins were conceived in the fitting room," she muttered to herself.

Rebecca just about choked on her drink. "How do you know?"

"I think Courtney should go next," Megan blurted out. "Since this was her idea."

"Okay." Court downed the last of her drink and set it on the carpet where it tilted over on its side. "Despite what everyone here thinks, I haven't had a lot of crazy sex before. But I did do it on the hood of a car once."

"Was that with Grant?" Avery asked with a sly grin.

Courtney's eyes hardened. "Please do not say that name in my presence."

"Who's Grant?" Megan asked.

"Sorry," the other woman answered with an eye roll. "I meant the lying, cheating rat bastard."

"What am I missing here? Who's Grant?" Megan demanded again.

Lacy stretched her legs in front of her. "Grant was Courtney's fiancé that none of us knew about."

Courtney shook her head. "We were never engaged."

Rebecca shot her friend a droll look. "Court, you had a ring."

"Lying, cheating bastards don't have the right to call

themselves 'fiancé'." Courtney tossed her hands in the air in an exasperated gesture. "How did we even get on this subject anyway?"

"Well, you said you'd done it on the hood of a car, then Avery asked if that was with Grant," Rebecca said, knowing it would get even more of a rise out of her friend.

"All right, smart ass. Why don't you go next?"

Rebecca lifted a shoulder in a nonchalant shrug. "That's easy, I've never done it anywhere crazy."

"Oh, come on," Lacy whined "I told you about conceiving in a dressing room. There's no holding back here."

"I'm honestly not holding back," she urged. If only her sex life had been that exciting. Until recently. "A bed is the only place I've done it."

Rebecca looked around as all the women in the room stared at her in disbelief. Why was that so hard to believe?

"What?" she asked.

"That can't be true," Avery announced.

"Not even the shower or a kitchen counter?" Elisa asked.

Rebecca shook her head. "No."

Avery sipped the last of her drink. "Okay, at least tell us who your first was."

No way. She'd rather bathe in sewage.

"Is it someone we know?" Lacy asked.

"Nope," she answered quickly.

"Let's move on," Avery said in a bored voice. Just as she looked at Megan, Courtney spoke up.

"I know who her first was."

Rebecca shot her friend a startled look, who was looking back at her over the rim of her wine glass. She took a deep swallow of the Chardonnay, then gazed at Rebecca with a poker face.

What was she talking about? How could Courtney have possibly known about that? Unless R.J. had told her. But why would he do that?

"Tell us," Avery urged. "Is it someone we know?"

Rebecca shook her head, even as anxiety coursed through her blood. "No. Court's just had too much to drink."

"Don't play dumb, Rebecca." Courtney waved a hand in the air. "Your conditioner has a very distinctive smell."

"What?" she squeaked out.

"It was all over him the next morning," Courtney said, matter-of-fact, as though she hadn't just outed Rebecca's darkest secret to half the family.

"What are they talking about?" Megan whispered to Lacy.

Lacy shook her head. "I don't know, but I—" Her attention shot to Rebecca and she gasped. With wide eyes, she placed a hand over her mouth. "No way," she said in astonishment. "You're not talking about R.J., are you?" she asked Courtney.

"Who else would I be talking about?" Rebecca's traitorous friend countered.

"Wait a minute," Avery said with a raised hand. She pinned Rebecca with a confused look. "You slept with R.J.? When?"

"I don't know why everyone is so shocked," Courtney said casually.

"I'm actually not that surprised," Lacy quipped. "I'm only surprised we didn't know about it sooner."

Rebecca tapped down her annoyance and reminded herself these were her friends. They didn't mean anything by it, *and* had alcohol in their systems. Which meant all bets were off. And Courtney was a loud mouth on her calmest day. What annoyed her was that the encounter and been let out before she was ready to talk about it.

Then again, would she ever really be ready?

Maybe this was the best way to exorcise R.J. from her system.

She shook her head and stared down into her drink. "It

happened nine years ago. It was just a one-time thing."

They all stared at her, waiting for juicy details. They weren't going to get them.

"And?" Elisa prompted.

"And nothing."

Avery rolled her eyes. "That can't be it."

"Sorry, but it is," Rebecca said, because she wasn't willing to discuss it any further. They knew. End of discussion.

Lacy watched Rebecca, then graced her with a tiny smile. "Let's move on," she suggested.

****

"Sorry for letting your secret out like that," Courtney whispered. "That's what happens when I drink too much."

Rebecca and Courtney were lying on their sides, facing each other on the living room floor. It was sometime around two a.m. and Lacy and Avery had claimed the only two couches in the room. Megan had forgotten to pack an overnight bag so Elisa had driven her home around midnight.

Sleep hadn't come easy. Rebecca had tossed and turned for a couple of hours, then woke to find that Courtney too hadn't been able to sleep. They'd been talking for the last couple minutes, while trying not to wake the other two women.

"It's okay," Rebecca said. She picked at a stray thread on the area rug and glanced at her friend. "I can't believe you've known all this time. Why didn't you ever say anything?"

Courtney shrugged. "I figured if you wanted me to know, you would have told me."

She was right. Rebecca hadn't wanted anybody to know, which was actually pretty stupid. At the young age of nineteen, she'd been incredibly naïve and vulnerable. Her worst fear was for people to see through her to the deep love she had for R.J. Courtney would have picked up on it in a second. Just as she had picked up on Rebecca and R.J. spending the night together.

"We've known each other a long time," her friend continued. "And you've always opened up to me about everything. Except my brother. You always clam up about him. Plus, I saw how it changed your relationship with him."

"How do you mean?" Even though she knew what Courtney meant. R.J. had never treated her the same after that night. She'd always assumed she'd been the only one to notice.

"I don't know exactly," she whispered. "It was a subtle shift, but enough for me to notice." Courtney's thin brows pulled together. "Almost like he became afraid of you."

Rebecca doubted that. She shook her head. "There's no way R.J.'s afraid of me. You'd have to notice a person to be afraid of them."

"Is that what you've always thought?" Courtney asked with her head tilted. "It's not the way he looks at you, Rebecca. It's the way he *doesn't*."

Which made absolutely no sense.

Courtney sighed and shifted her position on the floor. "I know you don't know much about my father, but the way he treated my mother had a huge impact on R.J."

R.J. hardly ever spoke about his father. But Courtney had told Rebecca that their father had repeatedly cheated on their mother, until she drew up the courage to divorce him. Carol had walked away from the marriage scarred and insecure.

"Anyway," her friend continued. "When our dad left, R.J. swore he would never be like the man. That's why he's never been in a committed relationship; he's so afraid of history repeating itself. He doesn't want to be the same disrespectful bastard my father was who hurt women over and over again." Courtney paused as though trying to gather her thoughts. "But something about you triggered something inside him. You mean more to him than all those other women." A half laugh popped out of her. "He thinks I don't know any of this;

that I don't see right through him. Everyone thinks I'm the airheaded younger sister."

Rebecca placed a hand on her friend's arm. "I don't think that."

"That's because you're a good friend."

"We really know how to put ourselves in an impossible relationship," Rebecca commented.

Courtney's smile didn't quite reach her eyes. "R.J. would never do to you what Grant did to me. He has too much respect for you."

Rebecca studied her friend and saw the old hurt darkening the depths of her eyes. An old hurt that still lingered three years later. It was obvious Courtney had strong feelings for Grant, and probably still did. The whole family had been blindsided by the fact that they'd been engaged. Courtney had always been very secretive of the relationship. And years later, she still hadn't given anyone the full story of what had happened.

"What happened with Grant?" Rebecca asked.

Courtney averted her gaze and stared down at the threadbare area rug. "I don't want to talk about him."

"Court, come on," she urged her friend. "It might do you some good to get it out." When Courtney remained silent, Rebecca added, "How about I spill another secret first."

"It depends on how juicy it is," she said with a half-smile.

Rebecca licked her suddenly dry lips. Why did she always get anxious whenever she talked about R.J.? "There was more than that one night nine years ago." Rebecca paused to allow the words to sink in. "You don't look surprised," she commented when Courtney just stared at her.

"I'm not. You think the fact that you and my brother have gotten naked together twice is shocking to me?" she asked when Rebecca rolled her eyes.

"You act like we're doing it all the time," she countered.

Courtney patted her arm. "Just give it time. You'll get

there."

Why did she agree to open up this subject with her friend? Courtney was blunt to a fault, but it was one of the things Rebecca loved most about her.

"Okay, your turn."

"I changed my mind, I don't want to do this," Court muttered.

"I just told you two things I never wanted anyone to know. Come on, it'll do you good to get it out because I can tell it's been eating you up."

When Courtney only stared at the floor and ran the tip of her finger along the edge of the rug, Rebecca urged her on. She scooted closer to her friend and lowered her voice. "You said Grant lied to you and cheated on you. What happened?"

Courtney licked her lips and tucked a strand of hair behind her ear. "I met Grant about six months before things ended. We'd only been engaged for about a month."

Rebecca waited in silence while Courtney sorted through the story in her head.

"Anyway, the night of my accident I'd gone over to his condo because he was supposed to cook me dinner. But I was running late," she grinned. "You know me. Could never keep track of time."

"So what happened when you got there?" Even though Rebecca knew this story wasn't going to end well. She already had a feeling what was going to happen next.

"Grant lived in one of those buildings where all the entrances to the condos were in indoor hallways. And the door to his unit was open and I could hear voices coming from inside. His and a woman's."

Just as she suspected. "What were they saying?"

Courtney swallowed, then said in a low voice. "I heard Grant apologize. But it wasn't the sorry itself that made me stop. It was the tone of his voice. Like he really was sorry." She looked at Rebecca. "There was genuine regret in his voice.

And I stopped just outside his door because I had this horrible feeling in the pit of my stomach.

"Then I heard the woman say, 'You promised me, Grant. Pretty soon the money you're sending isn't going to be enough. Money doesn't take the place of a father.'"

Rebecca's eyes widened as she listened to the pain in her friend's voice; listened to her retell the story that had caused her so much despair.

Courtney licked her lips and inhaled a deep breath. "Then Grant said, 'I don't know what you want from me, Melissa. I've paid for all your medical expenses and prenatal care. Right now, that's all I can give you.'"

"Oh, Court."

There was a slight tremor in her voice when she spoke next. "And the woman said," Courtney closed her eyes and cleared her throat. "She said, 'When I first told you I was pregnant, you told me you'd take care of me, that we'd be a family. You need to break things off with this woman you're engaged to and handle your responsibilities.'"

Rebecca's heart cracked open for her friend. But she didn't interrupt the story. Courtney had bottled it in for too long and needed to get it out.

"After that, I couldn't stand to hear anymore. I walked into the condo because I needed some kind of explanation from Grant. I found him in the living room with a very pregnant woman." Courtney shook her head as a small smile graced her sad face. "She took one look at me and stormed out the door."

Behind them, one of the women stirred. Rebecca glanced over her shoulder to see Lacy turning over on the couch.

When she looked back at Courtney, there was a single tear running down her cheek.

"Court, you don't have to keep telling me this."

She shook her head. "It's okay," she whispered.

"So, did you question Grant about it?" Rebecca wanted to

know.

"You really think I would have backed down from that confrontation?" Courtney asked with a smile that didn't reach her eyes. "His explanation was that she was an ex-girlfriend whom he'd ended things with a few months before he met me. Right after we started dating, Melissa told him she was pregnant. He told me he didn't want to be with her, but he'd been giving her financial support and checking in with her to make sure the pregnancy was progressing smoothly."

"And he never told you any of this?" Rebecca asked, wondering how anyone could keep a secret like that.

"No. He said when he found out, we'd hadn't been together long and he didn't want to scare me away. Then more time went by, and he'd started to develop serious feelings for me. He just kept saying that he never knew how to tell me."

Rebecca narrowed her eyes. "Didn't he know that you'd eventually find out?"

"That's what I asked him. All he said was that he was sorry. Over and over again he kept apologizing, saying how much he loved me and asking me to forgive him." Courtney's eyes dropped closed and she inhaled a deep breath. "I mean, how could he keep something like that from me? And how could I forgive him after lying to me like that?"

The pain in her friend's voice broke Rebecca's heart. No wonder Courtney had never wanted to talk about it. Having your heart broken by the man you loved could take a person years to get over. And some people never fully healed from something like that. Courtney had dealt with it the best way she knew how, and she'd gone through it alone. Had grieved for the loss of the relationship alone.

Rebecca wished she'd known so she could have been there for her friend. Offered some kind of…well, something.

"You said he cheated on you…" Rebecca tried to recall Courtney's words. "But he told you they'd broken up before he met you."

Courtney nodded. "Yeah. He told me Melissa was just a few weeks away from her due date, but she didn't look all that big to me. Instead of nine months she looked more like five or six months." She lifted her shoulders in a tired shrug. "If he hadn't been honest with me about a baby on the way, how do I know he wasn't being honest about other things?"

Rebecca's brows lowered. "So, you think he was two-timing you with this woman?"

"Why not?"

"Okay, at the risk of playing Devil's Advocate, some women don't get very big when they're pregnant. I mean, Lacy was huge with the twins. But with Abigail, she was tiny."

"I know, and the whole cheating thing may have been said out of anger more than anything else. But I can't overlook the fact that he kept a very important part of his life a secret from me." She pinned Rebecca with a desperate look. "How can you say you love someone and keep something like that from them?" Tears spilled over Courtney's lashes and ran down her cheeks. "Rebecca, I loved him so much," she said through her tears. "I feel like I've been robbed, like something was stolen from me."

"I'm so sorry," she said, swallowing past the lump in her own throat. How could Courtney have kept this to herself for the past three years? How could she stand do go through this alone?

Rebecca tried to fight off her own tears as her friend silently wept; wept for the man she'd loved and lost, wept for the life she used to have before everything had turned upside down in one night. Courtney was so much stronger than people gave her credit for. Her entire life, everyone underestimated her, and continually pegged her as the flighty younger sister who had no direction.

The truth was Courtney was stronger than anyone Rebecca knew. Her strength made Rebecca feel like a fraud, because she was always pretending to be this independent woman who had her shit together.

She was on the verge of losing her medical license and kept giving her heart away to a man she couldn't have.

Rebecca rubbed her hand over Courtney's hair until her sobs subsided. She wiped her nose with the edge of her sleeve. After a couple of sniffs, she looked at Rebecca with red-rimmed eyes.

"Whatever happened to Grant?" Rebecca asked.

"When he came to see me at the hospital, I told him I never wanted to see him again. I found out from his sister a few weeks later that he and Melissa had moved to Kentucky and got married."

"Oh, Courtney, I'm sorry."

"It's just as well," she said as though it were no big deal. "The relationship wouldn't have worked with another woman in the picture."

"But you still love him."

One corner of Courtney's mouth turned up. "I broke up with him because I was mad at him. Not because I stopped loving him."

"And you never hear from him? I mean, he never came back to try and win you back?"

Courtney shook her head. "I see his sister, Emily, sometimes, but she never mentions him. I think she pities my poor broken heart."

"Courtney, I wish you would have confided in me. I hate that you've gone through all this alone."

"No, it's okay. The months following my accident were a very dark time for me. I needed time to heal both emotionally and physically before I could let people in."

"You do seem a lot happier. Like you're at peace with yourself." Even if she was different, Courtney was happy with her life and that was all that mattered.

"It's been a long uphill battle, but I'm getting there."

SIXTEEN

R.J. WAS STILL IGNORING her.

Rebecca checked her phone when she left Courtney's house the next morning. No text messages, no missed calls.

More than a week had passed since she'd seen him. More than a week since she'd heard his deep voice and had felt him moving inside her. Up until now, Rebecca had never realized how much she enjoyed their banter, how much she looked forward to seeing him.

The urge to place another phone call was so strong, that she actually pulled her phone from her purse and started to dial his number. But would that make her the typical needy woman who whined about not being called after a one-night stand? Because, in all honesty, that's what they'd had.

Just one hot night of lying beneath him, feeling his strong body pinning her to the bed as he stroked deep inside her.

And wasn't that what R.J. did? Didn't that make her no better than every other woman he'd been with? Roll around between the sheets for a few hours, then move on to the next.

She'd become exactly what she'd always told herself she was better than. And it was no one's fault but her own.

All morning Rebecca had been unable to clear her head, to keep these thoughts from poisoning her mind. So she'd taken her frustration out on her bathroom walls, stripping the paper with a wicked vengeance. She ran the scraper over the paper so hard that her knuckles had started to ache. Her shoulders burned and sweat dripped down her backside. When she was finished with her project, she'd have a new bathroom, but her heart would still ache. That sick feeling in the pit of her stomach and the squeezing sensation around her heart would still be there. No amount of wallpaper stripping would heal her internal struggle.

Her fear over her uncertain future. How much she missed R.J., and not just sharing a bed with him. She missed his smartass comments, how he always found an excuse to touch her and the way he looked at her. He made her feel special, beautiful, and wanted. Even when he infuriated her, she still couldn't get enough of him.

And the bastard was ignoring her.

Rebecca loosened a section of paper and ripped it off the wall so hard, that she swayed on the step-stool.

Calm down.

She did not need to go falling down off a step-stool and breaking something. Lord knew, she had enough problems right now.

The front door opened, then slammed shut. She could only guess it was her mother, who'd come back to probably do a load of laundry or shower.

"Rebecca, is it true?" her mother demanded in a tone that told Rebecca she was to answer or else.

"Hi Mom," she said from her spot on the stool. Instead of getting down or turning around, she ran the wet sponge over the top layer of wallpaper.

Her mother's shoes crunched over the scraps of paper on the floor. "I just heard from Jane that her daughter, whose son is a patient of yours, said the practice was shut down.

Something about fraud. *And* that Dr. Gross was arrested."

"Yep," she said instead of playing dumb or apologizing. She didn't have the strength to do either.

"That's all you're going to say?" Patsy wanted to know.

Rebecca sighed and dropped her sponge in the bucket. She was hot, stressed out, and hadn't slept in several days.

"It's true, Mom," she agreed when she'd climbed down to the bathroom floor.

"People are saying that Dr. Gross is dead. That someone killed him, or that he left town and killed himself." Worry lines bracketed her mother's mouth.

Rebecca had known that keeping this from her mother would only create more of a problem. But she hadn't wanted to worry the woman. Plus, she didn't even know the full extent of what was going on, or what was going to happen.

"That's a bit extreme, don't you think?" Rebecca said. Dr. Gross dead?

Patsy placed her hands on her hips. "You know how news spreads in this town. A friend tells a friend, and everything gets lost in translation. Besides, I should have heard it from you," she pleaded as she placed her hands on Rebecca's shoulders.

Her mother was completely right. It had been wrong of her to keep her parents in the dark. What's more, Rebecca's secretive ways had likely hurt her mother's feelings. In the past, she'd always told her mother everything, even about men. The older woman wasn't going to understand why Rebecca had kept this one thing a secret.

"I'm sorry I didn't tell you," she admitted to her mom. She kicked aside a pile of discarded wallpaper. "I was having a hard time processing the information, and it happened so fast. I think I was kind of in denial."

"Honey, that's perfectly understandable. But you can imagine my shock when one of my best friends tells me my daughter's practice got shut down because of fraud."

"I know—"

"Just tell me you had nothing to do with it," her mother demanded.

"Of course I didn't," she shot back immediately. How could her mother even ask that?

Patsy sighed and leaned against the bathroom counter. "I'm sorry for asking. But Jane heard some people say that you and Dr. Gross were partners in some kind of fraud."

What?

How could anyone who knew her think she'd do something like that? And where in the world had anyone gotten that idea? Unless someone had started that rumor on purpose.

Two people came to mind with that thought.

Danielle and Dr. Gross — the two people who had everything to lose if charges were filed.

Could it be that Danielle leaked Rebecca's name to the DEA in order to detract attention away from Dr. Gross? So that her meal ticket would still be intact to service her needs?

The idea made perfect sense to Rebecca. And someone whose mind was muddled by drugs wouldn't be thinking coherently. A druggie would do everything they could to get their next fix, and that didn't always apply to the hard stuff. Addiction was addiction no matter what the substance. The only thought on a substance abusers mind was getting their hands on more drugs. If Dr. Gross went to jail, where would Danielle go? Who would she turn to?

The two of them needed Rebecca to take the fall, and it was clear neither one of them cared if she went down in flames.

The whole idea made her sick to her stomach. What had she ever done to deserve this?

"Honey, just start from the beginning," her mother asked. "Tell me everything that's happened."

Rebecca took a deep breath, knowing her mother would

break down in tears at any moment at the thought of her baby girl in pain. Patsy was an emotional woman who often went from hot to cold in a moment's notice, a trait she'd passed down to Rebecca's sister.

As she recounted the confusing and complicated story, her mother remained composed, only flattening out her lips at certain parts. Rebecca gave her mother as much information as she could, fully expecting the older woman to collapse in hysteria.

"I'll kill that son of a bitch," Patsy stated when Rebecca finished speaking.

"Mom," she chastised. Her mother *never* cursed.

"Don't you tell me to calm down. I ought to go over there and give him a piece of my mind."

Rebecca watched as her mother paced from the shower back to the counter. "You can try, but you won't find him."

Patsy shot her daughter a look. "So it's true about him leaving town?"

"I went over there already, and they weren't home. A neighbor told me she'd seen them packing up their car and leaving late the night before."

"Well, I'll be damned if I'm going to let you take the fall for him."

"There's no *letting*, Mom. This is one of things times where there's nothing you can do."

"There has to be something I can do," she stated with conviction that had Rebecca smiling.

Say or do anything you want to Patsy Underwood. But mess with her kids, and she'll bring down the wrath of God Almighty Himself.

"Mom, I appreciate your concern," Rebecca started. "But this is one of those times where you aren't going to be able to help me. I have to just be patient, wait this out and testify against Dr. Gross if I have to."

Patsy's eyes widened. "You think it'll come to that?"

"I have no idea. All I know is that they shut the practice down, then came back with warrants and took all our patient files." Lord, to think of all that personal information out there, being seen by uncaring, unsympathetic eyes… it was enough to send a cold shiver through her.

Her mother placed a hand on Rebecca's arm. The touch was comforting and brought back a flood of memories of her childhood. Her mother holding her in a warm embrace when Rebecca fell off her bike and scraped her knee. Telling her the other kids could go screw themselves when they laughed at her daughter's braces.

Her mother's support brought the unwanted sting of tears to her eyes. Dammit, she'd done enough crying and didn't have the strength to expel any more emotion.

"A friend of a friend knows Melinda Gross. I might be able to have one of them call her to find out where they are."

Rebecca shook her head. She didn't want her mother involved in this. "No, that's okay—" She stopped short when she remembered something that might be of help. "I need to go out for a while and clear my head," she told her mother. "I'll be back later."

"Okay," Patsy said in an uncertain tone.

Her plan was a long shot, but it was the only thing she could think of to locate Dr. Gross's whereabouts. She grabbed her purse from the front door and didn't bother to clean herself up. She didn't really give a damn about the scraps of paper stuck in her hair or the wet glue that had been slung on her thighs.

Once in her car, Rebecca fished her cell phone from her purse, then backed out of the driveway.

Lacy answered on the third ring. "Hello?" she said. One of the kids screamed in the background. "Mason, give that back to your brother," she chastised her son. "Sorry. They play so quietly, and as soon as they see a phone pressed to my ear, all hell breaks loose."

"That's okay," Rebecca replied automatically. She drove to the end of her street and made a left. "Can I ask you a really huge favor?"

"Sure," Lacy said slowly.

"You attend a playgroup with one of Patrick Gross's daughters, right?"

"Yeah. Hey, wait a minute. I got this weird letter in the mail—"

"I know, but I can't get into it right now. I'll explain the whole thing later." Rebecca rushed on as she turned onto Main Street. Let's see R.J. avoid her when she showed up and demanded he face her. "Can you find out from his daughter where Dr. Gross and his wife went?"

Lacy wouldn't understand, and Rebecca felt terrible for putting her friend in an awkward position. But she didn't know where else to turn.

"Um... all right," she conceded. "Can I ask why?"

Rebecca sighed and came to a stop at a red light. She knew she wasn't supposed to talk to Dr. Gross. Agent Reinhold had already made that clear. But she needed to know what happened to him. "Can you just see what you can find out?"

One of Lacy's kids screamed in the background. "I'll ask Stephanie next time I see her."

The light turned green and Rebecca pressed forward. "Thanks." She disconnected the call and tossed her phone into the cup holder. There was nothing more she could do about the matter, so she tried desperately to shove the issue out of her head. The only problem was that made room for thoughts about R.J.

Then again, no matter how full her head was, thoughts of R.J. always haunted her. Seems as though these days it was more of a plague. They'd become a way of life. And she wasn't used to R.J. not speaking to her. Smart-assed comments she could handle; scorching looks were the norm. But the silent treatment?

That wasn't R.J. at all, and Rebecca wasn't sure what to think. The last time he'd done this was when he'd taken her virginity. Of course, they'd eventually fallen back into their old routine, which was the way she preferred it. Sort of.

They were grown adults for Heaven's sake! They couldn't very well go around avoiding each other like a couple of teenagers.

Given their long history, Rebecca felt like she deserved an explanation. She was better than a bang-and-run. It was way past time the two of them were honest with each other.

In fact, the more she stewed over being ignored the more it had her blood boiling. Was that all she'd been to him? Just some woman he could roll around in the sack with?

She wasn't about to let him stroll away from her this time.

She rounded a turn and his shop appeared. It was well past hours of operation, thank goodness, because she really didn't want to have a confrontation in front of employees.

The place was dark, with only the bay lights shining through the small windows. The street lights hadn't kicked on yet, but twilight was well underway.

The parking lot was empty, and Rebecca maneuvered her car into the first slot. She tossed the gearshift into park and exited the car. With her keys tucked away in her shorts pocket, she yanked open the office door and allowed it to slam behind her. No sense in being quiet, and she wasn't in the mood for pleasantries anyway. With each step she took, her agitation grew. She was stressed out, exhausted, and R.J. was about to get a piece of her mind.

She stomped into the shop area, fully intending to launch into a tirade of why R.J. was like every other shallow guy, when she stopped short at the sight of him.

Some old piece of shit with gray primer and no wheels had the hood popped, so that the inner guts of the car were exposed. Rebecca hardly spared the thing a glance because the man standing in front of it commanded all her attention.

Every word she had prepared for him, to put him in his place, dissipated in the amount of time it took to give him a good once over.

And once was all it took to have her heart ratcheting up to super speeds.

Feet braced wide apart, long legs encased in a pair of camo pants and a strong, tightly-muscled, *naked* backside...

Ah, shit.

One quick glance and suddenly she couldn't make heads or tails of a single thought. She'd successfully compartmentalized each and every one, and now they were a jumbled mess. Infuriating man!

She'd come to give him a piece of her mind and all she could do was stare at the beads of sweat decorating the bronzed skin of his lower back.

But why should she let him do this to her? It was the same trap she always fell into, and for once she needed to get a grip. Just take a deep breath and remember why she was here.

Scrumptious man or not.

With sure steps, she made her way across the concrete floor, her determination growing as she got closer to him.

Finally she reached his side and eyed the greasy towel covering one bulky shoulder.

"Why are you ignoring me?" she demanded.

His hands, those big, dirty, blunt-fingered hands dug around the innards of the engine. "I've been busy," he bit out in a gruff voice. His tone said, "Stay the hell away if you know what's good for you."

Well, she had no intention of doing that. "That's not good enough," she shot back.

Apparently he didn't care, because he kept his focus on the car and not on her, which had her fuming even more. She was standing right in front of him, and he was still ignoring her.

"I've sent you text messages, called you…" She let the statement hang in the thick air between them. Nothing. Nothing but the clanking of metal and his heavy breathing.

"Dammit, R.J., you can't keep doing this to me. You can't sleep with me and pretend like I don't exist."

A muscle in his stubble-covered jaw clenched.

"And you can't go on pretending like what's between us doesn't exist either."

He whipped the towel off his shoulder and tossed it on the engine. "You think that's what I'm doing?"

"What the hell else am I supposed to think?" she asked with the last shred of composure she had. Damn him for dragging this side out of her.

"It's for your own good, Rebecca," he bit out through clenched teeth. "If you're smart, you'll get the hell out of here. Go find yourself a man who can give you what you want."

She took a step closer to him. "And you're not that man?"

"No."

"How do you know? You've never given it a chance." The accusation didn't go over well if the look he pinned her with was anything to go by.

His usually playful green eyes were stormy and anything but friendly. Rebecca wasn't used to seeing them like that. The inauspicious look in his eyes and the hard set of his jaw caused a frisson of unease to wash over her.

He lowered his face to hers so their mouths were a breath apart. For a brief second, Rebecca prepared herself for his kiss. It would be hard and furious, just like the man she couldn't bring herself to stay away from.

But there was no kiss. No passionate touch or words of love.

"Leave," he said just above a whisper.

He wanted her scared. Wanted her to think he was a big insensitive asshole who had nothing to offer her. But he was forgetting. She'd seen him vulnerable. She'd seen him grieve over the loss of his brother and felt firsthand just how tender his touch could be.

"No," she pushed back.

He gripped her shoulders and hauled her up on her toes. His fingers were rough on her arm, the bite of them borderline painful.

"You're asking for it," he warned.

"Finally something you notice," she said, which was probably taking her own life in her hands.

"Are kidding me?" He gave her a gentle shake. "I've spent the last fifteen years trying *not* to notice you."

His green eyes burned with passion he no doubt had been trying so hard to keep hidden. They bore down into her, seeing into her soul where all her darkest secrets lived. Where her love for him lived.

"Stop trying so hard," she pleaded.

One minute they were staring each other down, as though sending out silent dares to make the first move. The next R.J. was crushing his mouth over hers, immediately sweeping his tongue inside and taking her breath away.

Rebecca didn't protest, nor did she waste any time. They both had wasted too much time dancing around the tangible attraction for each other. Her arms went around his thick shoulders, savoring the feel of all that hardness, all that male splendor pressed against her much smaller, more feminine frame.

No one made her more aware of how very female she was than R.J. Every ridge, every sinew of muscle was a direct contrast to the curves and softness of her own body. That feeling alone was as much of a turn on than anything he could do with his hands.

Well, almost.

Actually, it wasn't even close.

Rebecca became aware of the fact when R.J. brought his

hands around to her back and squeezed her rear. The action brought her even closer to him, where she was able to feel the rigid bulge beneath his jeans.

There was nothing else but this. No work scandal. No ex-lover trying to send Rebecca to jail. No uncertain future. There was only R.J. and the feel of him and the musky scent that wrapped her in a cocoon of masculinity she always associated with the man. His hands were everywhere, all over her body, under her shirt, in her hair.

His kisses were rough, borderline bruising her lips but not painful. They exhibited how much he wanted her, how much he'd been holding himself back and was finally unleashing that inner sexual beast.

The fact that she could get him to come this unglued had her smiling against his lips.

"What're you grinning at?" he asked as he whipped her shirt over her head and tossed it aside.

"Nothing," she replied with a sly grin. "I just like seeing you all unhinged."

"You think this is unhinged." He reached up with his right hand and slammed the hood of the car shut. The sound was loud and echoed off the concrete walls, which mirrored the pounding of her heart inside her chest.

In one swift move, he had her off her feet and settled on the edge of the hood. The position allowed him to step in between her spread legs.

His eyes darkened when he gazed at her. It was a look of passion that made her feel like the only woman in the world, the only woman he had eyes for and the only woman he wanted.

Okay, let's not get ahead of ourselves. Right now is all that matters.

"Do you know what you're getting yourself into?" He growled into her ear.

"Oh, yes," she answered on a breathy sigh.

The passion R.J. showed her on the hood of the car was soul-shattering and deep, and Rebecca knew she'd never be the same after this; knew she'd never look at this man the same again.

When their breathing slowed and the room stopped spinning, she returned her legs to the floor.

R.J. shot her a lopsided grin, one that had the ground shifting beneath her. "I'm sorry," he muttered.

She jabbed a finger at him as she slid off the car and reached for her pants. "Don't you dare start apologizing for that."

He stepped into his pants and pulled them over his hips. "I was just saying sorry for not being gentler. Don't women want finesse and shit?"

"I didn't want gentle." He handed over her shirt, which she accepted. "Finesse and shit?" she asked.

One corner of his mouth kicked up. "You know what I mean."

He stepped closer to her and framed her face with his hands. They were rough and warm, like the man who thought he wasn't good enough for her.

"Thank you," he whispered against her mouth.

"For what?"

The kiss he pressed against her lips was soft and tender, not at all like the down and dirty lovemaking they'd just shared.

"For just being you."

****

The deep male grunts coming from the shop assaulted Danielle's ears and made her skin crawl. The sound was one she was all too familiar with and remembered with stunning clarity. Unfortunately for her, she was used to them being used with her and not some other bimbo R.J. would no doubt tire of in record time. Hearing the unmistakable sounds coming from the shop wasn't a shock to her either. R.J. often played where he worked, because the man had no scruples when it came to sex.

At one time, she loved that side of him. Now it just made her sick to her stomach, and she'd wished she'd chosen any other night to come snooping in the office.

She tuned the sounds of sex out and rifled through the drawers in the dark. Fumbling around in the pitch dark hadn't been part of her plan, but she certainly didn't want to alert R.J. and his flavor of the week to her presence. All she needed to do was gather evidence that she hadn't screwed up those orders. There had to be something here somewhere exonerating her of wrong doing.

But after pulling open the first drawer, Danielle knew her task would be harder than she thought. Someone had ruined her perfectly organized files. Nothing was in the right place, and some of them weren't even in the right drawer. Panic flooded her already anxiety-ridden body. With trembling fingers, she opened the second drawer, just as her gaze lit on a pile of invoices and work-orders on the desk.

A female cry followed by R.J.'s deep groan came from the shop. Danielle forced herself not to look out the office window as she picked up the top invoice and glanced the thing over. It was dated for a month ago and labeled "not paid." She'd collected the bill for this, hadn't she? The only way to find out for sure was to look up the record in the computer. But she didn't want the light from the screen to alert the two people in the next room, so she set that one aside.

The next slip of paper was a parts list stapled to the list of parts received. The lists didn't match; in fact they weren't even for the same job and had different dates. Had she stapled these together? The handwriting was hers, and she always kept her list of parts with the parts received stapled together. But these two didn't make sense.

Quickly she realized the pile was all the slip-ups she'd made. There had to be thirty to forty invoices and work orders piled on the desk, and she hadn't made that many mistakes had she? She'd always been very meticulous about her work, and detail-oriented about everything. That's what the medication was for. So she could keep up with everything.

No. There was nothing here to help her. Coming into the shop had been a mistake. Not only did her visit not solve anything, but she'd been forced to endure R.J.'s raunchy rendezvous.

As she turned from the desk, Danielle caught a glimpse of curly red hair through the office window. Her former boss was pulling up his pants and smiling at the meddling doctor bitch who'd ruined Danielle's life.

They'd screwed in the office several times over the past two years, but he'd never looked at Danielle the way he looked *her*. She was so disgusted that she couldn't even bring herself to think the woman's name.

The woman who'd opened her big mouth and got Dr. Gross in trouble.

Danielle's heart dropped to the bottom of her stomach as R.J. caressed the other woman's cheek and pressed a soft kiss to her mouth. Bile rose on her throat, and she fumbled in her back pocket for the bottle of pills.

Obviously the one she'd taken this morning hadn't been enough. Two more ought to do it. Just two more and she could place her mind to more important things.

Things like making them pay. They'd done this to her and, by God, she'd find a way to make them suffer for ruining her life.

SEVENTEEN

"YOU KNOW, IF YOU didn't have a career rebuilding cars, I'd say you could make it as a chef," Rebecca stated.

The shirt she had on was one of his old ones that she'd taken the liberty of digging out of his dresser. And instead of dressing in her own clothes, she'd pulled his shirt on and only fastened three of the buttons. The thing was huge on her and hung off one shoulder and hit mid-thigh. Every time she moved, the shirt slid father down her arm and came dangerously close to exposing her left breast. The same breast he'd feasted on for the past two hours. Also the same one she'd held his head to while he'd ravished it with his tongue.

Rebecca was an incredibly responsive woman. She had erogenous zones that drew him like a magnet and drove him out of his mind. If it hadn't been for her growling stomach, R.J. would have spent the rest of the night licking every inch and discovering even more sensitive areas.

As it was, they'd already spent two hours making love like two people on death row. And that was after the impromptu frenzied sex on the hood of a 1968 Mercury Cougar.

He'd stayed away from her for her sake, but after burying himself inside her tight body he found he no longer had the strength or the desire to stay away. Seeing her in his shop tonight had only confirmed what they both knew would happen.

And he couldn't say he regretted falling back into bed with her, although leaving Rebecca had never been about regret. In fact his only regret was that he'd inadvertently put that very idea in her mind and caused her pain. He hated himself for that and would do what he could to make it up to her.

After they pulled themselves from his bed, R.J. had dressed in a pair of old jeans and cooked the two of them some burgers. Rebecca had settled at the table next to him and dove into the meal like she hadn't eaten in days. In the meantime, he'd pushed his plate aside and used the opportunity to go over paperwork from the shop. The same paperwork he and the guys had been trying to make sense of.

"Seriously, these are really good," Rebecca reiterated.

R.J. cocked a brow at her. "No need for the flattery, you already got yours. Twice," he stated with a jerk of his head toward the bedroom.

She took another bite of the burger and swallowed. "Yes, that was nice." A smile pulled at the corners of her mouth, which she attempted to hide with a sip of her drink. Her poor attempt didn't fool him.

"Nice?" he repeated with a snort. "You screamed so loud I'm surprised my neighbors didn't report a domestic disturbance." Not to mention the scratches she'd left on his back.

Somewhere along the way sex between them had become more than just sex. And Rebecca had become more than just that woman he had crazy lust for. The line between lust and love had grown hazy to the point where he didn't know where one ended and the other began. One thing he did know was that lust didn't make his heart squeeze in his chest. It didn't make him lose track of his thoughts or feel unsure about himself.

In the past, she'd been about scratching an itch. But what did it mean when the itch didn't go away? And the itch grew and grew until it felt dangerously close to the L word?

Tonight had been more about getting laid, and he'd known that when he'd taken her on the hood of the car. And like an idiot, he'd done it anyway knowing that he'd be unable to deny his own feelings afterward.

He loved her.

No, not just love. He'd fallen deeply, head-over-heels, life-changing in love with Rebecca Underwood and there wasn't a damn thing he could do about it

Despite that, he still felt like she deserved better than him. What the hell did he know about being in a relationship? More importantly, what did he know about taking care of a woman? Especially one as special as the woman sitting next to him.

"I may have over-exaggerated a bit," she said in response to his teasing statement.

His answer was a snort as he glanced over an invoice. Exaggerated? No one could fake a reaction like the one she'd had in bed with him. R.J. was pretty sure no woman he'd been with had faked it, and he'd like to think he could tell. But what Rebecca had experienced had been far from fake. The trembling of her body hadn't been fake. The hot juices that had milked him hadn't been fake.

"You're awfully sure of yourself," she added.

He picked up a pink piece of paper, glanced it over and set it aside. "You're not going to sit there and tell me that wasn't genuine."

"How would you know?" she countered.

"I just do."

When she didn't answer, he set his paperwork down and

leaned back in the chair. "So you're telling me all that 'Oh God, yes, R.J.' business was for my benefit?"

She lifted a brow and took a bite of her burger.

"Okay, smartass explain this." He leaned forward in his chair and pointed to a tiny red mark on his bare shoulder from where she'd bitten him.

When her climax had slammed into her, she'd clamped her teeth down on the hard flesh of his shoulder. Her teeth had left actual marks, which had turned his skin red.

"See, I don't think you like to admit that I can make you scream," he said in a low voice.

A gorgeous shade of pink colored her high cheek bones. Busted. It wasn't that she didn't react to him. She just didn't want him to know exactly how much she reacted to him.

To prove his point, he leaned closer to her and slid his hand along her bare thigh. Her position on the chair had forced the hem of his shirt up to her hips. She shifted in an attempt to move away from him, but his fingers at the juncture of her thighs held her in place. Her nude body beneath his shirt tempted him to abandon their meal and drag her fine ass back to bed. If he did that, he wouldn't let her leave until morning, and he had work to do.

Even still, she sucked in a breath when he placed a soft kiss to the sensitive skin just beneath her ear.

"You can pretend all you want, Rebecca, but I know you," he whispered in her ear. Her soft moan was like an aphrodisiac to his overactive libido and fed the fire of his desire for her. "Every time you move, you'll remember it was me who made you scream," he taunted, just to remind her that she wanted him just as much as he wanted her.

To drive his point home, he worked his fingers to the liquid heat between her thighs and tested how ready she was for him. And she was more than ready. All it would take would be for him to slip the shirt over her head and she'd let him do whatever he wanted to her. And he'd do it with a smile on his face and an even bigger smile on hers.

She turned her head and caught his mouth with hers. Her lips were soft and moist and immediately opened for him. Their tongues slid around each other, slow and torturous and driving him out of his mind.

When he lifted his head, her eyes were heavy and her lips were swollen and still so very tempting. The pulse at the base of her neck was rapid and matched her rapid and shallow breathing.

"Just so we're clear," he said in a gruff voice. Hell, she wasn't the only one affected. He'd done that to prove a point to her and proven it just as much to himself:

That he couldn't touch her without losing his head.

She cleared her throat and tugged at the hem of the shirt. Her hands trembled when she picked up her burger. "So glad we cleared that up."

A little while later, they were back in his bed, naked and satisfied but far from exhausted. The comforter had been kicked to the floor, leaving only the sheet to cover their sweaty, limp bodies. They lay on their backs next to each other, both of them staring at the ceiling and trying to get their breathing under control.

R.J. had told himself, after they'd finished eating that he wasn't going to take her again. That he was just going to crawl beneath the sheets next to her and enjoy a night of feeling her sweet body pressed against his. But then she'd peeled that damn shirt off, allowing the thing to fall to the floor and pool around her feet. He got one look at that sinful body and knew there was no way he'd keep his hands to himself.

With a wicked smile, Rebecca had climbed onto the bed, shoved him onto his back and took control.

Damn, but he loved a woman who knew how to assert her dominance.

They'd ended with Rebecca on her back and now they were trying to recoup.

"That was..." the woman next to him let out a deep breath. "Incredible."

Incredible was an understatement, yet R.J. couldn't think of an exact word to describe what they'd just shared. Because he'd never experienced anything quite like that.

He folded one arm behind his head and smiled.

Yeah, it had been incredible. So fucking incredible that he actually had no words, because he didn't trust his voice to come out even. He didn't trust himself to speak without spilling his guts like some lovesick teenager. And what would he say? "I love you, but we can't be together?"

Some hero he was.

So why did Rebecca look at him as though that's what he was to her?

She turned her head on the pillow and stared at him out of those fathomless green eyes; eyes that drilled down to his soul and saw way too much.

He kept his focus on the ceiling because he didn't have the strength to look at her and see her love for him.

"What're you thinking?" she asked in a soft voice. Was that uncertainty he detected?

"Nothing."

The silence that stretched between them hovered like a storm cloud. Rebecca's once relaxed body went stiff, then slowly she sat up, clutching the sheet to her chest. The glass of half-drank red wine, which she'd brought into the bedroom earlier, was still on the nightstand where she'd left it. Without saying a word, she reached over, grabbed the glass and took a slow sip.

They sat in the quiet each trying to gather their own thoughts. Only R.J.'s were too complicated to gather neatly enough for him to understand. Part of him wanted to push her back to the bed and wrap himself around her. The other part wanted to run the opposite direction and continue to live with the denial he'd been living in for more than a decade.

Rebecca's red hair was a mess of frizzy curls and tumbled halfway down her back. He loved knowing he had the ability to tousle her normally perfect locks. Against his better judgment, R.J. reached over with one hand and fingered the ends of the strands. They were so soft and silky, slipping through his fingers like feathers.

His hand continued its exploration, going from her hair to her back. Her skin was warm and satiny beneath his fingers, giving him a gentle reminder of how she felt pressed against him. He ran his hand in slow circles over her back, just savoring the feel that was pure Rebecca.

She tossed back some more wine, then stared down into the glass. "What are we doing, R.J.? How do we keep ending up here?"

He lifted a brow and ran the tip of his index finger down her spine. The small shiver that washed over her gave him a minute amount of satisfaction. "You know how," he responded.

"That's not what I mean."

Yeah, he knew that. But shit, what could he say? She wanted more from him than he could give her.

She glanced at him over her shoulder, and the look she gave him just about cracked his damaged heart open.

"I don't know what you want from me," she said in a quiet voice.

Hell, he didn't know either. He wanted her, but the thought of hurting her was like a tight fist around his heart. "Rebecca," he said on a sigh. Sex with her was like having a holy experience. She always gazed up at him with eyes full of trust and glowing with love. Every time he emptied himself inside her, he tumbled farther down the never-ending hole of unrequited love.

So why was he such a chicken shit?

Why did three little words scare him more than anything else?

He stood from the bed and dug a pair of clean boxers from the dresser drawer. After pulling them on he turned to face her.

And man, was she a sight. A sight that always stole his breath and tilted the ground beneath his feat. Flaming red hair, a wild mass and tumbling around her shoulders, framing her stunning face. The dark bed sheet barely covering her generous breasts, which were the perfect shade of creamy and had little raspberry-colored nipples that tasted like sweet heaven.

"Stop looking at me like that."

The strain in her voice pulled him from his inappropriate thoughts.

"Like what?" *Don't play dumb, asshole.*

She tilted the wine glass to her full lips and sucked down another sip. Then she set the glass aside and stood from the bed. His fingers itched to wrap themselves around her curves, but her jerky movements told him she feeling anything but cuddly.

"You know exactly like what." One corner of her underwear barely peaked out from under his bed. Rebecca yanked them off the floor and stepped into them. "It's a look you've perfected over the past fifteen years."

Playing dumb never worked with her.

Regret tugged at him as she shimmied her petite derriere into those skimpy bottoms. He had to force his eyes to remain on her face and not ogle those breasts which were hanging free.

When she turned to face him, her brows were pulled down low over her green eyes. "When I'm around you, I always feel like I'm playing a game that I don't know the rules to." She walked around him and picked up his jeans off the floor. After scanning the ground, she dropped them, then looked under the bed. "I mean, one day you ignore me and the next we end up like this." She accented the last statement with a gesture between the two of them. Her breasts swayed when she yanked the comforter off the floor, then tossed it onto the bed. "Where the hell is my bra? Didn't you take it off in here?"

She was irritable as hell and looking to take it out on him. With a heavy sigh, he retrieved one of his shirts off the floor and handed it over to her.

The look she shot him was anything but grateful, but she accepted the shirt anyway and slid her arms into the sleeves.

Now probably wasn't the best time to tell her that seeing her in his shirt turned him the hell on. Not in the mood she was in. Flattery coming from him would only turn her cheeks even redder than they already were.

"Your bra's in the living room," he informed her as he sank to the edge of the bed and tried to gather his thoughts.

He'd known for the past several weeks this discussion was coming. Rebecca was smart as a whip and had too much self-respect to fall into the same trap all his other girlfriends fell into. Hell, they weren't even girlfriends. One and two-night stands, and Rebecca was better than that.

It was the moment of truth. The moment when she was going to call him on his bullshit and start demanding an explanation.

He braced his hands on his knees and watched the woman who'd stolen his heart years ago. The light from the full moon streamed in through the window, highlighted her high cheek bones, glanced off her trim thighs, and caught the triangle of flesh in the open vee of the shirt. No woman took his breath away like she did. No woman made his heart split open at the sight of her.

His gaze moved over her face as she took a hair tie off her wrist and piled her curls on top of her head. If her hair down was hot, then pulled back in a sloppy knot, with little wispy strands skimming her cheeks was the sexiest thing he'd ever seen. Her beautifully slender neck was exposed, tempting him to place his lips there just so he could hear her gasp.

"I can't keep doing this same dance with you," she said. "I like to think we're friends, but how many friends do you know get along better in bed than they do out of it?"

None. And R.J. didn't make it a habit of forming a friendship with a woman he'd slept with. "You know as well as I do we've never been friends," he told her as she gazed down at him.

Yeah, she knew. He wasn't the only who was well aware they couldn't maintain any kind of platonic relationship. Thinking they could was only a smoke screen, and a thin one at that.

"Besides, I don't want to be your friend." His voice came out harsher than he intended.

"Then what do you want?" she whispered. "Because I can't keep going on like this." She turned from him, paced to the other side of the room and crossed her arms over her chest. "How many times can we sleep together and still tell ourselves there isn't more going on? Because you know there is."

Yeah, he knew. And hearing her say the words for him wasn't any easier. He'd never been the sort of person who had a hard time telling things like they were. But with Rebecca... Hell, she made him tongue-tied. His thoughts became a jumbled mess of shit that he couldn't make sense of.

The woman scared him. "What do you want?" he countered, even though he already knew what her answer would be.

"I want *you*."

Simply stated, which was what he'd asked for.

"And not the R.J. who climbed out of my window nine years ago and pretended like that night never happened."

One side of his mouth kicked up. "You didn't exactly ask me to stay, remember?"

She uncrossed her arms and came toward him. "I'm not saying I'm not blameless, but at least I'm honest. So I'm going to ask you again: what do you want? Because if this is all there is, then we need to go our separate ways right now."

He snagged her hand and tugged her toward him. She came willingly, brushing her supple inner thighs along the outsides of his legs. The contact shot erotic fire directly to his groin. He shifted in an attempt to ward off the hard on he felt coming.

"What am I to you, R.J.?" she asked in a low whisper, while threading her hands through his hair. Her touch was sweet and gentle, everything he wasn't.

His eyes dropped closed as her fingers worked magic on his skull, scraping over his scalp to the ends of his hair.

When he was with her, she made everything better. She chased away his demons and made him feel like he was worth a damn. As though he was more than the object of women's fantasies who could bring them to orgasm with his hands. The fact that she believed in him that much was reason enough to love her.

"You're special," he whispered. Then cleared his throat past the lump forming. "You're special to me, Rebecca." He wrapped his arms around her, ran his hands up the backs of her thighs until they came to the softness of her round bottom. "You always have been."

Her eyelids fluttered closed when his touch traveled to her waist and farther up her torso. Only when he came to the tender underside of her breasts did he stop, allowing himself to graze the bottom swell of her boobs with his thumb.

"Special enough for you to stick around?" she wanted to know. The slight hitch in her voice told him that no matter how upset she was with him, she would succumb to his touch every time.

"Special enough for me to try." He cupped her cool cheek with his palm and stared up into her eyes. "You deserve so much better than me."

"Why don't you let me decide what I deserve?" she countered. A small smile pulled at the corners of her full mouth. "And what makes you so sure I'm too good for you? Have I ever done anything to make you feel that way?"

"It's not you," he responded absently while brushing his thumb across her lower lip.

"Then what?" Her voice was breathless from his touch. He flattened his palms against the column of her neck, ran it south until he could tease the cleavage just peeking above the top button of his shirt.

"My father was a heartless, cheating son of a bitch who constantly hurt my mother." In the past, thoughts of his father always created a fiery pit on the bottom of his stomach. Even though the man was hardly worth sparing a thought for. But being with Rebecca took the resentment and pain away, as though with her by his side he could conquer all of his demons.

"Courtney told me." Her breath hitched when he found one of her nipples and pinched. "We were talking about you the other night," she said with a smile.

"I hope it was about how huge my package is."

"No."

"Hmm." He undid the bottom two buttons of the shirt and placed a light kiss on her belly. "Then was it about how you scratch the shit out of my back when you come?"

"You would like that, wouldn't you?" Her teeth sank into her lower lip when he unfastened another button. "We didn't talk about sex. Although she does know about us."

"Because you told her?"

"No, she figured it out on her own." She paused while he removed the last button, then slid the shirt over her shoulders where it fell to the floor. "Would you care if I had told her?"

He molded his hands over her breasts and tested their weight. "No. I never said anything to anyone because I figured you didn't want me to. Was I wrong?" he asked with one brow lifted.

"No," she replied with a sigh.

"We're getting off subject here. What did you and my sister talk about?"

She stood, helpless, in front of him while he played with her breasts, pushing them together and burying his face in their plumpness. "How am I supposed to think straight when you touch me like that?"

"Try really hard."

"But you're distracting me."

"I know," he said with a wicked smile.

"You're shameless."

"I know that too."

The look she gave him could have scorched his clothes off, if he'd had any on. With a heavy sigh, he lowered his head to her stomach. "You're going to make me talk about this, aren't you?"

"Yes." She ran her hands over his hair. "And you're the one who wanted to talk about it."

He placed a kiss on her belly button. "No, I just asked what Courtney told you."

"Yeah, I know. And yes you need to talk about it."

Damn woman was going to yank this from him like pulling a rotten tooth. He lay back on the bed and stared at the ceiling. "Doesn't the fact that I never talk about my father mean that maybe I don't like talking about him?"

"I know why you don't talk about him." The bed dipped beneath Rebecca's weight when she crawled up next to him. "But you need to. And I want to hear it from you, not your sister."

He glanced at her out of the corner of his eye, and disappointment tightened his muscles when those glorious breasts disappeared beneath his shirt. Of course three times in one night was a lot, even for him. That last release of his was more than enough to get him through the next day. Or at least the morning.

This was not how he envisioned the night going.

Talking about his father.

Son of a bitch.

"Is your father still alive?" Rebecca asked in a soft voice.

"Last I heard," he answered with as little emotion as he could. It wasn't hard, considering he felt nothing for the man. From what he understood, his old man contacted Courtney about once a year. The only reason she ever took the calls was so she could use the opportunity to make the man feel like shit. Nick Devlin knew better than to call R.J. The last time they saw each other, R.J. had made it clear he wanted nothing to do with his father.

"Courtney talked to him about eight months ago," he continued. "He's in Southern California somewhere."

"Does your animosity toward her father have something to do with your brother's death?" she wanted to know.

R.J. folded one arm behind his head and used the other arm to maintain contact with Rebecca. The skin on her thigh was cool beneath his hand.

"Partly. Although things were unraveling before Trent died." He slanted her a look. The moonlight poured in from the windows and cast her face in a creamy glow. "Did I mention he was a cheating bastard?"

"Yes. Courtney said something along those same lines too."

"She was being kind." Had it been this difficult to talk about before? R.J. forged on, trying to ignore the sour feeling in the pit of his stomach. "Courtney's unusually soft when it comes to our dad. I think she keeps waiting for him to beg our forgiveness."

"And you don't think he will?"

A snort popped out. "Hell, no. The man doesn't know the meaning of the word."

"Does he ever get in touch with your mother?"

"He's not that stupid. He knows I'd hunt him down and kill him if he ever tried to speak to my mother."

Rebecca placed a hand on his shoulder. Her touch was reassuring and was just enough to beat back the horrible memories he'd suppressed for so long. "Your mom is very lucky to have someone like you looking out for her."

Yeah, he was a real prince. All those nights when he would find any excuse to sleep at a friend's house while his mom and dad fought. Leaving Courtney and a sick Trent there to deal with what he wasn't strong enough to handle. Only when his father was out of the picture did R.J. had the balls to stand up to the old man.

Too many years, he'd put of a façade of being a cocky badass who'd been left unaffected by his father's callous actions. The truth was Nick Devlin's infidelity had left a gaping hole in R.J. as well as their entire family.

"I didn't do nearly enough." He cleared his throat when his voice came out rough. "I was the oldest. I should have done more to shelter Courtney and Trent."

Rebecca narrowed her eyes at her. "You were a kid. What could you have done?"

Courtney had always said the same thing to him. Funny how the words did little to ease his conscience.

"Did your mother know what was going on at the time?" Rebecca asked.

A humorless laugh popped out of him. "My father never made an attempt to hide his affairs. I don't think he cared about us enough to be discreet." The familiar dark cloud that always hovered when R.J. thought about his father, grew bigger. "I remember one time, right before Trent died, my father showed up at the hospital with one of his girlfriends. She asked my dad if Trent was his nephew or a family friend."

"You're kidding?" Rebecca gasped. "That must have devastated your poor mother."

One side of his mouth kicked up, remembering the brave front Carol Devlin had put up in front of her kids. "At that point, nothing surprised her. She just smiled at told my father that if he ever showed his face there again, she'd take her hunting rifle to his midsection."

Rebecca shook her head. "I had no idea your family had such a hard time. How horrible for your mother to go through all that, then lose a child."

"My mother is the bravest woman I know. After Trent died she finally stopped putting up with his shit and slapped him with divorce papers. He gladly signed them."

"I don't understand how any parent could do that to their own family. Was the divorce the reason you came to Trouble?"

"For the most part, yeah. My mother always hated Billings and wanted to live in a small town. The only reason we stayed there was because my father refused to move. After Trent died she finally asked herself why she was living her life for a man who didn't give a shit."

Rebecca placed a hand on his shoulder. Her touch was gentle, reminding him of everything she was: good, beautiful, and sweet.

"You're not like him, R.J.," she said softly. "I know you think you are. But you're nothing like him."

"Aren't I, though?" he counted as he placed his attention on her. Wisps of red curls had escaped her sloppy bun and gingerly graced her cheeks.

"You would never deliberately hurt someone like that."

"But I have. I hurt you over and over again."

Her gaze dropped down to her lap, only confirming what they both knew, but never wanted to talk about. For years, he'd not only lived in the denial of his love for her, but the denial that he'd been the only man to break her heart. While attempting to not repeat his father's mistakes, he'd only succeeded in doing what he'd tried so hard not to.

And he hated himself for it.

Rebecca had every reason to hate him. She had every right to tell him what a bastard he was and stay far away from him. And yet, they always ended up together. Despite their tumultuous past and differences, Rebecca always gave herself to him. As though forgiveness came so easily for her, even though he didn't deserve it.

"We were kids, R.J.," she finally said. Was she trying to convince herself or him?

"That's no excuse," he said roughly. "There's never an excuse for that. I've tried so hard not to repeat my father's mistakes, and I ended up no better than him."

"Stop saying that," she argued with a touch of desperation. "Do you think if you had no redeeming qualities, that if you really were the heartless bastard you seem to think you are, I'd still be here with you? Or I would have told you how much I wanted to be with you?

Unable to keep his hands to himself, he reached out and cupped her cheek with his palm. No one moved him like Rebecca. No one felt like Heaven and sin all wrapped up in one graceful package.

"That's because you see the good in everyone, whether they have it or not. It's one of your best qualities." Only one of many.

She grinned and held up an index finger. "That's not always true. There were times when I cursed the day I met you."

"Oh, I don't doubt that." He bolted off the bed and rolled her beneath him, capturing her startled gasp in his mouth.

She didn't protest when he swept his tongue inside the hot cavern of her mouth. Of course, he didn't expect any objection from her. As soon as his tongue touched hers, her lips immediately opened wider and allowed him exploration. Their hips fit perfectly together, his own thighs cradled by her much smaller ones.

How could he ever think that pushing her away had been a good idea? Far too many years had been spent in the arms of other women, when the one he'd really wanted was right beneath him.

He broke the kiss to trail his lips over the column of her throat.

"Get the idea that you're not good enough out of your head," she whispered in his ear. The bottoms of her feet traveled up his calves. Her feet were wonderfully soft compared to the coarse hair on his legs. "If I ever hear you say anything like that again, I'll kill you myself. Understand?"

"Yes, ma'am," he muttered against her collarbone.

EIGHTEEN

R.J. HAD NEVER BEEN so reluctant to leave a naked woman in bed. Even with the promise of more sex, he always walked away knowing he'd never be back for more.

While his heart had told him not to be a dumbass and climb back under the covers with Rebecca, his head debated otherwise. Unfortunately for him, his head made a much more realistic argument. Things to do and people to see, and all that unnecessary shit he didn't really want to do. Despite his *playing hooky* attitude this morning, there were cars to be built and other business to be taken care of.

The *other business* part consisted of paying one final visit to Danielle. What he hoped to accomplish, he had no idea. This visit was likely to end much the same way as all the others. With him coming off as the big jackass for firing the single mother. The well-being of his shop had forced him to get over his own self blame for making Danielle unemployed. His business came first, no matter what.

Even so, R.J. still felt as though he had some unfinished business with the woman. She had a serious problem, and despite what had transpired between them, he still cared about her. She needed help and for some reason he felt solely responsible for making sure she conquered whatever demon was plaguing her. If he had to tie the woman up and drag her kicking and screaming to rehab, then so help him God, he'd do it.

Danielle's daughter at least deserved to have a sober mother.

R.J. pulled up to her house with a plan action ready to be enacted. But by the time he'd rang the doorbell three times and knocked twice, a feeling of dread had settled over him. Lindsey should have answered the door. Then he remembered that the girl was probably with her father, who lived somewhere outside of Trouble.

Something didn't set right and R.J. wasn't going to slink away without finding out what it was.

Thankfully, Danielle had told him where she kept the spare key. He figured she'd always wanted him to use it and surprise her with roses and a candlelight dinner or some romantic shit. Needless to say, he'd never done so, which Danielle had never failed to remind him of, as though they were some kind of couple.

The spare key came in handy now, and he let himself through the front door. The interior stank to high Heaven of rotten food and garbage. Thick draperies and dusty blinds blocked out any sunlight that would have otherwise made the home more appealing. Danielle was nowhere to be found, and even as he called out her name there was no answer.

A trail of ants led the way from a beneath a baseboard to a plate of a half-eaten sandwich, which had been left forgotten on the coffee table. R.J. discovered the source of the rotten smell with an open bag of garbage. The thing looked as though it had been ravished by wild animal, then left abandoned after it had picked out all the scraps of food.

He held his breath as he stepped over the mess and walked toward Danielle's bedroom. The room down the hall wasn't in much better shape than the rest of the house. The mattress in the middle of the room was bare, save for one pillow which lay at the foot of the bed. Light flickered from the muted television on top of the dresser. R.J. paid no attention to the 1980s movie as he dodged a pile of discarded clothes and called out Danielle's name again.

No answer.

He was about to give up his search when a bare foot caught his attention. The baby pink toe nail polish had him booking it to the bathroom, where he stopped short and let out a string of colorful expletives.

Even though it looked like she'd been attacked, with the bruises on her body and the plastic shower curtain, which had been ripped off the rod, R.J. knew exactly what he was looking at.

Half a dozen pill bottles were all over the bathroom floor, as though they'd been tossed there after being emptied. In the middle of the whole mess was Danielle, wearing nothing more than a thong and a solid gray t-shirt.

"Danielle," he barked, hoping his voice alone would be enough to rouse her.

But in the shape she was in, it was unlikely that anything would get through to her. Except maybe a stomach pump. Or something much more serious.

Holy hell, every single pill bottle was empty. How many had she swallowed? Enough to kill her.

R.J. quickly dismissed that idea when his fingers found a faint pulse at the base of her throat. Weak, but existent. A few light taps to her cheeks didn't prompt any sort of reaction either.

"Danielle," he said louder this time.

Nothing.

"Shit." He hurried out of the bathroom, snagged blanket from the closet and draped it over her half-naked body. Then, he withdrew his cell phone from his back pocket and dialed nine-one-one.

After reciting the address, R.J. filled the dispatcher in. "I need an ambulance. I have a woman here who's overdosed on some pills."

He listened to the instructions, answering questions when asked, and tried to fight off the guilt that was damn near making him sick to his stomach.

****

Whoever coined the phrase "When it rains, it pours," must have owned an auto shop and had a close, personal relationship with Charlie. The man had been waiting for R.J. bright and early that morning with a beat-up 1928 Rolls-Royce. The car had been an impulse buy to show with the other two cars in Reno next month. Apparently Charlie thought R.J. could wield magic. And while he appreciated the vote of confidence, and didn't like to turn down business, another car on a rack was the last thing he needed.

He was already up to his eyebrows with more business than he could handle. Fortunately, he'd finally found a replacement for Danielle in the form of a fifty-two year old man named Ryland Forbes. Ryland was a widower with two grown kids and thirty-two years' experience of working in an auto shop. The past ten of those had been spent with him running a sizeable repair shop in Rock Creek. His appearance in Trouble had been impeccable timing and saved R.J.'s ass right when it needed saving. With four more cars to rebuild, he needed his guys focused on the job at hand and not pushing papers and paying bills.

Another blessing had come yesterday when he'd hired another mechanic who specialized in electrical. Poor Mitch, R.J.'s only electrician, had been pulling overtime, mostly on Charlie's cars. The twenty-two year old kid who'd decided to skip college to be an auto mechanic had already proved his worth.

Not that R.J. condoned throwing away a college education, but man, was he grateful. With the extra two employees, there was a good chance he could finish all three of Charlie's cars. Of course, it had helped that Charlie had offered to pay triple whatever the normal cost of rebuilding the Rolls. And it would be pricey, considering he'd have to have all the parts overnighted, not to mention putting several of his other cars on hold.

But despite the overload in business, R.J. couldn't concentrate. He'd been having that problem a lot lately. Since kissing Rebecca good-bye two days ago, he hadn't seen or spoken to her since. He couldn't climb into bed or pick up one of his shirts without smelling her or feeling her presence. Or lack of it, since she hadn't attempted to get in touch with him. Not even a text message.

As he picked up a nearby towel and wiped his greasy hands, R.J. told himself it was for the better. Even though their relationship had shifted into another category, and even though he was crazy in love with her, R.J. didn't know the first thing about dating. He only did raw, primal sex. A night or two of headboard banging love-making was all he was capable of. Rebecca knew that as well as he did, yet she still believed he was better than that.

But was he? Or had he been selling himself short for most of his adult life?

You've just been too scared to try.

Yeah, he knew he was a coward. Beneath his I-Don't-Give-A-Shit exterior was the same scared little boy who'd been too chicken shit to stand up to his old man. Too much of a pussy to defend his own mother. Oh, he was all about defending her now. After she'd been too broken and defeated from the infidelities of her husband.

Nothing had changed, even though he told himself he wasn't the same kid he used to be, or that he was nothing like his father. He was still a puss. Too scared to tell one woman how he really felt about her. Which was exactly why she deserved better than him. No matter how much he thought otherwise.

R.J. went back to work on a 1970 Charger when Sam appeared by his side.

"I'm taking the Monte Carlo over to paint," the kid said. "And Tim just finished with Donald Underwood's car. The orange turned out really great."

R.J. ought to know, he'd personally picked out the exact shade of orange for Mr. Underwood's car. Along with almost all the other details.

"Okay. Let me know when it's ready to test drive," he responded while working on removing the steering wheel from Charlie's latest project. The other two cars were at the tail end of their rebuild and could be painted soon.

Sam grunted in agreement, then walked away.

For the rest of the afternoon, R.J. worked while trying not to think about the other woman in his life. The other woman he felt oddly responsible for, even with her addiction.

Upon seeing her on the bathroom floor, his anger and resentment toward her had melted away. Although, he suspected he'd never truly been angry with her, that it had only been a mask for pity.

Now he pitied her more than ever. He may never understand her reasoning for turning to drugs, but it was pretty clear Danielle was a lonely woman. And perhaps that was why she'd tried to latch onto him. Had she always had problems getting a man in her life?

That didn't make any sense. Danielle was beautiful and smart. He'd always enjoyed her company, when she hadn't gone all wiggy on the drugs.

Despite her being in the hospital, and knowing she was in good hands, he still worried about her. They hadn't let him see her when she'd first been admitted, saying she'd been too critical for anyone other than family. Her daughter Lindsey was the only one they'd let through the doors. The poor kid had been visibly shaken at the sight of her mother hooked up to monitors.

Not being able to do more for Danielle had made him feel like a helpless fool. So he'd done the next best thing and had researched rehabilitation centers in the area. The Central Wyoming Counseling Center was near Casper and seemed to be a good fit for Danielle. She didn't know it yet, but R.J. had every intention of driving her there himself and paying for it.

But he needed to see her. Despite her behavior and poor choices, he cared about her and needed to see for himself that she was okay. That the Danielle he knew was in there somewhere.

Luckily, he'd gotten a call from Lindsey that morning saying her mother had already been released from the hospital. They'd pumped her stomach and kept her overnight for observation, then sent her home.

All day, he'd debated whether or not it was too soon to bombard her with the plans he'd made for her. Then right around the time he'd started ripping apart the guts of Charlie's Rolls Royce, he decided the hell with it. Spending a night in the hospital wasn't going to heal Danielle. The sooner she got into a program, the sooner she could start putting her life back together. Maybe he'd even help her find another job.

At 6:30 R.J. shut the place down and headed across town. For the second time that week, he pulled into Danielle's driveway. Someone had watered her flowers and removed the pile of newspapers from the driveway. The cleanup job made the house seem less forlorn, but a shabby feel still poured out of the peeling paint of the black shutters framing the windows.

Maybe he could also hire some gardeners to come by and tend to the yard.

Lindsey answered the door after R.J.'s third knock. The girl's eyes were puffy, her blue eyes shiny from recently shed tears. Dammit, the kid shouldn't be crying over her mother's condition. They should be going to spa treatments together and shopping sprees. Mothers and daughters did those kinds of things together, didn't they?

"Hi," Lindsey said as she rubbed her nose on the sleeve of her shirt. "My mom's in bed." She stepped back to let him enter.

"Is she asleep?" he asked. The interior of the house was in slightly better shape than before. The garbage and food had been cleared, the curtains opened and the floors vacuumed. R.J. guessed Lindsey had done all that. And now the girl had been tasked with taking care of her mother.

"No, she's awake. She's watching T.V."

R.J. started down the hallway, then turned back to Danielle's daughter. "I thought you were with your dad."

Lindsey's eyes flickered to her surroundings. "I wanted to be here with my mom." She pinned R.J. with the saddest look he'd ever seen from a ten year old. "She can't take care of herself," she whispered.

And there went his heart. Cracking open over softly spoken words from a kid. He seemed to be having that feeling a lot lately.

His soft spot for vulnerable kids got him again. He stalked back toward Lindsey and gathered her in his arms. She came willingly, wrapping her skinny arms around his waist and squeezing tight.

He ran his hand up and down her back, hoping to offer whatever comfort he could give her. She pulled away from him, but he gripped her shoulders to keep her in place. "Listen, why don't I take care of all this, and you can go back to your dad's house? You shouldn't have to be here cleaning."

"I don't mind." She tucked a long strand of hair behind her ear and directed her gaze to the floor. "She needs me and I like to take care of her."

R.J. suspected the other way around was true as well.

Mother and daughter had always been close. Danielle and her husband and divorced several years ago, and Lindsey saw the man one weekend a month. From what R.J. understood, Lindsey had a good relationship with her father, but was much closer with her mom.

He squeezed her shoulders and dropped his hands. "I understand. If you need anything from me, though, give me a call."

"Okay," she offered him a weak smile that didn't reach her eyes. Then she turned around, grabbed a rag and a bottle of Pledge and swiped the surface of the coffee table.

Did Danielle know what a wonderful daughter she had? Did she have any clue how close she came to killing herself and ruining poor Lindsey's life?

The bedroom down the hall wasn't the gloomy cave it had been before. Clearly Lindsey had taken more care with that room than any other. As though she wanted her mother's surroundings to be as pleasant and cheerful as possible. Perhaps the girl thought that alone could cure her mother's weird not-quite-mid-life-crisis.

The curtains were pulled back from the windows so the sunlight could come in and hit the vase of daises on the dresser. They looked fresh and were in a clear vase with a red ribbon wrapped around them. Red was Danielle's favorite color.

The carpet in here had been vacuumed as well, and the clothes and been tidied off the floor.

Danielle was propped against the brass headboard with the comforter tucked tightly around her legs. Several magazines were piled next to her with a tray of half-eaten food.

R.J. perched on the edge of the bed. "Your daughter's quite the housekeeper."

"She's the best, isn't she?" Danielle said in a whisper.

Her murmured words turned into quiet tears, and little

by little, the woman in front of him crumbled. The tears, he suspected, had been a long time coming and had probably been a weakness Danielle hadn't allowed herself. As though they were a sign of admission of defeat or that she needed help.

Tears were never a weakness. In fact, his respect for her grew as he watched her bury her face in her hands and sob out all her demons. It was the sign he'd been waiting for that Danielle knew she had a problem and needed to change.

To offer his comfort, he placed a hand on her shoulder and yanked a tissue from the nightstand. She accepted it from him and dabbed the moisture from her cheeks.

"I'm sorry, R.J. So very sorry," she pleaded.

The desperation in her voice was like an iron-hot poker to his stomach. At one time, he'd cared very much for Danielle, even though what had transpired between them had only been sex. Sure, he'd never loved her, but she deserved better than what she'd done to herself. He wasn't going to try and understand it, nor was he going to ask for an explanation. The only thing she could do now was move forward and try to piece her life back together. And he intended to help her.

"Don't be sorry," he said in a low voice.

She worried her lower lip and played with the tissue in her hands.

"How can I not be? After the way I treated you when you'd only been trying to help me?" More tears leaked out, which she soaked up with the ragged tissue. "Waking up in that hospital bed and watching my daughter cry for me... hearing her ask me if I was going to die."

She broke down again, sobbing into the ragged tissue until all she could do was take deep breaths to gain her composure.

What could he possibly say to her? I'm sorry? It's going to be all right? Don't worry?

He couldn't promise her any of those things, and he

doubted she'd want to hear them anyway. She was in a serious state of self-pity, which was typical of recovering drug addicts.

He handed her another tissue, which she used to wipe her nose. "I'm sorry," she said again.

"Stop saying sorry, Danielle. I just want you to get better. So does Lindsey."

"I know. And I promised her she would never have to see me like that again." She let out a heavy sigh. "She shouldn't have to see me like that in the first place." Her dreary blue gaze shifted to his. "I don't know where I'd be if you hadn't found me. Thank you."

"That's what friends do for each other."

She gave a half laugh, which sounded more like a snort. "Are we friends, R.J.? Even after the way I've treated you?"

"Of course we are. I may have been mad at you, but I still cared." He gently touched her arm. "Besides, I knew it wasn't you. Those pills messed your mind up."

"Even though they're out of my system, I still feel that craving for them." She shifted positions on the bed, scooting herself up higher against the headboard. "I'm restless and anxious and I feel like I'm running a fever."

"That's why you need professional help. This isn't something you can kick overnight from having your stomach pumped. You need to go into a program."

"A program?" she asked with a panicked look on her make-up free face. She was still thin, her cheekbones hollow and her eyes droopier than normal. "I don't know," she went on with a shake of her head. "What if it doesn't work? And what would I do with Lindsey?"

He expected doubt, but wasn't about to stand for it. "The Central Wyoming Counseling Center has a really good reputation. And they do both inpatient and outpatient."

"I couldn't possibly afford something like that. Especially since I don't have a job."

"That's why I'm paying for it," he stated simply, waiting

for the objections to start flying.

"No," she replied in a firm voice. "I can't allow you to do that. Why would you want to after how I've acted?"

He leaned toward her and tucked a chunk of tangled hair behind her ear. "Because you can't go through this alone, and professional help is the only way you're going to get back on your feet. If my paying for it is the only way to accomplish that, then so be it. Besides, you owe it to Lindsey to try."

Her tongue darted out and swiped across her lower lip, which was always a sign of nerves. "I'm scared, R.J."

"I know. But admitting you have a problem is the first step. I'll be there to help you the rest of the way." He squeezed her arm. "I promise."

"I don't deserve your charity," she said in a low whisper.

"Don't do the self-pity thing. You're better than that. And it's not charity." He offered a smile, one he hoped would convey his sincerity. "I'm simply helping out a friend."

"I'll pay you back," she offered.

R.J. shook his head. "No—"

She leaned forward toward him. "Yes. I may be a train wreck right now, but please allow me to have some dignity. I'll pay you back no matter how much it costs."

If nothing else, he had to admire her tenacity and will power to keep her head high, a trait that had run strong in her for as long as he'd known her.

"All right. You can pay me in installments," he added with a grin. "By the way, there aren't any more pills around here, are there?" When she tossed him a scathing look, he held his hands up in defense. "I had to ask."

The small smile she showcased softened her features, although she still looked exhausted and older than her years. "I know. I made Lindsey throw what was left of them out." A defeated sigh slumped her shoulders over. "I hate myself for putting her in that position. She should never have had to do that."

"You're her mother and she loves you no matter what. And she's willing to do anything to get you well." He tilted her chin up with his finger. "You've made some bad choices, but what matters is if you've learned from them."

Her chin trembled with more tears. "Seeing my baby girl cry while I was in that hospital bed was the wakeup call I needed. But even so, I can still feel that God-awful craving. The anxiety and restlessness are killing me." Sweat beaded on her upper lip, which she swiped away with the back of her hand. "I'm all hot and feverish, like I want to come out of my skin."

"You're going through withdrawal. That's why you need professional help." He stood from the bed and checked his watch. "I'm going to call the center as soon as I get home. Hopefully we can get you down there soon."

She nodded, then stopped him when he turned to leave. "Wait a minute. Um…" Her fingers ran along the edge of the comforter, tracing the patterns and working the seams with a nervous movement. "About your friend Rebecca…"

This was the one thing he'd hoped wouldn't come up. Although Rebecca had been a major player in pinpointing Danielle's habit, and Danielle had blamed her, she was still a weird subject for the two of them. R.J. didn't want to talk about her, most of all because his feelings for her were too new. Or maybe they weren't. Maybe his realization of them were too fresh to the point where he needed to digest them some more.

"I was wrong to take my anger out on her. Especially given how you feel about her." She glanced at him from under long lashes, as though she expected him to deny he had any romantic feelings for Rebecca. He supposed, despite how adamant R.J. had been about keeping their relationship professional, Danielle still held out hope they'd get involved. How many other ways did he need to say it? Even if he'd been looking to settle down, it wouldn't be with Danielle. He'd just never felt that way about her. That didn't take away from the fact that she deserved to be with someone who could make her happy. Just not him.

He held up his hand to stop her from going any further into a subject he didn't want to broach. "You don't need to say anymore. And I don't feel..."

What? Was he really about to say he didn't feel anything for Rebecca? Even to Danielle?

"Don't deny it for my sake, R.J.," Danielle argued with a shake of her head, because apparently, he really was that transparent. "Anyone can see how you feel about her. Except maybe you."

He opened his mouth to argue, but she cut him off. "I know this because you look at her the way I wanted you to look at me."

Well, if that wasn't like a knife to the heart, he didn't know what was. "I'm sorry," he said lamely, because what the hell else could he say?

"Don't you dare apologize. I'm not in the right frame of mind to hear you say you're sorry for not loving me." She waved a hand in the air and leaned back against the headboard. "And, anyway, it's not your fault. I knew what I was doing. And I knew what *you* were doing, which wasn't the same thing that I was doing."

"I'm not sure what you mean." *Yeah you do, dumbass.*

Her tongue swiped across her lower lip. "I mean your heart was never in it. Mine was. And I pushed the issue, even though I knew you weren't built that way."

Ah, shit. The fact that she'd hit the nail on the head didn't make him feel any better. "Danielle..."

"It's okay." She shook her head. "I'm not trying to make you feel guilty, or anything. I just wanted to say sorry for the way I treated her."

He cleared his throat because he didn't trust his voice to come out even. Everywhere he went, his love for Rebecca was just... *there.* There was no escaping it, even if he wanted to. Hell, his feelings were even obvious to Danielle.

"I appreciate it." *Now time to get the hell out of here.* "I'll be in touch." On that note, he spun around and stalked down the hallway toward the front door.

"See ya later, kid," he called to Lindsey, who paused in the act of dusting the mini blinds to offer him a smile.

As the sun crept closer to setting and a light breeze settled in, R.J. hoped in his car and left Danielle's house with no particular destination in mind.

The most important thing was clearing his head. If he was going to have a conversation with Rebecca, a much overdue conversation, then he needed to be thinking coherently. She deserved better than some idiot who fumbled over himself just at the sight of her.

Confessing his love for someone wasn't something he had a whole lot of experience in. None, in fact.

What if he screwed it up? What if she'd already decided she didn't want to be with him?

But hadn't she told him she already wanted him?

But wanting someone and wanting to be *with* them weren't the same thing.

Maybe he'd misinterpreted her words. And had she ever actually used the L word? Had he assumed wrong?

Ah, shit. Now he was even more confused than before. Bad enough he didn't know how to handle his feelings, now he wasn't even sure of Rebecca's feelings.

As he left Danielle's neighborhood, R.J. realized he needed to do a lot more thinking before making any monumental announcements.

NINETEEN

R.J. DIDN'T EVEN MAKE it home before his cursed cell phone rang. The thing was one blink away from being chucked into the garbage can, and not because he was tired of it ringing. But because his fingers itched to dial Rebecca's number and he wasn't ready to confront her — yet.

All in due time.

When he knew what the hell he was going to say to her without tripping over his words like an ass.

Could it be that hard to say *I love you*?

Since he'd never said it to a woman before, he had no idea.

He pulled to a red light and picked up his cell phone. His sister's name blinked across the screen, and with it the promise of some rambling story she just *had* to tell him. While he loved her to death, conversations with Courtney had a way of sucking the life out of him. Since there wasn't that much of it in him at the moment, he allowed the call to go to voicemail.

However, as soon as the phone stopped ringing, it started again. He pressed forward when the street light turned green. Damn it all to hell, he wasn't in a conversational mood right now. All he wanted to do was go home, suck down a couple of beers until he passed out.

With a muttered curse, he picked up the phone. "Make it snappy," he demanded.

"Have you seen Rebecca today?" Court asked.

The concern in her voice had his knuckles gripping the steering wheel until they ached. "Not for a couple of days. Why?"

Background noise came from the other end, as though Court were rustling papers, or something equally annoying in his ear. "I don't know. I just talked to her and I can't shake the feeling that something's wrong. It sounded like she'd been crying."

Probably crying over him because he was the jackass who kept pushing her away. "And?"

His sister sighed. One of her annoyed sighs that dragged on for about half an hour. "And, I don't know… Do something. Go tease her until she smiles. You're good at that."

Dark clouds were rolling in from the south, undoubtedly bringing in a spontaneous rainstorm. Or they could be coming to join the dark clouds that were already swirling over his head. He'd gotten so used to their presence that a few more couldn't hurt.

"I'm not sure where you're going with this, Court. Rebecca's had a lot on her mind lately. She's going through some stuff with work."

"I know, that's why I'm worried about her. It's not like her not to talk to me." She paused. "Can you just find her please?"

"Yeah, no sweat. I'll just use my internal GPS tracker that I always use to find people." It was a joke, but so very true when it came to Rebecca.

The expletives that flew from Courtney's mouth would have made a trucker proud. "I'm serious, R.J. You'll find her. You always manage to find Rebecca."

Click.

Beating around the bush was never was one of his sister's strengths. Most of the time he admired that about her. She didn't take shit from anyone and always called it like she saw it. Sort of like him.

But at times like this, he needed her unabashed honesty like he needed a manicure.

Shit.

Just as he pulled in his driveway, where the solitude of his house waited, his cell vibrated.

Text me when you know she's okay.

Ah, hell. Why was he pretending that he was going to go in his house and be all relaxed and shit? He knew damn well he would eventually go after her. Going inside would only delay the inevitable. He'd toss his keys on the kitchen counter, grab a beer, pace for thirty minutes, then get back in his car.

Courtney was right to call him because she knew dropping Rebecca's name would get his attention. Even though he'd pretended otherwise, like he didn't give a damn. As though Rebecca's comings and goings weren't of concern to him.

"Son of a bitch." He tossed the gearshift in reverse, and backed out of the driveway. Without even thinking, he knew where to go because he *did* know Rebecca's comings and goings. In the past, he'd paid way too much attention to her, keeping one proverbial eye on her while trying to manage his own life. It hadn't been easy, serving more of a distraction than pleasing his appetite for her. Nothing pleased his appetite unless he was touching her. Kissing her. Holding her. Slipping deep inside her.

But even that wasn't satisfying. In fact, it was the equivalent of dipping his toe in a refreshing pool on a sweltering day. He needed, no craved, to jump head first, in the deep end and drown himself until he couldn't even see the surface anymore.

He wrapped his right hand around the shifter, tossed it in third gear and cruised toward Crown Liquors. While he had no intention of getting her drunk, he had in mind something that would, at least, put a smile on her face. And really, wasn't that the whole point? Didn't he love to make her smile more than anything else? Rebecca without a grin was like steak without potatoes. Like... apple pie without ice cream.

After grabbing some essentials, R.J. left the liquor store, and headed toward the neighborhood where Lacy used to live. Hopefully the rain would hold off a while longer. The clouds were drawing closer, brought on by the strengthening wind. Getting soaked wasn't in his plans nor did it sound like the least bit of fun.

John T. White Middle School was surrounded by a neighborhood that had been established back in the sixties. The place badly needed repairs and expansions. But the gymnasium was only fifteen years old and hadn't yet reached the decrepit state of the rest of the school. The roof, in particular, seemed to be a popular hangout among kids or anyone looking to get a great view of a sunset or the Fourth of July fireworks. The place had easy access with a ladder on the side of the building that anyone could climb. The school had made no attempt to keep people from making the roof of the gym their second playground. Not even the suicide attempt by a high school student who'd jumped and had only succeeded in breaking his leg.

Rebecca had liked to venture there just like everyone else. He knew she went there sometimes after work to clear her head or watch the sun set. Not that he'd ever followed her. He just *knew*.

He parked in a spot labeled *staff*, grabbed the two bottles from the passenger seat and headed to the ladder that would take him to the roof. Carrying two full bottles of beer while trying to climb wasn't going to be easy, and something he hadn't thought out very well.

"Shit," he muttered as he looked from the ladder to the bottles in each hand. Maybe if he shouted loud enough he could get Rebecca to come down.

Not likely.

She'd gone up there for a reason, most likely to be alone. It would take some coaxing to get her to leave.

He shoved the bottles in his front pockets, praying like hell they wouldn't fall out and shatter on the ground beneath him. Then he would just be the dumb shit who couldn't climb a simple ladder with full pockets. *That* would earn him a smile if nothing else would.

He made it to the roof without any catastrophes and spotted Rebecca right away. Her red hair caught his attention first, with its loose, unruly curls tumbling down her back and almost touching the cement where she sat. He wanted to go to her, grab a fistful of the stuff and bury his nose so deep until her scent intoxicated him. That familiar feeling happened again, the one where his heart shifted inside his chest and threatened to explode. He recognized the phenomenon for what it was, didn't even try to force it away or ignore it. That would only leave him more agitated.

Forcing some semblance of confidence, he walked toward her, carrying both bottles in one hand and thinking of something to say to her. The slump in her shoulders wasn't a good sign, nor was the sniffing. Her knees were tucked to her chest, encased in the cocoon of both her arms. In one hand was a ragged tissue, which she used to wipe both her eyes.

She sniffed again and shoved the tissue away in her pocket. "I knew you'd find me here," she said in a low voice. Its normal singsong beauty was tainted by tears she'd obviously been shedding.

The knowledge that something had sucked the vibrancy out of her had him wanting to smash both the bottles over someone's head.

He sat down next to her and handed her the pumpkin

beer. The sight of her favorite drink brought a momentary smile to her lips. "Where's your car?" he asked.

She twisted the cap off and tossed it aside. "Walked."

He paused with his own bottle halfway to his lips. "You walked here all the way from your house?" That had to have taken at least thirty minutes.

Her delicate throat muscles worked when she chugged a long sip. "Yep," she stated after lowering the bottle.

The corners of his mouth kicked up, then he sampled his own drink. "And what were you going to do when those clouds over there opened up on you?"

A humorless laugh popped out of her. "Get really wet."

"And that was your plan? Come sit on the roof of the middle school gym and get rained on?"

"Didn't really have a plan."

They sat in silence for a few minutes, both watching the dark clouds loom closer and closer. R.J. guessed they had maybe twenty more minutes before the sky let loose.

"Courtney's worried about you," he said. When she didn't answer, he pressed on. "Is something wrong?"

She set the bottle down and hugged her knees closer to her chest. "I don't want to talk about it."

Definitely something going on, but he didn't pressure her. Sometimes the best way to get a person to open up was to leave them alone. "All right."

A low rumble of thunder sounded from the distance. The wind picked up and blew Rebecca's curls around her face and over her shoulders. His arms practically twitched with need to wrap around her shoulders and pull her close. To offer comfort for something he didn't understand. Whatever internal battle she was dealing with had taken the light from her eyes and stained her cheeks with tears.

"Dr. Gross killed himself," she said in a voice so low he almost didn't hear her.

Then, he decided there was no possible way he heard that

correctly. Dr. Gross dead? Suicide?

Before he could ask her to repeat herself, she spoke again in that same defeated voice. "The DEA agent called me."

All the puzzle pieces of her whereabouts and the tears clicked into place.

She blamed herself. He could tell her from now until the end of time that it wasn't her fault. That Patrick Gross had been a grown man who'd made his decisions, fully aware of the consequences should he get caught. And he had gotten caught. Despite Rebecca stumbling across his illegal activities, the authorities would have found out sooner or later. In fact, hadn't Rebecca told him exactly that? That the DEA had already been aware of the prescription fraud going on in the practice? Rebecca had been an innocent bystander, simply doing her job in the wrong place at the wrong time. Yet, she'd been hurt the most, betrayed by someone she should have been able to trust. A mentor was supposed to take their protégé under their wings and teach them everything they knew.

A fresh wave of murderous anger washed over him. At the risk of being an insensitive asshole, R.J. would kill the man all over again if he could.

No one, but no one, put tears in Rebecca Underwood's eyes.

His heart cracked open when she let out a sob and buried her face in her hands. Instead of saying something menial like, "Don't cry," or "It's all right," he put his arm around her and tugged her close. She came without protest, most likely because she didn't have the strength to argue with him or push him away. Her tears dampened the skin on his neck and seeped through his t-shirt. He paid no attention to the trivial thing, and thought he'd soak up a bucket of her tears if it meant consoling her in the least.

Her fingers fisted in his shirt, as though holding onto him was the only thing that gave her strength. The thought, even if it was his own wishful thinking, gave him the illusion of doing even a trivial thing to comfort her.

She cried for several minutes, the sort of sobs that came from some deep, dark place in her soul that she'd locked and thrown away the key to. They shook her whole body and made him feel like a helpless wretch who could only sit there and hold her. When they subsided, only to the point where she could inhale a breath, she lifted her head and wiped her eyes.

"I never meant for any of this to happen," she said through a stream of tears.

"I know. Here." He whipped his shirt over his head, removed his undershirt and handed it to her. The tissue had practically been whittled to dust and wasn't doing her a bit of good. She accepted the shirt, and he put his own button up back on. "You can't sit here and blame yourself. Dr. Gross made his choices."

"I know, but..." She used the hem of his undershirt to dab the excess moisture from her cheeks. Her lips and eyes were swollen, her hair was a tangled mess and he'd never seen anything so beautiful. "I keep thinking maybe if I'd stayed out of it and minded my own business—"

"Things would have ended exactly the same," he reiterated. Her big, green eyes blinked back at him when he took her face in his hands. "You were a victim, Rebecca. Don't ever forget that."

She pressed her eyes closed tight, as though trying to rid herself of the memories. "I just keep thinking about his wife and kids. His grandkids..."

He used his thumbs to swipe away more tears that had leaked out. "He should have thought of them when he dug himself into the hole he was in. Patrick Gross was a nice guy. I liked him a lot. But he made some poor decisions."

She rested her forehead against his. "I still feel so terrible."

"That's because you're human. I'd worry if you didn't

feel anything at all."

The laugh she attempted came out more as a snort. "You probably think I'm some basket case who can't keep her act together."

Was that really all she thought of herself? Was that what she saw when she looked in the mirror, and not a beautiful, intelligent woman?

He forced her gaze by tilting her face up with his hands. "I don't ever want to hear those words come out of your mouth again, understand?" When she nodded, he continued. "You're anything but a basket case, Rebecca. You put yourself through medical school and are the best pediatrician in town. You have the biggest heart of anyone I know and you always put others' feelings before your own. That..." he grazed her bottom lip with the tip of his thumb. "Is what I love most about you."

When her eyes grew wide, the full impact of what he'd said was like punch to the gut. Had he really just used the word *love*? Without even thinking? Had it really been that easy to fall out of his mouth?

At the same time, he didn't want to have this discussion with Rebecca. Neither of them was in the right frame of mind for those kinds of revelations. At least not right now. She was grieving in so many levels and needed some time alone. Just telling her she wasn't responsible for Dr. Gross's actions wouldn't be enough. In order to fully recover, she needed to come to that realization on her own and accept it. That could take time. A lot had happened to her in a short amount of time and her brain hadn't had a chance to play catch up. The fierce release of tears tonight was a start, but there would be more to come.

She'd also need a shoulder to lean on. He'd be that shoulder, and more, if she wanted. But until this cloud cleared, he'd keep things simple between them.

The questions in her eyes were already forming. He knew

her well enough to know that she was already analyzing his words in that over-active brain of hers. Because that's what Rebecca did. She analyzed shit to death until she could fully understand and explain every piece of the puzzle.

Well, he had no intention of explaining anything at the moment. Not even an, "I mean that metaphorically." He needed to get her out of here, not only before they both got drenched, but to get her someplace where she could rest.

And not ask him questions.

He'd take her back to his house.

Yeah, that's good place. Go home where you'll be alone together.

His home may put the two of them in close proximity, but he still felt the need to watch over her and take care of her. To make sure she had everything she needed, including a sturdy shoulder should the waterworks start again.

"Come on," he said, tugging her to her feet. He grabbed both their bottles and pulled her by the hand across the gym roof.

"But—"

"The rain's almost here. We need to get indoors." *Yeah, that's a good excuse. Blame it on the weather.*

A burst of wind shot around them, whipped the strands of Rebecca's hair in front of her face. She let go of his hand so she could hold her hair back to see where she was going.

He climbed down the ladder first, then helped her down, trying not to pay attention to the soft curves of her hips beneath his hands. She kept her eyes on him as they climbed into the car, then pulled away from the school. Just as he got back on the main drag, the rain started. Big, fat drops plopped on his windshield, slowly at first, then gaining speed until they were surrounded by a steady downpour.

"Good thing you came along, or I'd be stuck in this," she muttered.

He glanced at her, while keeping one eye on the sheets of

rain. The moisture in the air had turned her soft curls into wild frizz. The transformation her hair made whenever it rained had always been the bane of Rebecca's existence, and one he'd never failed to give her shit about.

Oddly enough, he'd always liked the unruly frizz and the way it sort of gave her a wild look. It almost reminded him of an old Brooke Shields Calvin Klein ad. In his opinion her curls were her best feature, and he never wanted her to change them.

She didn't protest or question him when they pulled into his driveway. To avoid the rain, he cruised the car into the garage, then got out. He'd planned on opening the door for her, just because he was in a chivalrous mood, but she beat him to it. She either didn't give a shit about chivalry, or she was eager to get inside. He'd guessed it was the former.

She didn't say a word when he went in ahead of her and flipped on some lights.

"Are you hungry?" he asked.

"No," she replied in monotone.

"Thirsty?"

"No."

Her gaze was directed at the floor, but the pulse at the base of her neck beat wildly. Was she expecting him to coax her into bed with him? Could she still be thinking about the L word that he'd accidentally dropped?

She didn't seem to be in a chatty mood, not that he blamed her. So he ushered her down the hall to his room where he turned the lamp on. He felt her gaze on him like a couple of heat-seeking missiles. For some reason, he couldn't bring himself to look at her because he'd see the knowledge in her eyes. The fact that she knew how he felt about her, and she knew damn well that he knew. It was an odd feeling, wanting to comfort her and get the hell away from her all at the same time. Like his mind and his body were pulling him in two different directions and the result was a bitch of a headache.

He had no idea if she even wanted a bath, but he needed to do something to occupy her so he could slink away and think.

The tub in the bathroom had jets and all sorts of gadgets he'd never used. Courtney had talked him into putting the thing in. But honestly, what red-blooded man sat in a bathtub with massagers and neon lights and shit?

Rebecca would no doubt be into it, so he ran warm water. When the tub was full enough, he pushed the button to activate the jets, then draped a towel over the side.

"I don't have bubbles or any of that stuff," he told her. She'd moved to the bathroom doorway and just stood there. She was just leaning against the jamb with her arms hanging down at her sides like she didn't give a damn about anything. Which she probably didn't. The ends of her hair hung down over her breasts, and he tried not picturing her naked with her bare boobs hidden by her silky curls

You're supposed to be comforting her. Not growing a hard on.

"There's a towel here." He gestured lamely behind him, because he didn't know what the hell else to do. Or what to say.

Her silence wasn't making the situation any easier. The blank stare pinning him down was like a different person looking back at him. It had to be shock. The reality of Dr. Gross's death was hitting her hard and she didn't know how to deal with it.

"Take as long as you need." He moved toward her and almost made it out of the bathroom when she grabbed his hand.

She lifted those gloomy green eyes up to him and the sight damn near ripped his heart through his ribcage.

"When you're done, just grab whatever you can find to sleep in and take my bed. I'll sleep in the other room."

Her brows tugged together in confusion. "You're going to leave me in here alone?"

Ah, shit why did she have to ask him like that? Didn't she know how hard it was for him to keep his hands off her? His will power was on overload just trying to stay out of touching distance. Then she had to go and touch his hand, gaze at him and use that soft voice that felt like a caress over his skin.

He was trying to be noble, but she was making it damn impossible to keep his good intentions up.

"I think it would be for the best," he managed to say. How his voice came out that even, he had no effing clue.

And then, damn it all to hell, what was left of his will power snapped. Her skin just looked too damn luminescent and soft. With his free hand, he touched her cheek, cupping her cool and delicate jaw, trying his hardest to keep the contact at a light stroke. His jeans grew tight from just skimming the side of her face with his hand.

This was why he needed to leave her alone tonight. With the way he was feeling, he'd likely be rough with her and she didn't need that. She needed time to heal, not some oaf like him manhandling her and pinning her to the mattress until her thighs quivered.

On that thought, he dropped his hand and walked away from her.

TWENTY

NORMALLY, THE PATTER OF rain on the windows and the low rumble of thunder coaxed her to sleep like a baby's lullaby. And tonight, more than any other night, Rebecca needed that gentle nudge into the blissful REM stage where she could lose herself with dreams. Reality didn't exist in dreams. Only the edge of her subconscious where the fanciful and ridiculous reined.

The rain against the windows was doing its job to create that relaxing atmosphere. Her mind had other plans, and those did not include getting some much needed shut eye. Anxiety coursed through her blood like a poison, causing an uneasy restlessness that had her flip-flopping all over the mattress. The sheet, although soft and probably had a five-hundred thread count, felt like sandpaper against her skin. But the full blast air conditioning made sleeping without any sort of barrier damn near unbearable. Why did R.J. have to set his thermostat so low?

Probably because the man was a natural furnace.

All that muscle generated enough heat that the harsh Wyoming winters were probably of no concern to him.

She ought to know.

Too many times in recent weeks she'd felt them up close, under her fingertips and pressed against her body. She'd been especially aware of them tonight, straining against R.J.'s soft gray t-shirt, begging to be stripped free of their constraints so she could savor them.

Then she'd remember how R.J. found her and the state she'd been in, and all her erotic thoughts dissipated. Not only that, but she felt like the worst person in the world. The lowest of the low. Pond scum. Amoeba. The fungus that lives on the pond scum and feeds off the amoeba.

A man was dead. His family torn apart, his wife and children grieving, not understanding why he would take his own life. So many questions unanswered and Dr. Gross had taken most of those answers with him when he'd put a pistol to his head. Rebecca had never understood what went through a person's mind in the moments before they ended their lives. Were they sorry? Had they any idea of the impact their death would have? Why had they felt there was no other way out?

She supposed, now, all that was moot. Dr. Gross was dead and nothing would change that. And even though she knew it was irrational, she still felt responsible. As though she'd been the one to place the gun in his hands. And an even worse feeling, he'd been more than just a boss. He'd been a friend who'd taken her under his wing and had promised her the thing dearest to him: His practice.

Oh Lord, the practice. What would happen to it now? All their employees and patients? What was to become of her?

A fresh wave of grief and helplessness stole what was left of her peaceful mind. She rolled over to face the window as another tear leaked out and rolled to the pillow beneath her. Funny, but she didn't think she had anything left inside her to shed. So many tears already, and yet she still had it in her to pour out. She used the edge of the sheet to dry her cheek, but more tears came. They didn't stop for as much as she tried to hold them back.

For several minutes she cried silently, the moisture running down her cheeks mimicking the rain streaming down the windows. One was supposed to have a calming effect and the other... well, not calming. Just another metaphorical contradiction like everything else in her life.

When she couldn't stand anymore and had resigned herself to the fact that she couldn't sleep, she tossed the sheet aside and got out of the bed. The only thing that had held her there that long had been the seductive scent of R.J. lingering on the linens.

Another ironic contradiction was the smell of him driving her from the bed. Because every time she rolled over, another memory of them fought for space in her mind. She couldn't lie where the two of them had lain, making love, and expect to slip into a restful sleep.

If she couldn't will herself to sleep, maybe she could just tire herself the old-fashioned way.

The master bedroom was apart from the other bedrooms in the house. She strolled through the dark living room, dodging a pair of R.J.'s running shoes, and went to the kitchen. The pitch dark was so absolute that it was a freakin' miracle she hadn't tripped over something and twisted her ankle. She flipped the kitchen light on and opened the fridge. Several bottles of water sat on the middle shelf. She snagged one, twisted the cap and took a long chug. The liquid was ice cold and felt like sweet honey going down her throat. She hadn't realized how thirsty she'd been until the cool water had touched her lips.

After draining half the bottle, she replaced the cap and set it back on the shelf. R.J's fridge was surprisingly full for just one man. Most of the contents were leftover containers filled with food he'd cooked. A smile touched her lips at the memory of him feeding her pulled pork. Who knew R.J. Devlin turned into Emeril Lagasse in the kitchen?

Curiosity had her picking up one of the containers and lifting the lid. Fried chicken with gravy. Another container was full of mashed potatoes. A gallon sized plastic bag held about a pound of sliced brisket.

The man sure liked his meat. He also liked his leftovers. Why in the world did he cook so much?

Ketchup, mustard, BBQ sauce, and an industrial-sized container of mayonnaise lined the shelves. All manly food. Why had she expected any less?

The freezer was almost empty, holding nothing more than a bag of ice and some frozen pizzas. No ice cream, popsicles or anything sweet. Actually nothing that was found in her freezer was anywhere in R.J.'s. Complete opposite. Kind of typical given their relationship.

The door closed with a soft thump, and she turned from the kitchen. On the coffee table were several issues of *Sports Illustrated*. She picked up the top issue and thumbed through it. There was an article on some hot new rookie pitcher, photos of football players tackling each other, and the editor's picks on the wild card race in baseball. Honestly, who read this stuff? How could anyone possibly find it interesting?

Obviously R.J. did, given his collection. Meat and sports. Pretty much all man that pumped through his veins like his life's blood.

But wasn't that why she was so crazy in love with him? Why would she want to change any of that?

And, wasn't he just down the hall? Only about twenty steps and she'd be in his room. Where he was in bed. Probably naked. Because she knew he slept naked. The sheets were most likely kicked to the floor, leaving nothing but all that bronzed, perfect flesh that covered hard sinew and toned muscle. His good genes afforded him a low percent of body fat. However low, she had no idea, but it was, like, nonexistent. Her tongue and tips of her fingers knew just how little fat obscured the chiseled muscle.

R.J.'s bed was so big; too big, really, for just one person. And the sheets were cold without him. Why would she want to go back to that, alone? She knew what he was doing, trying to give her space.

He thought she needed time, and she did. But not by herself. She needed him, needed to feel his strong, reassuring body pressed against hers. His unwavering presence and constant strength were the only things proven to chase away her gloom. And as much as she loved feeling him inside her, it wasn't even about sex. She just needed to be near him. To know that no matter how many things went awry in her life, R.J. Devlin was the one thing she could count on to always be there. Because he'd always been there. Even when he hadn't, he'd still been there.

As weird and backward as that was, it somehow made sense to Rebecca. He was her lighthouse in the dark storm that always tossed her against the rocks.

His words *I think it would be for the best,* floated through her mind as Rebecca walked to the other side of the living room and passed through the rounded archway that led to a hall. There were three doors. One she knew was the bedroom and the middle one was probably a bathroom. She had no idea what the last one could be, nor did she care to contemplate it. The first door, which she knew was the guest room, was closed. The blasted thing squeaked when she opened it, which would no doubt alert R.J. to her presence.

She knew him to be a light sleeper. Another area where they were opposites, because she was a very deep sleeper. His form on the bed was discernible, even in the pitch dark. The drapes were pulled closed and the ceiling fan spun at jet-propulsion speeds even though the air had to be set at an uncomfortable seventy-three. Honestly, how could he stand to have that much cold air blowing on him?

Not only that, one sheet was pulled up halfway so the thing barely covered the goods in between his thighs. Good

Heavens, the man looked like he was doing a photo shoot for some men's calendar. Nude, sculpted chest and wide shoulders completely bare, taking up most of the bed. Arms spread out at his sides with heavy biceps roughly the size of tree trunks. And there. Right *there,* the edge of the dark patch of hair just peeking above the top of the sheet. One tug and she'd get an eye full of lean hips and all sorts of other goodies she could *not* think about.

On second thought, maybe this was a bad idea.

"Come or go, just make up your mind."

His deep voice, rough from sleep, startled her out of the silence of the bedroom. A second ago his eyes had been closed and now he stared at her from beneath heavy lids.

"I couldn't sleep, and..." *And what?* "I couldn't sleep," she said again, as if there was some other reason she'd be prowling his house in the middle of the night.

Without saying a word, he used his left hand to toss back the sheet on the empty side of the bed. She took that as an invitation and crawled onto the plush mattress beside him. The heat radiating off his body was already warming her in the way she needed it to. As soon as she got next to him, all the tension that had been humming through her body eased away by slow degrees. Just his heavy weight on the mattress next to her was enough to bring a blissful smile to her lips.

This was what she needed. No seduction or kisses or softly spoken words. Just being next to him was enough.

The both lay on their backs, staring at the ceiling, neither talking nor moving. Then, she couldn't stand the isolation or the silence anymore. She couldn't be this close to him and not touch him. She rolled over, rested her head on his outstretched arm and curled up against his side.

His warm skin smelled of soap, the same familiar scent she always associated with him. It surrounded her in a sensual masculinity that had always been the hook, line, and sinker. Even though she hadn't come to his room to seduce him or be seduced, her body still reacted. Heat gathered between her legs, which she tried to ignore. All she wanted was a good night's sleep.

Slowly, his arm came around her, as though he were hesitant to have too much contact with her. His noble intentions were still in the forefront but at the same time he wanted to touch her. At least that's what she told herself and that his contact with her wasn't out of pity.

His hand came to rest on her hip and he gently nudged her even closer.

"Better?" he asked in a gruff voice.

He had no idea. "Yes," she replied. She bent her knee and draped her leg across his. The movement had caused the sheet to slip, uncovering the impressive package beneath.

"I'm naked," he announced.

An amused smile tugged at the corners of her mouth. "I know."

He yanked the sheet back up, as though the sight of him stark naked was inappropriate. Frankly, she'd never minded looking at R.J. in the nude. However, this time she was grateful for the discretion because seeing his stuff hanging out there had been a major distraction.

Now she could focus on getting some shut eye and not mounting him like a wild animal.

His free hand cupped her head and massaged the back of her skull. She couldn't remember the last time someone had taken care of her like this, or had simply known what to do. The pressure of his fingers digging into her scalp was hypnotic and had her eyelids growing heavy.

The rain outside picked up, beating against the window even harder than before. A clap of thunder shook the house, jerking her out of her relaxed state. R.J.'s fingers didn't let up, but continued to knead the back of her head, as though he sensed the growing tension in her body.

"Relax," he whispered. His fingers threaded through her

hair, dragging all the way to the ends and starting over again. "Just try and go to sleep."

A flash of light illuminated the room for a split second, followed by another crack of thunder. Instead of allowing the jarring sound to suck away her euphoria, she focused on R.J. and his hands. His voice. The thump of his heart beneath her hand, the steady rise and fall of his chest.

After a moment, her eyes drifted shut and her muscles relaxed, despite the storm warring outside. R.J.'s magic had succeeded in making her feel human again. She loved him for that and the words were on the tip of her tongue, dying to come out and let him know just how she felt about him.

However, Rebecca wasn't one hundred percent sure how he felt about her. One minute she was sure he returned her love, and the next she was second guessing herself. Oh, she knew he had some feelings for her. And she was pretty sure they resembled some kind of love. But suspecting and hearing them for sure were two different things.

Once bitten, twice shy. Years ago, she'd gone out on a huge limb and told him she loved him. A stupid act that had been part of the afterglow of their love-making. He'd rejected her, flat out. Told her she needed to save her love for someone who could give it in return. Yes, they'd been so young, but the insecurity his denial had caused remained with her to this day.

There wasn't a part of her that wished to revisit that. So, she kept her feelings to herself. And waited. Just like always.

R.J.'s chest expanded when he pulled in a deep breath. He was still wide awake because he wasn't allowing his body to relax.

Was he not at ease lying next to her like this? Was he sacrificing his own comfort to make her feel better? That hadn't been her intention, but at the same time the idea surrounded her heart with a warm feeling.

"What does R.J. stand for?" she asked him, mostly because she needed to hear his voice.

Silence stretched between the two of them, then he finally answered. "Roland James." His thumb slid over the back of her neck. "I've never told anyone that before."

She was pretty sure she fell asleep with a smile on her lips.

****

The storm had finally passed, leaving nothing but faint rumbles of thunder in the distance. The sun had yet to rise, but her body told her morning wasn't far. Years of getting up before the sun had trained her mind to pull out of sleep at ungodly hours. These early hours were no different than any other day, except for one thing:

The man curled around her, pressing his hard thighs to the back of hers.

His thick arms enclosed her in a shelter of his warmth and strength. He shifted, pressing even closer to her, the rough hair on his legs grating against her bare ones. She let out a content sigh when he dropped a kiss to the curve between her shoulder and neck.

Then he was gone. Pulling away from her and the quiet solitude that precluded sleep was yanked away. He left the bed without a word. Not a, "I'll be right back," or "Try to go back to sleep."

Hadn't they moved past this?

He must have seen the questions in her eyes, which she hated. Her best poker face was laughable and probably more like a neon sign on her forehead.

With gentle and slow movements, he pulled the covers over and tucked her in. All nice and sweet. Kind of like a big brother.

It made her want to scream.

The soft caress to her face stopped any protest that had been moments away from flying out of her mouth. Her eyes dropped closed and she turned her face into his palm, unable to stop herself from reacting to his touch. The man was leaving her again. She knew it. He knew it. And yet, she still savored any sort of minimal contact from him, as though he was going to change his mind and climb back into bed with her.

"Go back to sleep," he whispered.

Her heart dropped to the bottom of her stomach when he left the room, shutting her in the darkness by herself. And, suddenly, her melancholy turned into a full blown ache in her chest when she realized what had just happened. The intimacy they'd shared from simply sleeping next to each other had been about an expression of love.

He'd been saying good-bye.

TWENTY-ONE

THE AFTERMATH OF THE storm left an overcast day with tepid temperatures and a gusty breeze. The overall effect was gloomy, which matched Rebecca's state of mind. Just as R.J. had commanded, she'd gone back to sleep, only because the few hours she'd already caught had been insufficient. When she'd woke a few minutes past seven a.m., the house had been eerily quiet. R.J. had gone, leaving nothing more than a handwritten note in his wake.

She'd supposed he'd written it to make her feel better. At one point in time it probably would have. Call her crazy, but she felt like they'd moved past the casual one-nighter they seemed to repeat over and over again. The commitment thing was still a hang up for him, and she'd be damned if she'd let him slink away that easily.

It's not like she was asking for a wedding ring. Just a shot at something more.

However, the note he scrawled made sure she knew he'd be busy all day. His cop-out way of hiding from her.

I'll be at the shop all day. Sleep in if you want and help yourself in the kitchen. Talk to ya later.

Talk to ya later. Like they were all chummy with each other. As though he hadn't spent the night gracing her with soft kisses, easing her anxiety and holding her while she cried.

Coward.

Fine. She'd give him some time, if that's what he wanted. But sooner, rather than later, she'd come after him. They needed to have an all-out, and she'd force him to come clean with his feelings for her. Until then, she'd bide her time.

Plus, the free time gave her the opportunity to do something she'd been contemplating for the past several weeks.

Whether or not visiting Danielle was a smart idea, Rebecca felt like it needed to be done. The two of them had gotten off on a serious wrong foot and maybe the woman had the wrong impression about her. Rebecca was a people person who strived to get along with everyone. Danielle had been the first person she'd met who'd outright hated her. Such negativity was a foreign thing for Rebecca, and she couldn't stand it.

Who knew if the woman would actually speak to her, but Rebecca couldn't let it go without at least trying. Under any other circumstances the two women may have been friends.

Luckily she'd been able to look up Danielle's address through Lindsey's medical file. Not a very kosher thing to do, but what the hell?

On her way, she stopped at the market, picked up a bouquet of flowers and purchased a vase to arrange them in. They were cheerful, something that was seriously lacking in the current weather. Hopefully they would at least put a smile on Danielle's face and convince her that Rebecca wasn't the devil.

Danielle lived on a heavily tree-lined street with old fashioned lamp posts and cracked sidewalks. Her home was on the small-side with a one-car garage and overgrown bushes. She slid her car along the curb and got out. A tabby cat with a sagging belly came *this* close to tripping her, which would have ended with the vase of flowers shattering to the cement. Somehow she managed to hold on to them and retrieve the day's newspaper from the front stoop.

Flowers and a newspaper.

She should at least get a half smile.

The newspaper slipped from under the crook of her arm when she rang the bell. The stupid thing fell out of the plastic, forcing Rebecca to set the flowers down so she could shove the paper back in the bag. The door opened in time for her to gather both items and right herself so she didn't look an idiot.

The last thing she needed was to make her already unfavorable impression get worse.

"Hi," Rebecca greeted with what she hoped was a friendly smile.

The shock of Danielle's appearance threatened to wipe that grin away. The other woman didn't look at all the way she did the last time Rebecca had seen her.

A few weeks ago, her hair had been shiny, if not a little ratty and she'd been about ten pounds heavier. Presently, her dull black hair was pulled back in a sloppy bun with wayward strands hanging out all over the place. Her sallow skin and heavy-lidded eyes made Danielle look ten years older than she really was. And a sharp collar bone protruded from the neckline of her baggy t-shirt.

All in all she didn't even remotely resemble the same stunning woman Rebecca had been mildly jealous of.

She held the newspaper out. "I picked up your paper for you."

Danielle eyed the thing as though Rebecca were trying to hand her a poisonous snake. Did the woman really think so little of her?

Thoughts of leaving had just entered her mind, when Danielle's features softened and she accepted the plastic bag. "Thanks."

Hurdle one crossed.

Now if she could just get inside and say her piece.

"Can I come in?" Rebecca asked when Danielle made no attempt to move the conversation further.

"All right."

The admission came much faster than she expected. Danielle stood back, allowing Rebecca to enter, and closed the door behind them. She tossed the newspaper down, probably because she had no intention of reading it. Whatever. At least Rebecca had tried.

"I just wanted to come by and..." She glanced around and tried not to grimace at the cluttered, unkempt state of the home. "Well, I just wanted to see how you were doing."

Danielle crossed her arms over her chest, a classic defensive move. "I'm unemployed and just had my stomach pumped. So not too well."

Wait, stomach pumped? What was she talking about? R.J. hadn't mentioned anything about Danielle having an overdose. Unless he hadn't known.

"R.J. found me," Danielle added, as though she'd read Rebecca's mind. "If it hadn't been for him, I'd probably be dead."

Okay, so he had known. Not only that, he'd been the one to find her and get her in the hospital. Why hadn't he shared that information with her?

The omission was like a dull, rusty knife twisting in her heart. She shoved the feeling aside, which wasn't easy, and tried to think of something appropriate to say. "I'm sorry," she muttered.

You're sorry?

She was a doctor for crying out loud! Her days had been spent comforting people and putting their minds at ease. And all she could think to say was sorry?

"I mean," she stumbled. "It's a good thing R.J. found you." Okay, that sounded slightly more sensitive.

And just what was R.J. doing here in the first place? He hadn't mentioned anything about coming to see the woman he used to sleep with.

Really? You're going to be jealous right now?

Danielle shrugged the words off. "It was my own fault. Anyway, it was the wakeup call I needed."

Rebecca almost said "good" but held herself back at the risk out shoving her foot in her mouth again.

Instead, she held out the vase of flowers. "I wanted to give you these. As sort of a peace offering," she added. "I think we just got off on the wrong foot with each other. I don't know about you, but it's kind of been eating away at me."

Judging by the look on Danielle's face, it hadn't been eating away at her. In fact, she probably enjoyed it.

To Rebecca's surprise, Danielle accepted the flowers and lowered her nose to a Carnation.

"They're really beautiful," she said in a sort of soft tone Rebecca hadn't heard from her before. "That was nice of you."

The kind words eased some of Rebecca's worries, but not completely. It had only been few minutes. Plenty of time still for Danielle to toss Rebecca out the door.

However, she planned on doing what she could to make amends with R.J.'s former employee.

"So, how are you doing now?" She wished she could say Danielle looked good, but Rebecca couldn't bring herself to embellish that much. Besides, she was a terrible liar. Best to keep the words to herself.

Danielle placed the vase of flowers on an end table and turned the glass around in a half circle. "I'm pretty weak. Basically I'm trying to keep things together until I go into a program."

Rebecca took a step toward her. "You're going into a program? That's great." The news was just about the best thing she'd heard all day. Or all week, for that matter.

"Yeah, listen..." Danielle's gaze darted around the room.

It touched on the flowers, the muted television in the corner, then the floor. "I've been thinking about everything's that happened and... well, I just wanted to apologize for the way I treated you. I never gave you a fair chance, and that was wrong of me."

O-kay. *That*, she was not expecting. While the admission sounded completely heartfelt, it totally threw her off-guard. True, Danielle hadn't given Rebecca a fair chance. And she hadn't been entirely friendly. But after a while, Rebecca hadn't cared about hearing the other woman say sorry. She just wanted to put things with each other on the right track.

Rebecca cleared her throat and tried to think of what to say without sounding ungrateful. "I really appreciate that, but you don't need to say you're sorry."

"Yes, I do," Danielle said with her eyes closed. "This isn't easy for me, so just bear with me."

Rebecca nodded and kept her mouth shut.

Danielle ran the tip of her fingernail over the wood grain of the end table. "I wasn't in a good place when we met." She inhaled a deep breath and pressed her lips together. "I didn't like the way R.J. looked at you. I saw you as a threat, and I disliked you on sight."

Well, then. She'd known part of the problem had been Danielle's feelings for R.J., but Rebecca certainly hadn't expected that kind frankness. Though it wasn't a surprise.

"Okay," Rebecca said, because what else could she say? She hadn't exactly liked Danielle either.

She slanted Rebecca a look out of the corner of her eyes. "He loves you," Danielle said, matter-of-factly. "I know because I used to look at him the same way he looks at you."

A wave of heat washed up to her cheeks. "I really don't think—"

"Yes, you do." Danielle turned to face her with her arms crossed over her chest. "Like I said, this isn't easy for me. I knew when I got involved with R.J. that it was a bad idea."

She laughed but the sound wasn't genuine. "I really have no one to blame but myself."

Rebecca didn't say anything. Couldn't, really, even if she wanted to.

Danielle licked her lips. "The relationship ended long before I wanted it to. Actually, I guess you could say there never was a relationship. At least not that R.J. wanted."

With those words, Rebecca remembered what R.J. had said to her about his fling with Danielle being only sex and no feelings. At the time, Rebecca had been willing to bet all the money in her bank account that hadn't been true for Danielle. So hearing her say the words wasn't shocking. As one woman to another, Rebecca totally understood where Danielle came from.

In fact, for the first time since she'd met the woman, Rebecca had a semblance of understanding for Danielle. One might even say that Rebecca felt sorry for her. Both had loved the same man, both had been heartbroken by him.

That feeling wasn't easy to forget, nor was it easy to get over. Years of practice had made Rebecca a pro at that.

She took a closer study of the woman standing a few feet away from her. Danielle must have been in much deeper than Rebecca had originally thought. Sure, she'd come off as bitchy and abrasive, but she'd been recovering from having her heart trampled by one very sexy man.

Who was Rebecca to say how a person grieved from that sort of loss? And it was a loss, no doubt about that. One that could take years to get over. It had been years for Rebecca. Danielle only mirrored on the outside what Rebecca felt on the inside.

"Danielle—"

"You don't need to say anything." She held up a hand and shook her head. "I know the two of you are involved, and I need to just get over it. But the point I'm trying to make is that it was wrong of me to judge you the way I did."

Rebecca slowly nodded, waiting for the "but" to come. "Okay. Thank you," she said.

"Don't thank me yet. There's something else I need to confess."

Just as Rebecca expected. And she had a feeling she knew what was coming next.

Danielle's nervous energy was like a third person in the room with them. She fiddled with the flowers, touching the petals and adjusting the bow tied around the vase. Then she righted a stack of magazines that had fallen to the floor. Once she had them stacked neatly, she moved to the throw pillows on the couch, fluffing them, which really didn't do a whole lot to improve their appearance.

While Danielle bounced from one thing to the next, Rebecca waited.

"I've made some really poor choices that I'm not proud of," Danielle finally said. Her attention was on a picture of Lindsey, which hung on a wall. "I mean, I honestly didn't think I was hurting anyone."

That's what most drug addicts thought. They rarely took their loved one's feelings into consideration.

Danielle, like most addicts, probably thought she'd been different from other people who suffered from the same problem. The truth was she was exactly the same.

"I didn't realize how much harm I actually caused," the other woman said in a quiet voice. Then she pinned Rebecca with her pale blue eyes. "I'm sorry about you losing your medical license. That was entirely my doing."

Bingo. The exact words she'd been waiting to hear. Drugs had made Danielle completely irrational and desperate, a common side effect of abusing. Not to mention paranoid. Rebecca had posed a threat to Danielle's safe little bubble, and she'd done what she felt had been necessary. Which didn't justify her actions by any means. But Rebecca didn't hold Danielle solely responsible. Dr. Gross had created the problem. Now he was dead, and hopefully Rebecca could work on putting things right again.

Despite that, she listened to Danielle's confession, knowing the woman needed to get the words out.

"When you came along, asking your questions, it scared me," Danielle said. She turned from the photos on the wall, but still wouldn't look Rebecca in the eye. "I didn't know what to do, so I panicked. I'm not saying what I did was right. Calling the DEA and dropping your name was crossing a line that I never intended to cross."

And doing drugs wasn't crossing the line?

"But I was afraid Dr. Gross would go to jail, and I'd lose my security blanket."

Rebecca took a step forward and tried to force down the resentment that threatened to overflow. "And you thought trying to get me sent to jail for something I didn't do was okay?"

Danielle lifted her tear-filled eyes to Rebecca. "I know what I did was wrong. I understand that now. But at the time I wasn't thinking clearly and…" She shrugged. "I guess it doesn't really matter now. I just needed to tell you how sorry I am and hopefully one day you can forgive me."

Well, it was a start, even if Rebecca wasn't completely enamored. Her life had been turned upside-down, and her name would never have come up if it hadn't been for Danielle. But she appreciated the attempt to make amends and was willing to acknowledge that much at least.

"I appreciate that," she responded. Danielle hadn't acted like she had any clue of Dr. Gross's death, and Rebecca decided to keep the news to herself. His passing was still fresh in her own mind, and Danielle looked like she couldn't handle much else on her plate. In fact, she looked a hair away from cracking, and the suicide news would likely send her over the edge. Or back on drugs.

Rebecca glanced at her watch, as though she had other

pressing issues to attend to. The truth was, she wanted out of there. "I need to get going so... yeah," she stated and turned toward the door. Danielle made no effort to keep Rebecca from leaving. Apparently she felt the conversation had run its course also.

When Rebecca reached the door, she paused with her hand on the knob. "I'm glad you're getting the help you need. Good luck with everything."

The half-smile on Danielle's face was the friendliest thing Rebecca had seen from her since meeting the woman. "Thank you. And good luck to you too."

Rebecca stepped out into the cool air, thankful that unpleasant experience was now over with. She'd wanted to right things between them, which she had. Even if it wasn't exactly the start of a new friendship, at least she could move on.

But she couldn't entirely move on, because there were still so many lose ends to tie up. What would happen to the practice now that Dr. Gross was dead? And what of the DEA's investigation? Would they continue even though their prime suspect was no longer living?

All those questions had been dying for answers, but Agent Reinhold had rushed her off the phone the other day. Her frustration coupled with grief had caused nothing but speechlessness while his phone had gone "click" in her ear. Since then, she'd meant to call him back but hadn't been in the right frame of mind for that conversation. But still, she deserved some kind of conclusion other than "Patrick Gross took his own life."

How much longer could she live in limbo like this? Were they still planning on questioning her? Letting her keep her license?

Even though the prescription fraud was over, it wasn't quite over for her.

As she opened her car door, her cell phone rang from

inside her purse. She practically dove for it, thinking it would be R.J., saying something like, "I'm desperately in love with you, let's run off and get married." And since that wasn't likely anyway, Rebecca wasn't surprised to see it wasn't him.

The number wasn't local, but she knew it to be Agent Reinhold's. With her heart in her throat, she answered the call.

"Hello?"

"Dr. Underwood, it's Agent Reinhold with the DEA," he clarified, as though she knew some other Agent Reinhold who would be calling her. "I apologize for rushing you off the phone the other day. And normally I would bring you in to talk to you in person, but I'm swamped right now and wanted to reach you as soon as possible."

As ominous as that sounded, Rebecca held her breath and told herself that nothing else could go possibly wrong. "All right," she said as she slid into behind the wheel and started the car.

There was some rustling in the background, followed by other voices. Agent Reinhold muttered something to someone, then spoke to her. "I wanted to inform you that we are officially closing our investigation and I'm being reassigned."

Rebecca just about crashed into the curb when she backed out of the driveway. They were closing the investigation? "Wait, are you serious? You're really closing the case?"

"Well, our suspect is deceased. There's nothing left for us to investigate." His words were so matter of fact, as though she should have figured it out on her own.

"As for you," he continued. "You'll be receiving your license back along with all your files. The process could take a few weeks, so bear with us. We're overworked and underpaid." His chuckle wasn't infectious, nor was the joke funny. Even though it was good news, Rebecca couldn't bring herself to laugh at anything involving what had happened.

She made a left at the stop sign and adjusted her grip on the cell phone. "I'm really getting my license back? Just like that? And I can go back to work?"

Agent Reinhold waited before answering. "I know this wasn't an easy thing for you, Dr. Underwood. And we never considered you a serious suspect. Really, you were nothing more than a witness for us. Suspending your license is standard procedure and had nothing to do with guilt on your part. I apologize for leading you to believe that, but when you're running an investigation, you can't go around sharing details like that. But now that the case is closed, I can be more forthcoming with you."

"I understand," she said, trying to see his side of things when her fear had obscured her vision and her confidence in the system. "But how can I go back to practicing medicine, when there's no practice to go back to? All our patients have been referred to another pediatrician."

"I agree, that is another matter entirely. But between you and me, the practice is up for sale."

"Up for sale?" Her grip on the phone tightened. "What do you mean?"

"You know Dr. Gross owned that building, right?"

"Yes."

"When I spoke with Mrs. Gross I got the impression she was going to sell the building and the practice along with it. Might be something you want to look into."

Buying the medical practice? Her? Although she'd always dreamed of running her own place, it had never occurred to her to buy one out. But her student loans alone were overwhelming enough.

"I'm not sure," she considered. "All our patients are gone. It could take years to rebuild the kind of base we had."

"Sounds like you have some thinking to do. But I would imagine the other pediatrician in town is probably overwhelmed with all the new patients they have. He might be happy to hand them back to you. I would even imagine he'd be more than thrilled to have you on staff."

Yes, going to another practice was something she'd considered. She could just step in and not have to worry about building the place from the ground up. On the other hand, it wouldn't be her own.

"I appreciate you calling," she said, because anything else was too much for her brain to handle.

"Just doing my job, Dr. Underwood. And for the record, I'm sorry for the way things ended."

His words sounded genuine, as did the tone of his voice. And really, none of this was his fault. As he said, he had just been doing his job.

"Thank you."

She disconnected the call, and set her phone down.

The storm had passed, but she still felt the after-effects of the rain and thrashing wind. What was it she really wanted?

Running her own practice was her ultimate dream, but pulling together the cash could be difficult. A mortgage and student loans was more than enough debt than she wanted to deal with. Did she really want to add more loans on top of it?

If she joined the other practice, she could jump right in and go back to treating all her patients. And, really, that was the most important part for her. She'd worked hard to build some lasting relationships with some amazing children. Not to mention their parents. Interacting with those children on a daily basis was what she missed most.

As she turned toward her neighborhood, Agent Reinhold's words came back to her. Yes, she definitely had some things to think about.

TWENTY-TWO

THE RE-BUILD FROM HELL was officially over. At 10:15 last night, R.J. and his guys had put the finishing touches on all three of Charlie's cars. After pulling all-nighters for two straight weeks, they'd managed come in on time and only slightly over budget. That part was a miracle in itself, considering the man kept calling and adding on more stuff. R.J.'s patience had barely remained in check when Charlie had called at the last minute and changed the paint color for the Mercedes.

Sam had threatened to quit if Charlie so much as added an extra seatbelt. R.J. had to remind the kid of the big, fat paycheck that was going to put an enormous smile on all their faces. With those words, Sam had wisely shut the hell up.

They could all breathe collective sighs of relief. Donald Underwood's car was finished, so four of their cars would be gone today, significantly lightening their workload. Maybe he'd take a few days off and figure some shit out. Like the fact that it was way past time for him to set things straight with Rebecca. Two and a half weeks ago he'd left her in his guest bed.

Two and a half weeks since he'd felt that soft skin and

inhaled the sweet honey scent of her hair. Two and a half weeks too long if you asked him. But he'd needed time to make sense of his feelings and figure out a way to put them into words. Not to mention he'd been working his ass off. From six a.m. to midnight every night trying to finish Charlie's cars. By the time he left work, standing on his own two feet was challenging enough without adding an emotional conversation to the mix. Especially since he had little to no experience with emotional conversations.

He needed to be prepared, and now that his biggest project was done, he'd have more time on his hands.

Last week, when she'd come in to pay the remaining balance on her father's car, R.J. had had to shove his hands in his pockets to keep them to himself. Her springy curls had been loose and especially touchable. And there'd been a light in her eyes that hadn't been there the last time he'd seen her. Then the light became uncertain when she'd seen him, as though she was just as unsure about where they stood as he was.

She was probably waiting for him to make the first move. And she was right. He should. Especially since she'd already told him she wanted to be with him. But shit, he had no experience with this. He'd never found a woman worth staying with, much less saying the words to her.

How much longer are you going to be a chicken shit? Do you expect her to wait for you forever?

She'd already waited more than fifteen years for him to come to his senses. How much longer could she sit around a wait for him? Women like Rebecca got snatched up left and right. One of these days she was going to grow impatient and run off with some guy who drove luxury sedan and ate at five star restaurants.

R.J. would never drive a luxury sedan, but hell, he could do a five star joint every once in a while.

"I've never seen this place so busy."

R.J. turned and clapped eyes on his older step-brother, Chase, who was holding the hands of his twin boys, Kevin and Zack. The kids were three, rambunctious as hell, and asked a thousand questions. Although they were cute as shit, with their parents' blonde hair and angelic looks, they were a disaster waiting to happen. Add their four year old brother, Mason, to the mix, and the kids could rival Hurricane Katrina.

"On kid duty, huh?" he asked his brother, who already had to grab Kevin, or maybe it was Zack, from running off and cracking his head open on a shard of metal. Honestly he had no idea how Chase and Lacy told the two kids apart. Even their hair was cut the same.

Chase bent down and picked Zack, or maybe Kevin, up off the floor and tossed the kid over his shoulder. The boy kicked his legs and demanded to be put down. The other twin giggled.

"Yeah, Mason's playing at a neighbor's house and Abigail's asleep. I told Lacy I'd give her a break."

Kevin, or maybe Zack, looked up at R.J. with big, round eyes. "And Daddy had to pick up dog shit. But he told me not to say shit."

R.J. glanced at his brother, who'd been trying to stifle a laugh. "Nice," he said.

"Yeah, Lacy ripped me a new one over that." He ruffled his son's hair. "I told you not to say that. It's a grown up word."

"He also said 'damn.'" The other kid announced from Chase's shoulder.

R.J. grinned. "Maybe you should stop cursing in front of your children."

"I don't need that shit from you," Chase grumbled. "Don't say shit," he warned to the twin still on the ground.

"Daddy, you said we could play on the cars." The twin standing up tugged on Chase's hand.

"I said maybe. But I don't trust you and your brother."

"What's trust mean?" The boy tossed over Chase's shoulder asked.

R.J. gestured to Mr. Underwood's car. "They can sit in that one over there. It's all done, so no one's working on it."

Chase set the kid down next to his brother and tapped both of them on their bottoms. "You can play in the orange one over there. But if I see you leave that car, no ice cream for either one of you."

The kids took off, barely dodging Alex in their path. The one in the blue shirt opened the door and the two of them climbed inside.

"Which one is which again?" he asked Chase.

Chase lowered his brows and shot him an accusatory glare. "You can't tell your own nephews apart?"

"Half the time you can't either, so shut the hell up."

Chase lifted a brow, and R.J. wanted to kick himself for losing his temper. Rebecca had him tied up in so many knots, now he was snapping at his own brother.

"Get up on the wrong side of the bed today?" Chase asked with half a smile. "Or maybe whatever's wrong with you starts with an R and has curly hair."

Ah, well shit. He thought he'd been sneakier than that.

"Don't act like it's a big secret," Chase went on. "The whole family knows you belong together. The only one who hasn't figured it out yet is you."

He rubbed the back of his neck. Was that a headache he felt coming on? "How did you figure it out with Lacy?" Because, Lord knew, Chase's romance with his wife hadn't been a matter of a few candlelit dinners. He'd been just as resistant toward admitting his feelings for Lacy as R.J. was for Rebecca. Okay, so fifteen years was a bit long, and Chase hadn't been that obstinate. But R.J.'s relationship with Rebecca was unique. Not at all the way Chase started his relationship with Lacy. Theirs had been immediate and explosive.

"Right around the time Brody punched me," his brother

admitted.

Oh yeah, R.J. remembered that. Brody had simply been protective of Lacy, but Chase had deserved it. He hadn't taken Lacy's surprise pregnancy well and had needed some sense knocked into him. Literally.

"Yeah, but you were being bull-headed," he reminded his brother. Not to mention R.J. hadn't tossed out a marriage proposal without thinking.

Chase placed a hand on his shoulder. "My friend, you are the epitome of bull-headed. In fact, you're so bull-headed that you can't even see it." A mock smile curved his lips. "Maybe I ought to send Brody over here to smack you around. He's good at that."

"Try it and see what happens," he warned his brother.

Besides, stubbornness wasn't the problem. Was it?

No, he'd merely been protective of Rebecca, keeping her away from damaged goods like him so she didn't end up with a bruised heart.

Chances are her heart is already bruised. So what good has all that done you?

Well hell, how was he supposed to have known she'd keep on loving him? And how could he have possibly predicted that her absence would only magnify his feelings for her?

Because you're too bull-headed to see it.

Ah shit.

Wasn't this the same problem all three of his brothers had when they fell in love? Hadn't they displayed the same unwillingness to accept their fate?

"You know exactly what I'm talking about," Chase went on. "You just can't admit it. Something about her terrifies you." He lowered his voice. "Look, I know what you're going through. Men are stupid when it comes to women. And trust me when I say, she doesn't need your version of chivalry. She just needs someone to love her."

R.J. shook his head. "She deserves better than me," he muttered.

"What she deserves is for someone to allow her to make her own decisions." Chase directed his attention over R.J.'s shoulder. "Kevin, don't jump on those seats. I know what you're doing," he said to R.J. "Because I made all the same mistakes with Lacy. You think you're doing the right thing, but you're not. I'd better get out of here, or my kids will make scrap metal of your cars."

Chase stomped over to Mr. Underwood's car, where he unceremoniously grabbed both boys by the backside and hauled them over his shoulders.

"I don't know how my wife does this every day," he said to R.J. as he walked out of the shop. The twins were kicking their legs and demanding to be put down. Chase laughed at their non-authoritative tones and practically tossed them in the back seat of his pickup.

R.J. turned back to his work and tried not to dwell on his step-brother's advice. They were wise words from a man who'd been in the same position five years ago. If R.J. had any sense, he'd listen. Not only that, he'd get in his car, find Rebecca wherever she was, and kiss her until she admitted how much she loved him too.

Instead, he got back to work because there was too much of it for him to ignore. Plus, he needed to work out exactly what he wanted to say.

Several hours later, his mind wasn't in any better condition than it had been before. He was still confused, scared, and downright anxious. Funny how one woman could bring out such foreign feelings in him. Come to think of it, they weren't all that strange. Rebecca had always made him feel that way.

Actually if he were to be completely honest, and it was way past time for that, *not* being with Rebecca had made him feel that way. When he was with her, he felt right. Everything clicked, as though his surroundings could fade away and not a shiver of doubt would cloud his mind. Being with Rebecca made him a better man.

Being without her just made him stupid.

As though conjured by his very thoughts, the woman herself walked into his shop, all sleek and beautiful, just as always. Just the slightest glimpse of her had his heart ratcheting up his throat. Her long, trim legs were wrapped in faded denim with tattered holes that gave him a glimpse of petite knees. A form-fitting, long-sleeved shirt fell to her hips, with a neckline that revealed delicate collarbones. She was so very... Rebecca.

Just as breathtaking and sweet as she'd always been.

And he'd been trying to stay away from her?

She greeted some of his techs, and her soft voice washed over him like a forbidden whisper. The sound gave him actual goosebumps, something he'd only designated to women. He adjusted his package beneath his jeans because the material had grown tight in the ten seconds she'd been in the building.

How predictable of him.

Sam said something that made her laugh, a genuine, deep-throated sound that hadn't come from her in a long time. R.J. grinned at the sweet innocence of her happiness, because it was long overdue.

He supposed she had a lot to be happy about, seeing as though the DEA had officially closed their investigation and surrendered Rebecca's license back to her.

Somehow he managed to hold his shit together when she approached. The tent in his jeans bordered on embarrassing, but thoughts of the time when he accidentally saw his grandmother naked took care of the problem in a snap.

"My dad's car looks really good," she said in that bedroom voice of hers. The one that always haunted him when he slept. "You did a fantastic job with it." She leaned against a Dodge Challenger and tilted her head. A strand of curl fell from her loose bun and graced cheek, sort of the same way he used to touch her.

Used to.

It doesn't have to be in the past tense.

His hands weren't that dirty, but he picked up a rag anyway because if he didn't occupy himself, he'd bend her over his arm and embarrass them both.

"Thanks," he managed to grunt out. "I was just about to take it for a spin." Lie. "Want to join me?"

Her tongue swiped across her lower lip, which damn near gave him an aneurism. "Okay," she replied.

Ten minutes later, they were cruising in her father's brand-new car with orange paint, white leather seats and a kickass manual transmission. His team had outdone themselves with this car, and he knew Donald Underwood was going to love every surface of the vehicle.

"It's like a completely different machine," Rebecca said in awe as she ran her hand over the dash. "It even rides better."

"Think your dad will be pleased with it?" he asked, even though he knew the answer. He just needed something to say so he didn't swallow his own tongue.

She twisted in her seat to glance behind her. "He's going to love it." Her green eyes fixed with his. "You're really talented, R.J."

He moved one shoulder, which was more nerves than anything else. "It's my job."

"It's more than just a job," she argued. "Cars have always been your passion. You're lucky you get to do what you love."

He glanced at her just before turning to the baseball fields. "So are you."

"More or less," she said with a sigh.

"You got your license back, Rebecca. Why don't you seem happier?"

She unbuckled her seatbelt when he parked in front of one of the baseball diamonds. "Believe me, I am happy. But I can't help but feel like I'm selling out by joining Dr. Scarboro's practice."

That was his overachiever. Always feeling like she could reach higher.

"You're not selling out. You're being smart." He draped his arm over the wheel and looked at her. "Joining another practice allows you to get back to work right away. If you build a new place from scratch, it could take you years to get going."

She glanced down at her hands, and her uncertainty was like someone scooping out his guts with a spoon.

"But I finally had a chance to have everything I wanted, and I didn't take it. What if this opportunity never comes again?" She pinned him with eyes full of questions. "I feel like I let my dreams slip through my hands."

Rebecca had always had more confidence than anyone he knew, and rightfully so. To hear her question herself had his protective instincts coming out. He turned in his seat and abandoned his personal vow not to touch her.

He smoothed her hair back from her face. "Rebecca, whether you realize or not, you're already living your dream. You put yourself through medical school, you're a great doctor, and your patients love you. What more could you ask for than that?"

Her mouth opened, then shut, as though something was on the tip of her tongue. The urge to kiss her was so strong that he actually leaned across the seat. But something stopped him short. Maybe it was the fact that he didn't want to start something he couldn't finish. Maybe it was the look in Rebecca's eyes, all hope and need and things that still made him hyperventilate.

Just as he pulled back, she leaned forward and pressed her lips to his. The kiss was soft and light, but still elicited a response from him. His hand tightened around her head, holding her closer to him even though he knew it would be smart to just drive her back to work. But damn, he couldn't help himself. It wasn't a very passionate kiss, but he still didn't want to let her go. Even the smallest of touches with Rebecca could send his world in a tailspin and his heart punching through his ribcage.

Rebecca broke the contact first. Even though he ought to be grateful, disappointment wrapped around him just the same.

"I know what more I want," she said in a near whisper. "I love you, R.J."

The words weren't a surprise to him, but they knocked the breath from his lungs anyway. All he needed to do was say it back to her. Be honest. The familiar tightening in his chest started again.

"Rebecca—"

A flash of darkness clouded her eyes. It was instantaneous, but he knew her well enough to recognize the shadow of pain. Dammit, how did he always manage to come off as an ass?

"It's okay, you don't need to say anything." She sank back into the seat with defeat slumping her shoulders.

"Rebecca, I was just going to say—"

"I need to get back to work."

R.J. wasn't sure if not enough had been said, or if too much had transpired between them. Their relationship had become diluted with the same predictable conversations and arguments. Yet, each time they expected a different outcome.

He'd spent the last fifteen years being a condescending asshole and trying to drive her away. How could she expect any different from him? He'd programmed her to feel this way, and here he was trying to cry wolf.

With frustration burning in his gut, R.J. pulled away from the baseball fields and drove Rebecca back to work. The heavy silence that stretched between them was as oppressive and thick as a dense fog. Rebecca was coiled so close to the car door, her arms and legs crossed tightly, that she practically melted in the thing.

Okay, he got it. Once again he'd stuck his foot in his mouth. Only this time, he didn't want to leave things like this between them. Rebecca, at the very least, deserved him to be honest with her. The time for being a lying bastard was over.

Humility was a bitch of a pill to swallow.

She had the door open before he even came to a stop. The endings to dozens of lame chick movies came to mind, as he made a half-hearted attempt at stopping her.

"Rebecca, just wait a minute—" The door slammed in his face.

Yeah, she was good and pissed. He didn't blame her.

"You know where to find me when you know what you want, R.J."

The parting words were simply spoken in a calm voice, but were no less cutting.

He caught a glimpse of his future disappearing as she walked into the building.

****

The only thing that brought a smile to Rebecca's face that afternoon was Carly Foster's giggle when she tickled the two-year-old's bare foot. The girl's mother had brought her in because of a lingering cough and fever.

"Corinne will be right in with your prescription," Rebecca told her patient. "And before you leave, check in with Janet to make an appointment in ten days."

"Thanks, Dr. Underwood," the young woman said with a grateful smile.

She opened the door and faced her patients. "My pleasure. Have a great evening."

As the last patient filed out, Rebecca retreated to her office to finish her paperwork. Normally paper-pushing, a necessary evil in medicine, gave her solitude after a hectic day of fussy kids and screaming newborns. Her customary headache was in full swing and showed no signs of slowing down. Even after the three pain relievers she'd washed down with a bottle of water. And also thinking about what to cook for dinner. She hadn't realized how much she missed her mother's cooking until her parents moved back into their house last week.

But the sharp pain in her head wouldn't cease, and she knew why. It wasn't because she'd been on her feet all day. And her head had already been throbbing before her first after-lunch patient.

The source had sandy-blond, wind-blown hair and soul-searching green eyes. He had broad shoulders, a lean-against-me chest and a way of ripping a woman's heart right out of her chest.

The damn thing was still beating, despite the fact that R.J. had repeatedly stomped it into the ground. Especially after she'd given him ample opportunity that afternoon to finally come out with it. And told him she loved him.

Like the love-sick, foolish, glutton for punishment she was. Had she really expected anything less? R.J. Devlin didn't commit. He didn't fall in love and wine and dine women.

He had notches on his bedpost. He gave curl-your-toes orgasms, made you feel like the only woman in the world, then moved on. And made some other wide-eyed optimistic woman feel like that.

She glanced over the same form for a third time and had no clue what she was supposed to write. The words didn't make any sense. The left-over turkey wrap didn't look appetizing, and the sunset outside held no appeal. Normally, she'd get through with work so she'd get to see the last remnants of day; to catch the last rays of sunshine before they retreated behind the foothills.

Now she didn't care. Let the sun go. The night-time

would come and only mirror what was inside her; nothing but darkness because the only thing that had ever mattered to her had never really cared.

Despite the bottomless despair and debilitating heartache, regret wasn't in the mix. How could she regret being honest? What if she'd spent the rest of her life not knowing? In her muddled mind, that was far worse than putting oneself out there and being rejected.

Even with the proverbial door slammed on her love life, the world would still turn. The sun would still rise tomorrow, and her paperwork wasn't going to do itself. She set her mind to finishing work and barely paid attention to the office door opening, then closing. Barely heard Janet's laughter and the sound the hard-soled shoes coming down the hall toward her office.

The dark figure that appeared in her doorway stirred the air around her with a crackling sexual awareness that always came when R.J. Devlin was near. Rebecca knew him by feeling alone, but didn't take her attention off her paperwork. He'd surely see the heartache in her eyes and pity her like the pathetic creature she was.

Rebecca could handle anything but that.

"You're not getting rid of me that easily." His deep voice cut through the silence of her office like a warm caress on the sensitive spot beneath her ear. How could a near whisper sound that close?

Had she been trying to get rid of him? Funny, she thought he'd been doing the same with her.

Although, she hadn't given him a chance to respond after her confession. Her pride had gotten the better of her on that one.

She leaned back in her chair and placed the cap on her pen. "I've never tried to get rid of you, R.J." At least not recently.

He stepped forward into her office with a brown paper

bag grasped in one hand. "Oh, yes you have. I'm not saying I'm innocent, but you've played the game as well as I have."

"It was never a game to me," she whispered. Who was she trying to convince? Why couldn't she admit she was just as much to blame as him?

His green eyes narrowed. "It may not be anymore, but in the beginning it was. You know that as well as I do."

She stood from her chair and walked around the desk in order to show him out of her office. "If you came here to mess with my head again, I'm not interested." She held the door open, and stared at the ground. If she made contact with those deep eyes of his, she'd give into her urge to melt into him. And she couldn't allow herself to go there again. "If you can't be honest about your feelings for me, then you need to keep your distance."

"See, that's why I'm here. To be honest." He took a step closer and held out the brown bag. "And to give you this."

Her eyes swept up to his, and she was blindsided with her overwhelming love for him. Would she be knocked to her backside like that every time she looked at him? Or was around him? She reluctantly accepted the bag and opened it. A pinkish-yellow mango was inside. A fresh wave of nostalgia slammed into her almost as hard as the realization that she loved him.

She glanced at him without taking the mango out of the bag. "You're giving me a mango?" Her attempt at sounding nonchalant and blasé was pathetic.

"It's not just a mango," he corrected. A hint of a smile pulled at the corners of his mouth. He reached inside and removed the fruit. His hand was huge and masculine compared to the pink mango. Sort of like the way he'd palmed her breasts...

"Do you know what this represents?" he asked while testing the weight of the fruit.

"The knot on your hard-headed skull?"

The smarmy comment earned her a grin, one that shot directly to her midsection and spread fire down to her toes.

He flicked the end of her nose with his index finger. "You always know how to bring a guy to his knees."

How could he be so damn comfortable? She was about to come out of her skin.

"That's going to land on your head if you keep it up," she warned. Although a smile almost broke across her face. She'd never forget the look he shot when she'd dropped a mango, just like the one he held, right on top of his head.

"You may have given me a hell of a bruise with one of these," he said, ignoring her comment. "But you also did something else."

Taken her life in her own hands by getting on his bad side?

"You made me fall in love with you," he blurted out.

She froze in front of him, thinking if she even blinked he'd take the words back and her reality would continue to sink in. The same reality she'd been living in for too long, the one where R.J. didn't love her.

"Did you hear me?" He took step closer and gripped her shoulders. "I said I love you, Rebecca."

"I heard you." She swallowed past the grapefruit-sized lump in her throat, and tried to keep her knees from buckling. "I don't understand," she said with a shake of her head. "This whole time... I mean, all these years you've been so indifferent."

"That's what I wanted you to think. I guess I did too good of a job," he added with a half-smile.

"But... why?"

His eyes dropped closed, as though still battling with some internal insecurities. "I told you about my father and the issues I've always had with relationships. I just..." His forehead pressed against hers. "I wanted you to find better than me."

"And *I* told *you* to let me decide what I do and don't deserve."

"I had a hard time letting go of that control." His work-rough hands cupped her face. "My pride got the better of me."

His admission had her grinning, because he was only telling her what she'd known all along. "I know. For a long time I thought you'd never come around."

"You're too smart for your own good." The look on his face sobered. "I'm sorry."

She tilted her head to one side. "For what?"

His laugh was more of a snort than a sound of happiness. "For always being a stubborn ass. For torturing you all those years. For doing my damnedest to push you away." He paused and took a deep breath. "For making you think I didn't care. I was trying to do you a favor, but I regret that now."

She took one of his hands in hers and placed a kiss on his palm. Just the feel of his warm skin on her lips sent tremors through her. "Don't do that. I don't have any regrets. You may have been incorrigible at times, but you always made me feel special in a way no other man has."

"I guarantee you it's not a tenth of the way you make me feel."

His words melted her heart. She wrapped her arms around his neck and kissed him, because they'd already spent too much time talking. Too many wasted years of dancing around each other and playing games when they should have been sharing their lives together.

Her lips molded to his with a perfection that knocked the breath out of her. When he swept his tongue inside her mouth, she squeezed her eyes tight and shut everything out of her mind. There was only this; only R.J. who'd always been the one thing that had mattered to her more than anything else.

The times when he'd been absent from her life, the long nights of medical school, had been some of the loneliest and meaningless. The spark in her life had been missing, and she hadn't even realized. Now that she had him, really had him, she was never going to let him back away again.

He pulled away from her and picked up the mango. The devious glint in his eye she'd grown so familiar with was back. "Now I'd like to take you home and explore some interesting ways to enjoy this baby."

She eyed the fruit and welcomed the little flutters of anticipation that danced in her midsection. "Luckily for you, this paperwork can wait."

"Luckily for me?" He grabbed her hand and led her from the office, not even giving her a chance to clean up her desk. The look he shot her over his shoulder was hot enough to singe the hairs off her head. "You obviously don't know me well enough."

Keep reading for a preview of the next book in the Trouble series, *The Trouble with Trouble.*

THE TROUBLE WITH TROUBLE

THERE WAS A TWO-HEADED beast out there, bound and determined to suck the humanity straight out of Courtney's soul, and the son-of-a-bitch's name was Murphy's Law.

Yeah, she was well-acquainted with Murphy and the bastard's entire family. Hell, she was practically on a first name basis with the entire Murphy clan.

Okay, so there technically wasn't such a thing as The Murphy Clan. This Murphy person, or whatever the hell it was, flew solo but inflicted as much damage as a flash flood. In downtown New Orleans.

But never mind any of that, because Courtney Devlin was an independent, strong woman who could handle anything tossed her way. And yeah, those babies were usually thrown by a major league baseball pitcher. And she was the minor leaguer at home plate who got drilled in the head every time.

Earlier that morning, for example. Her insurance company had all of a sudden decided that her migraines were "pre-existing conditions" and could no longer cover her medication. Never mind the fact that they'd been covering it for the past two years. A fact of which she'd had to remind them of, very and unnaturally calm thank you very much.

But did they care? Not one flying rip.

Useless, self-serving corporate jerks.

That had started her day off on such a sour note, that dealing with the cantankerous air conditioning in her car suddenly going kaput, seemed like a trivial thing. And anyone knew that driving around with no air conditioning in the middle of a Wyoming summer, the hottest summer on record, was anything but trivial. By the time she pulled into the parking lot of her brother's restaurant, the cherry blossom body spray she'd used had faded to *Eau de* sweat.

And forget the way she smelled, because really what was a little perspiration? The sight of her hair alone, was enough to scare Medusa away. And that chick had really bad hair.

The unruly, yet not quite bouncy, waves, with a touch of frizz was thanks to a fried coil in her cheap ass hair dryer. Not that she couldn't afford a nicer hair dryer. Because she could. But Courtney had always been a bargain shopper, no matter how much money she had in the bank. Clearly buying the less expensive version, because it had been twenty bucks cheaper, had not been the wisest thing.

Like she said. Murphy's Law.

Luckily it was only Chase and he wouldn't care what she looked like.

Only her ability to decorate the shit out of his restaurant, which she could do with her eyes closed. Which was why he'd specifically requested her. Or so her boss, Cynthia Wright, had told her. That "The guy at McDermott's had asked for her by name." Although, why Chase had called Courtney's boss and not Courtney herself was a little strange. But whatever. The end result was still the same.

Project score for her.

Chase had told her that one of his first wishes as the new owner was to give the interior a complete overhaul. Martin, Chase's father and Courtney's step-dad, may know how to make restaurant gold, but the man's taste in décor was about on par with Courtney's baseball skills.

Translation: *they sucked.*

Somehow her step-father had done a good job with The Golden Glove. But that place was sport-themed and really didn't require a whole lot of creativity or imagination. McDermott's was in some serious need of flare.

In other words, the Courtney Devlin touch. Because flare was one thing she had a lot of.

The parking lot was almost empty, on account that the restaurant was officially closed for renovations. She parked her car in a spot in front of the entrance and cut the engine.

Hopefully they had the air conditioning cranked inside because, *damn*, it was hot.

She got out of the car, and rounded to back to the trunk, where she kept the necessary items for that first-time consult with a client. She draped a tote bag over her shoulder, which held a tape measure, a clipboard for notes, an architectural scale, a paint deck, and swatch books for fabric and flooring. The damn bag weighed a friggin' ton.

Once she had everything in hand, literally, she made her way to the door, and only by a miracle was she able to get the thing open with two full arms.

The interior of the place was quiet and practically deserted. She spotted her brother, looking crisp and handsome as always. Tan slacks with creases so sharp, they could have cut glass, and a royal blue polo that had an odd way of making Chase's blue eyes seem even bluer. Lacy, his wife, had probably hand-picked the outfit and then starched the slacks.

Chase was whipped like that.

A fact of which Courtney never failed to remind him. Because she was a supreme sister, and that's what sisters did.

"You're ten minutes late," her brother blurted out like the nice guy he was.

"You don't want to know the morning I've had," she

warned him.

He grinned, which didn't make her feel any better. "You're right, I don't."

She dumped her stuff on a nearby table and rolled her left shoulder from carrying a heavy bag.

"So…" she rubbed her hands together in anticipation of starting a new project. This was always her favorite part. "Want to see what I brought? I already have tons of ideas."

Chase shook his head, and his mouth flattened to a thin line. "Not me," he said, then jerked his thumb over his shoulder. "Him."

She shifted her attention over Chase's shoulder to a man seated at one of the tables, flipping through a stack of papers. She lowered her hands, and they fell to her sides like fifty pound weights.

Short, spiky dark hair. Dark like the black coffee her mother Carol liked to drink. Hazel eyes with the perfect mixture of green and brown, and the ability see past her tough exterior to the vulnerabilities underneath. Wide, corded shoulders that narrowed down to a trim waist and loose hips, then gave way to a perfectly rounded, sculpted rear-end that could bring a lesbian to tears.

Shut. The front. Door.

"I'm sorry," Courtney said with a rapid blink of her eyes. "What am I seeing here?"

Chase opened his mouth to explain, probably some stupid calm-down speech that he knew wouldn't work on her. But she placed a hand on his arm and dug her fingernails into the hard muscle of his forearm.

"Please tell me you found some Grant Blackwood look-alike and not the real Grant Blackwood," she whispered, which sounded strained even though it was a whisper, for crying out loud. "You know, the same guy who punched his fist through my chest, yanked my heart out and fed it to a tree chipper."

Both of Chase's golden brows lowered over his eyes. "Okay, *that's* a bit dramatic."

Her hand tightened on his arm, which was tight enough given the flare of her brother's nostrils. "I'll show you dramatic, Chase."

He pried her hand off his arm, one finger at a time. "It's been four years, Court."

"And what part of 'I don't ever want to see him again,' do you not get? Is that four years or less in Chase world?"

Her older brother heaved a heavy sigh. "Courtney—"

"Did you hire me to play some sick and twisted game of matchmaker?" she asked with her arms crossed over her chest. Maybe if she crossed them hard enough she could keep her heart from thumping through her ribcage.

"He didn't hire you, I did," Grant said in a low voice.

Damn it, she'd been so hell bent on reading her brother the riot act, that she hadn't noticed Grant approach them. Courtney hated being caught off-guard. Made her feel out of sorts. She took a step back, because having her ex-fiancée standing next to her brother was way too close to *her*. Plus, the farther away she was, the less strong his... scent was. And by *scent* she meant, eyes-rolling-back-into-the-head-stomach-dipping manliness. Hell, she had no idea what he put on himself, but it was damn good. Still.

Courtney glanced around, looking for the video camera that someone had planted when they decided to play a practical joke on her. "Apparently that door I walked through was a door to the Twilight Zone," she muttered to herself.

"Quit kidding around, Court," Chase said.

She whipped her gaze back to her brother, who was going to get a serious ass beating later on. Via his wife. Who'd back Courtney up any day. "You think this is funny to me?" She jerked her thumb in Grant's direction. "And this guy, seriously? Of all the people to hire."

"Your confidence in my abilities is overwhelming," Grant

stated.

"Give us a minute," Chase said, then placed a hand on Courtney's shoulder and guided her to a spot where they could speak alone. When he had her cornered, and there was really no other way to describe the situation she was in, he crossed his arms over his chest. "I know you're kind of pissed."

"Kind of?" she repeated. *Kind of?* She was so stinkin' mad she wanted to ram bamboo shoots under her brother's nails.

"Just hear me out," he urged in a calm voice. "I hired Grant because he's good at what he does, and he hired you because you're good at what you do. None of this is personal, Court."

"The flattery is nice and everything, but I thought *you* hired me."

Chase shook his head. "No, the redesign is his thing. I've got nothing to do with it."

"So he's the one who asked for me, and you didn't think to warn me?"

"Would you have come if I had?"

No. "Yes."

"Okay, that's beside the point, even though I don't believe you. Can you do this job, or not?"

Being able to do the job and wanting the job were two entirely different things. In fact, they weren't even in the same universe. "Of course."

"Then do it," Chase said with a lift of one shoulder.

Someone please kill her now. "Chase…"

Then Grant piped in because that was all she needed. "If she can't handle this job, then we should bring in someone else."

Courtney tossed him a look that normally made all four of her brothers zip their mouths shut when they pushed her too far. "I told you I can do it."

Grant lifted a shoulder in an elegant shrug. "Prove it."

Did he really just challenge her? Didn't he know better than that?

"Prove it?" she repeated. "How old are we?"

"I'm just saying. If you think you can handle the job, then we shouldn't have any problems."

She opened her mouth to argue, but nothing came out. Because really, what could she say or do? Grab her stuff and leave? How unprofessional was that? She supposed she could demand that she work with Chase only, but again, what good would that do? Certainly she was adult enough to work side by side with her ex without killing him. Or herself.

Yeah, she could do it.

Totally.

She shot Chase a look, who'd been doing nothing but glancing back and forth between her and Grant. "Fine." With her chin raised, she brushed past her brother, who was *still* going to get an ear-full from her later on, and approached Grant.

The guy stood there, with a half-smile pulling at the corners of his mouth. His *full* mouth, which used to kiss the hell out of her until her brain ceased to function.

Don't think about that!

"Let's just get started then," she muttered.

ACKNOWLEDGEMENTS

I have such an awesome support system, that I don't even know where to start. My fellow writer besties, Rachel Lacey, Shannon Richard, Jessica Lemmon, and Rachel Van Dyken. You are all so amazing and make me laugh when I don't feel like laughing. Jessica don't ever stop posting Henry Cavill and Charlie Hunnam photos. And Rachel VD, your support, help, and resources have guided me when I didn't know where to start. THANK YOU.

To my loyal and enthusiastic street team and beta readers: Kim, Meghan, Sarah, Kelly, Amanda and Bette. Having your support and love means more to me than I can say. Thanks for sticking with me and for waiting the eons it's taken me to get a book published.

And lastly to my husband, who's always had my back. Thank you for always being proud of me and telling perfect strangers on the train about your wife who writes romance. And always giving away copies of my books to every neighbor we have.

Made in the USA
San Bernardino, CA
29 August 2014